Kiss Me TONIGHT

MARIA LUIS

KISS ME TONIGHT

PUT A RING ON IT

MARIA LUIS

ALKMINI BOOKS, LLC

I had it all.
The Super Bowl rings.
The hot shot TV gig.

Then I got fired.

Now I'm living in middle-of-nowhere Maine, playing assistant coach to the woman of my nightmares.

Did I mention that she and her son are my new neighbors?

If you talk to the locals, they'll tell you Aspen Levi is the queen of high school football.
But if you ask me, my new head coach is a pain in my left nut sac.

She's too blonde.
Too peppy.
And way too sexy for my peace of mind.

Only, one minute we're fighting, and the next I can't keep my hands off her. One hot kiss. One forbidden touch. I don't do love but . . .

What I want, I take, and what I want is Aspen Levi.

Cover Photographer: Wander Book Club Photography

Cover Designer: Najla Qamber, Najla Qamber Designs

Cover Models: Thiago & Elise

Editing: Kathy Bosman, Indie Editing Chick

Proofreading: Tandy Proofreads; Horus Proofreading

❀ Created with Vellum

To you—yes, you. Believe in your dreams. Reach for the stars.
Achieve the impossible.
And then find a new dream to conquer.

☜

Good job, honey.

PLAYLIST

"Girl Like You" — Jason Aldean
"Lovely" — Billie Eilish ft. Khalid
"Face My Fears" — Hikaru Utada (English Version)
"Start Again" — OneRepublic ft. Logic
"The Night We Met" — Lord Huron
"Bad Company" — Five Finger Death Punch
"Blue" — Eiffel 65

ASPEN

LONDON, MAINE

*H*andling balls isn't for everyone.

But here I am, playing with the decades-old football that the Golden Fleece keeps around for whenever a Levi enters the pub.

Growing up, I always pretended the honor was bestowed upon us because someone in my family did the world a good deed. You know, something inspiring, like curing a rare disease or establishing a school for god-knows-what or proving, once and for all, that aliens exist and Earth isn't the sole survivable planet. I don't know, something monumental, something that carries weight and importance—something more than the truth.

And the truth is, us Levis are notoriously notable for only one thing: football.

The town of London loves us for it. Loves *me* for it, even though I have two strikes against me. My lack of penis being the first, and my status as a "traitor" trailing behind in a close second place. The minute I eloped with Rick, the general manager for the Pittsburgh Steelers, heads started to roll. My mother's included.

No New Englander betrays the beloved Patriots like I did and lives to tell the tale.

Luckily for me, Londoners are the sort to forgive, if not forget, a fact I've never been more grateful for than when Shawn, the pub's long-time bartender, flips over a fresh pint glass, fills it to the brim with Guinness, and plunks it down in front of me with a *we-knew-you'd-come-crawling-back-at-some-point* gleam in his dark eyes.

Out loud, though?

No questions asked.

No snide remarks about how my ring finger is surprisingly bare since we last crossed paths or that I'm already straddling the thin line between sober-and-boring and drunk-and-dancing-on-pool-tables.

It's probably for the best that the Golden Fleece isn't a pool table kinda place. It's the oldest pub in town, built sometime just before the turn of the twentieth century, and the only technology in here is wired to the cash registers, the jukebox blasting Aerosmith like the 90s have risen from the dead, and a massive TV hoisted behind the bar. The bathrooms are hooked up to electricity, too, but that's to be expected. The rest of the place is a waltz back in time, complete with tapered candles, which sit dead-center on every table, and equally fancy sconces decorating the walls.

I've missed the quirkiness of the place.

I sigh into my Guinness. Fifteen years is a heck of a long time to be away.

Catching my eye, Shawn drops his hands to the bar, a damp rag slung over one shoulder. "Never thought I'd see the day when Aspen Levi walked back on in here."

Might not look like it, I want to boast, *but I'm in celebration mode.*

Celebrating my return to the motherland, as well as my

new teaching job at London High. History isn't my passion —not like football. Which is why I'm even more thrilled to take over as the new head coach for the Wildcats. The football field is my home away from home. Whistles blowing, refs charging up and down the turf, the sound of bulky pads colliding as players make contact, like modern-day knights hurtling toward victory.

I graze my thumb over the football's cracked leather laces and breathe through the lingering grief. I'm here because Dad's not. Not at the Golden Fleece, not at London High, not anywhere. He'd be disappointed to learn about the events that led to my return to London. His baby girl was strong, a badass on and off the field, intensely focused—and I'm . . . divorced, for one. An expert at putting on a brave face and a cheerful smile, for another. Unfortunately, I haven't felt like a badass in years.

Beneath the football, my knee jiggles up and down. Dad may have passed away three years ago, but it's Mom who wore me down eventually and convinced me to come home.

You're not happy in Pittsburgh, she told me almost weekly.

Rick's a good-for-nothing cheating bastard.

We need you, Aspen. I need you.

Mom hasn't asked me for anything since I dropped out of Boston College in my senior year. Back when I was the first female kicker in all of the NCAA. Back when the NFL— for the first time in history—was considering drafting a *woman* to the professional level.

All my life, my parents urged me to rock the boat.

Push at sexist, big boys' club sensibilities.

Show the world at large that just because I was born with a vagina, that didn't mean I couldn't make my mark on a league dominated by cocks and balls. It was nothing but an unlikely pipe dream.

Let's put it this way: I had the world at my fingertips, and I lost it all.

No, that's a lie—I *gave* it away.

And all because I met an older man with a slick smile and a magic penis. Scratch that. There'd been nothing remotely magical about Rick's dick. Just because he was packing below the belt didn't mean he knew how to use it, but I'd been young and inexperienced and naïve enough to fall for false promises of love and happily-ever-afters.

Stop ruminating and count your lucky stars.

Idly plucking at the laces, knowing that Shawn's waiting for me to get my shit together and answer, I count out three doses of luck:

I'm grateful for having a job that pays me to do what I love.

I'm grateful for divorcing Rick the Prick a year ago—finally.

I'm grateful to Mom, who ditched her knitting club tonight to watch Topher so I can socialize with people over the age of thirty.

Actually, the last one came from Topher himself, my fifteen-year-old-son, who shouldered on up to me, rapped his knuckles on my forehead, and confessed, "I think you need to adult, Ma. I love you, but maybe I could—I don't know—play video games tonight without you hovering over my shoulder?"

I think I'm failing at this adulting thing.

The locals are keeping their distance, Shawn is eyeing me like he can't trust me worth a damn, and at this point in the night, I've shared more intellectual conversation with my Guinness than with anyone in possession of a heartbeat.

"Couldn't imagine staying away forever," I lie to Shawn, hoping he won't hear the tipsy tremor in my voice. I balance the tattered football on my bent knee, wishing the Golden Fleece rocked more than candlelight so that I might be able to make out my dad's signature scrawled across the textured leather. *I miss you, Dad.* Miss his hearty laugh and the crazy knack he had for staring at a group of players and bringing out the best in every one of them. Holding this football, the same one he caught in the end zone back in 1982, when he played for the Pats, makes me feel a little less lonely.

When Shawn's silence stretches on uncomfortably, I paste on a happy-go-lucky grin. "Oh, c'mon. I know you secretly missed me. No point in denying it."

Shawn's expression radiates all kinds of *in-your-dreams* vibes. "The last time you stepped foot in here, I served you your first legal drink."

Wiggling my brows to tease him, I give my pint glass a little swirl. Tap it down on the bar in an informal toast. "If I remember correctly, it wasn't the first drink you sent my way. How old was I the first time? Eighteen? Nineteen?"

Finally, the tightness around his eyes softens. Internally I rejoice when he lets out his familiar, raspy chuckle. "You ever tell that to your mom and I'll be dead by morning."

"If she has it her way, you'll be dead no matter what."

"Nah." He cups the back of his neck with a weathered hand, then swipes the rag from his shoulder. "What? Gossip doesn't reach as far as Pittsburgh?" With gusto, he wipes down the already polished mahogany bar. "Your mom and I have set aside our differences. I'm nearin' seventy, Levi. You think I care about what happened fifty years ago?"

I blink. Stare down into my dark stout and wonder if I'm already drunk enough to be hearing things that can't possibly be true. Then I blink again for good measure because the up and down motion of my head is not doing me any favors.

At thirty-seven, you'd think I'd be a pro at managing my liquor intake, but drinking has never really been my thing.

I press a stabilizing hand to the bar and pray for soberness. "You really want me to believe that Mom forgave you for dumping her at Homecoming?" Everyone knows the story here in London. And if you *don't* know the story of how Shawn Jensen declared his love for someone other than my mother at 1971's Homecoming—that "someone" being her ex-best friend—then you're one lucky son of a gun. I've heard it retold so many times I can recite the night's itinerary down to the second. Last I heard, Mom went so far as to ban Miranda Lee from joining her popular knitting club a few years back. *Some* gossip reaches Pittsburgh, it seems. "She hates you, Shawn."

The muted light emphasizes the silver strands in Shawn's surprisingly thick head of hair as he snags a cocktail glass from where it hangs upside down from a rack. "Hate's a strong word."

Is it?

I have a whole list of things that I hate. Pickles. The band Journey. Drivers who don't know how to navigate a four-way intersection. Ex-husbands named Rick.

"Has she baked you her famous casserole pie yet?" I ask, swishing the beer in my glass before taking another heavy gulp. Mom is an absolute sweetheart, but apologies aren't really her thing. She prefers to gloss over *I'm sorry* with homemade casserole and a good amount of booze.

Shawn's bushy brows knit together. "Casserole?"

"Yup."

Hand-delivering a (store bought) casserole to my mom's front door was the first order of business when I moved back a month ago. As expected, she'd laughed, ushered me inside, then promptly informed me that I had shit taste in men.

No surprise there.

"I hate to be the bearer of bad news but . . . without the

casserole"—I shrug, feeling only slightly evil about messing with Shawn—"you're not in the clear yet."

"What the hell do you mean, I'm not in the clear?"

"The casserole is the gateway to forgiveness."

His thin lips flatten—all the better to play the role of grumpy old bartender—even as his dark eyes light with humor. "That might be the stupidest shit I've ever heard."

Before I have the chance to respond, a guy three stools down from me summons Shawn with an empty glass hoisted in the air.

I wave Shawn off with the promise to behave.

"It's not your behavior I'm worried about," he tells me, his tone as dry as the Sahara. "In case you haven't noticed . . . no one's come to welcome you back into the fold yet."

No need to rub my lackluster reality in my face quite so bluntly.

Ugh.

Peering over my shoulder, I meet the eye of an older gentleman who used to sit front row at my high school football games. He hasn't changed at all—aside from his shiny, bald head and the Wildcats T-shirt that's been swapped out for a flannel button-down. "Him," I say, just short of pointing at the man as I swing around to look at Shawn, "I remember him. What's his name again?"

Shawn grumbles under his breath. "Elia Woods. Don't initiate conversation."

Don't initiate conversation?

Sounds like a challenge if I've ever heard one.

I stare at Elia a little harder, keenly aware that I'm balanced precariously on the edge of my bar stool. "What? Does he have fangs now? Claws? Some sort of air-transmitted disease?"

"Heya! Shawn! I need a refill, man!"

Shawn taps me on the top of my head with his knuckles, the same way he did when I was a kid waltzing in every spring to sell him Girl Scout cookies. "Not Elia, Levi. He's had it rough the last few years."

That's great. Okay, not *great*. But that gives us something to talk about. I have my divorce and shitty ex-husband and he has . . .

Well, time to find out.

I slip off my bar stool and land on my sneakered feet without a hitch.

Around the pub, unwanted attention swivels in my direction. Elia himself lifts his head from where he's drawing in a notebook—on second thought, it looks more like a crossword puzzle—and stares at my face.

Oh, goody.

Eye contact.

Giddiness (and Guinness) swims in my veins. We're off to a great start.

My hand finds the back of the chair opposite Elia's and, below the gravelly undertones of Steven Tyler belting his heart out from the jukebox, the wooden legs screech like a banshee as I pull the chair out.

Be friendly. Smile big. Be the girl they all used to love!

Riffing off my mental pep talk, I wave at him like a lunatic even though I've already invaded his space. "Hey there! Elia, right? I'm not sure if you remember me. I used to play for the Wildcats years ago."

I sit down.

Elia promptly stands up, confirmed crossword puzzle in hand, and moves two tables over.

Like I don't even exist.

The tiny hairs on my arms stand up in a melee of dejection and embarrassment.

Tipsy me thinks it's a great idea to try again, but just as I clamber to my feet to make my move, a deep voice calls out, "Figures you'd only come home when it was time to take your dad's old job."

Oh, boy. I should have known news would travel fast.

I find the source of the voice, then rack my brain for the accompanying name. Stuart. Stewart? *Doesn't matter.* He was two years behind me in school and we played football together during his sophomore and my senior year. From what little I've seen of him on social media, he married his high school sweetheart and popped out a brood of dark-haired children.

A smile hitches to life on my face. "Stuart!" *Stewart? Oh, my God, stop thinking about it.* "It's so good to see you! How's Beth-Anne?"

His expression darkens to a veritable glower. "Dead."

I—I . . .

There are a few snickers to my left. My heart threatens mutiny with a virtual white flag of surrender.

With empathy and humiliation warring inside me, I manage a hushed, "Stuart, I'm so, so sorry for your loss."

More snickering.

The chair squeals again as I launch to my feet.

"Your beer is waiting," Stuart/Stewart sneers, flicking his fingers toward the bar in a casual dismissal. "Wouldn't want it to go flat on you."

He doesn't need to tell me twice.

I flee with my nonexistent tail tucked between my legs, hopping up on my recently vacated bar stool. Immediately, I snatch up my phone and shoot off a quick text to my younger sister, Willow.

Me: Beth-Anne is dead?!!

And even though she totally claimed to be too busy

tonight to come out with me, Willow answers almost immediately.

Willow: Who the hell is Beth-Anne?

*Me: Stuart's wife!!! Stuart—football player, dark, curly hair,
definite beer gut. He was in your grade. Remember your small
penis theory?*

**Willow: Ohhh HIM. Yeah, I still stand by that theory.
Husband #1 proved it.**

Willow: Also, Beth-Anne?

Willow: Do you mean Annabeth?

Fingers flexing around my phone, I glance back, just in
time to see Stuart sniggering into his beer. Considering I
brought up his dead wife only minutes ago, the man doesn't
look perturbed in the slightest. No crease in his brow. No
sorrow lines bracketing his mouth. No defeated posture.

**Willow: Who told you Annabeth is dead? I saw her at
the grocery store this morning when I was buying
condoms.**

Because, of course, my sister would ditch me to get laid.
Who's surprised? Not me.

Me: I think I've been played.

**Willow: Welcome back to London, dear sister. We've
missed you!!! Now stop texting me. I'm on a date.**

I don't know whether to laugh at finding myself alone in
a place that should feel like home or whether I should go
ahead and call it quits before I end up looking like an even
bigger fool. I knew the transition to London life wouldn't
necessarily be a smooth one. With a population of under
two thousand, tight-knit doesn't even begin to describe our
tiny coastal town.

*Figures you'd only come home when it was time to take your
dad's old job.*

Stuart's words ring painfully loud in my ears.

Is that what everyone thinks of me? That the only reason I'm back is because I want to take up the Levi crown?

The false judgment burns like acid.

If they only understood how much of a "fairytale" life I had with Rick, they'd know that coaching the Wildcats is nothing but a salve on a festering wound. I took the job because it was offered to me and I'm good at what I do. Because living in Pittsburgh, a year after my divorce was finalized, felt just as hellish as surviving my marriage. And because I'd be a fool to move to a different state without a single source of income, especially since Rick left me high and dry in the divorce settlement.

When successful, *powerful* men like Rick Clarke sway a judge with the promise of some extra Benjamins, there's no hope for women like me: washed-up college athletes who are long past their prime.

Ugh. Thinking like that is *not* doing me any favors.

Planting a hand on the bar to steady myself, I lift my gaze to the old Patriots game Shawn has playing. It's nice to see that some things haven't changed around here—for as long as I can remember, Golden Fleece management has always gone out of their way to record every Pats game. By 9 p.m., Monday through Friday, Londoners have claimed their booths and their booze in preparation of watching their favorite players storm the small screen.

And the game Shawn's playing now? I remember this one oh-so-vividly, if only because Rick raged about it for weeks afterward.

Tampa Bay Buccaneers against the New England Patriots, circa 2015.

Rick had obsessed over recruiting Tampa's hotshot player, Dominic DaSilva. MVP winner. Super Bowl champion—twice. Best tight end in NFL history, even topping out

Tony Gonzalez who had III touchdowns to his name before retiring from Atlanta.

Pretty sure each time Rick watched DaSilva play, he popped an instant boner.

Until DaSilva refused to enter negotiations with the Steelers. Didn't matter that he was a free agent at the time. Didn't matter that he could have made more money playing for Pittsburgh than he did for Tampa Bay.

It pissed off Rick to no end.

Hadn't mattered to me in the slightest. DaSilva played a big game but he talked big too. To the press, to other players. Guys like him might have the stats to back it all up, but a little humility never hurt anyone.

That's what I try to get across to my players. You can be the biggest badass to ever step on the field, but if you're an asshole off of it? No one's gonna respect you for long. No one's going to want to go to bat for you. No one's going to want to take a chance on a player once the stats stop rolling in and the excitement bubbling around you dries up and all you have left is a big bank account and an even bigger attitude problem.

And I use Dominic DaSilva as an example of What Not To Do, each and every time.

I mean, the man went on a *dating show,* of all things, and proceeded to be the biggest douchebag of the season.

Not that I've been watching *Put A Ring On It* every Wednesday night when it airs—much.

Gaze locked on the TV, I sip what's left of my Guinness. I'll head home as soon as the game is over. Third quarter, three minutes left on the clock. Tampa Bay has the ball. They look a little too cocky, considering they're trailing behind by a touchdown and a field goal, or maybe that's just number twelve—DaSilva himself—radiating enough arrogance to power an entire electrical plant as he slicks his gloved hands over his thighs and drops into position.

Someone in the bar hollers, "Thirty seconds, guys!" to the cacophony of raucous laughter and requests for more booze.

I hope Stuart chokes on his beer.

Twenty seconds.

The whistle blows. Grown-ass men charge toward each other like raging bulls on speed. Helmets clang, bouncing ping-pong style. Shoulders work like cranes heaving boulders out of the way. DaSilva rounds the cluster, arms pumping fast, and the camera pans out for a better angle of him sprinting down the field.

Eyes glued to the TV, I tighten my grip around my empty pint glass.

Wait for it . . .

Wait *for it . . .*

Tampa's quarterback finally makes the pass, and the football spirals through the air like a cannonball hurtling into enemy territory.

DaSilva cuts around a Pats player, dodging one way, then quick-stepping in the opposite direction. He twists his big body, and I swear there's an arrogant quirk to his mouth as he leaps in the air, bulky arms raised high.

His hands connect with the football.

And then he comes down.

It's all so, so wrong.

Players rush him from all sides, and even though I've watched this clip more times than I can count—it became Rick's favorite after all the times DaSilva told my ex-husband to fuck off—I still grimace.

Because if you don't feel an ounce of sympathy when a person's bone tears through their flesh to wave Queen-of-

England-style at the crowd, then there's something intrinsically wrong with you.

Feeling my own limbs clench in phantom pain, I hiss between my teeth. "Not even assholes deserve that."

A big body slides onto the neighboring stool, seconds before that same big body rumbles out, "Deserve what?"

ASPEN

$\mathcal{M}$y spine snaps straight with awareness as the stranger gets comfortable beside me.

I don't even have to look at him to know that he's massive in a way most men aren't.

So tall that he can sit at ease with one foot planted on the floor and the other languidly parked on my stool's footrest. *Who needs personal space nowadays, anyway?* Not me, apparently. His bent knee is flush with my left thigh, and it can't all be in my head—tipsy brain or not—that I catch him angling his big body to face me.

Like he's possibly intrigued by what I have to say.

Even though I don't know him from a hole in the wall.

Out of the corner of my eye, I watch as he flattens one hand on his thigh. Casual. Confident. No jittering knees—guilty—or any sign of flushed cheeks. Also guilty. Thanks to the candlelight—and, admittedly, the beer goggles I've donned since round two—he's nothing but olive skin revealed by rolled-up sleeves, a hard jawline dusted with dark scruff, and the crooked bridge of his nose.

The black baseball hat he's sporting unfairly obscures the upper half of his face.

After taking a moment to flag down Shawn and order a Bud Light, he props one forearm up on the bar. Then the distressed bill of his hat—not that store-bought frayed look, but honest-to-God tattered—swivels unerringly in my direction.

Oh, boy.

I blame the Guinness for the way my heart feels like it's trying out for *Fear Factor*, Adrenaline Edition.

Better to blame the beer than admit the truth: I don't remember the last time a man other than Rick paid me any attention.

Don't be weird. Act normal.

You can play it cool—

"Deserve what?" he asks again.

Here we go. I keep my gaze centered on the TV, where DaSilva is being carried off the field on a stretcher. "Having their tibia play peekaboo for the entire world to witness."

Shawn shoots me a reprimanding glance at the graphic visual I offer, then slicks the Bud Light across the bar with an indecipherable grumble.

Who's surprised when the stranger next to me catches the bottle with a cool flick of his wrist? Not me. He's got the confident vibes of an athlete—and the bulky size to match.

I turn a little.

Just in time to watch him grasp the glass neck with three fingers. Full lips, the bottom one plumper than the top. They wrap around the bottle's puckered mouth, then suck down the beer, his throat working smoothly.

Slow, precise movements.

For as Hulk-like as this guy is, he moves with a compelling grace.

Then he speaks again, and the idea of "grace" gets launched out the closest window.

"Happened to a guy I know. Hurt like a goddamn bitch." Another deceptively nonchalant draw from his beer. "Can't say anyone deserves a hit like that, asshole or not."

Rough around the edges.

Gravel-pitched voice.

Clearly, he's a fan of players like Dominic DaSilva, who retired from the league a few years ago. Much to Rick's delight.

My cheeks warm from the embarrassment of being over-heard. "You say it like you're a hardcore fan."

His bottle hesitates midway down to his knee. "Of DaSilva?"

I nod.

"The guy's a goddamn legend." That full mouth of his ticks up in a lazy grin. "Asshole or not, he knows the game inside and out. You can't deny that."

Sure, I can't *deny* it. But knowing the game doesn't give him a free pass for everything he's done off the field. I mean, this is the same player who told my ex-husband that Rick could offer him all the pussy in the world, and DaSilva *still* wouldn't consider taking the Steelers up on their multi-million dollar offer.

I've read the email.

DaSilva didn't even bother to asterisk the heck out of the word pussy. Simply left it there—bold and brash and completely insolent. Just like him.

Feeling the Guinness-fueled adrenaline in my veins, I eagerly shift my weight to face the Hulk. Football has and will always be my kryptonite. Give me a chance to talk shop, and you'll be begging me to call it quits within the hour.

But this guy sat down next to me—his first mistake—

and Topher *did* suggest I hang out with people my own age. My boy knows me too well. He also knows that his good-for-nothing dad preferred to pretend that his "dear wife" was way too busy to be included in Steelers business.

Oh, my wife? I can almost hear Rick say to any number of his peers. *Yeah, she couldn't make it out tonight. Too much on her plate, the dear thing. Now, how about we grab a drink at that strip club you mentioned last time I was in town?*

I'm not sure when Rick decided I was too much of a liability to bring around his fancy friends, but at this point in life, I don't give a damn. He can take his holier-than-thou attitude and shove it where the sun hasn't shined a day in his life, and I can . . .

Scrunching my nose, I survey the Hulk with a critical eye. Or as critical as it can be since I'm swaying ever so slightly and he's swaying right along with me. On second thought, pretty sure I'm actually the only one swaying. *Thank you, beer.* "How old are you?"

He barks out a startled laugh. "Legal." As if to prove it, he lifts the Bud Light and pointedly watches me as he takes a swig. "Does that count?"

Probably. As if I'm about to impart some big, crazy secret, I motion for him to meet me in the middle when I lean in close. "I told my son I'd come out tonight and get some adult conversation in. He thinks I need socializing."

Another slow pull of his beer, and like a moth to a flame, my attention drifts to the way his bottle reflects the TV's glowing screen. *Focus.* Nails scraping my pint glass, I look up at his face—or what's visible of it, at least.

Even though I can't see his eyes, I get the feeling that he's studying me shamelessly. Elbow planted on the bar, the bottle hovering millimeters away from his mouth. When the curve of his lips deepens into a smirk, like he can't help but find me amusing, I'm momentarily struck dumb.

"Socializing." He draws out the word on the cusp of a dry, masculine chuckle. "Well, in case you're concerned about corrupting a youngin', let me tell you a little secret . . ." Lowering the Bud Light to the bar, he shifts forward until his mouth brushes the sensitive shell of my ear and a shiver shimmies down my spine. "I don't have an innocent bone in my body."

My breath hitches. "Not even one?"

"You sound disappointed."

I blink. "Do I?"

"Nah, not even a little bit. But I don't regret lying." Warm lips graze my cheek. "You blush real pretty."

Oh. *Oh.*

I jerk back, nearly teetering off the bar stool. "Hold on." Tipsy me thinks it's a *grand* idea to lift my hands, palms up, despite the fact that I'm on the verge of going ass-down to the floor. "Are you *flirting* with me?"

As though he's used to putting up with the drunk and disorderly, he smoothly catches me with one of his mammoth-sized paws and hauls me upright. My naked bicep—thank you, universe, for creating tank tops—tingles at the warmth of his touch.

The physical connection lasts only seconds. One moment he's saving me from absolute humiliation and, in the next, he's sipping his beer again, cool as a cucumber. Slowly, he dips his chin.

Is he checking me out?

It certainly feels that way, especially when his chest inflates with a sudden intake of breath. In the year that I've officially re-entered singledom, I haven't given much thought to dating. I revel in going to bed and not worrying about slamming doors or living with a man who has no concept of kindness. I don't particularly miss sex, especially when my sex life with Rick dried up years ago.

He preferred the company of other women and, after the initial hurt of discovering my husband in bed with someone who was decidedly not me, I grew to treasure every moment that I didn't have to fake my orgasm for the sake of stroking his ego.

But I think . . . well, based on the way I'm squirming on my stool and sneaking peeks at this man's pouty mouth—to say nothing of the broad expanse of his shoulders or the hard pecs that stretch the fabric of his shirt—maybe I wouldn't mind flirting.

At least, I don't mind flirting with a guy like him. Whoever *he* is.

Finding a small seed of sexual confidence that has long lain dormant, I arch my brows and bait him for a response. *Is* he flirting with me? God, please let his answer be yes. "Well?" I ask boldly, going so far as to twirl a finger around a strand of my hair like the hot chick out of a romantic comedy instead of being, well, *me*.

"Old habits die hard."

Come again?

I'm blinking so fast, I'm half-convinced I've developed a sty in the five minutes since he sat down and interrupted my otherwise boring evening.

Quiet.

I meant my otherwise *quiet* evening.

Snapping my head to the side, I press my hand to my ear in disbelief. "I'm sorry. Did you just say *old habits die hard*?"

What. A. *Jerk.*

It's one thing to confess he's not attracted to me, and another to go in for the *moment*—you know the one—the meaningful look, the throaty, sexy laughter that all but signals foreplay, orgasms, and expert make-out sessions—and play a game of takesy-backsies.

Takesy-backsies shouldn't even be *allowed* once you've spotted your first gray hair in your pubes. And I'm five in, ladies. *Five.* Maybe more. I wouldn't know, since I have my esthetician regularly wax the suckers out and call it a day.

Good*bye,* evil age reminders.

I reach for my clutch by my empty pint and pop it open. I'm fully prepared to drop cash on the bar for Shawn and get the hell out of dodge when the Hulk grunts out, "Look. Listen."

Hands clasped together, I turn to him, brows arched in expectation.

Unfortunately for him, I'm not in the habit of accepting casseroles in place of apologies like my mother.

I spent fourteen years kissing Rick's ass and I'll be damned if I do the same for a stranger. I don't care how muscular his arms are or that his chest is wide enough for me to curl up and take a nap alongside my nonexistent cat.

The Hulk hooks a finger in the collar of his black shirt. Then drops his hand to the bar, fingers closed in a fist. "Listen—"

"You said that already."

That tight fist unfurls until his fingers are digging into the mahogany bar, leaving me with the distinct impression that I'm poking a not-so-hibernating bear.

Bring it.

"You're cute," he says, like I should be grateful for the assessment. Like I'm not a woman closing in on forty with a teenage son and goddamn gray hairs threatening to sprout at any moment from my nether regions.

A puppy is cute.

A kid in kindergarten is cute.

I am *not*—

"Cute," he repeats with oblivious male arrogance, "but I'm not looking to pick anyone up tonight."

For possibly the first time in my life, I'm rendered mute.

If Topher knew, he'd commemorate the moment by marking it as a national holiday.

If my mom knew, she'd whip out her phone and get me on the first dating app she could find—all before I could protest about not wanting to meet a guy right now.

Which I don't.

I'm *not* looking, which doesn't at all explain why I'm contemplating rearing back an arm and busting this guy in the jaw. Clearly, this delicious-looking douchebag has inspired a bout of insanity—it's the only reason I have for envisioning the dimple puncturing the center of his chin being used as bull's-eye practice for my fist.

Wishing his hat wasn't in the way, so I could, at least, stare daggers at him with surefire accuracy, I growl, "No wonder you're taking up for Dominic DaSilva. Kindred spirits, after all."

"Yeah?" He drains his Bud Light. When he pulls the bottle away, his damp lips glisten. Then they glisten even more when he runs his tongue along them. Unwanted heat gathers in my core, just as he taunts, "How's that?"

Feeling emboldened by how much I'm growing to *dislike* this man, I leverage my weight by dropping my hands to his single bent knee. Beneath his dark-washed jeans, hard muscles flex and unclench under my fingers.

"Here's a clue," I clip out succinctly, "you're both assholes."

A moment's pause.

I hear Stuart/Stewart at the back of the pub arguing

about the merits of the Patriots drafting a rookie quarterback next season.

I hear Shawn taking a new patron's order.

And then—

And then the knee beneath my hands is quivering because the damn bastard is laughing. *Laughing!* Head tipped back. Throat elongated. One hand lifting to his chest like if he presses hard enough, he might have a chance to stem the flow of mirth.

I'm momentarily drunk-tracted by the sound.

Husky.

Low.

Sex bottled up in the form of masculine enjoyment.

I hate him on principle alone.

Grabbing my wallet from my clutch, I sloppily pull out a twenty and toss it on the bar. No change needed. There's not a chance in hell I'm gonna wait around for it, all for the entertainment of the douchebag propped up next to me who thinks it's *hilarious* that I dared to imagine he might be interested in me.

When I make a move to leave, the Hulk halts me with a hand to my shoulder. "Hey. You can't drive home like this."

"Ninety-percent asshole."

If I could see his brows, I bet they'd be sky high right now. As it is, his mouth opens and then slams shut. "What?"

"You heard me," I mutter, drawing my clutch to my chest like a shield from his overwhelming masculinity. "I don't know where you're from, buddy, but you're clearly not a local."

"California." When I jerk my head up, he clears his throat. "Originally, I mean. I'm from San Francisco."

Well, that explains it.

I met a *lot* of Hollywood folks early on in my marriage to

Rick, back when he still enjoyed toting me around like his toy of the month. Some were nice. Most were phony. All had a certain scent of privilege permeating through their pores. And this one here . . . my gaze catches on the gold Rolex encircling one thick wrist.

Yeah, he might be wearing an old-as-shit hat, but the watch weaves the complete story.

Rich.

Entitled.

Just like my ex-husband.

No doubt the Hulk is vacationing here in London, just like Rick was when I first met him that summer before my senior year.

"Word to the wise," I say, pulling up the Uber app on my phone, "Londoners talk. A lot. If you're sticking around long enough to give a shit about whether or not they talk about *you*, I suggest digging deep into that non-asshole ten percent and learn to be a good person."

"Be a good person, huh?"

I tap the screen to pull up the new street address that's belonged to me for all of a month.

"Mhmm." Without glancing up, I pat his shoulder like he's a good dog. "It'll be tough for you, considering all those *old habits* you're going to have to kick to the curb, but I have faith in your abilities to turn your life around."

"How gallant of you," comes his soft, sardonic murmur, "considering you just met me."

Satisfied that the Uber is only minutes away, I drop the phone into my clutch. "A memorable meeting, for sure. It's not every day I start dreaming of ways to punch a hot guy in the face after only ten minutes of conversat—"

I go down.

As in, I go *down*.

Weak, alcohol-inflicted legs.

Numb feet.

Worst-case scenario doesn't even come close to doing this moment any justice—not the way I collapse, knees buckling, and go face-first into the Hulk's crotch.

Face.

First.

Someone just put me out of my misery.

In my desperation to not end up on the floor, my hands snake out and find purchase wherever I can.

His legs, I think.

There's a masculine grunt, loud enough for my sloshed brain to pick up on and send SOS signals sparking to high alert in my system.

Abort! ABORT!!!

The grunt is followed by a big hand cupping the back of my skull, and I'm *distinctly* aware of the barely restrained tension lacing those fingers. Pull me closer, push me away. He's clearly stuck in limbo, and I'm on the verge of holing up in my house and becoming a hermit until the day I die.

I'll miss the sunlight, but when the alternative is this . . .

"Jesus fuck."

His obscenely uttered curse springs me into motion, which seems to shock him into action too. That hand drops to one of my shoulders, followed by the other one doing the same. He tows me upright so easily that air swoops in under my feet as my sneakers leave the floor.

"Jesus *fuck*."

And I thought my dad had a potty mouth. Dad had nothing on *this* guy.

Lurching backward, out of reach, I step back. Then do so again. Anything to put some much-needed space between us.

His hands find his narrow hips, his barrel chest expanding with an unsteady breath. "You're absolutely trashed." He says this like it's a massive inconvenience, something he proves a moment later when he snags his wallet from the back pocket of his jeans and drops cash on the bar. "I'm taking you home."

I stare at him. "I don't get in the car with strangers."

"Considering where you just had your face, I'd say we're practically best friends at this point."

Heat stings my cheeks.

Shoving his wallet back in his jeans, arm muscles visibly bunching with just that slightest movement, he stands there, and I'm forced to tilt my head *back* to look up at his face. Holy cow, is he tall. Way taller than I anticipated. Six-five, maybe. Six-six, probably.

"I ordered an Uber," I inform him stiffly, if only to maneuver the conversation away from my all-too-inappropriate nosedive.

With a chuffed breath, the Hulk steers me toward the front door of the Golden Fleece. "The irony of modern-day living. You're totally fine with jumping into some random person's car without knowing anything about them but you won't get in mine even after our delightful talk."

"Delightful" sounds anything but, given the hostile way it comes out of his mouth.

Together, we step out into the crisp, Maine night. The scent of woods and ocean mingle like the most intoxicating cocktail. I inhale sharply, dredging up all that fresh goodness into my body. Living in Pittsburgh may have worked for my lifestyle with Rick, but Maine is the soothing balm to my soul. Like a salve being smoothed over all my cracked crevices and sharp craters.

The Hulk is ruining my salve.

"For the record," I mutter, "I don't know anything about *you* either."

"You know I'm a ninety-percent asshole."

Sharply, I spin around, catching him off guard. We're close. Close enough that my hands land on his chest and I look up, I see more of his face than I have all night. His features . . . they're familiar.

Strangely so.

"Ninety-five," I counter weakly.

His lips press together. "Tacked on another five percent, did you?"

"Collateral damage that you can earn back."

"Yeah?"

Maybe it's just me, but I *swear* his voice just dropped an octave. Could be the Guinness talking. My tipsy, sex-starved body hoping. Either way, I rise up on my toes, putting our faces as close together as humanly possible, considering our height difference, and murmur, "Never mention that *moment* from inside again, and you'll be set to go."

His chest shakes with silent laughter. "You're assuming we'll be running into each other again."

"If you're living in London, we'll be lucky if we're not neighbors."

Leaning down, putting his mouth next to my ear, like he did when he first sat down next to me, he husks out, "Might want to give me a perfect score, then."

I squeeze my legs together. "Oh, yeah?"

"Yeah." He steps close, one foot in my direction, but it's enough to bring our chests flush together. *Oh, boy.* "I'm a guy who can't walk away from a challenge. So unless you want me goin' out of my way to look for you all over town . . ."

He lets the threat dangle out in the open.

He's flirting again, and I . . . I swallow over the thick lump in my throat. "I'd rather you didn't."

A car honks its horn behind me.

My ride.

I stumble back, gravel crunching beneath my shoes. "See you when I see you?"

Moonlight splices across his face as he lifts his ball cap for the first time all night, and for a moment—a split second in time—my heart stutters in a quick tattoo that echoes to the beat of *oh, God no*, because the Hulk, the stranger whose jean-clad crotch I met without preamble, looks a *whole* lot like Dominic DaSilva.

I scrub my eyes with the heels of my palms, disregarding the makeup I'll be washing off as soon as I walk through my front door in ten minutes.

There is *no way* it's him. DaSilva, I mean.

A famous, former football player camping out in London, Maine—population three thousand at the peak of tourist season?

Impossible.

Blearily, I blink my eyes open.

His hat is back in place, and he's standing there watching me, feet spread wide like a cowboy ready to wrangle a steer. "Forget something?" he calls out, that gravelly voice of his surrounding me like dark smoke.

It's not him.

It can't be.

Go home, brain. You're drunk.

Beyond drunk, apparently. There's no other explanation for me closing the blinds of my new home an hour later, only to see a truck pull in next door . . . and the Hulk-Definitely-Not-Dominic-DaSilva clamber out.

With my hand pressed to the cool glass window, I watch,

slack-jawed and swaying on my bare feet, as that now all-too-familiar massive body strides up the driveway to the house that's had U-Haul trucks parked outside it all week.

He pauses at the front door.

My heart gathers in my throat.

(Or maybe that's the beer-induced vomit already threatening to make an appearance.)

And then he goes *inside*.

I let the curtain fall, obscuring my view of the street. Twist around. Let my body slip against the glass window until my ass is on the floor, my forehead is parked on my bent knees, and I'm forced to admit out loud:

"Guinness is the devil."

And I'm never drinking it again.

DOMINIC

"*A*ssistant coach."

It's all I can do not to spit out the words as I sit opposite London High's athletic director.

Adam Brien and I go way back—we both played on the offensive line at Louisiana State University. During the off-season, we partied together until the sun crested the horizon. I suited up and attended his first wedding in Rhode Island—I was out of the country for his second—and I regularly send gifts for every one of his kids' birthdays.

Normally, hanging out with him would be cause for celebration. Pop open a beer can. Kick my feet up on the desk. Ruminate about all the good times we shared when we were fifteen years younger.

This situation is anything but normal.

I stare down at the contract, my fingers splayed over the London High School crest printed at the top of the page. Drag my gaze up, up, up until I'm looking my old buddy in the eye and feeling my mouth twist in a sneer. "You've got to be fucking shitting me."

Brien drums his fingers on the desk, his expression, for

once, giving nothing away. "You can't be droppin' F-bombs like that around the kids."

Without missing a beat, I point to his signature scrawled at the bottom of the first page. "If they saw this shit, they'd be dropping F-bombs too." Hands flat on the desk, I lean in. *Keep your calm. Don't lose your shit.* Swallowing down all the four-letter words that are wanting to join the party, I grit out, "A month ago, you promised me the head coach position. I just fuc—"

And, repeat: no F-bombs.

Clearing my throat, I try again. "I just moved across the country, bought a house that looks like the backdrop to a 70s porno, with floral wallpaper and shag carpet everywhere, all so I could do you a solid."

That makes Brien laugh. Uproariously. "Do *me* a solid? DaSilva, you were *fired*. You, man, not me."

If I were the sort of guy who blushed, my cheeks would be flaring red right about now.

And, yeah, there's no denying it. I *was* fired, though that particular call had nothing to do with me and everything to do with inner-company politics. Hollywood is a firepit of snakes, and I was more than willing to play the game, so long as the checks kept coming in too.

Go on that new dating show, my former boss at Sports 24/7 told me.

Network ratings are down and a publicity stunt, like you falling in love on national TV, could do us all a favor, he said. *Put A Ring On It? Hell, all you need to do is stick around for a few weeks before getting yourself booted off.*

So, I went.

And I stayed longer than just a few weeks.

Because I'm all about taking one for the team and doing the dirty work. Blame it on foster-care syndrome, if you want, or we can just call a spade a spade: Hollywood is a cesspit of the mundane, a real-life version of *Groundhog Day* where the same shit happens day after day. I was more than willing to go on an adventure and get paid while doing it.

Maybe that makes me an asshole.

I'm more inclined to think it makes me an opportunist.

An opportunist with a heart.

Lips clamping shut, I rake my fingers through my hair, tugging at the ends in frustration. "Brien, you called as soon as news broke of the network letting me go." They'd fired me for the same reason they'd asked me to go on *Put A Ring On It*: network ratings. Only, Sports 24/7 hadn't appreciated their cover being blown post-production. Within months, I went from being the alleged forerunner on the show to the man who went on for all the wrong reasons. Once the episodes began airing a month ago, Sports 24/7 cut their losses. In other words, I got kicked to the curb. "You said you had a gig all lined up for me here," I add, keeping my temper in check. "Teach P.E. Coach ball. I bought a house—"

"With how much money you've got, it's more of a tax write-off than a forever home, man. Don't get it twisted."

He's not wrong about that.

I bought a two-bedroom cottage on a cul-de-sac that needs some serious Chip and Joanna Gaines sorta love. Floral wallpaper. Pink, Pepto-Bismol carpets in the bedrooms and bathrooms. Laminate tile throughout the rest of the house. A garage that can't even fit a lawn mower, never mind my truck. Wood-paneled walls.

The house is a complete train wreck, and the only reason I bought the place is because it has one of the few exclusive accesses to a private beach here in London that won't run me over a million bucks. Had I wanted to, I could have easily purchased one of the mansions up on Madison Drive. Moved into it with absolutely no work necessary. Lived the same damn life I've been living in Los Angeles for the better part of four years.

And I'd be just as bored too.

So, yeah, I passed on the mansions for a thirteen-hundred-square-foot home that'll prove to be a sound investment once I do some major renovating.

Private beach. Larger profit margins. Cheap mortgage.

It was a no-brainer.

Faced with my silence, Brien drops his head back with a sigh. He's wearing a London High polo shirt with the Wildcat mascot stitched into the fabric. Swap out the red-and-white colors, erase the gray hairs coming in at his temples, and I can almost believe we're shooting the shit just like we did back in college.

Almost.

"Levi came back, man."

It's all he says, but it's enough for me to sit up a little taller and narrow my eyes. "What sort of secret local code is that? Give me the translation."

Looking a little on edge, Brien's hand comes off the desk to pinch the bridge of his nose. "The Levi family is football royalty around here. Grandpapa Levi played for the Buffalo Bills, then came home to coach the Wildcats once he retired. Papa Levi did the same, about twenty years later, once he was out of the NFL."

I look to the contract, a sinking sensation swirling in my gut like spoiled milk. "So, what? Levi Junior is back home and ready to claim the throne?"

"Something like that."

Jesus.

Nothing like small-town politics to remind you that you're an outsider.

Unfortunately for London—but fortunately for me—the first half of my life was spent outside the proverbial glass walls, my hand raised and waving, hoping someone would take pity on the poor-as-shit kid with a chip on his shoulder the size of California and the perpetual hope in his gaze that just wouldn't quit.

The hope is long gone, but the chip's still got permanent residence.

Thing is, the only person who has the power to make you feel like a forgotten soul is you—and I don't give a damn what Londoners think of me.

"The school board doesn't care about your Super Bowl wins, DaSilva," Brien goes on, finally dropping his chin as he cuts his gaze away from the ceiling. "They don't care that you were MVP multiple seasons in a row. They don't care that you won the Heisman trophy back in college or that, until someone comes around and demolishes your stats, you're the best tight end the league has ever seen."

Hearing my accolades dished back to me has me shifting uncomfortably in my seat. I've won a lot of trophies over the years. I've beaten a shit ton of records. I've earned more money than I know what to do with.

But none of it really matters at the end of the day—

The Bucs let me go after an injury kept me hospital-bound for weeks.

Sports 24/7 cut me loose when I made the ultimate mistake in thinking, for just one second, that maybe it was fate that led me onto *Put A Ring On It* and right into the arms of Savannah Rose.

My gut clenches at the memory of her. Not because I'm in love but because spending time with her, even with a dozen other guys milling around on set, proved to be more illuminating to my own psyche than anything else I've experienced so far in life.

Savannah Rose was kind. Open. America's adored sweetheart.

Good as I am at flirting like my life depends on it, I can say with complete honesty that there's not a soul on this planet who truly knows me. Not even Nick Stamos, my best friend and fellow *Put A Ring On It* contestant, or Adam Brien, who I've known for years, or Savannah Rose, who should have been so easy to trust.

Welcome to the life of Dominic DaSilva, party of one.

"Levi's a Londoner," Brien tells me, hands clasped together on the desk, a no-BS expression on his face. "You could dance naked in front of the board, and they'd still pass you over."

"You sure about that? The cardboard cutout of me wearing nothing but briefs is regularly sold out on Amazon."

"That's because Good Samaritans buy that shit and use it as kindling for fire."

Laughter climbs my throat. "Asshole."

"Nothing I haven't heard before. My wife calls me that like it's a goddamn endearment. Honey who?"

Fingers scraping over my skull, I slouch down and spread my thighs wide to avoid smacking my knees on the underside of the desk. "Assistant coach," I muse dryly, shaking my head. "Someone, somewhere, is taking way too much joy at my expense."

Brien lifts a finger. "That'd be me. Remember when you convinced the guys to play dead every time I dropped back to make a pass for a week straight?" His eyes narrow, like he's being confronted with the long-ago memory of the entire LSU offensive line going belly-up on the field, our legs and arms sticking straight in the air like a herd of fainting goats. Watching Brien lose his temper—a true rarity —made every lecture about unprofessionalism from Coach Wynters worth it. "Think of this as long overdue penance," he adds without a single trace of heat. "Payback's a bitch, motherfuc—"

"Mr. Brien, *language!*" a voice admonishes from behind me.

Twisting around, I lay an arm over the back of the chair. Make eye contact with the elderly woman hovering in the doorway. "I've told him the same thing twice now, Miss . . ."

Reaching up to fluff her gray bouffant, she shoots me a welcoming smile. "Irene. Irene Coleman."

I never met my grandmother, but if I had, I'd like to think she would look like this woman. Crinkled crow's feet. Big smile lines bracketing her mouth. Bright, eye-blinding clothing that looks more at home on a parakeet in the tropics than a small, New England town.

"Nice to meet you, Irene." I flash her one of my trade-mark grins. *Old habits die hard.* It's what I told the woman in the pub last night right after I caught myself leaning in to lay it on thick. And right *before* I reminded myself that I was done with shameless, meaningless flirtations. At thirty-five, I'm not looking to settle down. I'm not even looking for a fling. What I am is fucking exhausted with playing the same role everyone expects from me.

Bad-boy Dom. Flirty Dom. Devil-may-care Dom.

I may have given Brien's initial proposition some thought because he's a longtime friend—but I ultimately moved to Maine because I'm in desperate need of a reprieve.

A reprieve that doesn't include taking home cute blondes for one-night-stands.

Feeling my smile weaken, I mentally push the damn bastard back into place. "Sorry, long few weeks," I say smoothly, by way of apology. "I'm Dominic, the—"

"New assistant football coach."

Fucking Brien.

Irene pushes her wire-rimmed frames up her nose with a single finger. "Oh, you'll just *love* it here, Coach. The kids are really, really great. I'm the athletic department's secretary. I handle it all . . . basketball, soccer, gymnastics, the works. If you ever need anything, you just let me know, dear."

Don't stop smiling. "Will do, Irene. Thanks in advance for all your help."

She gives a little hop on her heels, then waves goodbye to us both.

I wait for the chipper staccato of her footsteps to fade before I turn to my former teammate with a scowl. "I didn't say yes to the position."

"You didn't say *no* either."

I didn't say no because I'm far too deep into my escape-the-Hollywood-vultures plan to turn back now. With *Put A Ring On It* finally airing on TV, Los Angeles has become stifling. Paparazzi pop out of bushes to sneak pictures of me. Recently I was cornered in a grocery store, cucumber in hand, and asked by a camera-wielding stranger, "Is that thing the same size of your member, Dominic? Readers are dying to know." Last month, I even sued a "journalist" after she followed me into my gym's locker room and took pictures of me showering.

I'm not a prude—never have been—but cross the line and I guarantee I'll be the last man standing.

As if following my train of thought, Brien pulls open a drawer and slides a ballpoint pen across the desk. "We both know Maine isn't a forever stop for you, man. You're gonna stick it out long enough to lick your wounds and flip that house you bought. I'll be more than happy to write you a letter of recommendation when you're done playing small-town-living and ready to head home to the city of smog."

At his letter of rec dig, I flash him the bird.

Even as my heart tangles in a knot.

I don't know when the thought of Los Angeles won't make me want to reach for a beer and drain it dry. Two months, maybe. Eight months. Three years. With no property to tie me down in California—I sold it all—my life is up in the air.

Much as I don't want to admit it, I know Brien's suggestion is the way to go.

I refuse to be the asshole coach who lets his team down, no matter the fact that I don't know any of the kids who'll show up bright-eyed and bushy-tailed for the first day of practice. What if Brien is right and, halfway through the season, I decide I can't hole up in Maine anymore? What happens to the kids then, if I fight for the head coach position?

I hold way too much respect for the sport to put its players at a disadvantage, and my old teammate knows it. As for the teaching physical education part of the gig, it's not like the job can't be filled ASAP if I do dip out. It's all temporary at best.

Taking the assistant position is smarter—and better—for everyone involved.

Bitterness tightens my grip as I put ballpoint tip to paper, the black ink curdling on the page in a heavy drop. From NFL player to TV host to high school assistant football coach. I'm on a downward trajectory that burns like cheap vodka going down the wrong pipe.

Contract signed, I cap the pen.

Brien grins at me. "Congrats, man. You're officially a London Wildcat now." He spins on his chair and nabs a cardboard box from the ground. Out comes a T-shirt, which he tosses over to me. It's a XXXL, big enough to fit over my shoulders and arms, and not risk turning into a belly-revealing crop top. Red fabric, white font.

My surname is printed on the back, and then, right below, it reads: *Assistant Coach.*

My gaze leaps up to meet Brien's. "You knew I'd agree?"

He shrugs. "I hoped your pride would let you."

Pride is a fickle mistress, though, and as I fold the T-shirt over my shoulder, all I can hope is that this Levi dude doesn't make me regret my decision to stick around.

4

ASPEN

*T*hree days after the Golden Fleece Incident, I'm strangling the non-existent life out of my seat belt. Car wheels squeal as Topher bangs a hard uey to head the opposite way down Main Street toward the high school. His brown hair, so much like his father's, is longer up front, and he blows upward out of the corner of his mouth to get the strands out of the way.

The tactic fails him as he rolls right past a stop sign.

"*Stop!*" My back jerks against the cushioned seat as my baby boy slams on the brakes like his life depends on it.

But instead of looking remorseful for almost driving us into a busy intersection, he slips a hand from the steering wheel and tries to pat the top of my head. He misses and catches the slope of my nose instead.

"You're fine, Ma. Deep breaths."

I swat his hand away. "Ten and two, Toph. Ten and *two*. What in the world are they teaching you kids at Driver's Ed nowadays?"

He hesitates, the pause more than a little obvious since the radio is off and there's nothing but the sound of my *I'm-*

going-to-die breathing to keep us entertained. He digs his tongue into the inner flesh of his right cheek, a nervous tick that's stayed with him since childhood.

Immediately on the alert, my eyes narrow. "Nuh-uh, bud. Pull the car over and spill."

"We're gonna be late for workouts," is his only excuse as he pumps the gas and clears the intersection. "Which means we'll be late on our very first day. We can't let that happen, Coach."

The little speed demon accelerates, and my stomach does this topsy-turvy thing that has nothing to do with it being my first day coaching the Wildcats and everything to do with Topher's shoddy driving skills.

A car honks to my right, daring me to glance in that direction and see all the reasons I made the wrong call this morning by letting Topher get some driving practice in on the way to the football field.

Hello there, Bad Decisions, it's awful to see you again.

As delicately as possible, I sip coffee from my Dunkin' Donuts traveler mug. Once caffeinated, I breathe a little easier. "I know you're worried about the other kids, baby."

His narrow shoulders twitch as he circles the steering wheel, heading north to the school. "Don't . . . you aren't gonna call me that around my teammates, right?"

"Baby?" I ask, keeping my tone light and unassuming. This is new territory for us, me coaching where he attends school. In Pittsburgh, I always worked in a different district, preferring instead to give him space to live without his mother hanging around at all times. But the enclave of Frenchman Bay is tiny, Mount Desert Island being even smaller. I've counted my lucky stars ten times over that London was even hiring and gave us a chance to leave Pittsburgh.

And Rick.

Ten and two-ing the wheel, Topher gives the most imperceptible nod.

"What would you rather I call you?" I settle into my seat, legs crossed at my ankles. Quickly, I think of crazy nicknames off the top of my head. "Gangster Toph? Hey, You? Giraffe Legs?"

The sound of Topher's laughter fuels my own happiness. There's been so, so little of it over the last year, ever since he caught Rick in bed with a woman who was decidedly not *me*. Scratch that—two women. Instead of waiting for the embarrassment to reemerge, as it always does, I drink more coffee.

Maine is the fresh start Topher and I both need.

"I like Giraffe Legs, I think." Topher jerks his chin toward where his legs are powering the pedals. "It fits."

At five-ten, I'm no shrinking violet. And yet, just the other day, Topher stood next to me in the kitchen, while he grabbed a bowl from the cabinet, and we were shoulder-to-shoulder. Give him another few months and he'll shoot right past me.

I try not to cry. Life was so much simpler when I could push my baby boy around in a stroller all day and not worry about him driving us into a ditch.

"Left here into the parking lot," I tell him, gripping the seat-belt strap a little tighter in preparation for the final leg of our whopping ten-minute journey. This morning, it's felt like ten minutes going on a hundred. "Slow, Toph. Take it *slow*."

Honk! Honk! Honkkkkkkkk!

Oh, *crap.*

A red Volkswagen Beetle powers toward us. "Right!" I shout, darting out a hand to yank on the steering wheel. "To the right." My precious car cries its little heart out as it hurtles back over the yellow lane markers.

"Mom, we're going to miss the turn—"

"Nope." Blood pounds furiously in my head. Is this what it means to have a near-death experience? It certainly feels that way. "Keep going. We'll make the U-turn up ahead."

A pregnant pause. And then a hushed, "I didn't mean to almost kill us."

"I know, baby, I know. But I'm not kidding when I say I'm gonna have a talk with your Driver's Ed teacher. Eight-hundred bucks, Toph. That's how much I spent on those classes, and clearly the man can't even explain to you proper turning procedures—right here, ease up on it. Slow . . . yeah, there you go. Now turn."

Topher decelerates to a crawl, maneuvering into the turn at such a halted pace that my foot is pressing a gas pedal that doesn't exist on the passenger's side of the car.

I sip my coffee and pretend it's something stronger.

Once in the parking lot, Topher breaks into a wide smile. "I did it! Right, Ma?"

"Yup, you sure did."

If he hears my relief, he doesn't call me out on it. He's too busy bopping his head along to the rhythm of tires rolling over cracked gravel while he searches for a place to park. His hair flops across his forehead again, and, knowing that I'll be in Coach mode for the rest of the morning, I push it back for him.

No matter the fact that he'll be trying out for varsity at the end of the summer, he's still the same little boy who used to beg me to throw the football around with him in the backyard when his dad was away at Steelers games and we were left behind.

He shoots me a crooked-tooth smile. It's all joy, mixed in with a bit of restless energy.

His emotions are a mirror image of my own.

Adam mentioned over the phone last night that I'll be meeting the new assistant coach today. At first, I couldn't help but feel a pang of annoyance over not being able to pick my own staff like I've done at every school since I started coaching. But I've always been a firm believer in knowing when to make waves and when to hold your grievances close to the vest. With people like Stuart under the misguided impression that I feel entitled to lead the Wildcats because of the Levi name, now is *not* the time to rock the boat.

No matter what they think, I'm not some insolent brat ready to throw a temper tantrum because I didn't get my way. I've spent years living outside the Levi home base, where my surname meant jack squat—not to the school board or to the parents of the players or, even, to my own husband.

I'm an expert in biding my time and waiting for the opportune moment to strike. In the meantime, I trust Adam's opinion. If he thinks this new guy will be a solid addition to the team, then I'm willing to rally behind the cause.

For now, at least.

Pointing to a row of mostly empty spots lining the pathway down to the fields, I murmur, "Right there. Careful of that truck, Toph."

"I got this, Mom."

"Of course you do, baby."

Two seconds later, it's clear to everyone involved that he does not, in fact, *got this.*

Instead of leaving enough space between the two vehicles, he cuts in close, no doubt trying to slip my Honda Civic between the parallel white lines, and bumps right into the parked truck.

Fun fact: two vehicles making it to second base releases the most godawful squeal you'll ever hear.

It sounds like thousand-dollar paint jobs and the joyous, *pay-up* applause of car insurance companies all around the world.

"*Topher!*"

My car skids alongside the truck's profile, dragging and whining, as Topher panics and accelerates instead of hitting the brakes. More squealing. More dollar signs flashing before my eyes. The truck emits a murderous *beeeeeeeeep!* and I give up all pretense of not gripping the oh-shit handle.

The forward momentum dies a second later, as does my soul.

"Mike—Driver's Ed Mike—he likes to tell us stories about how he did a whole lot of drugs when he was younger and once ran from the cops through a forest of marijuana."

A *forest* of marijuana?

I blink.

Refocus on the Tom Brady bobblehead thrashing around on my dashboard.

Open my mouth and mutter, "Now's not the time for a confessional."

"I thought I was gonna die."

"Sorry to disappoint, bud, but you're still kicking."

And long enough to promise the owner of that truck that you're going to repay all the damage you just caused.

Abandoning my Dunkin's in the cupholder, I crack open the passenger door and round the hood of my car. With firm resolution, I keep my eyes rooted to the concrete instead of checking out the probable mutilation of my poor Honda.

I hear a door slam shut, followed by clipped footfalls that are way too heavy to belong to Topher.

Deep breath in. Deep exhale out.

My lungs give a shallow, *eff-you* pump.

Looks like all the meditation I do every morning isn't going to help me in a real-world crisis.

Figures.

Hands on my hips, I raise my gaze from my hot-pink sneakers to the massive feet encased in black running shoes. No socks that I can see. I trail my eyes up, over strong calf muscles dusted with dark springs of hair to black mesh shorts clinging to thick, tree-trunk thighs. Up some more, to the familiar red-and-white London High polo I'm also wearing, and oh, boy, but there goes my breakfast.

My stomach churns uneasily, a sick, foreboding sensation tumbling through me.

Fight or flight.

Since my kid just wreaked havoc on this guy's truck, fight it is.

Recognition spears me like a two-pronged fork, right in the jugular, as I take in that familiar jawline and that equally familiar cleft chin.

The Hulk.

Whose crotch I face-planted on.

Who called me "cute."

Who I swear, in my drunkenness, I saw waltz into the house next door to mine, late on Friday night. In the three days that have passed since, there have been no U-Haul trucks or other vehicles parked out front for me to inspect.

I gulp, audibly, and finally look all the way up.

Firm lips are flat and unamused as they part to growl, "Is this what you had in mind when you said, 'See you when I see you?'"

I'm not prepared for what happens next.

Not the way he flings his baseball hat on the hood of his truck.

Nor the way he drags his fingers through thick, inky-black hair.

And most assuredly not the way my pulse kicks into overdrive when my eyes settle on his rugged features and my suspicions are confirmed.

Standing approximately three feet away, looking like a total, pissed-off male, is none other than Dominic DaSilva.

God help me.

5

DOMINIC

*S*he knows who I am.

Inside the candlelit world of the Golden Fleece, there was no doubt in my mind that the cute, drunk blonde didn't recognize me. We'd sat side by side with her mouthing off about how much of an asshole Dominic DaSilva was.

Is.

Shit, does it really matter? End of the day, the anonymity gave me an unexpected thrill. Like an adrenaline junkie watching the ground rise up fast, just before the release of the parachute, I'd done nothing to reveal that I was the same "asshole" clutching his leg on the TV.

Had it been uncomfortable to watch the lowest point of my life play out on screen while a bunch of strangers hollered their joy from every corner of the pub?

Yep.

Had I cared, especially once she ditched the prim and proper attitude and loosened up?

Not even a little.

There's a special circle of hell reserved for people like you.

A visual of her calling me an asshole just like him—*me.* *Just like me*—springs to mind, only to be cast aside by the memory of her landing face-first on my dick.

Embarrassment had pinkened her cheeks and sharpened her tongue, and there'd been one heavy, electric moment when I nearly said "screw it" to my mission of staying in my own lane and away from women and dating and relationships.

Because those pink lips of hers had beckoned. Strongly.

Now, standing mere feet away from her, I'm glad for resisting the urge to lean in and discover how she likes to be kissed. Aggressive, with warring tongues and nipping teeth? Or slow and soul-wrenchingly sweet?

Doesn't matter.

Considering how she's gaping at me, *oblivious* is no longer her middle name. She knows exactly who I am.

I shouldn't have taken off the damn hat.

Too late now.

Her jaw is hanging open and her eyes are the size of saucers.

One slender hand lifts to clutch her shirt collar—the same one I'm wearing—and an ominous feeling slicks through me.

Red-and-white London High polo.

The Wildcat mascot, paired with a football in motion, is printed over her left breast.

My gaze drifts south, over her loose shorts and the neon-pink tennis shoes on her feet. She's decked out in workout gear. Her blond hair is tugged up into a high ponytail, the tips of which brush her right shoulder. Unlike the other night, her face is completely devoid of makeup.

Though her lips are still the same berry shade that made me think twice about turning her down. *Au natural.* They're full and plump and instead of curving up in a smile like she's excited to see me, they're shaped in an *O*.

"Fuck me."

At her hushed whisper, I jerk my eyes away from her mouth like I've been caught with my hand inching toward the proverbial cookie jar. "What did you say?"

Her hand drops away from her shirt to point an accusing finger at me. "No."

It's all she says. *No.* And yet that one syllable rocks my entire world.

Because if she's here at London High, dressed like that, at seven in the fucking morning on a Monday, there's only one conclusion to be made here and we both know what it is:

"Levi."

Blue eyes, the color of San Francisco Bay at sunrise—so deep a shade they almost don't appear blue at all—blink back at me, her throat working hard with a swallow. "You know my name."

I rest a hand against the still-warm grill of my Ford 1-50. "I didn't then."

We both know what "then" I'm referring to.

"You let me think you were someone else."

And I enjoyed every second of stepping out of "Dominic DaSilva's" size sixteen shoes. Enough that I wouldn't change a single thing about the hour we spent talking at the pub, including the tense moment when we went from strangers to the intimately acquainted.

I've spent the last three days picturing her blond head buried in my lap.

Not that I'll ever admit that out loud.

Grasping my old hat off the truck, I swipe it against the outside of my thigh. Then shoulder past her so I can check out how much damage we're looking at here. "A slip of the tongue," I tell her, fitting the ball cap on my head and squaring off the brim. "We'll call it even."

"*Even?*"

"Even," I confirm smoothly. "You jacked up my car."

"You let me call you an asshole and didn't even have the decency to clue me in that I was making a complete fool of myself!"

"Are we talking about before or after you used my lap as a personal pillow?"

When silence greets me, I glance over my shoulder to see her miming strangulation. No need to question whose throat she's envisioning caught between her slender hands. I flash her a shit-eating grin. She flashes me the bird. And then I hear a teenage voice shout, "No middle fingers, Ma! Your rules, not mine. Pizza's on you tonight!"

Ma?

I duck down, one hand planted on her car's roof, and spot a teenager lounging in the passenger's seat. As though sensing my stare, his head swivels to the left. I watch his mouth move—"*Oh, crap,*" he mutters, I think—right before he throws open his door and scrambles out into the parking lot. He zips around the car, nearly careening into Levi, who cuts his stride short with a hand to his shoulder.

They're the same height but look nothing alike.

The kid's got dark hair flopping over his forehead like a wannabe Justin Bieber. He's lanky across the chest, wiry down the arms, and his legs could pass for string beans.

Oh, the joys of teenage boyhood.

I remember growing like a weed, too.

"You've got to be kidding me," Levi hisses to the kid, her hand still locked over his shoulder. "You moved to the *passenger's* seat?"

Her son has the good grace to dig his shoe into the gravel and look ten shades of apologetic when he mutters, "It seemed like a good idea at the time. I panicked, Ma. What if my permit got taken away? What if I couldn't play football anymore? One minute I was sitting there with my hands on the wheel and then, before I knew it, I was crab-crawling over the shifty thing."

"It's not called a 'shifty' thing." She throws up air quotes and I bite back a grin. Flustered is a good look on her— objectively speaking, of course. "And I can't believe you . . ." She sucks in a sharp breath, and I'd have to be blind not to notice the way her ample chest lifts with the inhalation. "It's bad to lie."

Then she turns to me, no pointed fingers in sight. Not that they're necessary when she's already glaring murder in my direction.

Blue. Her eyes are most definitely blue.

I drop to my haunches and inspect the peeling gray paint. With the heat of the sun beating down on my shoulders, I trace the claw-like scratches marring the side of my truck. It looks like it went to battle with a bear instead of a four-door sedan.

With exaggerated, good guy charm, I murmur, "I agree with you on the lying front."

Clearly caught off guard, she echoes, "You *agree?*"

"Yes, ma'am."

I swear I can hear molars grinding, all the way from over here. "You did not just call me ma'am—"

"Take Brien, for instance." Hands on my bent knees, I shove up to my full height. Six-foot-six in bare feet. Tall as Levi is for a woman, I still dwarf her. And, despite the decades separating who I am today and who I was at her son's age, there's still a mischievous part of me that finds great delight in knowing she has to tip her head way on back to maintain eye contact with me. *If looks could kill, I'd be skewered and left in a ditch by now.* "He let me assume you were a man when he downgraded me to the assistant coach position."

"A man." She spits out the words like they're the most vile thing she's ever heard.

"Assistant coach?" the last bit comes from the kid, whose face promptly lights up like it's his birthday and Christmas all rolled into one. "Hell yes!"

Levi catches her son's arm just as he's about to raise it for a fist-pump. "Heck," she corrects stiffly, never letting her gaze wander away from my face. "No cursing."

His shoulders don't even slump at the reprimand, he's too excited. "This is the best day ever! *Dominic DaSilva* is our coach?"

"*Assistant coach*," she snips distastefully, those blue eyes of hers flashing with a heat that has nothing to do with naked bodies or orgasms. Gone is the soft, flirty woman from Friday night. She's been replaced with a hard-ass. "Don't get ahead of yourself, Topher. He does whatever I say he does. Nothing else."

But there's nothing left she can do to dissuade her son —*Topher*—what kind of hippie dippie name is that?—from letting out a *whoop! whoop!* and spinning away. He hauls open the driver's side door, narrowly missing my truck, and tugs out a duffel bag. With it slung over one shoulder, he gives me an enthusiastic wave.

Not wanting to risk looking like an even bigger prick in front of his mom, I wave right on back.

Throwing an excited glance my way, Topher announces, "I'm gonna head down to the field. Give the news to the team, you know? They're going to be *pumped*!" That's when I see it—those blue eyes that are the same deep shade as Levi's. He might not have her fair coloring, but he's clearly her son in every other way.

He shuffles backward. "You two just take your time now. The guys will understand. Holy *crap*, Dominic-freakin'-DaSilva." He utters the last bit under his breath in complete amazement like I'm some sort of superhero. Louder, he adds, "Sorry about your truck, Coach. My mistake."

"*Topher*. It's more than a mistake. You damaged his—"

"I'm really sorry, Coach!" The kid doesn't stop at his mother's chastising tone. He just keeps on waving as he heads to the field, never turning his back on us. "She's always right!" he shouts out two seconds later. To me, I think. "Just remember that. Aspen Levi is always right!"

Aspen.

Her name settles on my tongue, reminding me of white winters, and crisp, icy breezes, and tumblers of whiskey sipped before a lit fireplace.

Aspen Levi doesn't fit her namesake.

She's spitting fire, sunny days, and currently turning my way with that finger already within striking distance.

I catch it with my right hand, demolishing her pretty, little speech before she even has the chance to get started.

"I'm not very good at following orders," I murmur, slipping my palm fully against hers.

Her nose turns up. "Not good at following orders in general? Or those coming from me because I have a vagina?"

"The first."

Because I spent eighteen years being shuffled from place to place at the snap of someone else's fingers.

I don't know Levi nearly well enough to give her the truth.

Then again, even those I know best know nothing about me at all.

Nothing besides the façade I've paraded around over the years.

A façade that's currently biting me in the ass as *Coach* Levi warms up her argument with squared-off shoulders and a glacial look in her eye. If I hadn't earned a paycheck off my quick reflexes, I'd already be moving my hand to protect the family jewels.

"This is just a game for you," she snaps, yanking fruitlessly at her captive hand. "You don't care about those boys down there. I don't even know how you got this job, but I can tell you right now that—"

"Boys like your son?" I lower my head, tugging her imprisoned hand down to her side until I'm intruding in her space. "Brien—college teammate, by the way—told me all about how the Levis are football royalty around here." Her lips tighten at my mention of her boss, like she hates the idea that she might be stuck with me. *The feeling is entirely mutual.* "Grandpa Levi kicked the whole family legacy off, is what he told me. Then your dad, and now . . . you."

Her brows furrow. "So what?"

"Looks to me like London has a little taste for nepotism."

That gets her hackles roaring. "*Nepotism*? I'm sorry, but you did not just say that we're . . . that I would *ever* stoop to—"

"Should I remind you that we don't know each other?"

Letting her go, I recline against the side of my truck,

crossing my legs at the ankles and my arms over my chest. Like I'm ready to stand here all day and hash this shit out with her. I could, too. There's nothing that gets me more fired up than a good debate. Probably because I spent so many years not talking to anyone before LSU pulled me out of the hell I'd been living in.

"Should we anticipate Topher taking your spot in about ten to fifteen years? Four generations of Levis all owning this town's successes." I whistle low, heavy on the sarcasm. "From where I'm standing, it doesn't look too good, Coach. You need some fresh blood. Just offerin' an opinion."

"*Your* opinion." She growls the words seconds before she pushes past me to yank open the back door to her car. She bends over, ass up in the air, and *Jesus fu*—

My fingers curl in, blunt nails biting into the calloused flesh of my palms. Completely unaware that I'm halfway to a full hard-on, she grabs her belongings and innocently— correction: *unknowingly*—sticks her perky ass up and out as she digs around for whatever the hell she's gathering in her back seat. The hem of her shorts creeps north, revealing more creamy, pale skin.

My dick, traitorous bastard that it is, goes from half-mast to instant erection.

Look away. Right now. Do not *keep staring.*

I hike my chin up, eyes lifting to the sky, because it's either that or crawl into the backseat with her, and, amazing ass aside, I'm not interested in a woman like Aspen Levi.

Single mom.

Ball-buster extraordinaire.

So damn cheerful—the last ten minutes notwithstanding—that I'm just waiting to learn that she commands both the sun and its rays, along with the happiness of all humanity.

"—And for the record," she rants, turning with a bag hanging from one shoulder and a clipboard clasped to her breasts, "I don't care *what* this town thinks of me." The clipboard escapes the confines of her embrace to prod me in the center of my chest with its rounded corner. "I don't care what *you* think about me. You might have played for the Bucs, you might have shiny Super Bowl rings that you kiss and coddle every night before bed, but no one knows this game better than I do. No one."

I quirk a brow at the vehemence in her tone. "Sounds like you're worried you have something to prove, Coach."

Another bump of that clipboard against my chest. "Kiss my ass, DaSilva."

The end of her ponytail thwacks me in the chin as she whips around to head toward the field. Her hips sway angrily, her gait short and clipped like it's taking everything in her power not to jump in her car and finish off what her son started. Given the right circumstances, I have no doubt she'd run me over and not lose any sleep because of it.

I glance at the two vehicles, to the mirror-image paint scratches.

Once she's almost reached the path that leads down to the fields, I holler, "Good thing you have that head coach's salary, Levi!" She darts a suspicious look over her shoulder while I point to my truck. "You're gonna need it."

For the second time in less than an hour, she flips me the bird.

And then, because I can, I pretend to catch the "bird" mid-flight, cup its invisible tiny body in my hands, and kiss its furry little head.

"See you when I see you!" I call out, throwing her own words from the other day back at her. I'll be seeing her within minutes for the Wildcats' first practice, but knowing it'll rile her up? Knowing that she'll be seething all damn practice and thinking of ways to get rid of me when we both know Brien won't allow it?

Yeah, there's something about messing with her that feels real damn good.

And if that makes me the asshole she so wants to believe that I am, so be it.

6

ASPEN

Surprise, surprise—the players love him.

And when I say *love him*, I mean they've been catering to his every whim and desire all practice.

"Coach, you look like you need some water!" one kid exclaims when he spots Dominic's temple beading with sweat, right before he bum-rushes two teammates for a Dixie cup at the watercooler.

"Coach," another one says during warm-ups, while he's bent over at the waist with his fingers dangling toward his toes, "I want arm muscles like you. What'd you do to get 'em? Like a hundred push-ups a day or something?"

"Coach!" shouts another as he lines up at the scrimmage line, knuckles already planted in the turf, rearing to go. "Watch me hustle this play like the time you caught that sixty-yarder in the Super Bowl!"

It's sickening.

Downright vomit-worthy.

Especially when you factor in how old these kids are. Even the seniors were barely preteens at the height of Dominic's career. They're babies—half of them can't even legally drive—and yet they watch Dominic, slack-jawed, as though he's a . . . a *legend*. A bonafide idol stepped down from the heavens to share his wealth of knowledge with them.

Even Topher's doing his fair share of hero-worshipping, and he's spent his entire life around pro football players. Thanks to Rick's job, Topher's no stranger to meeting NFL players and coaches and physical therapists—I mean, the kid celebrated his first five birthdays at Pittsburgh's Heinz Field.

He's never been star struck . . . until now.

Until Dominic DaSilva stormed into my little hometown like he owns the place, doling out high fives and bicep punches and advice like he's some sort of sage wise man who knows everything there is to know about everything.

Breathe in. Breathe out.

I'm grateful for my job.

I'm grateful Topher didn't kill us on the way to practice—although the two of us are going to have a nice, long talk about taking responsibility for our mistakes later tonight.

I'm not *grateful for the way Dominic's shirt keeps riding up to expose that tight V above his shorts . . .*

Damn it.

My lucky stars trick is not doing it for me.

It's the first day of summer camp for both JV and varsity, and my blood pressure is already skyrocketing. If I have to hear one more praiseworthy comment tossed Dominic's way, I'm going to—

"Coach?"

My heart turns over, and sure enough, a fresh-faced kid is standing there, helmet clasped to his practice jersey with dirt caked on his chin. Hope gleams in his dark eyes. "Yes"— I sneak a quick peek at my clipboard, where I've printed a photo of every player on the team alongside basic facts about them—"Timmy? What's going on?"

He's a few inches shorter than me. A freshman, too. New to London High, new to the team. I watched him play in the scrimmage earlier, while both Dominic and I surveyed the field with a keen eye as we rotated players in and out of positions to determine their natural fit. I'm leaning toward wide receiver for Timmy. He's lean and fast and shows no sign of being scared to run and keep on running.

Possibly on varsity, if he can hack it with the older kids.

Shifting his helmet from one hand to the other, he rocks his weight onto the backs of his cleats. "Coach Levi, do you think . . . maybe . . . like, I'm just wondering—"

I stare at him, silently urging him on to get on with it.

You can do it, Timmy. I know you can.

I keep the cheerleading to myself and offer him an encouraging smile instead.

In a burst of speed, he spits out, "I know phones aren't allowed during practice but when we breaked for water, I texted my mom about Coach DaSilva. She *loves* him. I mean, not that she knows him personally or anything. But yeah. And then *she* texted some of the other moms, and now they're on their way here. They want to take pictures. With Coach DaSilva. And us kids." He barely stops to breathe before tacking on, "I'm sorry, Coach Levi."

Pictures.

With Dominic.

Is that the sound of my soul crying or just my teeth gnashing together in an effort to keep on smiling?

I'm suddenly confronted with the visual of *Finding Nemo's* Dory when she sings, *Just keep swimming, just keep swimming, just keep swimming, swimming, swimming.* Dory knew what the hell she was talking about.

My smile doesn't budge.

Clipboard clenched between my hands, tight, like I'm imagining it to be someone's neck—one guess as to whose —I lift my chin and search for the man in question on the field. *There*. About ten yards away, doing squat jumps with the kids. He's easily double their size and when his legs straighten to propel himself upward, it's almost comical how much more height he gains.

Also, unless I'm mistaken, I think he's free-balling it . . .

Up, he jumps. Down, he lands.

I should look away, turn my attention back on Timmy. Dominic DaSilva is a high-rolling jerk-bag. His humor is pointed and aggressive, his baritone voice is laden with mischief—like he's withholding a secret I'll never know— and that's not even taking into account the fact that he has no business being on this field. He doesn't care about these kids, about this town. I know it. He knows it. Adam *should* know it.

When he swings his arms up and over his head, his T-shirt rides high on his flat stomach, exposing that tight *V* again.

Heat zings up my spine, quickening my pulse, and I bite down on my bottom lip.

Unfair. It is so ridiculously unfair that a man like him can have such an obnoxious, rub-me-wrong attitude and yet be the hottest guy to grace this field. Hell, to grace all of Maine.

The thought alone ignites my temper all over again.

Though it doesn't stop my gaze from betraying me. Against my will, I zero in on his shorts as I hear him bellow —"One! Two! Bobby, make sure your feet are comin' all the way off the grass! Four! Five more, guys! Remember to breathe or you'll pass the hell out!"—as all his disciples work in overdrive to please him.

Topher's in with that group too.

I don't know whether to applaud Dominic for earning the boys' respect the old school way—getting in the trenches alongside them—or hate him more because now I'll be expected to do the same.

I've always been a hands-on coach.

I run drills. I point out mistakes and start from the ground up to rework a player's bad habits. I've never been the sort of person who holes up in my office and lets my staff run things for me. Not once in the almost ten years that I've coached middle and high schoolers.

But watching Dominic during the last two hours of our first summer camp practice has made me feel . . . hot and bothered. *No.* Not that. Inadequate is a better way to phrase it, and even that doesn't quite capture the riot of emotions racing through my head.

Uncool.

Yeah, that's the word I'm looking for. Up against the muscular magnificence of Dominic, I feel like the loser coach.

None of these kids care that I was the first female kicker to join the collegiate level of football. None care that, had I not ended up pregnant with Rick's baby, I would have been the first woman drafted to the NFL too.

To them, I'm a Levi. They know my name, if not my face. They know that Levi's have always done well by the team.

In their eyes, there's nothing particularly exciting about me.

Certainly no mothers have ever rushed to practice to take pictures with me.

Then again, I don't have washboard abs, a sexy, *I-know-you-want-to-do-me* smirk, and an athletic bubble butt that should be illegal everywhere but on a *Got Milk?* advertisement.

Dominic has all that in spades.

And Timmy's mom wants a piece of it.

Exactly how many minutes of every practice am I going to spend fending off mothers who are looking for a little Dominic DaSilva side-action?

I face the energetic freshman, noting the way he keeps darting looks behind me toward the parking lot. Keeping my voice light, I ask, "Is your mom married, Timmy?"

"No." He grips his helmet a little tighter. As brave as he is on the field, he's still a kid. An innocent kid with big ol' dreams. "Just me and Mom. Dad left when I was five."

Oh, no.

Instantly, my heart aches for him.

The mom in me wants to pull him in for a big, comforting hug. But a male coach wouldn't do that. A male coach would chuck him on the shoulder, praise him for staying true to his momma and having her back when things got tough, before directing the conversation back to the game.

Back to football.

Finding that perfect blend has always been my biggest struggle.

So, I knock my fingers on the top of Timmy's helmet, once, twice, and then angle him to face Topher, who is currently squirting water from his bottle all over his face.

"See that kid?" I ask.

Timmy nods. "Yeah."

I drop my hand to my hip. "He knows what it's like to have a father not be around." I don't think there was a day in my fourteen-year marriage that Rick remained faithful to me. He enjoyed the chase, and once he caught me, it was as though he didn't know what to do. He didn't want me but neither would he free me—and because of that, Topher's relationship with his father might as well be the retractable string on a yo-yo.

Whenever I tried to leave, Rick made things difficult for Topher. When I retreated into myself and stopped struggling, suddenly Rick was the perfect father figure to our son. By the time we finally divorced, I'd already seen beneath my ex-husband's polished façade to the cracked and angry interior. He never asked for more than holidays with Topher, and his phone calls to our only son over the last year have been sporadic at best and nonexistent at worst.

I may have suffered years of living under Rick's thumb, but it was Topher who suffered the minute we signed the divorce papers. The last words out of Rick's mouth, when he called Topher on our last day in Pittsburgh, were, *See you when I see you.*

That's it.

No promises to visit.

No mentions of *I love you* or *be good for your mom now.*

Just *see you when I see you.*

Topher cried the first leg of the journey, though he did his best to keep his sniffles to himself. With each mile marker we passed, my rage burned a little hotter. And each time my baby boy voiced the question, "Why doesn't Dad care anymore?" I heard what he was really asking: *Why doesn't Dad care about* me *anymore?*

Because snakes don't give a rat's ass about anyone but themselves. Because you can give them loyalty and love and, soon enough, their skin will always peel and reveal their true colors.

Rick Clarke's colors are nothing but narcissistic tendencies and abusive behavior.

He left me to pick up the tattered pieces of our family, to glue the fragments back together again, and show Topher that *we* are a team. Me and him. Always and forever.

Blinking away the memories, I nudge Timmy in the shoulder. "Trust me, I think you two would be good friends."

In a tone weighted with hesitation, Timmy whispers, "He's a sophomore," like it's the biggest obstacle in the world.

Oh, to be fourteen again.

"Yup." I nod, not bothering to refute that fact. "But if you keep playing like you did today, varsity might not be out of reach for you come the end of the summer. By then, age won't matter so long as you bleed red and white."

The kid's smile makes me feel like I've hung the moon, all the planets, and the damn sun, too, for good measure. "I'm gonna bleed red and white, Coach. Just you wait."

"See that you do, Timmy."

He thumps a hand over his helmet in excitement. "Oh! There's my mom."

I turn, clipboard tucked under one armpit.

And nearly cramp a muscle from smiling so freaking hard.

Timmy's mom has brought the brigade.

Women flank her on either side, like geese trailing their leader. Ten in total. I hear their laughter from here, and yeah, maybe it makes me a *little* bit evil to know Dominic's afternoon is on the verge of being disrupted by Chanel perfume, kitten heels—bad idea on grass, that's for sure—and a group of women determined to cozy up to him.

Leaving *me* to take control over the last thirty minutes of practice.

Bull's-eye.

Mission in place, I pat Timmy on the shoulder and swoop forward to meet the moms halfway.

"Coach Levi!" greets a woman with pageant-worthy brown hair. Instead of sticking out a hand in introduction, she wraps an arm around me and pulls me in for a tight hug. Surprise ricochets through me, stiffening my frame, just as she lets me go. "You probably don't remember me."

Should I?

As subtly as possible, I study her features. Big, blue eyes. Dimples twinkling in her cheeks. An imperfect scar bisecting her right brow, leaving me with the impression that the end of the tail has been penciled in.

That scar.

Why is that scar so familiar?

"Meredith," she tells me when the silence clings a little too uncomfortably. "My maiden name is Bweller. I was a year behind you in school . . . you played football with my older brother?"

That scar.

"You tried keeping up with one of our pickup games," I say, my voice low as the memory rises up from the ashes of my youth, "and ran—"

"Directly into a parked car." Her stained red lips tug up in a wide grin. "*Yup*, that was me. Not the highlight of my teenage years, of course. Then again, that's the problem with youthful infatuation, right there. I wanted Steven's best friend to notice me in a big way."

Ouch. I wince in sympathy. "Nate, right?" I readjust the clipboard, holding it with both hands in front of my hips. "I never realized you had a crush on Nate."

"Oh, girl." Her exaggerated eye roll is one for the books. "Crushing doesn't even begin to cover it. I was a Grade-A stalker. The only thing stopping me from sneaking into his bedroom window at night was that he slept on the second floor and the universe cursed me with no lattice to climb like in the movies. It was a travesty."

"Well, it worked out, didn't it?" interjects one of the other women. "You married him and now we all have to watch the two of you frolic together on the beach every Sunday morning."

Oh. *Oh.*

I drop my gaze to her left hand. Sure enough, there's a dainty little diamond nestled next to a simple gold band on her ring finger.

The diamond, in particular, sparkles under the sun, as she fiddles with the ring, her thumb moving it back and forth. "Seven years later this fall." Her chin tips in the direction of the field. "You have our son out there. Bobby. Curly hair like his dad. Blue eyes like me. Crazy good manners. He has my husband to thank for that last one."

Out of all the players this morning, Bobby was the only one to walk up to me and introduce himself after we finished warmups. I didn't recognize his last name from my notes—Sutter, if I'm remembering Nate's correctly—but he impressed me with his openness and maturity.

He's also one of the older kids in the group. Sixteen.

Which means that there's a story there with Meredith and her teenage crush, and their son who was born years before they tied the knot.

When I return my attention to her, her smile has dimmed. Just enough for me to acknowledge the hard challenge in her eye, daring me to call her out and say something rude about Bobby.

You're barking up the wrong tree, I almost confess. I'm the last person who will ever judge a relationship. I mean, look at me—my track record is pure shit. Rick "the prick" Clarke didn't earn his nickname simply because it rhymes. The way I see it, all relationships come with a beginning, a middle, and an end. It's not my or anyone else's business to dig our noses where they don't belong and demand the full details on a story that doesn't include us.

Catching Meredith's eye, I make sure to hold her gaze when I murmur, "Bobby's lucky to have you both. And I'm incredibly lucky to see what he can bring to the team. Here's to hoping he has more of Nate's football skills than yours— no offense, Meredith."

She cracks a grin at my bad joke.

Turning my head to the other moms, I wonder, briefly, if I'm in the wrong for wanting to sic them on Dominic.

Maybe.

Probably.

I don't let it faze me. I'm here to do a job that I love, and while Dominic is proving to be a pain in the butt, his oh-so-holy presence may solve another one of my problems . . .

"Ladies, as the Wildcats' head coach, part of my job is to kickstart fundraising opportunities. I know the season is months away, but when I took this position, I told the athletic director that there was one tradition I wasn't willing to leave behind at my old school."

One woman lifts a hand, her coffin-shaped nails practically clawing at the air. Her features are almost an exact replica of Timmy's—his mom, I assume—a fact she confirms when she barks out, "Tim's mom!" A tiny pause follows, in which she stares me down like I'm all that's standing in her way. "We want to meet Coach DaSilva."

Feeling not the least bit guilty about using my assistant coach as bait, I promise, "And you will."

Okay, I feel a *little* guilty.

But Dominic is a big boy, both literally and figuratively. He can handle it. Hell, based on what I've read online over the years, he's *more* than used to fending off women at every turn. He fended off *me* just this weekend, even.

Old habits die hard.

I hate myself a little for letting his words impact me so greatly. In the grand scheme of things, Dominic's opinion of me means jack squat. So what if he doesn't find me attractive? There are plenty of guys out there who don't make my lady parts tingle. Attraction isn't always a two-way street.

And there *is your hang-up*, my conscience announces like a little traitor.

I promptly shove it into a mental box and flip the lock. I refuse to give any more thought to emotional hang-ups, specifically those that include my ex-husband making me feel like less of a woman.

Big smile now.

It creaks across my face like the reaper of death.

You. Are. Grateful. For. This. Job.

"Having Coach DaSilva on staff will no doubt open some doors for us," I tell the moms, forgetting about my smile as my love for coaching filters into place. "In the past, I've always capped off the end of football camp with a weekend retreat for the players. *Every* player—even those with families who can't afford the expense—deserve to go." One by one, I catch the eye of every woman standing before me in a semi-circle. If I can convince even a quarter of them to help me out, I'll consider this a success. "It'll be fun for the boys after two months of hard work, and it's a great way to solidify their bonds and friendships off the turf, as well as on it."

Meredith looks to the field, a pensive expression on her face. "What're you suggesting, then?"

"A parents' and staff meeting at the Golden Fleece," I say, barely leashing my excitement, "maybe this Friday? It's time to brainstorm and think of ways we can foster a family environment for the Wildcats."

Instead of a volley of voices rising to meet the cause, I hear the collision of pads and the occasional squawking of seagulls swirling above our heads.

I look to Meredith, hoping she'll help a girl out. She sways on her feet, announces, "I'm with you!" and then retreats back into the fold.

My clipboard feels like a hundred pounds in my arms. Sweat gathers under my pits. It's almost laughable that I was put out that not a single one of my players was willing to go to bat for me at the watercooler. Here I am facing down the firing squad—er, their *mothers*—and I'm an army of one.

Life must be so damn easy being Dominic DaSilva.

I take a moment to meet the gaze of every woman staring back at me. "While I can't promise that every one of your boys will end up playing for JV or varsity, I can say with absolute certainty that an experience like a camping trip will be something they remember—"

"Will Coach DaSilva be at the meeting?"

I feel my brows go sky high. "He's our assistant coach, so . . . yes. His duties aren't isolated to whenever he's blowing a whistle and telling the boys to give him more burpees."

"*Oooo,* we should have him do a naked calendar!" someone calls out from the back of the pack.

What? "Absolutely not—"

"It's a calendar for *kids*," Meredith counters dryly. "You all do realize that, right?"

"It's also for charity," Timmy's mom declares, her hands folded demurely over her chest. "And we're the ones in need."

"I *need* to see his naked chest," crows someone else.

"September ought to be the month we have him pose with his dick in a sock."

Startled, I stare at the thirty-something-year-old woman suggesting Dominic wear nothing but footwear on his penis. She has the good grace to look sheepish when she catches my open-mouthed gawking.

Not sheepish enough, though. "The sock is to keep the picture PG-13," she defends with a loose-limbed shrug. "Plus, September is my birthday month. Happy birthday to *me!*"

"Have you guys seen DaSilva on *Put A Ring On It*? The only reason I'm hooked is because he's *totally* dreamy. There's this one shot of him pulling himself out of a pool, and let's just say, his dick-print is what wet dreams are made of. I mean, I'm guessing he didn't win the show since he's here and all . . ."

"Does your husband know you're salivating over someone else, Belinda?"

Belinda, a blonde who looks like she spends her days on a treadmill, only grins. "May I present to you all what marriage looks like after twenty years, ladies? We each have a celebrity free pass. His is that actress from *How To Lose a Guy In Ten Days*, and mine is Dominic DaSilva. It's like the gods have answered my prayers because here he is in little old London, looking fine *as heck* out there in those shorts."

As one, the women peer around me to check out the view.

Don't turn around. Don't tell them you know that even unaroused, Dominic DaSilva is packing more down there than any guy you've ever seen naked.

Which isn't a whole lot, anyhow. Two guys, including Rick.

Okay, minor correction: Dominic DaSilva is packing more than any guy I've ever seen, both in real life and in porn.

Sue me.

"I hope he jumps around like that all day," Belinda breathes out.

"I swear I can see his dick bouncing in his shorts from here," Timmy's mom echoes in awe. "Five bucks says he's not even wearing boxers."

Sweat beads on my brow as I clamp my clipboard to my chest.

"Friday at five, ladies," I say, hoping they can't get a read on me. I can only imagine what they'd hear: *Oh, Dom? Psshaw. A complete tool but whaddaya know? He is* packing, *ladies. The big kahuna, if you know what I mean. The Weiner schnitzel of all Weiner schnitzels.*

Oh. God.

I clear my throat, my cheeks burning. "Meet at the Golden Fleece. I'll email the rest of the parents. Please bring your spouses or any family members—anyone who would like to be involved in the fundraising process."

"Who are you bringing?" asks Miss Dick In a Sock.

I lift my chin and hope all they see is a coach ready to do anything to give her players an experience they'll never forget—even if they don't make the cut, even if they get stuck on JV instead of varsity, even if their wish comes true and they end up on the front line.

"I'm bringing Coach DaSilva."

Even if I have to drag his dead, limp body with me.

7

DOMINIC

*T*hree.

     That's the number of times in my life when I've felt absolutely blindsided by fate or the universe or whoever the fuck is pulling the strings behind the scenes.

The first time, I'd been absolutely sure that my top pick —the Atlanta Falcons—were going to call my name in the draft. After studying their roster, it didn't take a rocket scientist to know they were in need of a tight end. And, in collegiate ball, there'd been no one better than me. I had the record-breaking stats, the drive and the ambition, not to mention the heart to finally belong to something on a permanent basis.

They passed me over for a pimply-faced kid out of Utah, and I was left to await my fate on the metaphorical bench.

An opportunity that Tampa Bay didn't squander.

While all the players around me were surrounded by family, all ready to leap up and lose their minds in excitement, I sat alone with only my coach from LSU cued in via speakerphone.

I accepted my blank Buccaneers jersey and team hat alone.

Went back to my hotel room alone.

Celebrated with a bottle of Patron alone.

The second time, I was down on one knee before Savannah Rose, *Put A Ring On It*'s bachelorette. The producers and the film crew and the asshole director, who looked like a frat boy and talked like a douchebag, all had a front-row seat to what should have been a private, tender moment. Only, I didn't propose marriage to Savannah. Didn't even propose lifetime commitment because that sort of promise doesn't have a slot in my genetic makeup.

But I offered what I could give, what I'd never offered to anyone else before her and what I doubt I'll be offering again anytime soon: the chance to see if I could love. Fully. With every corner of my soul. Something I'd given to no one but the game of football.

For the first time since my early foster-care years, a thread of hope had sparked within me. Bleeding out of every crevice, locking my limbs tight as I waited for her answer. I had no ring. I had no flowery language or desperate words of love because that was the ugly truth: I didn't love Savannah Rose.

Not that it didn't stop me from hoping she'd take a chance on my emotional defects and see that I was willing to give our budding relationship my all.

She turned me down.

Blindside number two.

Following the Wildcat's first practice, driving down my street leads directly to blindside number three:

Levi's banged-up Honda Civic is parked in my next-door neighbor's driveway.

You've got to be fucking kidding me.

I rack my brain for details from Friday night. She ordered an Uber from the Golden Fleece. No car to take note of at the pub, and when I arrived home, I had no reason to look twice at the house next door. Over the weekend, I packed a duffel bag and drove down to Boston to visit my *Put A Ring On It* castmate, Nick Stamos, and his new fiancée, Mina.

With my foot on the brake, I scrub my palms over my face and then release the pedal to coast into my driveway. The scent of pepperoni and cheese pizza saturates the interior of my pickup, re-centering my attention on the two boxes resting innocently on the passenger's seat.

One box for today. The other for tomorrow, when I'll probably procrastinate once again with heading to the grocery store.

News of me moving to London has spread like wildfire.

When I stopped to gas up my truck this morning, an elderly man sidled up to me under the pretense of needing to use the squeegee on his windshield. He didn't even last twenty seconds before bringing up that dreaded 2015 game where I fucked up my leg and essentially ended my career.

At practice, I was bombarded by mothers, all of whom wanted a picture with me to post on their Instagram accounts. One lady—Belinda, I think—gave my ass a not-so-discreet squeeze when the flash went off.

Even the guy behind the counter at Pizzeria Athena slipped a bare napkin forward along with my receipt. It was a move I recognized well. Sign the damn thing, leave a good tip, or "Dominic DaSilva is an entitled dick" would be all over the internet by the 5 p.m. Evening News.

Maine was meant to be a reprieve from the bullshit of my normal life.

Instead, the only reprieve I've had thus far has come

from a blond-haired coach who doesn't seem all too impressed that I could buy this town three times over and still have enough money in the bank to last me a lifetime.

"Don't do it, man," I warn myself, already grabbing the two pizza boxes and climbing out of my truck. "Don't fucking do it."

I don't listen to my own advice.

Still dressed in the same clothes I wore to practice, I cross the strip of neatly trimmed lawn that divides our two properties. Whereas my place looks like the stage model for 1970s suburbia, Levi's Cape-Cod-style home is quintessential New England. Dark gray siding and snow-white shutters. Window boxes with colorful flowers peeking out, seeking the warmth of the afternoon sunlight. A cherry-apple-red door with a brass knocker positioned dead center.

Pizza boxes clasped in one hand, I step onto a ridiculous straw doormat that reads *"Home is Where the Tacos Are,"* and ring the buzzer.

You're making a big mistake. You don't even like her!

I don't, no.

But I don't dislike her any more than I generally dislike everyone else.

Two seconds pass before I hear a muffled, "Coming!"

Briefly I wonder if Topher's home or if he's out with friends. It's summertime, after all. No school. No deadlines. No commitments to anything but football.

The door yawns open.

"Sorry about that, I—"

Levi's apology cuts short at the sight of me on her front stoop. Eyes going comically wide, she lifts a hand to clutch the white towel wrapped around her head. Perspiration curls the strands that have escaped the terrycloth, so they peek out like little devil horns. Fitting, I guess, considering how much she rode my ass all day at practice. The woman is a menace with a whistle. My old Bucs coach would have bowed down to her in pure reverence.

Unbidden, my gaze slips lower, acting on its own accord, like a puppet controlled by the dancing strings of its master.

Spaghetti-strap tank top. The color reminds me of the muted pink shag carpet in my bedrooms. Unlike the thick, string-like carpet, however, Levi's shirt is thin and practically transparent with Tweety Bird printed over the center of her chest.

No bra.

Tweety does nothing to conceal the fullness of Levi's breasts. *I wish to hell it did.* It's all I can do not to notice the deep shadows beneath Tweety's jawline and the twin peaks thrusting up against the cartoon character's yellow cheeks. Levi's damp skin is not doing me any favors—it's rosy from her shower and dewy from what has to be some miracle blend of lotion and, *fuck,* but does she always answer the door like this?

My fingers tighten reflexively around the warm pizza boxes, even as I allow my eyes to wander south. Black gym shorts slung low on her hips. No shoes or socks, only yellow-painted toenails that remind me of Tweety Bird and hard nipples and deep cleavage.

A weak man would drop the pizza and send Tweety flying to the ground, all so he could get a glimpse of paradise under that shirt.

I've never been weak.

But I'd be lying if I say I don't feel a hint of annoyance that Tweety is smirking at me like a smug, little asshole from its vantage point across Levi's breasts.

This . . . this is a new low.

No fucking shit.

Levi's grasp on the door slips down a notch, like she's fully prepared to sling it back in my face and call it a day. "What are you doing here, Dominic?"

Just looking to spend some time with a person who hates my guts.

I bite back the caustic response and lift the goods for her to see. "I come bearing peace offerings. Topher mentioned pizza."

"Topher's not here."

She doesn't move, not even an inch.

Even though her pert, unconstrained nipples are doing a solid job of answering my question all on their own, I ask, "Are you heading somewhere?"

Her lips purse when I flick my gaze up to the damp, turban-style towel wrapped around her head. "Does it *look* like I'm going somewhere?"

"Didn't want to presume anything." I drop my shoulder to the doorframe, getting comfortable under the watch of her icy stare. "Who knows? That tank top could be your most prized possession."

As though remembering what she's wearing—and everything that she's not—she drops her hand from the towel to link her arms over Tweety Bird's face. Only, the towel's lack of support guarantees her nothing but a few precious seconds before she'll have to make a decision.

Bend over to pick the towel up off the floor once it falls —and risk the chance of giving me a full-on, braless peep show—or accept defeat in the form of me getting an eyeful of her puckered nipples by raising her arms and keeping the towel in place.

My vote is for the former.

She chooses option number three: ripping the damn thing straight from her head and letting her blonde hair fall down around her shoulders, completely untamed. "I liked you better when you were a nameless jerk at the bar."

I meet her gaze. "I liked you better before I realized we weren't just coworkers."

"What's that supposed to mean?"

Debating my next words, I rap my knuckles on top of the pizza box. "Back in L.A., I used to think about what it might be like to move to a small town. I figured there'd be cookies on my doorstep with a card saying something like, *howdy neighbor*. If not that, then at least a welcome to the neighborhood-block party."

Levi's blue eyes flash. "Your ego is limitless."

"My point being, Coach"—I drop my face so that we're nose to nose—"is that I've come with neighborly tidings, and the least you can do is welcome me inside."

DOMINIC

"*G*oddammit."

Sardonically, I cock one eyebrow. "I'll be honest, I was expecting more of a freak-out."

Levi mimics my brow lift, then, without asking, snags the pizza out of my grasp. "In my defense, I thought I was hallucinating when I saw you next door on Friday," she says, her back to me as she saunters past the entryway and deeper into her house.

With a kick of my heel, I close the door behind me. "Hallucinating?"

"Don't you dare suggest your presence left me scatter-brained."

"You said it, not me."

If she weren't holding the pizza, I have no doubt she would have gone oh-for-three and flipped me the bird.

Instead, she leads me past a contemporary-styled dining room and a half-bath that's on the smaller side. Unlike the godawful layout at my place, though, Levi's home is magazine praiseworthy. Spacious. Crisp-white walls with nautical-blue accent pieces. Sandy hardwood floors that are so glossy and freshly varnished I half expect to see my own reflection staring back at me.

Framed pictures decorating the walls catch my eye as I pause before them. Two are of her and Topher, both taken when the top of the kid's head was level with his mom's chin. In another, a young Topher sits on a front porch with his arm slung around the neck of a ginormous Bull Mastiff. The dog and Topher are rocking the same cheesed expression. Yeah, Topher's tongue isn't lolling out of his mouth but his smile is massive and his blue eyes are nearly closed he's laughing so hard at whatever is behind the camera. In the corner of the frame, the date is marked in pencil: *04/27/2014.*

I don't think I've ever smiled the way Topher is on that front stoop.

As I check out the last frame, a beach-themed oil painting that reminds me a lot of the wharf off Main Street, I almost expect to hear the *clip-clip-clip* of dog toenails.

There's nothing but the sound of my breathing and the soft whir of ceiling fans.

A college professor of mine once spent an entire lecture arguing against the theory of eyes being the windows to the soul. *Eyes deceive,* he'd said, camera strap slung over one shoulder, *but pictures . . . pictures reveal to us a person's truth and what they value the most.*

Based on the limited number of subjects within Levi's pictures, it's safe to say her life revolves around her son and this tiny town she left behind so many years ago. And a dog that's nowhere to be seen.

Tearing my gaze away from a younger-looking Levi, rocking a cute pixie cut, I look to the kitchen. It opens into the living room, the latter of which leads directly to a set of wall-to-wall French doors.

The view of Frenchman Bay is what ultimately sold me

on the 70s abomination next door, but here in Levi's house, it's a view like nothing else. No trees obstruct the sight of glistening, sapphire water. A brick-paved patio greets the eye, as does a hot tub and matching white outdoor furniture.

Either Levi knows someone who knows someone, who, in turn, clued her in about this property, or she got absurdly lucky and reappeared in town at just the right time.

Something tells me it's the latter.

She seems like the sort of person blessed with good fortune at every corner.

Without a glance in my direction, Levi drops off the pizza on the marble-topped island. Humming beneath her breath—or cursing my very existence, more likely—she folds the damp towel over the back of a bar stool and spares me a quick, searching glance when she reaches for one of the top cabinets. The hem of her Tweety shirt inches high on the curve of her belly, her bare nipples poking the fabric mercilessly.

Stop noticing her nipples.

Easier said than done.

Uncomfortably aware of the same heat flooding my body as when she took a nosedive into my crotch, I check out the rest of the kitchen.

Force myself to think of something else—anything else —besides the fullness of her tits.

Plates. Plates are safe.

I snag the two she's pulled out from the cabinet and set them down on the island, side by side. "When'd you move in?"

"You don't seem like the type to actually enjoy small talk."

Surprised by her astuteness, I watch as she shuts a

drawer with her hip, utensils in hand. "You read minds, too, when you're not coaching ball?"

"I wish. If I did, then I wouldn't have to ask why you're here." It's not exactly a question but I wasn't born yesterday. She's using her coach voice on me. It's a completely different pitch than the bubbly enthusiasm that kept my ass glued to that bar stool at the Golden Fleece. I may not have thought it a good idea to go home and fuck her, but her good humor and quick wit had made it hard to walk away.

She'd . . . Well, not captivated me. She'd *something'ed* me. Something. Jesus fuck. Even in my own head, I sound like a verbally incompetent jock.

Oblivious to my inner word conundrum, Levi tacks on, "There's no reason for you to be here right now. We both know you could have easily brought up our . . . neighborly living arrangements at practice tomorrow instead of swinging by today."

Is that what being neighbors is called nowadays? Neighborly living arrangements—uttered in such distaste?

When she hops up on the far bar stool, taking her plate with her, I read the boundary she's drawn loud and clear. Two stools down from her it is then. I flick open the pizza box to reveal America's most valued treasure. Greasy, cheesy deliciousness. Without waiting to see if Levi will make a move first, I rip out two slices and plop them down on her plate.

Then do the same with mine, except I opt for three.

You don't get to be six-six and almost three-hundred pounds of solid muscle by eating rabbit food all day.

Aware that she's waiting for a reply, I snag napkins for each of us from the glass dispenser to my right. "Let's put it this way," I murmur, handing her two napkins, "small talk serves its purpose."

"But you hate it."

I study her. The way the ends of her blond hair are starting to dry and curl. How her lips are flat and uncompromising, but her blue eyes are lit with barely leashed curiosity. "Maybe I wanted to come over and discuss what we're gonna do about the damage to my truck."

She pauses for only a moment, biting into the tip of the pizza slice and moaning like the damn thing is the answer to all her prayers. Or my prayers.

Women who prefer to be called by their surname shouldn't be allowed to moan like that.

They shouldn't, but not two seconds pass before she does it again.

Blue eyes squeezed shut. Head tipped back in bliss. Those unrestrained tits of hers swaying under the loose fit of her tank top.

Jesus.

I shift my weight on the bar stool, angling my hips away from her. Harden my voice and pray that she's so into the pizza that she won't notice how much my dick is into those breathy sighs of hers. "You don't believe me."

"Believe that you're here to demand that I pay up?" She cracks one eye open to stare me down. "Not even a little bit."

I fold my pizza in half, lengthwise like a paper airplane, and take a bite. Chew. Swallow. "Maybe you're wrong. Maybe I'm here because your kid hit my truck, and a paint job is gonna run me almost a grand, if not more."

A telltale blush warms her cheeks. "I am sorry about what happened. Really. Topher is just—"

"A teenager. We'll work out." Forearms propped up on the counter, I cock my head to the side when I catch her sucking her bottom lip between her teeth. *She looks like a woman trying to hold the words in.* I wave at her. "Go ahead. Spit it out."

Startled, her gaze snaps up to meet mine. "Spit what out?"

"All those thoughts you're trying to hold under lock and key right now. I can see the wheels spinning."

The blush staining her cheeks, though still there, takes a back seat to the glint in her blue eyes. Never once averting her gaze from my face, she says, "I just can't help but get the feeling that you're here because the whole town is buzzing about your arrival and you want to hide out with someone who doesn't get a lady boner just by breathing the same air as you."

Pizza halfway to my mouth, I freeze. Twist my head to get a real good look at the woman scarfing down God's best creation like it's her only job. "Did you just say—"

"Lady boner?" Wiping her hands on a napkin, she jumps off the stool and ambles toward the fridge. "I mean, I guess I could phrase it differently. Tingling nub, maybe. Swollen clit, for sure." She snags the stainless-steel handle then props open the door with her hip. Two seconds later, she's holding a bottle of water in each hand, one of which she deposits in front of me. "Don't tell me you've never revved up a woman enough to know what I'm talking about."

Revved up a woman . . .

Jesus fuck.

"Or maybe all the women you've slept with are too scared to clue you in that you're doing something wrong," Levi continues, unscrewing the bottle cap and taking a hearty swig. When she pulls it away, a bead of water glistens on her upper lip. She sucks it off with little aplomb. Then meets my gaze head-on. "I mean, if you're sleeping with a famous person, it's probably best to just lie back and think of England, especially if it sucks. Don't want to hurt their fragile egos."

"You're insane."

Another sip of water as she rakes her gaze down over my chest. "It's only an opinion, Coach." Her lips quirk up in a smug grin. "Sorta like the one you had about London having a taste for nepotism? Just like that."

Silence permeates the kitchen, and then the sound of laughter bulldozes the quiet into smithereens.

The sound of *my laughter*.

It sets my chest ablaze, and hell, but it feels crazy good to let go and give in. The pizza's tip droops like a wilted flower as I rub the back of my wrist against my face, right under my eye. Pretty sure I haven't laughed this hard in ages. Years, maybe.

Levi—*Aspen*—thinks she's got me all figured out. Her blue eyes are dancing; she's rocking onto the balls of her feet like she can't hold still as she waits for my reaction. So, I give it to her.

"Probably goes without saying that opinions are like assholes, everyone's—"

"Got one?" she finishes for me, reaching into the open pizza box for another slice. She nabs her plate and doesn't even bother to sit down as she digs right in, standing not two feet away from me. "Funny, I said the same thing to Topher's dad when we divorced. He said it was in his right to play around outside our marriage. I told him to shove his opinion up his ass and sign the papers."

Fucking prick.

Disgust swirls in my gut at her revelation. Sinks into my bones and reminds me of what little I know of my biological parents through court records. I let the past linger for barely a moment before I push aside the sympathy rising to the forefront, courtesy of her unexpected show of vulnerability. In my experience, people open up only so they can maneuver you to their liking.

Jaw clenched tight, I ask, "Why are you telling me this?"

She swallows her bite before washing it down with water. "You hate small talk. Figured we could go straight to a heart-to-heart."

"If you think we're gonna start braiding each other's hair now that you've opened up . . ."

"Dom—can I call you Dom?"

I reach for my water bottle. "If it works for you."

"Dom, then."

She leaves her empty plate on the bar and, hips swinging with confidence, closes the gap between us. With me on the stool and her standing, we're finally eye to eye. Close enough for me to spot the flecks of gray in her dark blue eyes. Close enough for me to see that her upper lip is perfectly imperfect with the faintest hairline scar piercing the bow.

If my aura was a bubble, it'd burst from her intrusion.

Pop.

Just. Like. That.

"Being a coach is nothing like playing the game." Her hand lands on the counter, off to the side of my abandoned plate. "You hate small talk? Better get used to it because parents are going to expect it. You don't feel comfortable with displays of vulnerability? Guess what. *Every* kid on your team is going to come to you with a problem." She gets in my face, her slender shoulders heaving with a heavy, frustrated breath. "Maybe you've forgotten what it's like to be in high school. Emotions are all over the place. Those kids still don't know what they want out of life. They're fighting for this *dream* and they expect to be led by someone who gives a damn about whether or not they achieve it."

She's not the only one feeling frustrated. And that little test she just put me through? The small-talk ploy? The 'give a little piece of herself because she wanted to see how I'd respond'—all so she can damn me for not giving the answer she wants to hear?

Fuck this.

My body sways forward, utilizing my size—even though I'm still seated—to intimidate. With my anger leashed like a rabid dog collared to a junk yard, I grit out, "You don't know me, Levi. One night at a pub and a day of practice doesn't give you nearly enough time to learn what I give a damn about."

Her chin hikes up defiantly. "I know enough."

"From what?" I laugh, the sound so much harsher than the one from a few minutes ago. This one sounds like *me.* Cynical. Bitter. My hand closes into a fist that I press to my thigh. "Tabloid magazines? Rumors in a league that you have no connections to?"

"Rick Clarke."

Surprise jerks my head back. "Pittsburgh's GM?"

An emotion I can't even begin to define sweeps over her delicate features. "My ex-husband."

My gaze flicks to her ring finger. It's bare. Probably should have been bare from the start, if I'm going for honesty here. I may not have the best history with women—uncomplicated one-night stands have always been my preferred level of non-commitment—but even I find Rick Clarke's inability to keep his dick out of women who aren't his wife completely revolting.

I knew he was married—but to *Levi?*

The pizza suddenly sits like toxic lead in my stomach.

I can't even recall seeing a picture of her with Clarke at any time over the years. Then again, I'm not too surprised. Pittsburgh's GM has long kept his family out of the limelight, actively touting his reasoning as a matter of separating business from personal. One time, not long after I retired from the NFL, he even flew to Sports 24/7 for an exclusive, sit-down interview about the toll the game of football has on its families, and how the rush of the celebrity-like lifestyle does more damage than good.

I know I'm not the only one who chalked up Clarke's silver-tongued speech about "putting family first" to be nothing but bullshit.

Clarke's extramarital affairs weren't a secret to anyone in the league, even to those of us who played for different teams. But knowing that he spouted all that nonsense while his wife was *Levi*? It's a tough fucking pill to swallow.

Aspen Clarke, not Levi.

While it's possible I've come across her married name before, it's not as though I make it a habit to hang out with scumbags like her ex-husband.

One look at her face now reveals nothing. No sign of vulnerability for miles around.

Temper held in check, I lower my voice. "I'm nothing like your ex."

Clarke and I exist on two different planes. The man might be a beneficial asset to the Steelers, but he lacks all human decency. The team keeps him around because he brings results. Women flock to him because he dotes on them with elaborate gifts and cars, all in exchange for getting his dick wet.

That Levi fell for his ploys, too, is a little disappointing.

"You are," she counters with a shake of her head. "Maybe you don't screw everything that moves. Maybe you're better with your money than he'll ever be. But that doesn't change the fact that you're on the run, and that's typical Rick behavior. You came to Maine because you want out of Hollywood, just like you came *here* because you didn't want to deal with locals asking you questions. You don't want small talk. You don't want to listen to their stories or hear about how football has changed their lives, how meeting *you* might be something momentous for them."

The vehemence in her tone stiffens my spine. "Aside from the fact that we work together"—and live next door to each other, apparently—"I don't see how any of that affects you."

"I divorced Rick, and he and I were married." Her blue eyes zero in on me, and I'm almost surprised I don't erupt into flames where I sit. "But you and me? We don't have a single bond tying us together, and we sure as hell aren't married. Don't think I won't hesitate to find a way to get rid of you if you can't be the coach those boys deserve."

Jesus, this woman.

Bubbly and happy one moment, ready to slit my neck in the next.

It's enough to give a guy mental whiplash.

"Your lack of faith in me is almost inspiring," I grind out, already shifting off my stool. Getting in her space. Forcing her to back up or risk a collision that she'll never win.

She glares up at me, her hands curled into tight fists down by her sides. "I don't see the point in stroking your ego when you have so many other people lining up to do the job."

I drop my head, my mouth finding her ear amidst all that damp, curly blond hair. "Less than a week ago you were more than willing to stroke something else of mine."

I hear her stifled growl, just before she turns her head to

meet my gaze. Our noses bump and still neither of us jerks away. "Less than a week ago," she mutters, her focus momentarily derailed by the proximity of my mouth, "I thought you were a random guy in a bar. Not my assistant."

Assistant.

I bet she loves thinking of me like that. At her beck and call. Her subordinate. Bending over backward to tick off all the little check marks on her endless task list.

My fingers dart up, instinctively finding the thin strap of her tank top. Whereas she just smothered that growl of hers, the same can't be said for the way she gasps now at the sensation of my rough fingers brushing her soft skin. I glide my thumb along the strap, moving north over the swell of her cleavage and the delicate jut of her collarbone. Her breath catches as I flick the strap down, exposing her shoulder entirely.

To torment her.

Or maybe to torment us both.

It would be so easy to coast my fingers over her pale flesh and follow behind with the imprint of my kiss on her skin. Even easier to back her up against the kitchen island, my body caging hers, as I swallow her anger with my mouth slanted over hers and my hands tangled in her untamed hair.

The old me would have no problems taking what I want; no thoughts to the potential consequences of my actions. What I wanted, I took. What I needed, I stole. And what I craved, I devoured.

Except that I've worked long and hard to see that the old me is dead.

The old me that maybe once looked a little like Rick Clarke.

Dammit.

Self-disgust puts me on the retreat. With a dismissive wave at the kitchen island, I mutter, "Keep the rest of the pizza for when Topher comes home."

Cornering Levi was a power-play move on my part. A calculated reminder that she may be walking around with *Head Coach* printed on the back of her Wildcats polo but I'm no wimpy, pushover assistant. I won't jump because she asked me to. I won't roll over like a good dog simply because she barked out an order.

My attempt at regaining control backfired.

I'm the one dragging much-needed air into my lungs to extinguish the fog of unwanted lust. My fingers are curling in and stretching out, like I'm desperate to hear that soft gasp in my ear all over again. To say nothing of the state of my hard dick, which I do my best to hide by twisting my body away to face the hallway.

I've got to get the hell out of here.

One step toward freedom.

And yet another.

"DaSilva."

DaSilva, not Dominic or even Dom.

I cut a sharp glance over my shoulder, only to see her fiddling with the strap of her tank. It's exactly where I left it, hanging loosely down by her elbow and narrowly exposing more than just her cleavage. Shock kicks me square in the gut when I catch sight of the intense look on her face while she stares down at the fabric. Her expression is otherwise unreadable, but the slight tremble in her hands?

That tremble tells a whole other story, one I'm not privy to learning.

Because you shut her out like an asshole.

Because you have no idea how to interact with people once the helmet's off and your jersey is strung up.

"What do you give a damn about?" The question is nothing more than a whisper, so low I need to strain my ears to hear every word.

I avert my gaze. Keep my emotions in check and do my best to remember that if this woman was married to Rick Clarke, then what she knows about me can fit in the same box as the rest of society's impression of Dominic DaSilva:

Charming yet cynical. An unfeeling asshole.

But still the greatest tight end the NFL has ever seen.

If I were to die tomorrow, that'd be what's written on my tombstone.

In my eulogy.

In the goddamn newspapers.

"Nothing," I answer after a moment, already feeling the weight of Levi's disappointment in me as I head for the door, "You were right. I don't give a damn about anything."

CELEBRITY TEA PRESENTS:

EX-NFL PLAYER DOMINIC DASILVA—FIRED FROM SPORTS
24/7, RECAP OF ONE-ON-ONE DATE WITH SAVANNAH ROSE,
AND MORE JUICY DETAILS

D ear Reader, America's favorite playboy contestant has been . . . FIRED. You read that right. According to the Sports 24/7 website (and some expert sleuthing skills from yours truly), Dominic DaSilva is out of a job.

Is his untimely departure from the network due to the scandal that went down on last night's episode of Put A Ring On It? *Probably not, due to the time lapse between filming and the airing of the show, but let's go over the details anyway, shall we?*

Last night, millions of viewers tuned in to watch as DaSilva romanced Savannah Rose in—appropriate, I suppose, given our bachelorette's name—Savannah, Georgia. We're talking a swoony carriage ride along East Bay Street, a picnic for two at the famous Forsyth Park, and a candlelit dinner at the always-a-must Olde Pink House. Romance bloomed in the air, and DaSilva sealed the date with a kiss that even turned me on . . . and we all know my soul is colder than the Arctic in the dead of summer.

Meanwhile, mayhem broke out back at the bachelor compound.

Richard Thompson (age 35, an investment broker out of NYC) claimed that DaSilva was not *on the show for "the right reasons."*

(For whatever that's worth coming from a man who showed up on the first night wearing a dinosaur onesie).

Not only did Thompson effectively throw DaSilva under the bus to his castmates while the latter was out on his date, he then went behind the producers' backs to sneak out of the compound before heading to Savannah's private apartments. In his words to America's favorite sweetheart, I quote: "You made a big mistake giving DaSilva a ring tonight. He's not here for you. He's only here for himself and his own fame."

What followed next are insane shenanigans involving flying fists, one man crying in a dinosaur onesie, and a visit from the show's medical team. All of which was an absolute joy to witness.

My favorite quote from the night comes from fellow castmate Joshua Hardman: "If DaSilva isn't here for the right reasons, then I'm the president of the United States."

Thanks to footage leaked earlier this winter, we're all well aware that DaSilva is one of the last two men standing on the show. We also know that Savannah Rose turned him down.

Is this troubled moment with Thompson the catalyst that began the end of DaSilva's reign as top dog of the season? Does it somehow correlate to DaSilva's abrupt termination on his long-time sports show?

As of right now, hearsay is all we have, but I'll be back next week.

Another episode. More grown men crying about their broken hearts. And all the spilled tea you could ever need.

You're welcome.

*T*he whistle blows, and Bobby sprints forward, shoulders hunched, as he snatches the two-by-four foam pad out of Topher's grasp.

Tweet!

Bobby takes my son's place, and the next kid comes barreling forward to repeat the drill all over again.

Tweet!

And again.

I let the whistle fall to my chest. "Guys, you need to explode from the hips and thighs! You want to end up with stress fractures in your back down the road because you took the easy way out?" I point to the second three-pound memory foam pad down by my feet. "Three pounds versus picking up Coach DaSilva. See the difference?" As one, they all check out the other side of the field where the man in question is running a different set of drills with Group B. "What're you gonna do when you're lifting guys his size and your arms are too weak to get the job done?"

"Uhh, we'll do more push-ups?" calls out a wiseass from the back of the line.

I want to hang my head in defeat.

We've been at this all morning. Honestly, I'm not sure what I expected in coming on to coach the Wildcats. Under my dad's leadership, the team was a powerhouse—and I'm not only talking about trophies and wins. Dad fostered their love for the game while instilling in them a sharp blade of discipline. By the time they graduated, those players had all the tools they needed to succeed, both on and off the field.

The kids staring back at me now look like the third-hand rejects off a football recreational team. I have no idea what my dad's successor did when he came in to work every day for the last three years. From where I'm standing, it looks like he did a whole lotta nothing.

At the rate we're going, summer camp is going to be nothing but undoing bad habits and rehashing drills they should have perfected in the youth, Pop Warner league.

The freshmen are a little easier to manage, considering they're fresh-faced and on the verge of pissing their pants whenever I blow the whistle, but the juniors and seniors are something else entirely. Angsty, pimple-faced teenagers are the worst.

I drag my palms over my sweaty face. "*Again.*"

Tweet!

I'm met with groans from all twenty-two kids in the lineup, including my own son. When they drag their feet, I blow the whistle for a second time and motion with my hands to get a move on.

They shuffle into place with so little enthusiasm I nearly start yawning.

The stark difference between Group A and Group B might as well be night and day. I check out the other half of the field, where Dominic is leading his group through a series of fire-out blocks that should have the kids wheezing on the ground. *Should* being the operative word here. Instead, every one of those boys looks like they're having the time of their lives as they sprint from the thirty-yard line to the twenty.

Dominic slaps the hands of the five guys who make it to the twenty-yard line first, then blows his whistle for the rest of the kids to line up in a three-point stance and wait for the pretend snap of the ball.

Tweet!

Dominic and I blow our whistles at the same time, our individual groups moving in sync even though we've barely exchanged a word in the two days since he stormed out of my house.

Yeah, I pushed him.

I pushed him because I care about the well-being of the kids on our team. I want them to feel as though they can come to us with whatever is on their minds—things that are happening at home, problems at school, worries about the game—without feeling as though we're going to turn a blind eye because we don't give a damn about them as individuals.

Football saves people. It can change the trajectory of a person's life forever. Give them confidence where they otherwise have none. Teach them the value of building a family that has nothing to do with bloodlines and everything to do with bonding with people who share similar goals and fears and dreams.

And I . . . I acted like Dominic—a vet of the game—understood nothing of that.

You were an insecure jerk and he didn't deserve your tongue-lashing.

I quiet my rebel conscience for no less than the fifteenth time in the last forty-eight hours and blow the whistle again, my gaze still fixed on my assistant coach.

Dominic's standing with his feet spread apart, hands squared off on his hips, a Wildcats baseball hat turned backward on his head. As I've come to expect from him, he's not sporting a smile though he does call out encouragements, rooting the kids on as they race to the next benchmark.

Does he want to be here? *Really* want to be here? My gut tells me no. Actually, it tells me *fuck no* and warns me that London is only a passing stop on his path to god-knows-where. Something I'd do well to remember the next time I grow tongue-tied around him. It's not every day a man like him looks at a woman like me—and it's *certainly* not a frequent event that a man like him nearly strips me naked in my kitchen.

For the third time since practice started this morning, my fingers drift to my collarbone. The fabric of my Wildcats polo bunches under my touch but does nothing to eviscerate the memory of Dominic's full lips parting on a heavy breath as he toyed with my tank top. Had he wanted to kiss me? Maybe the better question is: would I have let him?

Now is not *the time to be thinking about that.*

Wrenching my gaze away from his bulky form, I tuck the whistle between my lips and blow.

Tweet-tweet!

The kids nudge each other as they tromp over to the cooler setup by the bleachers. Each morning, I've arrived early to put together a snack station for the team. Granola bars on the first day. Veggie sticks on the second. Back in Pittsburgh, I came across too many of my players whose parents either didn't have the funds to send their kids to practice with something to eat or who simply couldn't be bothered.

Either way, my heart couldn't bear watching some kids

snack away while others sipped water from the cooler and pretended they weren't as hungry as their teammates.

It was a nonnegotiable tradition that I couldn't give up in returning to London.

Satisfaction skips through me now as I watch Timmy reach into one of the cardboard boxes for a bag of carrots and a bottle of blue Gatorade. I hide a smile behind my hand.

"Timmy's mom works two different jobs," says a familiar, dark voice to my left.

Dominic.

My chest expands with a sharp breath. That's four more words than we've exchanged at any given time since the other day. Keeping my attention on the team—and noting the way my baby boy takes a seat next to Timmy—I strive for complete nonchalance when I reply, "Being a single mom isn't easy." *Don't look at him.* But I can't not, especially when I catch the delicious scent of aftershave and sandalwood. His bicep brushes my shoulder, he's so much taller than me. "Did you—"

"Ask him?" He slips his hands into the pockets of his black mesh shorts. "I pushed him to elaborate after he dropped a hint on granola-bar day. Casually mentioned how his mom works at a late-night joint over in Bar Harbor in addition to waitressing at Cookies and Joe Diner in the mornings. I didn't get much else out of him before he asked if he could have two bars since his mom hadn't had time to make him anything to eat before she dropped him off at practice."

And there goes my heart.

I glance over to where Timmy and Topher are laughing together. My son's resting his forearms on his thighs, head bowed as he shoves a baby carrot into his mouth. As if sensing my stare, he looks up and gives me a short wave.

It's his *we're-at-practice-but-I-still-want-to-acknowledge-you* wave.

I kick my chin up in return, my silent *I-love-you* all he needs before he grins happily and turns back to his conversation with Timmy.

"Thank you for letting me know," I tell Dominic softly. "About Timmy, I mean. It breaks my heart to know that not all of these boys have it the best at home, though I'm sure Timmy's mom is doing everything in her power to give her kid whatever he needs." Despite her brash attitude on the first day of camp, she's never been late to pick her son up from practice, and I've even overheard her suggesting that Harry, a redheaded junior, spend the night when Timmy mentioned Harry's mom being out of town. "Raising him alone can't be easy for her, and I really appreciate you looking out for—"

"I was the Timmy back in grade school."

I jerk back, caught off guard by the gruff note in Dominic's voice. "I don't understand."

"Except that I didn't even have an overworked mom on my side. I won't bore you with the details." He lifts his hat up by the brim, then settles it back down over his head. After being outside in the sun every day, his olive skin appears even more golden now than it did a week ago. "Back then, I would have done pretty much anything to have a coach like you bringing in snacks and drinks. It would have appeased the hunger, especially during some of the rougher years."

Something tells me I'm not sure I want to know what he means by the "rougher years."

I remember reading something online about how

Dominic grew up in the foster-care system out in California. Back in Pittsburgh, one of my best friends, Mariah, takes in kids. She dotes on them all and has even adopted three—a little girl and two teenage boys—and still continues to do as much work in that world as she feasibly can, considering her day job keeps her continuously busy. The boys, especially the eldest, Zach, has been Topher's best friend since his adoption four years ago.

But I'm not so naïve as to think that all situations are as good as Zach and his foster siblings have had it with Mariah, and I can't quite stop my heart from plummeting at the thought of Dominic struggling as a child.

Without thinking, I loop my hand around his muscular forearm. "You can be that coach, too."

He grunts out something beneath his breath before his big hand slips over mine. His palm is rough, calloused from years of playing professional football. Once upon a time, mine would have been a perfect match. I never had been all that good about wearing my gloves, unless it was game time. Even now, if you look closely, you can see the scarred, bubbled tissue from years of lifting dumbbells and grappling with knotted, weighted ropes for conditioning.

Then Dominic's knuckles slide between mine, and I forget all about training and exercise as I stare at my paleness interlocked with his bronzed skin. The two of us are quite a pair—opposite in every way and yet forced to unite in order to lead a team of forty-plus teenage boys.

The team.

In touching him at practice, however unintentional, I crossed a boundary. I know it. He knows it.

And then he slips out of my grasp, putting respectable space between us again.

Right.

Right.

I sneak a peek to see if any of the kids witnessed our exchange, but they're all too wrapped up in their own conversations to notice. I swallow, hard, and peer up at Dominic's face. Cynical, dark eyes. A firm, unsmiling mouth. Sharp-as-glass cheekbones. I wonder if there's a soul out there in the world whom he freely gives his smiles to.

If such a person exists, they're incredibly lucky.

"We gonna switch drills and then wind down with some stretching?" he asks, fisting the whistle hanging from a black lanyard around his neck.

Get your head in the game, girl. Do what you do best—coach. "Yeah. Yeah, that'll work."

Dominic nods. "Sounds good, Coach."

Coach.

Tweet! His whistle explodes. "Let's get goin', guys! One more hour and then you're free to go home and play video games for the rest of the day."

That earns him some raucous laughter and high fives out of the kids. They ditch their water and Gatorade bottles on the metal bleachers, then toss their trash in the nearby garbage can.

I watch as Dominic turns away, his broad shoulders appearing even more massive today since his T-shirt is a little snug. My gaze falls to his round bubble butt. The man must do leg presses and squats all day to get impressive glutes like that.

Maybe working out is his escape from reality, what he does when I see his pickup truck parked in his driveway and heavy rock music blasting from his house. The music is loud and angry but every night when I climb into bed, I can't help but think that it also sounds a little lonely.

Like *he's* lonely.

Which is an absolutely absurd thought. Dominic DaSilva might be hiding out in Maine, but he still has the world at his fingertips. He could literally snap them and half of London would come scurrying over, despite the fact that he's an enemy of the New England Patriots, having played for Tampa Bay for over a decade.

I don't *want* to think more about Dominic than I need to, and I certainly don't want to be giving him any more of my headspace than he deserves. He's my assistant coach. He technically works for me. Who the hell cares if he's lonely?

You do.

Dammit.

"DaSilva!"

I'm not even sure what I'm going to say until he's wheeling around, hands lifted to the back of his head, where he's playing with his ball cap again. His T-shirt lifts, revealing a dark happy trail that disappears down into his shorts.

My heart jerks.

Or maybe that's just my starved libido thrashing around like a beached whale.

I can't make out his dark eyes from here, but his tense body language conveys all I need to know: he's on edge, ready to release the coil and spring, and I'm . . .

Curious.

"Why did you bring up the . . . rougher years?"

The heavy ropes of his arm muscles visibly tighten as he whips off his hat and slaps it against the outside of his thigh. He did that the other day too, when we first officially met after Topher drove right into his truck. A nervous tick, maybe?

After a moment, he shoves the ball cap back on his head, this time with the brim facing forward. Like at the Golden

Fleece, the upper half of his face is concealed, leaving me in the dark about his inner thoughts.

I release a pent up breath, accepting the fact that he's not going to answer. Which is *fine*, just fine. This won't be the first time in my career that I've had to work with someone who I get along with like oil and water. Sure it helps to be friends but it's not a requirement to get the job done.

And something tells me that Dominic and I . . . we're not on the path to friendship.

Not even close.

Just as I begin to turn away, ready to head back to my new group for more lift drills, he speaks up, voice low enough that I only hear it as it carries on the early summer breeze: "Because someone told me that if I want to hack it out at this coaching gig, I have to be prepared to get vulnerable." A small pause that catches my breath and fills my lungs with anticipation. "It's safe to say I'm a work in progress."

11

DOMINIC

T've discovered the tenth circle of hell:

The Golden Fleece after it's been ransacked by football parents.

"... And *then* I told Suzy to lay off the Cheetos before she starts pooping orange. She cried. I felt like a horrible dad and caved. Next thing I know, she's the happiest three-year-old on the planet, smashing Cheetos into her face like she's on the verge of starvation ..."

"... Naked boobs, Josh. You know how horrifying it is to walk into a room and see your son doing *that* to the daughter of a friend of yours? I screamed. Craig screamed. She screamed. We're all scarred ..."

"If he takes my car one more time without asking, he's grounded until he's so old, he'll have gray hairs coming out of his nose."

The scene before me is like a PTA meeting on steroids, and though I know I should be mingling and introducing myself, my ass has been parked in a booth for the last ten minutes and counting.

Where the hell is Levi?

This meeting was her brilliant idea.

"We're both new to the school," she told me yesterday after practice, "so we really should make an effort to introduce ourselves and let the parents get to know us."

Except that our peppy head coach is nowhere to be found, and I'm slowly beginning to suspect that I'll be forced to handle this shindig alone.

Looking at the impending clusterfuck objectively, nothing about this event is out of my realm of expertise. I spent four years faking smiles on TV for millions of people every week. Before that, when I played for the Bucs, I spearheaded a new, team-led charity where each player—myself included—mentored a child in foster care. Junior Buccaneers was a cause close to my heart, but I made the tough decision to pass the director role to another one of my teammates after I retired from the league.

The mission of the charity was always to cut out the trustee boards and all the inner-politics that inevitably comes from having too many mouths shouting their respective opinions.

Player-led.

That was the goal.

And when I wasn't a player anymore, I gave someone else the chance to do something good, something that makes a difference in a way most people will never understand.

What's the difference, then, between founding a charity and talking to a bunch of parents?

Expectations.

No, that's not it.

I take a drag from my beer bottle.

The difference is simple: I understood the kids who came through Junior Buccaneers. A long time ago, I *was* that kid. I never had a mom or a dad—not a set who played an influential role in my life, at any rate—and being shuffled from house to house meant that I never stuck around long enough to feel largely impacted by the women and men who took me in, either.

I'm a fish trying to swim on solid ground.

Doesn't mean that I can't do my best with what I've got.

I drain the rest of my Bud Light, then slide out of the booth.

Shawn, the bartender who I met last week, is hustling hard tonight behind the bar. Parents swarm him like locusts, no doubt feverish at the thought of being kid-free for an evening. Conversation closes in on me from all sides as I maneuver my way through the dense crowd.

". . . I heard Dominic DaSilva is the new assistant coach . . ."

". . . Oh, my God, did you see him two nights ago on that dating show? Girl, I *live* for the drama. When he punched that other guy, I swear my ovaries exploded . . ."

". . . What the hell was the athletic director thinking, bringing in a guy like him? Yeah, he's good on the field, but I hear he's a complete asshole . . ."

My molars grind together as I fight the urge to say *fuck this* and head home.

Playing for the NFL isn't at all like being a celebrity. For the most part, my reputation when I played for Tampa Bay was mostly hearsay. Even when I worked for Sports 24/7, the mass media didn't give a shit about me. Certainly nothing I ever said or did made headline news and landed me on the front page of every gossip rag in the country.

Then I went on *Put A Ring On It*.

Old tweets began to resurface. Old flings came out of the woodwork to reveal their side of our breakups to online gossip sites like *Cosmo* and, the worst of them all, the anonymously run *Celebrity Tea Presents*. Old acquaintances suddenly had an opinion as to why I behaved a certain way on one episode and acted completely different a week later.

In the three months since footage was leaked to the media, just after filming wrapped up in Bali, my life has been shoved under a microscope in ways I never fathomed were possible. And in the month since *Put A Ring On It* began airing every Wednesday night, my name has trended online continuously.

No wonder the pillars of Hollywood shake and crumble on the regular, until fresh blood pops up to stabilize the crippling foundation of bone-weary celebrities. Three months of putting up with this shit and I'm already done for life.

When I finally reach the bar, I flag down Shawn, who's sweating at the temples and looking totally frenzied.

"What?" he snaps as he pours wine into a glass, then shoves it into the hand of a waiting customer.

"I heard this place has a closed-to-the-public courtyard out back."

He sends me a look that would cut a lesser man at the knees. "So?"

Hands on the bar, I lean forward so he can make out every word: "So, hand over the key and let me lead the parents away from your regular patrons."

Shawn's brows tug together, just as someone shouts, "Hey, man! Where's my whiskey?"

That's all the convincing the bartender apparently needs because he reaches for the keys hooked onto his belt and shoves them in my open palm. "Five bucks a pop," he says, before I can call out to the masses to retreat to the back. "Half of them aren't drinking anything but tap water, and if the boss comes in tomorrow to find out that I let them all stay without—"

"Add it to my tab," I cut in, tossing the keys up in the air and re-catching them. "I'll get a head count before the meeting's over and you can charge me for it."

His dark eyes widen. "You sure? That's a whole lot of money."

I shoot a glance to the crowd. It's utter pandemonium.

Levi should have picked any other night but a Friday for this—and she's not even here to deal with the fallout.

"Yup, just do it." I clap my free hand down on the bar top, then pull away. "If you've got a microphone or something back there, make the announcement."

"I'll do you one better."

The next thing I know, Shawn is hauling his aging body up onto the bar and hollering for all London High football parents to follow the "Hulk" to the exclusive courtyard. I can't help but grin. Back in my LSU days, my teammates always called me the Hulk. Even among football players, I've always been on the big side.

Sure enough, though, Shawn's unconventional methods do the trick.

Like lemmings being led straight into the unknown, the parents fall into line behind me. Past the swinging doors that open up to the men and women's bathrooms on either side of me, a narrow hallway leads directly out into the courtyard.

A pergola, with lights strung up along the oak wood, catches my eye first. Then a full-bodied, clay chimenea that sits dormant and dark, off to the right. There's a motley number of patio furniture—nowhere near enough to account for the fifty or so people who have shown up for the meeting tonight—but beggars can't be choosers.

"Find a spot!" I bark out, motioning as I turn for everyone to get their asses in gear.

If Levi wanted this meeting to be eloquent, she should have shown up.

For the third time since I arrived, I pull my phone out of my jeans' pocket and check for a missed text or a call.

Nothing.

Again.

As I wait for everyone to situate themselves, I fire off a quick message to her:

Me: Where the hell are you?

Worry pierces me for a quick second while a million possibilities skip through my brain. Maybe she got in a car accident? Is something wrong with Topher? Did something happen from the time she left practice earlier today till now? It's only been six hours, give or take, and while six hours doesn't seem like nearly long enough for a catastrophe to go down . . .

My fingers fly over the glass screen one more time.

Me: You and the kid okay?

Then I pocket my phone and focus on the parents of my players. Players who, in the five days that I've had them running drills for three hours every morning, have come to mean something to me.

Think about how excited they are to have you as their coach.

All right. Time to make the magic happen—or die trying.

"Some of you may know me," I say, keeping my voice steady but raised, so the folks in the back can hear me too, "and some of you are probably wondering who the hell you followed into a dark courtyard you've never been granted access to before."

The joke earns me a few chuckles, mostly from the dads in the group.

"There were supposed to be two of us greeting you all tonight." I point to the invisible space next to me, hovering my hand about shoulder-high. "My partner-in-crime is on her way"—*I fucking hope*—"and you've probably heard of her family, the Levi's."

A few *hell yes we know her!* rise up, and I feel a modicum of relief that the group hasn't stomped back into the bar and left me out here alone.

"Aspen probably doesn't need any introduction." I ignore the fact that her first name sounds illicitly forbidden on my lips. *Levi* is familiar, safe, and not the name of a woman who moans when she eats pizza and forgoes wearing a bra around the house. "But I probably do," I continue, noting a few of the women tittering to themselves behind shielded hands. "Dominic DaSilva. I played for the Buccaneers for a decade and some change, then took a TV hosting gig with Sports 24/7. I'm excited to start this new journey with all of you here in London, and I'm *really* pumped to see how well your sons do over the next two months of summer camp."

"I was told we're talking about fundraising today," comes a voice from deep in the pack, out of my line of sight. "Coach Levi mentioned it the other day?"

Fundraising.

I haven't talked fundraising since college ball.

Swiping a hand over the back of my skull, wishing I hadn't left my ball cap on the dashboard of my truck, I give a clipped nod. "It's on the agenda for the night, yes—"

"I heard you agreed to do a calendar for the team," calls out a woman to my left. "A naked one."

"No, not naked!" shouts someone else. Another female, I

think. "We're keeping it PG-13. Remember? Someone mentioned his dick in a sock."

My dick in a sock?

In all my years playing for the NFL and working with various branding sponsorships, I've never posed naked. Not a single time. Briefs only? Yes. Briefs and cleats? Also yes. Briefs, cleats, and a football clutched in my hands? On multiple occasions, yes.

But not balls-hanging-free-dick-flapping-in-the-breeze naked.

Conversation erupts, groups of parents taking sides on whether or not I should be photographed with a sock covering the family jewels—or not photographed at all.

I'm siding with the latter.

One-hundred-percent.

Needing a drink to wash this nightmare away, and wishing I hadn't been so eager to finish my beer earlier, I hold up both hands and pray for divine intervention. *Sorry, Father, for I have sinned—but please, for all things holy, get Levi's curvy ass here right now and let her deal with this shit.*

"Whoa now, guys. I don't know who confirmed this calendar thing, but I can assure you that I won't be—"

"Coach Levi was the one who suggested it."

My stomach lurches. "Come again?"

The woman who brought up the sock bit shifts her weight, then sips from her cocktail. "It was the other day . . . at our first practice. She asked us all to meet here for fundraising ideas, and *she* said we should come up with ways to use you working for London High to our advantage. Oh, look, she's right there—Coach Levi!" the woman bellows, turning heads with the force of her shout. "Didn't you think Coach DaSilva posing with a sock over his member would be the best method to ensure calendar sales?"

I feel my phone buzz in my pocket at the same moment Levi stumbles up next to me. Her blond hair is wild and curly. Even in late evening light, it's hard to miss her panicked expression—the heavy-duty makeup caked onto her skin like she's bathed in the stuff is not doing her any favors.

Her blue eyes meet mine.

I don't look away as I grab my phone and quickly check the text, already knowing it's from her.

She doesn't disappoint.

Levi: I'm walking in now. I'm so so SO sorry. Ultimate disaster. Will explain later.

Her throat constricts with a visible swallow as she continues to hold my gaze, never once severing our connection while I pocket my phone.

I make a show of welcoming Levi to the faux stage, wrapping my arms around her tall frame. Her shoulders twitch when I make skin-to-skin contact, like she's either uncomfortable with me hugging her or she's fully prepared for me to turn the tables around and put *her* in the hot seat.

If I promised a group of people the chance to see her in nothing but nipple pasties and panties made of candy, I'd have a lawsuit on my hands.

Something she must realize because her mouth finds my ear—she's risen up on her tiptoes—and whispers, "It's a big misunderstanding, I promise."

"Nah, Coach," I return, my voice low and my nose grazing the curve of her jaw, "you sold me out."

12

ASPEN

*T*onight, Dominic smells like sandalwood, aftershave, and pissed-off man.

Full confession: I don't blame him for the latter.

I'm late.

I left him to the wolves.

And I . . . *feel so friggin' guilty*.

He's been mingling like a champ over the last thirty minutes, ever since I showed up and announced in no uncertain terms that a naked calendar would *never* be up for discussion. There was some grumbling of disappointment before more common fundraiser ideas were thrown into the mix: a bake sale, a car wash, and someone even suggesting a dog-walking stint on the weekends.

I smiled and laughed and took down names for whoever might be willing to help with what, but never once did I forget about the man beside me. Oh, Dominic chuckled right along with me and he certainly kept the conversation moving when a few of the parents shouted out rowdy suggestions. But we were standing elbow to elbow, only inches apart from each other, and it was impossible to ignore how he studiously ignored *me*.

The moment we were done, he was out in the crowd, shaking hands and even doling out hugs to those who asked for one.

He's sans baseball hat tonight, which means, whenever the moonlight slants across his face, I'm given full access to his austere features. Narrowed eyes. Flatline mouth. Hard jaw—hard enough that when he *does* laugh, I half expect it to shatter into a million little pieces.

My phone vibrates with the fourth incoming text since I made it to the Golden Fleece.

Willow. Again.

I last all of five seconds before unzipping my purse and grabbing the phone from the depth of my bag.

Willow: I'm sorry.

Willow: Like, when I say I'm sorry, I REALLY, REALLY AM.

Willow: Love me?

Willow: Okay, I screwed up. How was I supposed to remember Topher needed me to pick him up from a friend's house when I had Mr. McHotPants down MY pants??? Take pity, sis. One of us needs to be getting laid, and I'm MORE than happy to be the one to make the sacrifice.

I let out an undignified snort. This is a serious case of Classic Willow.

I can count on both hands the number of times Willow has actually shown up when I've needed her. My sister's track record is abysmal, and I spent most of my early life cleaning up her messes.

Until I moved to Pittsburgh with Rick and left her to fend for herself.

In the time that I've been gone, she's been married twice and divorced the same number of times. She's gone on to work in at least three different industries, and only settled on selling real estate in the last few years. Okay, I guess I can't be all that annoyed about her latest job change. If it weren't for her tendency to be extremely nosey and up in everyone's business, I wouldn't have bought my house fully furnished the day it was put on the market.

Despite the fact that my sister is a flaky serial dater, who drives a pink car with a license plate reading EXWIFEY, I love her dearly.

Doesn't mean I shouldn't have known better than to ask her to pick up Topher for me. But she's been begging me to let her spend more time with him, considering how she only saw him maybe once or twice a year until earlier this month, and I figured this would be a good first step.

Pick up Topher.

Bring him home.

Mission accomplished.

Only, Willow failed on obstacle number one because of sex. There are about a gazillion things wrong with this picture—the first being the fact that she forgot my son at his buddy's house—but I'm woman enough to admit that I'm also a little jealous too.

I miss sex.

Not necessarily sex with Rick because, well, he was something of a one-pump master—two for special occasions—but I do miss the intimacy of it all. The intimacy and the orgasms. Although it's been a heck of a long time (read: years) since I had one of the latter that didn't come from a little solo-play action.

Ugh.

I drop my phone in my purse and focus on the fifty or so people who have come out tonight to talk football, their kids, and their hopes for a successful season ahead of us.

Not that every kid attending camp will make JV or varsity. Morale needs encouragement, though, and I've always been of the mindset that confidence begins in the home.

Get the parents excited and involved in their children's dreams—step one. Foster unity and a sense of belonging—step two. Run drills and scrimmages until either your feet fall off or you become the next Tom Brady—step three.

I sidestep a couple heading back into the pub. Crane my neck and bounce up onto my toes to look for my assistant coach.

There. Standing beneath the pergola and looking like Lucifer himself. Dressed in all black—from his slacks to his leather shoes to the dress shirt molded to his bulky torso—Dominic casually reclines against the wooden railing while holding a beer bottle down by his hip. I wouldn't be surprised if his dress shirt was unbuttoned at the collar to reveal the sign of a . . . pentagram? Hexagram?

Doesn't matter.

The point is, he's rocking a nonchalant vibe like he doesn't have a care in the world.

Over the last week, I've realized that it's his M.O. How much would it take to crack his concrete resolve? It's a question I've wondered every night as I toss and turn in bed. Other than that moment outside his truck when he was blatantly messing with me, along with those tense few minutes in my kitchen, he's always kept his emotions in check.

Does he ever just *relax*?

God forbid he smiles for real or kicks that cynical twist of his lips to the curb. The world would probably end immediately if he did. And if not the world, then at the very least London would crumble right into Frenchman Bay like a modern-day Atlantis.

"You think Coach Levi was trying to save face up there? Belinda told me Coach is totally willing to let DaSilva strip naked for a high school calendar," says someone over to my right.

No.

The answer is definitely no, something I reiterated to the group at large, once I finally caught my breath, after Dominic swept me up in a tight, not-so-welcoming hug. Friendly it wasn't, but that didn't stop my breath from hitching as he closed the distance between us. Even now, my heart gives an extra thud, and I silence it with a palm to my chest. No extra beats are allowed for a man like Dominic DaSilva.

Wishing I had a cool glass of water to press to my heated cheeks, I move toward the pergola. I need to talk to Dominic. Smooth the turbulent waters before we're forced to swim through the murkiness all next week during camp. There's also a good possibility I'll need to give a closing statement tonight, just to make sure we're all on the same page here: *there is no calendar, PG-13 or not, starring Dominic as the centerfold model.*

I'm maybe five feet away from ground zero when I'm pulled to a stop with a hand around my arm and an enthusiastic, "Levi!" ringing in my ear.

Dammit. So, so close.

Swinging one last glance at the pergola, and at Dominic, I paste a smile on my face and turn to greet whoever stopped me. "How can I help—oh, Meredith!"

Her grin hitches wide at my greeting, and she doesn't miss a beat before leaning in for a quick kiss-kiss to my cheeks. "Listen, I don't want to take up too much of your time or anything," she says, one hand clutching the thick strap of her purse, "so I promise to be quick."

I wave her off. "No time limit." I'll find Dominic at some point tonight . . . or at home. *Bad,* bad *neighborly thoughts.* Immediately, I lead my brain in a safer direction, one that doesn't include ex-NFL players living conveniently next door to me. "We're here to answer any questions you might have. It's the point of tonight's meeting."

"I thought the point was to talk about Coach DaSilva's sacred parts in a calendar?"

Wouldn't Dominic just love to know his dick has been likened to something sacred. In his book, it probably is.

Struggling to hold back an unprofessional groan, I knead my temples. "For the record, that calendar is seriously never going to happen. Please tell me no one is still thinking about it."

"Depends on who you're talking to, I think. Belinda—Matthew's mom—is hopeful."

No high school in the history of high schools would ever allow a grown-ass man to strip naked for a calendar. It's called instantly landing oneself in jail, and I don't know about Dominic, but I'm just not a good fit for prison.

There's no good food, for one, and I rather like my nightly mug of hot tea to polish off the day's efforts and successes.

That's a luxury that jail will never afford me. Same with bath bombs, regularly scheduled appointments with a hairstylist to cover up my graying roots, and BBQs every Sunday in the fall to celebrate my favorite kind of ball. Football. I know my place, and it's existing without shackles on my limbs.

At my strangled silence, Meredith shrugs. "I think they're hoping if they push for it, you'll buckle."

"They're out of luck. There will be no buckling—not today, tomorrow, or five years from now."

Although I keep my voice even-keeled, I swear the remark earns me a few death glares from the people in close proximity. A man I've never seen before cracks a grin, destroying the whole death-glare theory, and then promptly whispers something to the woman standing next to him. She, in turn, giggles fiercely.

Her shoulders shake like a set of Mexican jumping beans.

What in the world is so funny?

Although it's been years since I schmoozed and cruised on Rick's arm for any number of his high-end functions—he preferred to leave his "small-town wife" at home—I'm no stranger to high school events with parents. These meetings, which I always try to host in a non-intimidating venue like a bar or a restaurant, are how I create personal connections with the parents. For me, coaching football isn't just about drills and plays—it's about the off-the-field victories too. I'm no therapist, and I would never claim to be one, but I've never felt more successful than when I've managed to help a mom or dad re-engage with their child, for whatever reason.

These initial meetings are my launching point—where I'm most in my zone.

And yet something is so, so off tonight.

I glance down at my shirt, immediately searching for something amiss. I haven't even had a single cocktail tonight, so the likelihood of a stain is close to nil. *My zipper.* Subtly, I sweep a hand over my pelvis, doing a little drive-by check to ensure I'm not showing the world my pink panties with little pineapples on them.

I'm a sucker for fun underwear—as opposed to sexy lingerie—and have a wide assortment in my drawer at home. Ones with funny sayings, ones with hilarious designs printed on them. It's a joke Rick never understood, which no doubt culminated in another check mark in the column titled Reasons Why I Should Have Never Married Aspen Levi. He tallied up many check marks over the years, starting with how I failed to lose the baby weight after Topher was born, and not even coming close to ending with how I never managed to fit in with his fancy acquaintances. Better to leave me at home than risk me getting in his way.

"Meredith," I start, when I catch another woman covering her mouth to hide a grin when she looks over at me. "I know we don't really know each other, but I have to ask . . . Do I have a sign on my forehead that I don't know about? Maybe a piece of paper taped to my back?"

The way I'm getting looks tonight, it's as though I'm a walking disaster.

Which, though often true, shouldn't be the case tonight. While I didn't have time to tame my hair into a sleek blowout the way I'd hoped to before the Willow fiasco, I still hit up the makeup I rarely use and also dressed in a flirty, lace top that gives the girls a nice boost. For the first time in a very, very long while, I feel feminine. Pretty. Someone to be desired, despite spending years with Rick, who made me feel like the ratty shirt in the back of your closet, forgotten and unwanted. More importantly, I feel like a woman, too, and not just a mom and a football coach who lives in workout gear like I was born in spandex.

Hello, my name is Aspen Levi and I'm the queen of leggings and oversized T-shirts. It doesn't have a memorable ring to it.

Faced with Meredith's silence, I glance over at her. Only, she's currently licking the pad of her thumb and rubbing her forehead with it over and over again.

Huh.

Maybe all those people aren't laughing at me but at her.

Jerks—all of them.

Don't they know how cruelty can damage a person's self-esteem?

Looking left, then right, I step close and lower my voice. "You okay?" I ask gently. "You seem a little . . . squirrely right now."

"Your eye . . ." Meredith rubs her forehead again a little more forcefully.

Is it code? Is she trying to communicate that someone around us has made her feel uncomfortable? Though she's only a few years younger than I am, I'm ready to go all mama bear and get to the bottom of it.

"She's trying to tell you that you have makeup all over your face."

13

ASPEN

$\mathcal{T}$he latter doesn't come from Bobby's mom.

No, I could never be so lucky.

Dominic Fucking DaSilva.

Is there a humiliation of mine that this man has *not* witnessed since we met? No, I don't think so. It's incredibly unfair. You'd think the universe would be tired of giving him everything: good hair, great muscles, a gorgeous face.

Okay, maybe "gorgeous" is taking it a bit too far.

Dominic's features are rugged, like the terrain of Cadillac Mountain southwest of London. But like the landscape of Maine, pieced together with the expansive sky, and the thick copse of trees, and the beautiful creeks and rivers, Dominic is a showstopper.

Handsome in a way most men will never be.

Heat effuses my cheeks, warming me despite the bite in the air tonight. I refuse to turn around and give him the satisfaction of seeing me blush. And, boy, am I blushing. Fingers twitching with the need to press them into the hollows of my cheeks and hide any redness, I look to Meredith, meeting her kind gaze. "I'm sorry, would you mind if I took off for a second to go and . . ." I wave at my face. "You know?"

"Oh, of course." In camaraderie or maybe in womanly support, she squeezes my arm just above the wrist. "I'll see you later?"

Unless I somehow find myself on the run after murdering the arrogant man standing next to me? "I'll be here. Thank you so much for coming tonight. We really appreciate it."

I shoulder Dominic out of the way with very little grace, heading straight for safety.

If there's anyone in the bathroom, I'm going to haul them out. Okay, no hauling will commence, mainly because I stopped doing push-ups right after I caught Rick cheating the first time—about four years ago—and opted for spoon-digging as my preferred method of exercise instead.

My biceps might not thank me for all the extra chocolate ice cream I've eaten over the years, but my emotional welfare says otherwise.

Speaking of emotional welfare, I'm *highly* aware of Dominic tracking me like a shadow clinging to a tiny seed of light. He even has the balls—literally, too, I suppose—to settle a hand on my lower spine, as if I actually need his guidance or support.

I don't need either.

I try to lose him around a group of parents, but then he's right back in my lane again with his palm kissing my back and his pace in step with mine.

Stubborn, infuriating man.

When I reach the restrooms, I cut my stride abruptly short. Send a quick thank-you up to the universe for keeping the crowd outside and away from this narrow hall-way. The space is quiet, locked between the pub and the courtyard, and when I wheel around to confront the broody man hovering at my back, he nearly mows me over.

My arms fly out to catch something to hold onto, and damn me if I'm not hand-delivered a severe case of déjà vu.

Only last time, it wasn't Dominic's arms I latched onto but his thighs, and my nose was buried in a place a lot more R-rated than the broad expanse of his chest.

I take a subtle sniff.

Yup. Sandalwood, aftershave, and ticked-off male.

Just my luck.

Yanking out of his arms, I feel my eyes narrow as I glare up at his face. "If you even think about pulling a tactic out of a romance novel and try cornering me in the bathroom, think again." I jab his hard chest with two fingers. Step back toward the women's restroom. "Don't follow me."

His only answer? A smirk.

Or maybe it's a sneer.

It's tough to tell with the pub's dim lighting. There aren't any candles back here, which means it's moonlight or bust.

Keeping my eyes trained on his face, in case he gets swept away by a bad idea, I reach behind me for the door-knob. My palm fondles a vertical handle. *Freedom, here I come.* I give the door a little push, and it's that two-second diversion of my attention that proves to be my downfall.

Dominic swoops in front of me, one arm wrapping around my shoulders as he spins us around. He backs me up. One foot then the other.

"Hey, hold on now—"

My heel catches on an uplifted step.

He draws his free arm up and over my head to plant it against something behind me.

The door.

It creaks open, swinging on its hinges as Dominic leads me in a tango of demise.

And then my poor nostrils are being assaulted by an odor so foul I nearly gag.

It takes only a second for my surroundings to register. Urinals line one wall, and two stalls grace the other. The walls are painted a muted gray, the floors are a dull black tile, and there's a guy tucking himself into his pants as he ambles over to the row of sinks.

Oh, God.

No more games. Time to go.

I attempt to sidestep Dominic, but he thwarts me off and I end up nose-to-nose with a full-body mirror.

Oh. *God*.

I'm not incompetent when it comes to makeup. I know all about proper blending and which setting sprays to use to lock the powders all in, but knowing any of that doesn't take into account the fact that I decided to get ready at the new vanity I purchased. The lights in my bedroom aren't nearly as illuminating as those in the bathroom, but I hadn't thought anything of it. I put on some fun music, wearing nothing but a bra and underwear, and dolled myself up. Doing so made me feel like a pampered princess, and after years of feeling undesirable by my own husband, I wanted the chance to get ready in style.

And I had—only, I'd unknowingly applied my bronzer with a heavy hand. The woman staring back at me from the mirror looks like a Kardashian sister, circa the 2000s.

"I'm a raccoon," I breathe out, staring at my reflection and wishing it was as easy to erase as mist on glass after a steamy shower. "A drunk raccoon that's done Spring Break in Miami, Mardi Gras in New Orleans, and St. Patrick's Day in Boston."

"I'm surprised the raccoon is still alive after all that partying."

Dominic's big body brushes past me. I barely register him.

I'm not sure what to do first: wet a paper towel and do my best to scrub off the atrocity on my face or deliberate the probability of a scientist discovering a time-travel machine soon enough that I can restart this entire night.

As though the universe is peering down at me and asking, *What? You aren't having fun yet?* It's at that moment when the guy at the sink notices there's a woman in the house. The mirror gives me the full, HD experience of watching his face pale as his hands dart to his crotch, fingers fumbling with the zipper. Once satisfied that he's all put away, he scurries past us, mutters something beneath his breath, and lets the door slam shut behind him.

Only the sound of the door clanging closed joggles my brain enough to register his parting words: *"Good to have you back in town, Levi."*

I drop my head on the mirror, ignoring the sting of my forehead meeting glass. "Please tell me he's not one of the team dads."

Dominic's footfalls cue me into the fact that he's moving around. There's the soft electronic whir of the paper-towel machine, then water splashing from a faucet. Then more of those heavy footfalls coming closer and closer until a hand is nudging mine.

"He's one of the team dads."

Unwanted laughter unfurls in my chest before making a break for it. "You're supposed to make me feel better."

"I'm going to, once you stop feeling sorry for yourself."

I snort, but begrudgingly roll my body so my back is flush with the mirror and my arms are down by my sides.

"Good to know that pep talks are not your forte. You're here-after banned from giving them. The kids will thank me."

"They gonna thank you for lying about that calendar too?"

Guilt slays me, even though the calendar was certainly not my idea. Opening my mouth, prepared to give it to him straight, I'm struck silent when big hands come into view. The one carrying a damp paper towel presses softly to my forehead while the other makes itself at home at the back of my skull, keeping me in place for his ministrations.

My heart, already on the fritz after a night of stress and embarrassment, loops into a fast rhythm. "What are you doing?" I whisper, almost fearful to speak too loudly and destroy whatever *this* is.

Not that there is a *this*.

Dominic's expression doesn't show a hint of softness as he works diligently. "Cleaning you up."

The paper towel drags down over my profile, skimming my hairline where the worst of the bronzer mishap is. "It's makeup. Water . . . water alone won't remove it."

"I added soap."

Three words that somehow gut me where I stand. He keeps the distance between us, our chests not even coming remotely close to touching. Neither do our feet. And yet, it feels as though we're tethered together as one anyhow. I breathe in and he expels the breath for me, ruffling my baby hairs that never take to my natural curl. His fingers graze my skin, and mine twitch of their own volition.

His touch remains gentle but his eyes . . .

Cynicism stares back at me, so much so that I can't help but wonder how he remains standing from the weight of it. Even after my divorce, I've retained a certain level of hope. Inner peace. Perhaps it's the mom in me—as lost as I've felt over the years, I've always had Topher as my due north. Letting my baby boy see my turmoil has never, ever been an option. No matter how bad things got with Rick.

"You're mad at me."

He doesn't dispute my claim.

Dark eyes meet mine, then skip away.

I try again, wishing he would actually look at me and keep on looking. "I'm sorry for being late. I asked my sister to pick Topher up from Kevin's house. Kevin from the team, I mean. Mistake number one, and that's on me. She forgot him and when he called, I was getting ready and now this —" I wave a hand at my face, careful of his working fingers. "I feel like I'm having an amateur moment when that's so far from the truth."

"Bet you got a lot of practice with socializing after being Rick's wife."

I almost snort out loud. "One would think."

"What do you think?"

"I think Rick likes having young women as arm candy. He likes it when the relationship is new and exciting, and there's nothing he enjoys more than waltzing into a party with a woman who turns heads and stops other men in their tracks." I had stopped men, too, but not because of my looks. In the beginning, Rick loved to brag about me playing football to anyone who would listen. In the beginning, it felt less like I was a freak-show case he paraded around and more like I was the mother of his child who he felt remarkably proud of.

Unfortunately, beginnings never last forever.

Staring at the shallow dimple in Dominic's chin, I continue, "Once I wasn't as young anymore, and my body not nearly the same as it had been before giving birth to

Topher, he drew the curtain closed on socializing hour. For me, at least. He never stopped going out."

Dominic's voice emerges as pure gravel when he orders: "Close your eyes for me."

My lids flutter shut on command. The rough pads of his fingers curl under my chin, lifting it up, as he carefully drags the paper towel over the most sensitive part of my face. Did Rick ever touch me so gently? So carefully? It hurts to answer the question, even to myself: *No.* Not even in those early days of our marriage, when everything smelled like roses and looked like unicorns, and he was still enamored with the idea of being with a woman who had fans fawning over her. Then the fans quieted the longer I was out of the game, and he grew to hate everything that made me *me*: my short hair and my lack of curves and my brash opinions.

"For the record, I'm not mad at you for being late. Annoyed? Yeah. Did I feel out of my comfort zone? Yeah, I'm man enough to admit it."

Something in Dominic's tone sends a shiver skittering down my spine. If he feels the tremor, he doesn't bring it up.

I swallow past the lump in my throat, my eyes still closed. "The calendar."

I sense the shift in his breathing. It comes a little faster, a little heavier, as it falls across my temple. "Like you, I took this job for a fresh start. You're back here because you divorced Rick and want a bite of the familiar. I'm here because I'm tired of pretending to be someone I'm not."

"Who's that?" The light behind my lids turns darker—a bruised purple—like Dominic has stepped directly in front of me and cut off my access to the rest of the bathroom.

The hand cupping the back of my head slips south, to where my neck and shoulder meet. Squeezes once. In warning? Lust?

"Gonna have to take a pass on answering. I'm not looking to be that vulnerable."

"I call bullshit."

His thumb traces my collarbone, exposed by my lace top. "Maybe it's not."

"Maybe you cornered me in this bathroom because you were actually worried about me." I saw his text asking if Topher and I were okay. Heard the concern through his written words, even if he'll never voice them out loud. Perhaps it's the fact that I can't see him that revs up my boldness, but I decide to call him out on the tangible tension radiating between us. He can pretend all he wants, but there's no way I'm the only one feeling this—this *heat* that just won't quit. "Could it be that you're regretting your decision to not . . . take me home the night we met?"

The gentle tracing stops.

As does my heart.

I blink open my eyes, unwilling to forego the opportunity to study his expression.

Stillness.

It's the only word that comes to mind looking up at him now. He's as still, as unmoving, as a glass pond.

Then I meet his gaze, and I feel as though I've been launched into a pit of flickering flames. Heat scorches my skin, tugging my knees together. My sex clenches—and though I try to remain perfectly still and wait out his response, my hips give the smallest roll. Needy. Wanting. The paper towel isn't as damp as it was at first touch, but I still seek it out with an almost keening desperation to ease the fire flaming to life beneath my skin.

I want Dominic—I admit it.

I wanted him that first night we met here at the Golden

Fleece and, standing here now with my body caged between his and the mirror, I want him even more.

With the damp paper towel acting as a barrier, he smooths his thumb over my upper lip, directly over the hairline scar that gives my smile a crooked flare. He drops his heated gaze to my mouth, to the slope of my neck, then traces the same well-traveled path back up again. To my disappointment, he curls his hand into a fist—the one that's been teasing me with caresses that make me want to nip his thumb playfully—and plants it on the mirror above my head. As though dug up from the rubble of the pits of hell itself, he growls, "I don't eat where I shit."

Do not be disappointed. He's thinking clearly and you're thinking with your . . .

My vagina. There, I said it. I've been thinking with what's in my panties. *Oh, God, I'm turning into Willow.*

I draw in a sharp breath. Then, just to needle him, and to get under his skin the way he's done to me, I tease, "Appropriate analogy, given where we are."

He doesn't laugh, not that I expected him to, but his mouth softens.

Success.

I push him again, just to see if he'll break. "I know we're all about opinions around here"—I peek up at him, hoping he'll recall the conversation we had at my house, but no, this joke doesn't make the cut—"but I think what you need is a night of fun. An orgasm would probably do it for you."

"*Levi.*"

"Okay, no orgasms. Your loss." Another blinding smile. I'm not above hoping he doesn't notice that I'm still struggling to regain my composure. I want to feel his fingers caressing my face again. I want to know if, had I said nothing at all, he would have taken it one step further. Boob touching. Man, he's got good-size hands, too. It'd be a perfect fit. *Focus. Focus.* "Mini-golf?"

Aha! A twitch of the lips, like he thinks I'm crazy.

He's probably right.

"Great," I murmur, "because I have the best cure for your brooding ailment. In case you're wondering about what ailment I'm referring to . . ."

"I'm not."

"You're no fun."

A real grin this time. Good Lord, he needs to warn a woman before unleashing that bad boy on humankind. *Dangerously sexy.* It's all I can do not to grasp the collar of his dress shirt and beg him to reconsider—even though I won't ever do that. I spent years begging Rick for scraps of attention. If I learned no other lesson from my marriage, it's that begging gets you nothing. Not affection, not your freedom, and certainly not a divorce.

"I believe that's why you're offering me a cure," Dominic replies, his voice still low, still growly, but not nearly as angry, "because I'm in need of some fun."

He still hasn't pocketed that smile of his, nor has he removed his arm from above my head. I'm entirely surrounded. By his heat, his masculine scent, by that smile that shines a little too bright and renders me mute.

Aware that my response is slow on the uptake, I laugh awkwardly. "You're right." *Sorry, don't mind me. I was just momentarily struck dumb by your smile.* Squeezing my eyes shut, I recapture my equilibrium. "Sunday, 1 p.m. You and Topher are going mini-golfing together."

I duck under his muscular arm before he can reject the offer.

"With Topher?" he asks my back, the curiosity evident in his voice.

I glance over my shoulder to stare at him. "My baby boy's my secret weapon. There's not a single day that he doesn't make me almost pee myself laughing. If there's anyone out there in the world that can make you ditch the pissed-off vibes, it'll be him. Plus, how bad of a time can it possibly be? You'll probably beat his score with your hands tied behind your back."

"Levi, I don't have—"

"You dragged me into a men's bathroom, Dominic."

He shifts his weight, then spirals the paper towel into the wastebasket.

A perfect shot.

Shocker.

"I did you a favor."

I lift a brow. "Sure, but not until after you let me walk around like that for thirty minutes and didn't say a word."

The grin he gives me then makes me want to flick it right off his face, sexiness be damned. "Consider it karma for standing me up."

"There's something seriously wrong with you."

"You're not the first person to think so, Coach." He says the nickname with emphasis, as though trying to redraw the lines between us. I wonder if it makes him feel any more in control than he did two seconds ago, when his fingers were brazenly caressing my face.

His long legs cross the distance over to me, his hand already reaching for the door above my head. Before he leaves, though, he pauses at my side. Lingers for a second too long to make me think he's wanting a casual hug goodnight, especially when we still have to go back and mingle with the parents who have come out to talk to us tonight.

Still, I wait him out.

Force him to open up and say *something*. Anything.

Then, "Don't ever offer me up again like I'm some sort of bargaining chip, Levi. And I'm not talking about the calendar—I'm a coach, just like you. I want what's best for the boys, just like you. Don't use me as a way to get the results you want, even if it's only parents showing up for a meeting. If you do . . ." He lets the warning dangle like a ticking time bomb between us.

"I'm sorry for that," I say with full sincerity.

He nods shortly.

Before he can make his exit, I give him a piece of his own medicine: "Don't ever touch me like you did tonight unless you plan to do something about it." At the sharp twist of his head in my direction, I angle my chin defiantly and give voice to the words that have lain dormant within me for far too long. "I'm not a toy. Not anyone else's and definitely not yours."

I stick my hand out.

He hesitates for only a moment before agreeing to the verbal deal by shaking my hand.

Later that night, back at home, I scrub my hands in hot water. It's either get rid of the brand of his touch or savor it all night like an idiot with a new crush. And after falling for Rick so swiftly—before watching my life implode in front of my eyes—I refuse to make the same mistake again.

Fool me once, shame on you.

Fool me twice . . . yeah, well, we all know how the saying goes.

Shame on me.

14

DOMINIC

I wake to the sound of fists pounding on my front door.

It's early. Too goddamn early for visitors.

Wait.

Since when do I have visitors in London?

Squeezing my lids shut against the light seeping in through the blinds, I reach blindly for my phone off the coffee table. My palm hits the TV remote, then accidentally tips over the plastic container that was topped off with chocolate chip cookies just last night—binging *Cake Wars* is not conducive to healthy eating—and, finally, lands on my phone.

More eager knocking pops off like rounds of gunfire as I bring the phone close to my nose and peer at the screen with only one eye open.

Eight in the morning.

Whoever's at my door has a death wish.

I roll onto my side, feet landing on the floor with a heavy thud, and take my sorry ass to the entryway. Knuckling aside the blinds, I spot Topher standing on my front stoop. His fingers are looped around the padded straps of his back-pack, and he's bouncing from foot to foot like he can't be bothered to tamp down his excess energy.

Sunday. Mini-golf.

Shit.

Fully prepared to do whatever I can to keep that smile plastered on the kid's face, I yank open the door and drop my shoulder to the frame. Cover my mouth to shield the yawn threatening to make an appearance.

"Teenagers are supposed to sleep in," I tell him, soft-ening my tone and hoping I don't sound like a gruff bastard. Mornings have never been my thing, not when I was in the NFL or when I worked for Sports 24/7. Not even a week of morning practices with the Wildcats has managed to do away with my bad habits yet. "Thought your mom told me we were going for one today?"

Topher only tightens his grip on the backpack straps. "I may have been a little excited."

"To play me in mini-golf?"

"To whip your ass."

I let out a bark of laughter. "I specifically remember your mom saying something about no cursing."

"Whip your butt. How's that?"

"Yeah, that'll work." The kid has spunk, I won't deny that. Pressing a finger to the awful, yellow-colored door that is in serious need of a repaint, I push it open another few inches. "You wanna come in and hang out while I shower real fast? If not, I'll come by and let you know when we're ready to roll out. I wasn't expecting you so early this morning."

I haven't even finished talking before Levi's son is already ducking under my arm and letting himself into my place. "I've been dying to know what this house looks like on the inside." He turns in a half-circle, eyes critically surveying the eyesore of a living room. "I was expecting cobwebs."

Ironic. I'd been expecting dildos hanging from the ceiling after the realtor sent the listing over to me last month. Aisha Smarts had promised the house would be a labor of love—the understatement of the year, in my opinion. This place needs less love and more demolition. I'm pretty sure there's mold growing under the nasty pink carpet.

Nothing wads of cash and my buddy Nick Stamos can't fix, though.

"This place is going to look great soon enough." I point to the far wall that's currently nothing but rotted wood paneling. "Floor-to-ceiling bookcase right there," I tell the kid. "It's gonna be a showstopper. And the ceiling is tall enough for a ladder, too, so we'll go all out."

"We?"

"Well, me and a buddy of mine, Nick. He does construction down in Boston." He was also the only guy on *Put A Ring On It* that I felt any compulsion to befriend. The rest of my castmates were nothing but gossip-toting crybabies. Having come from a team environment in football—all dudes, all the time for over ten years—I'd had similar expectations for the men who showed up for filming. I couldn't have been more wrong. It's not every day a guy shows up in a dinosaur onesie looking for true love. "I'm good enough with putting things together or tearing stuff out"—I tap the laminate floor with my bare foot, indicating that it too will be stripped from the house—"but in no way am I a designer or a visionary. Not like him."

Topher nods like that makes a whole lot of sense. "Oh, right."

Part of me can't help but wonder how much of a role Topher's dad has played in his life. Everyone in the league is fully aware of Rick's reputation. After all, the guy's been with the Steelers for nearly twenty years now . . . which has got to put him in his fifties, at least.

And a good deal older than Levi.

Was that part of his allure for her when they first hooked up? An older man paying a small-town girl a bit of attention, enough to sweep her off her feet and promise a world of fairytales? Being married to a man like Clarke . . . it must have been hell. Even my limited interactions with the guy have been less than stellar.

Back when my contract was up with Tampa Bay and I hadn't resigned yet, Rick Clarke pushed hard to get me in with Pittsburgh. He promised me all sorts of shit if I agreed to the trade: a Lamborghini as soon as I signed on the dotted line, exclusive access to women he promised were virgins, and the chance to come on the team as captain, never mind the fact that Pittsburgh as a team—and as a city—adored their quarterback captain, Jesse Evans.

I turned Rick down as soon as the email popped up in my inbox.

Call me an asshole, spread rumors that I'm lacking in the emotional department—I don't care. It's not as if those accusations are entirely unfounded. But don't ever think, for even a second, that I can be bought . . . or that I'm willing to loosen my morals for the sake of fame and fortune. Fuck that.

With Rick Clarke for a father, it's clear to me that Levi is to thank for Topher's good demeanor. His kindness, which is evident every day at practice when he seeks out the kids who haven't had any luck making friends yet. His dry humor, which has his mama written all over it.

Me and the kid—we've got something in common, I guess. Neither of us come from families with an ideal father figure.

Empathy has my mouth opening before I even work out what I'm gonna say next: "Nick will be up here in two weeks to help get the early demolition moving along. The tile and awful shag carpet in the bedrooms have got to go." I motion toward the floor. "You interested in helping out? We could use the extra set of hands."

Blue eyes, so much like Levi's it almost hurts, land on my face. The kid's mouth hangs open and he goes so far as to physically clamp it shut with the back of his hand. "For real? I mean, are you sure? I . . . I don't want to bother you or anything." His gaze turns downcast, his shoulders narrowing as they slump. "Or get in your way."

My rogue, dead heart gives a traitorous thump. It's the same sensation I always felt when I helped my mentees back with Junior Buccaneers. You can't change the world for every child out there, but one at a time . . . Yeah, those are the sort of promises I'll do everything in my power to keep. When it comes to kids, every single word matters and carries a lifelong impact on their psyche. That I know first-hand, though it's a life skill I could have done without learning so young.

"I don't say things I don't mean, Topher. If I'm askin' you to help, then that means I want you here."

His face visibly brightens with relief.

"Well, shit—" At my cocked brow, he points at me, finger-gun style. "You're right. Completely right, Coach. No cursing, just like Mom tells me. *Crap.* Is that better? It's gotta be since I'm all for expanding my vocabulary and—"

"Is that a yes for lending a hand?"

"Yup, it sure is!" Topher shoots me two thumbs-ups and

a crooked grin. "Now, I like to think of myself as a little bit of a businessman. Is there a possibility that helping might lead to . . . money?"

Damn if Levi wasn't right.

Admiring the kid's gumption, laughter breaks free from my chest. "You have balls for asking, Toph, I'll give you that."

"Is that a yes?" he asks, repeating my words verbatim.

I return the finger-gun salute. Cock the nonexistent safety. And "discharge" the weapon toward the space between us, like I'm laying down the law. "You owe both your mom and me a good deal of money after the car mishap, so let's look at it this way—every time you come over to help with the house, I'll knock a sum off your total. Sound like a deal?"

Grumbling, Topher shrugs a narrow shoulder. "Can't blame a guy for trying."

Nah, I can't.

At least he has the manners to ask, which is a lot more than I did back in the day.

I rap my knuckles on the wall. "Take a seat or grab something from the fridge. I'll be ready in five."

I'm halfway down the hallway, grabbing a towel from the linen closet, when I hear him call out, "If I take an apple, am I gonna have to pay you back for that too? How do you feel about the charity, *Feed Topher's Belly*?"

My mouth tugs up in an honest-to-God smile.

Pulling my phone from my shorts' pocket as I head for the master bedroom that I've yet to sleep in, I thumb down through my contacts until I get to Levi's name.

Me: Your son is a piece of work, Coach.

As if she's been waiting by the phone, her answer is immediate.

Levi: Have you smiled yet?

I spy my reflection in the mirror, and sure enough, I'm grinning like an idiot. I scrub a hand over my mouth, turn the hot water knob to get the shower running, and tap the glass screen to bring our message thread back to life.

Me: Twice.

Levi: See if you can make it a home run by the end of the day. I believe in you.

Me: Do you now?

Levi: Well, I believe in my baby boy. He never lets me down.

Me: We'll see.

Levi: Want some advice?

Me: Go ahead. I get the feeling you're gonna offer it anyway.

Levi: Topher's not above bending the rules to win.

Steam whirls around me, heating up the tiny bathroom off the master bedroom. Another section of the house that'll require some major renovation. No couple would ever want a bathroom this small as the master. The sink and toilet are nearly on top of each other, and the bathtub is the same shade of blue as Aladdin's Genie. Contrasted against the muted pink shag carpeting, this room is a disaster of epic proportions.

I strip out of my shorts, letting the material drop to the floor. Do the same with my T-shirt, which I whip over my head. No boxers or briefs to take off. I prefer to go commando.

The insane, devil-may-care part of me wants to find out what Levi would think if I let her know that we're texting while I'm naked. Would her cheeks turn the same red as my skin after I step under the hot jets? Would she care that I enjoy our easy banter—that it turns me on, despite the fact that I'm not looking for a fling or a one-night stand or anything remotely . . . *couple-y*? I'm not looking for it, but for reasons better left unanalyzed, Levi still manages to worm her way under my skin at the most inconvenient times.

In the men's bathroom at the Golden Fleece. At practice when she's running drills with the kids and her tits are bouncing. *Now*, when her son is waiting for me to hop in and out of the shower and take him mini-golfing so that I can learn what it's like to have fun.

One glance down past my stomach shows my cock on the rise—literally.

Jesus fuck.

It'd be so easy to slip my fist around the thick head and give it a slow, feel-good pump. Tight along the root, then looser, quicker, over the shaft. Imagine what it would be like to have those berry lips of hers pursed and ready to—

No.

No.

I drop my head forward, chin to my chest, fingers white-knuckling the lip of the Genie-blue counter. Suck in a heavy, labored breath. Remind myself that I'm here in Maine to avoid any and all entanglements.

Yeah? Is that why you cleaned her up at the Golden Fleece? Why you couldn't stop touching her, even after you wiped away all the caked-on makeup? I'd had no reason to keep caressing her skin. No other reason but that she'd felt soft and smooth and I'd enjoyed the hell out of watching the pulse in her neck flutter to life the longer I lingered.

My phone vibrates again.

Levi: Head's up. Topher's going to invite you over for dinner. He's wicked excited to have you living next door. I tried to tell him that just because we're neighbors doesn't mean we're friends but . . . kids. They pretend cluelessness to get what they want, and Topher wants you over for dinner.

I close my eyes. Pretty sure I'm already getting entangled, and I've only been in Maine for a week and a half.

I jump in the shower without responding to Levi's text. I wash my hair. Rinse out the suds. Purposely ignore my angry hard-on that's begging for some sort of release. When I accidentally brush it with the bar of soap, I swallow a desperate groan.

Head coach.

Assistant coach.

I've got to keep the lines between us firmly drawn.

If I give in . . . I have no doubt that I'll end up driving her away. I'll fuck her body and then somehow fuck up her life because that's generally the way things work out for me. And, as a single mom who's been through a divorce and probably a nasty marriage, Levi doesn't deserve having to deal with my hang-ups too.

Before we head out to the golf course, I send her one last text.

Me: Thanks for letting me know. I've got plans—I'll figure out a way to make it up to him.

15

ASPEN

"*O*h, hello there, sexy."

The words are crooned into the crook of my neck.

"Willow," I mutter, craning an arm behind me to swat at my younger sister's face, "seriously. Do you not know how to knock?"

She plunks down on the matching Adirondack chair next to mine. "Did you or did you not give me a key and invite me to visit whenever I wanted?"

Hand to the back of the laptop, I hastily snap it shut, all the better to keep my secrets. Dammit. I'm the worst sleuther in the history of sleuthers. Can't a girl catch a break and do a little online stalking in peace nowadays?

"I could have been naked," I protest, tucking a flyaway blond strand behind my ear.

"Seen it," Willow says with an exaggerated yawn. "Nothing I don't have myself. Plus, you stopped walking around naked the day Topher was born. I had nothing to fear."

Ugh. Touché.

Racking my brain for a counterargument, I settle on, "I could have been having sex?"

It's not supposed to come out as a question.

Willow only kicks up her legs onto the bottom of her chair, ankles crisscrossed, and turns her face up to the sky. She's wearing one of those sun hats that's three times the size of her face and looks good on her but would look absolutely ridiculous on me.

"Sex with what? That vibrator I got you for your thirtieth birthday that you *never used*?" She pokes up the front of her hat so she can still see me. "Sex isn't your thing."

I swear, younger sisters are put on this earth purely to torture their older siblings.

And Willow can be the worst.

"Oh, don't look so put out." She pats the back of my hand all sweet and innocent-like. "I still love you even if you're testing the hymen theory."

Since we were teenagers, Willow always liked to joke that without consistent sex, a woman's hymen regrows. I'm here as proof that the theory is wrong, even if it's a ridiculous theory to begin with.

Letting out a sigh, I roll my eyes. "Yeah, yeah. I love you too. Now will you please tell me why you're—*oomf!*"

All one hundred and thirty pounds of Willow Levi Lloyd land on my lap. I don't even have time to process the fact that my sister has jumped me before she's opening my laptop. Her back blocks my view, as does her massive hat, so all I see are her tanned shoulders and the tank top she stole from my closet three weeks ago and never returned. I buck my hips, trying to upheave her, but she holds on with enviable inner-thigh strength.

Oh, God.

"Willow."

Tap. Tap. Tap.

"I see you changed up your regular password, dear sister," she says, her voice muffled since she's turned away from me.

I have zero regrets about taking desperate action in the face of inevitable humiliation.

My fingers pinch the skin at her waist, twisting hard in the same way we used to do to each other when we were kids and fighting over toys.

"Ow!" she shrieks now, batting at my hand. "Rude."

"Willow"—I grab her hips and attempt to throw her off to the side, computer be damned—"you owe me after forgetting Topher at Kevin's. Remember? You forgot to pick him up!"

If anything, her ass only grows heavier in my lap as she lets me take on her full weight.

The. *Worst*.

Tap! Tap! TAP TAP TAP!

I'm seeing my life flash before my eyes. It's going to be horrible. I'm going to live in shame until the day I take my last breath. Which could be five minutes from now, given the chaotic way my heart is threatening to leap right out of my chest. And, honestly, it wasn't my fault. Not really. The internet is a strange, strange place, and one site led to another which led to another, and the next thing I know I was—

"Aha! Topher's birthday." More tapping ensues, and I hope—oh, I friggin' hope—she doesn't get curious and click on one of the open internet tabs. "You are so predictable—"

The sounds of moaning and ass slapping explode in my small courtyard, overtaking the chirping of the birds and the rhythmic lull of the waves slipping over the sand.

"Aspen."

Resigned, I close my eyes at the shock evident in my sister's voice. "Please," I whisper, heat charging its way up my throat, "please don't."

Because Willow's favorite thing to do in life is torment me, I'm treated to the *tap-tap-tap* of the keyboard before the volume hikes up and I'm forced to listen to the play-by-play happening on the screen.

"*Oh, Dominic! Dominic, right THERE!*"

"*Fuck yeah, baby. I'm gonna come all up inside you. You want this dick? How bad do you want this dick?*"

More moaning. More ass slapping.

More moments of me wondering what I did to deserve a sister like Willow.

She leans forward, her butt squashing my bladder. "That's not Dominic DaSilva."

This could not get any worse.

I drop my head back. "No, it's not."

"Fan role-play?" She sounds incredibly impressed. "Good for him. I want to be famous enough one day that someone pretends to be me in a porno."

"*Yeah, baby, ride that cock. Ride it, yeahhhhh.*"

Eyes closed in defeat, I beg, "Please turn it off."

Willow pokes me in the thigh. "Hold on, he's about to come."

"I can't take it anymore."

"You were the one who found this!"

"It was right *there*. On Google. I can't be blamed for clicking a link."

"That's what people say before they contract a computer virus and spread it around like herpes." A small pause. "Do you think DaSilva is actually uncut like this guy?"

"Oh, my God, I don't know!" I push at her back once

more, but she's too engrossed with the sex on the screen to pay me any attention. "It's not like he's coming over to my house, pants unzipped and ready to do the deed."

"Are you saying that if he *did* do any of those things, you'd be game to find out what he's rocking in his briefs?"

I swallow, thickly, then whisper, "I don't think he wears briefs."

"Boxers, then?"

I shake my head. "I don't know, Willow. All I know is that when he's running around at practice, sometimes I notice his *you-know-what* roaming a little too freely in his shorts."

"Dick, Asp. If you can sit here and watch porn about a guy who's pretending to be the hot football player living next door, the least you can do is use the right word. Or cock. Cock works too."

"Mom! Mom, are you outside?"

I don't know which one of us moves faster.

"Shut it down!" I hiss, reaching around Willow to grasp the laptop. Her fingers shoo mine away.

"Dammit, we were just getting to the good part."

I'm going to throw her off the patio and hope, for her sake, that she lands in the water below.

"*Willow.*"

"Oh, my God, calm down already, Grandma, it's closed." She leaps off my lap at the same time Topher appears in the open doorway. He's dressed in the same pair of cargo shorts that he left in this morning to go mini-golfing with Dominic, but his shirt is different.

Immediately, he jabs a finger to his chest, where a T-Rex has golf clubs for arms. Across the top of the dinosaur's massive head is a single word: *Unstoppable*. "Like it?" he asks. "Coach DaSilva bought it for me on the course." He glances to my left, then offers a small wave. "Hey, Aunt Willow. Did you find the house okay?"

My sister nods, even as her mouth twitches with the effort to hold back a grin. "You do remember that I sold this house to your mom, right?"

Topher rocks back on his heels, his expression eerily blasé. "Sure do. Just had to ask since you couldn't find Kevin's place the other day, and he lives a block over from you."

I cringe.

Willow, for the first time in her life, seems to struggle for words.

And then I hear *his* voice: "Ouch, kid. Rein in those T-Rex clubs, will you?"

Dominic steps out onto the patio, dressed in his usual black ensemble. The jeans, the shoes, the T-shirt, the black, tattered baseball hat. He's the devil come out to play and I just spent the last hour of my life stalking him online, where twenty of those minutes were spent watching a man who's not him pretend to *be* him as he screws some random woman.

Is it blisteringly hot outside or is it just me?

Dominic keeps his distance, hands shoved deep in the front pocket of his jeans, and then cocks his head to the side. Like he's curious about something. About me, maybe.

If only.

No! Not *if only*.

Clearly, the uncut penis on the screen has rattled my brain cells—even if it wasn't actually Dominic's.

"Dominic DaSilva, am I right?" Willow pokes me in the side as she sweeps forward, her blond hair curled to perfection as it hangs down her back under her hat. "I've heard *so* much about you. Aspen—weren't you just telling me that you love the way Coach DaSilva plays . . . ball?"

I'm going to kill her, it's official.

Lurching forward, I snake my arm through hers. "Dominic, this is my sister Willow."

Dominic peers down at her, his expression unreadable. "You the one with the EXWIFEY license plate out front?"

My sister practically preens beside me. "I have a morbid sense of humor."

"Doesn't morbid mean you like dead people, Aunt Willow?" Topher asks, narrowing his eyes in that way that always alerts me he's got something up his sleeve. "You know what? Now that I'm thinking about it, Uncle Larry always did seem a little *pale.*"

Willow audibly chokes. "I did not marry a vampire, kid. And you should probably invest in a dictionary because that is *not* the definition of morbid. Don't schools give them out free nowadays?"

"There's a thing called the internet. I don't need them to give me a dictionary." My son leans in, innocently batting his eyelashes. "You're too old to remember having internet at school, right?"

This time, I can't help but laugh out loud. It bubbles to life in my chest, making me gasp for air a little when I say, "You two are insane. Also, no fighting in front of strangers."

"Not quite a stranger anymore," Dominic cuts in, jutting a finger over my shoulder to point at his house next door. "Also, based on the way Topher here hustled me today, I should be awarded an honorary Levi medal. It was brutal out there."

In the midst of Dominic-wannabes and morbid word-play, it totally slipped my mind as to why he's here. In my courtyard. Particularly when he made it a point to mention that he has plans tonight . . .

Throat absurdly dry—from nerves? Guilt? Lust?—I only nod. Then blurt, "Thanks for bringing Topher home."

Fifteen-year-old boys are not known for their subtlety. Topher snickers under his breath. "Yeah, Mom, because he had *such* a far way to go."

The twenty feet separating our two houses suddenly feels even smaller than normal. I meet Dominic's dark gaze, surprised to find that he's actually removed his ball cap. It's dangling from a finger down at his side, but his attention is rooted on me.

"I thought you had plans?" I ask.

"He canceled them," Topher butts in before ambling over to Willow. "Coach said he needs to talk with you, Ma."

My eyes fly to the laptop, which is still perched on the Adirondack chair. It sits there like a beacon of impending disaster. Slowly, I move toward it. Only a step. Nothing too obvious. "About what?"

Did he hear the moaning coming from the laptop when he walked in the house?

I hope not.

Really, really hope not.

"Adult stuff, apparently," Topher says, which does nothing at all to alleviate my anxiety. "I don't know. Aunt Willow, want to grab some ice cream from Cookies and Joe?"

My younger sister narrows her eyes on her nephew. "Is this blackmail? I bring you to the diner and you forget about sitting on your buddy's front stoop for an hour?"

"Sounds like a fair trade to me."

Willow's grumbling is belied by the wink she sends my way. "All right, fine. You've twisted my arm, nephew. Ice cream it is."

"And then after you have to bring me to the video game store before it closes."

My kid is nothing if not an expert at maneuvering people to act in his best interests. Hiding a grin behind my closed fist, I watch my sister and son bicker their way back into the house. Over the years, they've built more of a brother-sister bond, considering how young I was when I first learned I was pregnant.

Willow was even younger. By the time of Topher's birth, she had only recently turned nineteen. I was a month shy of my twenty-second birthday.

"Your son's a swindler."

Jumping a little, I look swiftly to Dominic. "Figured that out already, did you?"

Without waiting for me to offer him a place to sit, he takes a seat on the Adirondack chair like he owns the damn thing. Long legs planted down on the brick patio on either side of the chair, arms crossed over his chest. He drops his head back, twisting it to the left so he can still get a read on me.

Lord, those eyes of his are the very definition of temptation.

Lips tipping up in a delicious grin, Dominic says, "He's ruthless. He'd wait till I was about to nail a ball in the hole and then—"

"Cross-check you out of the way?" I take the chair next to his, folding my legs beneath me so that I'm sitting cross-legged. "My boy did me proud."

Laughter greets my ears, the sound deep and husky and, boy, if he only laughed more often . . . he'd need sticks to keep the women away. "Like mother, like son?"

I bat my eyelashes innocently, much the same way Topher did, and it does the trick.

More gravel-pitched laughter that does something funny to my insides. And does way more for me than the pretend Dominic DaSilva going to town on that website. I'm not sure what this says about me, besides the obvious: the real Dominic intrigues me more than he should.

"Why am I not surprised?" he muses, sounding not the least bit put out about my kid screwing him over. "You were way too eager to have me take him mini-golfing. I should have known you were up to no good."

"I taught him everything he knows."

"And you said *I* have a big ego."

I shift forward, forearms propped up on my thighs. "Newsflash, Coach, you *do* have a big ego."

Letting out a low chuckle, Dominic shakes his head. Rubs a hand over his mouth like he's determined to kill off his lingering smile.

"What?" I ask.

"Every time I think I've nailed you down, you surprise me all over again."

It takes a lot of inner strength to ignore the more-than-obvious sexual euphemism in his words. At another time, in another world—in my dreams, if we're being honest—I wouldn't mind being nailed down by Dominic. Simply to scratch the itch, of course. Nothing more. Licking my lips, which suddenly feel dry, I murmur, "Is surprising you . . . is that a bad thing?"

"Nah." Black eyes flit from my naked thighs and then up, up, up to my face. I squirm under his intense stare, and all but pluck at the hem of my shorts to tug them as far down as they can go. His stare makes me feel exposed in a way that standing naked in front of a crowd never could. "Predictability is overrated."

Something in his tone piques my curiosity. It's the bitterness, I realize a moment later. It drips like the most toxic poison, forming in the twist of his mouth and hardening the glint in his gaze.

I sit up a little straighter. "Do you really think that?"

Sharply, he averts his face. Stares out at the crystalline bay and the green island beyond it. This part of Mount Desert Island is tucked away from the Atlantic Ocean, which means the waters in London are usually warmer than in other parts of the state.

Has Dominic made use of his private pathway down to the beach yet? It's just there, right over the four-foot hedge separating our small, individual courtyards.

Until this moment, I hadn't really given much thought as to how intimately our backyards are positioned. All it would take is one crook of his finger to invite me onto his side of the property . . .

"Predictability kills ambition."

I cut my attention away from the bay and revert it back to his face. "I don't agree."

I watch as his jaw clenches, then releases. Like he's making a controlled effort to go here with me—to be vulnerable.

"Give yourself three months in my shoes, Levi. You'd see it, too."

"Then take me there." I don't know what I'm suggesting, what exactly I'm inviting him to open up to me about. Feeling a pinch in my heart, I drop my bare feet to the patio, feeling the rough texture of the bricks graze my soles. "You want me to see it from your perspective? Then make me see."

He spears his fingers through his thick hair.

Then twists on his chair, too, so that we're facing each other. His legs, so much longer than my own, rest on the outside of mine. This close to him, it's hard to miss the thickness of his throat, the soft fullness of his lips, the overall harshness of the rest of his features. Put together with the all-black ensemble, and Dominic DaSilva should be a man I run far, far away from.

Instead, I scoot my butt forward. Allow my feet to extend out under his chair, between the *V* of his legs. Get all up in his business because this . . . I want to hear this. I spent years living with a man I thought I knew, only to realize that I didn't know him at all.

Didn't know why he stopped wanting me in the bedroom.

Didn't understand why he chose to spend his time with people who weren't his family.

Could never piece together how a man who vowed to love me until the day he died suddenly made me feel like I was a hindrance to his long-term plans.

Rick made me feel like an extra in his life, and when he wasn't making me feel like a secondary cast member, he simply made me feel miserable. Hopeless. *Help*less.

And while Dominic and I aren't dating—we aren't even remotely together—I won't lie and say that I'm not curious to understand what makes him *him*.

His chest inflates with a heavy breath. Then, as though he's preparing himself to go there with me, he drops his forearms to his thighs and comes pretty close to letting his fingers skim my knees. He doesn't make that final connection, much to my regret. Only keeps his head bowed when he says, "The only times in my life where I've felt true success have come after the rug has been ripped out from beneath me. In college . . ." He trails off, then lifts his head so I can see all of him. "You know what? Let me put it this way: I do best when I've got something driving me forward."

"So, what? You *like* having your world turned upside down?"

Dark eyes pin me in place. "I thrive on feeling like I've hit rock bottom and have come out of it alive."

I don't look away. Can't, I don't think, even if I wanted to.

Because the fervor in his voice has me locked all the way in.

"Say it."

At his rough demand, I press my tongue to the roof of my mouth, unable to find adequate words for the thoughts spinning through my head.

"*Aspen*."

My first name off his tongue is like a jolt of electricity to my system. I twitch—honest to God *twitch*—and fold my hands under my thighs to keep them still. My skin is sticky from the sinking sun, but even the mid-afternoon warmth heating the top of my head and shoulders can't strip away the pleasure sinking into my bones after hearing him say my name.

Aspen.

Other than my immediate family, everyone has always referred to me as Levi. Like it's some sort of rite of passage with becoming the next generation of Levi football royalty. After thirty-seven years, I've long since given up trying to convince people to use Aspen instead. Hell, even Rick called me Levi, and I was his *wife*.

On second thought, that probably should have been my first clue that we were doomed.

Brilliant epiphany to have fifteen years after the fact.

Go, me.

Aware that my voice is lower, more intimate than it has any right to be, I give Dominic the answer he probably doesn't want: "I think you feed off crushing people's opinions of you." When his eyes widen, ever so slightly, I take it as a thumbs-up to keep going, and recall exactly what I found online before Willow showed up. "If I had to guess, it's probably a direct result of you growing up in foster care . . . at least, how *you* grew up in foster care. The poor kid. The one no one wanted."

I slip one hand out from under my thigh and lay it on his knee, taking a risk when it's clear as day that Dominic isn't as hands-on as his public persona would suggest he is. "So, yeah, I think you get off on proving people wrong. It's not that predictability kills ambition—it's that predictability, for you, means that there's no fire behind your every move while you show the world that their vision of Dominic DaSilva is wrong."

The lines of his face sharpen.

"Predictability is an empty space for you, when all you have is time to think about your life, and what you'd change and all the ways you've taken the wrong path," I continue, because he asked for my opinion and I've never been one to shy away from delivering when called upon. *He wanted this.* It's what I remind myself when I add, "Isn't that the reason you went on *Put A Ring On It?* Because you were done with the quiet? Because you were ready, once again, to come out on top and feel . . . how did you put it? *Alive?*"

Silence ticks by, only interspersed by the sound of our breathing and a boat's rudder as it cuts through the choppy water out in the bay.

I bite down on my bottom lip. Internally curse myself out for speaking out of turn.

Dominic and I aren't friends who trade secrets and feelings and hidden truths that no one else knows but the two of us. *Remember that.*

Unfortunately, since coming back to London, he also feels like my *only* friend.

Even if the friendship is a bit one-sided.

Nothing you aren't used to in relationships with guys.

I shove the memories of Rick in a box, turning the key and visualizing it—and him—going up in flames. *Take that, you cheating, rat bastard.*

Dominic's jean-clad knee shifts beneath my hand. To my surprise, he doesn't shove me away as he scrubs a hand over the side of his face. Then, "There you go surprisin' me again."

And, like I said only minutes ago, I repeat the same words back: "Is that a bad thing?"

"It is when you're calling me out on shit that I . . ." His hand moves to cup the back of his neck. "No. No, it's not a bad thing."

"Maybe you're looking at the quiet times all wrong."

He quirks a single brow. "Oh, yeah?"

"Yeah." When I pull my hand away from his leg, his gaze tracks my retreat, and I wish—seriously *wish*—his expressions were more transparent. I'd give anything to know what he's thinking right now. "The quiet means safety," I tell him, hands tucked together in my lap. "Predictability means you've reached a point in your life where you feel good about who you are, who you're with."

His lips part. "Levi . . ."

I squeeze my eyes shut against the disappointment of being back where we started this conversation.

Not friends.

Not anything more.

Levi.

You'd think I would be used to it all by now.

Eyes still closed, I go on, revealing more of myself than I

have to anyone in years. "Predictability means not jumping every time you hear a door slam shut or see a number you don't recognize calling your husband's cell phone. It means that your son—the one person in your life who you would die to protect—no longer cries at night because his father is an asshole who wouldn't know love if it bit him in the balls."

"*Jesus fuck.*"

The first time I heard Dominic use that particular four-letter soundtrack in that cool, unfeeling voice of his, it shocked me right out of my skin. It's not unfeeling right now. Not even a little. I hear the emotion quaking to life, like a volcano ready to erupt.

Ragged.

Angry.

I pop up off the Adirondack chair, needing space between us.

Space between me and the place of my confession.

You need to breathe. That too. Talking about Rick isn't nearly the same as living in the same house as him—I don't need to mind my opinionated tongue or look over my shoulder every time I hear his voice echo in the house. I don't need to wait until I'm in my car, with the locks acti-vated, until I give into the tears. No, talking about Rick isn't nearly the same as being stuck with him but that doesn't mean my heart isn't racing or that I don't feel the least bit lightheaded from the memories.

Breathe in. Breathe out.

I'm grateful for divorce attorneys.

I'm grateful for little hometowns that feel like sanctuaries.

I'm grateful for being strong enough to have this conversation with Dominic and not outwardly break down.

"Thank you for hanging out with Topher today." I glance at him over my shoulder before I tuck my laptop under my arm for safekeeping. "I know he probably appreciated it more than he'll ever admit out loud."

Because Rick never took Topher mini-golfing. Hell, he can barely remember to call his only son now that we're well outside Pittsburgh city limits.

Slowly, like a panther unfurling in the wild just before it launches at its prey, Dominic rises to his full height. "The feeling's mutual," he husks out. "He's a good kid."

"He's the best kid."

"I won't deny that. Levi, I—"

"It's okay." I flash him a bright grin that I so wish I felt to the depths of my soul. "I didn't open up because I expected you to have something to add back, but I just . . . Well, I wanted you to step in my shoes, too. Predictability isn't always bad. It doesn't always mean that you're somehow failing or that your ambition has taken a walk and left you out in the cold."

"I see that." He steps close, eliminating the distance between us until he's not even a hand's width away from me. "You made me see that."

His fingers curl up, the backs of his knuckles hovering a hair's breadth away from my face.

And I *breathe*.

In and out, like I haven't sucked in real oxygen in years.

My gaze shoots up to meet his.

Behind the wide breadth of his shoulders, the sun has begun its descent. Pinks and mauves mar the horizon, turning the sky into my favorite color-painted mural. The sunsets in Pittsburgh never once came close to those here in my hometown.

In and out.

More clean, crisp air filtering in and out of my lungs. Fueling my soul.

"Dominic?"

Disappointment is swift and merciless as his hand drops to his side and he falls back a step. "I had you all wrong," is all he says cryptically, like that's supposed to make sense to me.

It doesn't.

I clutch my laptop to my chest. Turn away to head back into the house through the open French doors. "Topher said you wanted to talk to me about something?"

"It had to do with the team but . . . it can wait."

I look over at him. "Are you sure?"

"Yeah. It's not urgent."

He only makes it a few steps before he whirls around, hips squared off and his Adam's apple bobbing down the length of his throat. "I lied."

I blink. "About . . . ?"

"Having plans tonight. I didn't—I *don't*."

My arms tighten around my laptop. "I mean, I figured that was the case." I force a light chuckle in hope of easing his strained expression. "It's okay, Dominic. We're not going to hold it against you, even though I am a pretty good cook, if I do say so myself."

"I needed today and your kid . . . you were right." As if agitated, he rakes his fingers through his hair. "I came by because I wanted to say thank you. For giving me exactly what I needed when I didn't even know." With the smallest of smiles, he adds, "I hit a home run."

I hit a home run.

I know exactly what he means—Topher did that for him, made Dominic laugh the way he's always kept me seeing the good in people all these years.

Before I have the chance to respond, Dominic is striding through my living room to the front door like he's some good civilian letting himself out when we both know he could have just hopped the hedge between our yards and called it a day.

And then I sit on my sofa and open my laptop. I'm quick to click out of the role-play porno, but hesitate over the next tab. The one with an article dated to 2014, a year before Dominic's exit from the NFL.

I skim the headline once more and feel my insides twist with sympathy.

From Rags to Riches: NFL Player Dominic DaSilva (Tight End for the Tampa Bay Buccaneers) Looks Back on a Youth Spent in Juvenile Detention.

Although I already read the article minutes before Willow showed up, I find myself scanning through again, searching out Dominic's quotes that have been highlighted:

"Football is the reason I'm where I am today, no questions asked. It saved me when I had nothing and gave me a reason to live."

"No, I don't know what happened to the boys I was with in juvie. It's not exactly a place for bonding. You all did wrong. You all messed up. Time to pay your penance and do better once you're out—unless you don't learn your lesson the first time around . . . which, clearly, I didn't."

"I created Junior Buccaneers because those kids need a reason to get up in the morning and feel excited about life. They need someone on their side—so, yeah, I know what that's like. I guess I finally learned how to do better."

"I guess I learned how to do better," I whisper to myself, staring at the black-and-white photo the article has provided of Dominic in his Bucs jersey. The number twelve is printed across the front, half-hidden by the football he's holding. But when I take in his black eyes, I hear only the words he told me on the Wildcats football field a week ago: *I'm something of a work in progress.*

In the deepest, most secret parts of my soul, I can't help but wonder what Dominic might accomplish if his driving force wasn't ambition or a fear of predictability . . . but love.

16

DOMINIC

*T*he sun is overwhelmingly hot. The kids are sweating bullets. And I'm in a foul fucking mood.

I blow the whistle before calling for another round of breakthrough drills. Bobby sends me a glance that could wither unicorns where they stand. Timmy's shoulders cave as he tromps back into place. And Topher . . . Shit, even Topher eyes me like I'm the devil incarnate as he lines up and drops his hands to the grass.

The days of worshipping the ground I walk on are long gone.

Even Harry, a red-headed junior, who's a beast with the ball, didn't sandwich himself next to me during warm-ups to chat about my time in the NFL, the way he's done at every practice.

Your shitty attitude might as well be repellant.

Like a bad habit I can't quit, my attention drifts over to where Levi is running some intricate footwork drills with her group. Her blond hair is tied off in a bun on the top of her head that bobbles and trembles as she demonstrates how she wants the set performed. Despite the muggy weather, she's wearing baggy sweats that do nothing for her figure and an olive-green T-shirt that represents a team she's coached in the past.

The Hancock Tigers.

In the two weeks that we've worked together, she's never shown up in anything but Wildcats paraphernalia. Maybe we're both shaken up over yesterday's talk out in her courtyard.

I know that I am.

She demolished my walls and scraped out my emotions with a jagged-edged spoon. And she did it all with a gentle hand on my leg and a soft but challenging look in her gaze. *Don't run from the truth,* those sapphire eyes of hers dared.

I ran.

But I didn't run fast enough. I heard every word she spilled about Rick-fucking-Clarke loud and clear. I witnessed the moment when her eyes dulled, the bad memories of her ex-husband threatening to submerge her.

Just as my own bad memories have always come close to drowning me.

I've come as far as I have in life by using the shittiness of my childhood and teenage years as fuel in pushing me forward. Every holiday that I spent alone, every achievement I marked off as complete, became another reason to prove to the world—and to myself—that I didn't *need* more.

I had the big house. I had the fleet of fancy cars packed away in my five-car garage. I had the pool and the money and a string of women ready to sleep with me at a moment's notice.

And with a single glimpse into Levi's life, all of it—the cars and the investment properties and the shallow, inconsequential sex—carves a hollow notch in my soul. The semblance of peace Levi talked about? The sensation of gleaning comfort from the predictable? I have no idea how to find that. Wouldn't even recognize that level of calm if it stood in front of me in a fucking clown costume.

It's frustrating. Beyond that, it's left me feeling *lacking* all morning. Just as I did years ago, back when I couldn't help but wonder if there was something so intrinsically wrong with me that I went unwanted for so long.

Why I've gone unloved, even now.

"You look like you ate something bad for lunch, Coach."

Brien.

Goddammit.

Figures he'd show up to observe practice on the one day I'm spitting nails and feeling restless and exposed in my own skin.

I push my sunglasses to the top of my head, over my backward baseball hat. "What brings you down to the field today? Ran out of paperwork to push around on your desk?"

Brien steps up beside me, arms linked over his chest as he surveys the field. "You sure do know how to make a person feel included, DaSilva. Tell me, do you roll out the welcome mat for everyone or am I just special enough to warrant an invitation to your bad side?"

I bite out a harsh laugh. "Sorry, was I supposed to jump to attention and salute you?"

"I'm not opposed."

"You're pushing your luck, Bri."

"You're pushing those kids too hard, *Dom*." Uncurling one arm, he flicks a finger toward where my players are slinking back into position after running through the drill another time. Harry, the football whisperer, pushes his helmet up and tips back his head as he repositions himself opposite the five offensive players whose only mission is to keep him from exploding through their lines. Guilt hits me like a sledgehammer to the gut when Brien tacks on, "They're not in the pro's. You can't treat them like they're the next Tom Brady."

"New England's obsession with him is borderline neurotic."

"Don't be put out that none of us have a Dominic DaSilva bobblehead in our cars. Even Levi has a Brady one on her dashboard. You see it yet?"

Levi.

Hearing her name heats my blood immediately.

I reach for my hat, then force my hand to veer to the lanyard around my neck. *Tweet!* I wait for the boys to look my way then shout for them to take a water break.

Their relief is palpable.

My guilt threatens to drown me like quicksand.

"I didn't actually come out here to reprimand you."

"No?" With my arms linked over my chest, I watch the boys pile around the watercooler. "I figured you were tired of grounding your kids at home and needed another victim. Is Cody using your condoms as slingshots again?"

Brien's shoots me a quality-level side-eye. "That was *one* time and he was only four."

"Didn't he successfully tip over a glass of milk with nothing but his condom slingshot and a peanut to his name?"

"Once. Just once."

"Early signs of athleticism, if you ask me. Think about what kinda prospects he'll have one day with aim like that."

"Who has good aim?" Levi muses as she cuts over to us, one hand raised to shield her face from the sun. "Your son, Adam?"

The smile she sends my way is no different than her normal ones: bright and cheery and not the least bit intimate. I think of what she told me in the Golden Fleece's restroom: *Don't ever touch me like you did tonight unless you plan to do something about it.*

Last night, with her faintly scarred lips parted and her breathing heavy with emotion, I came damn near close to doing something about it. Came so close to it, even, that when I paused to tell her exactly why I had stopped by, I'd been seconds away from pushing her up against her glass doors and kissing that smart mouth of hers until her breathy moans belonged to me alone.

I wanted to soak up that calm she talked so much about. I wanted to devour her positivity and the hope that coated every inch of her, even when life has clearly tried to beat her down. I wanted, for once, to bare my skin and know that a woman like Aspen Levi would see more than just my nakedness when she looked my way.

Except . . . except she's got emotional baggage from her ex-husband and clearly I'm all kinds of fucked up in the head. Hooking up with a coworker is a bad idea. Hooking up with a coworker whose son you also coach? Now that's disaster in the making.

Maine is my calm. Maine is my reprieve. Maine *isn't* hot sex with a single mom who encourages her kid to play dirty at mini-golf and moans when she eats pizza.

Levi's hand brushes mine and, fuck me, but I hiss between my teeth at the unexpected contact.

"Don't mind him," Brien says to Levi with a dismissive nod in my direction, "all the grumbling he's doing is on account of stomach problems." He and I both know my stomach isn't hurting and he's only trying to bust my balls for being in a bad mood, not that he seems to give a shit when he blithely adds, "Is it wrong of me to hope it's painful? DaSilva's got a crap ton of bad karma to work off."

Feminine laughter loops around me, tightening the invisible noose circling my neck. "Are you prepared to die waiting for retribution? Something tells me Dominic here has bad karma in spades."

Her comment hits a little too close to home. And, after last night's heart-to-heart, it also grates on an already sore wound.

Sharply, before I even think about the words as they escape me, I ask, "Where's your Wildcat shirt?"

Levi twists toward me, berry lips parted. "Excuse me?"

The asshole in me—the one who despises feeling vulnerable and raw—digs its heels in deeper, refusing to listen to reason and shut the hell up. "Hancock High?" I nod to the tiger mascot printed on her shirt. "What? You weren't feeling the Wildcat school spirit? Or maybe you're just regrettin' your move back home?"

Her nostrils flare. "Jeez, what crawled up your ass and died today?"

"You did."

Shit, shit, *shit!*

She gapes at me, and I don't need to hear her response to know I've messed up. *And this is why you think before opening your big, stupid mouth.* It doesn't matter that she *has* gotten to me today. She's wreaked havoc on my head, on my thoughts, on my isolated, black heart. "Levi, shit. I'm sorry—"

"Screw off, Dominic."

"Whoa, whoa, whoa." Brien shuffles between us, his hands raised like he's concerned we might go at each other, battering-ram-style. "Enough of that." He points a finger at me. "Don't be a jerk." When he looks to Levi, his expression softens imperceptibly. "Don't sink to his level, Coach."

His advice feels like the worst kind of insult.

Thing is? I deserve it, one-hundred percent.

Giving me the cold shoulder—literally—Levi's cheeks burn red as she addresses Brien. "Get him out of here, Adam. I'm not dealing with the bullshit. Not today."

"No can do," my old friend sing-songs, palms raised to the sky in an *aw, shucks* pose if I've ever seen one. "I've got a journalist sitting in my office who drove up here from Portland. Three-hour trip, guys. He's determined."

"From where?" Levi asks with her profile to me.

"The *New England Sports Advocate*."

Not. A. Chance. In. Hell.

"No press," I growl. *NESA* might as well be the *Celebrity Tea Presents* of the sports-journalism world. It's a cesspool of social climbers all looking for their big break, each so-called "journalist" willing to write just about anything to catch the eye of a more established publication. That my old buddy is even considering it is . . . concerning, to say the least. "And especially not them."

Brien stares at me like I've snipped the wires to his favorite gaming set. "You don't have a choice, DaSilva. He's here and we could use the publicity."

Only, it's not publicity for the team that journalist is looking to expose—it's me. "Bri, are you seriously gonna sit there and tell me that *NESA* would be looking at London High if I weren't here?"

"Okay, I'm seriously over the ego trip." Levi fingers the hem of her shirt, not even sparing me a single glance. "Dominic can cover practice while I take care of the interview. Let the *assistant* do his job—how about that?"

It's a low blow and she knows it.

In the almost two weeks that we've been coaching together, we've taken on a partnership role with the team. Sure, she has the final say. But that hasn't stopped her from seeking me out and asking my opinion about a play or allowing me to run drills and scrimmages and everything else as I see fit.

The only place I've worked the assistant angle is when we met with the parents at the Golden Fleece, and even then I pulled my weight.

Feeling the sharp blade of annoyance pierce me, I mutter, "Don't even go there, Coach."

"What?" she baits, her finger digging into my chest like she's turned my own blade back on me. "You worried I'll mess up your mojo by making you look like a decent human being for the article and not like the jerk you actually are? You seriously are the only person I've ever met who takes pride in being a complete tool."

"*Ooookay* now." Brien's hand collides with my shoulder, pushing me back. "While I'd like to play babysitter and sit you both down for a time-out, unfortunately you're going to have to pull on your adult panties and get your shit together." Another thrust of his hand against my shoulder. "I've got a big-time journalist wanting to talk with you both about how your careers have landed you in small-town Maine. You will not screw this up for the team. Some of those seniors need a slice of hope, and a drop of their name in a paper with their circulation numbers could be a game changer."

I let the silence linger only momentarily. Then, "I haven't missed your pep talks. I thought maybe I would but . . . no. Definitely don't."

Brien sticks out an arm, head turned toward the field. "Go."

"The kids—"

"I played quarterback for LSU, Levi. I think I know what I'm doing. *Go*."

Like scolded children, Levi and I lurch into step and head for the school.

The silence is damning.

In the past, it's never mattered to me who I piss off. A coach? They'll get over it when they see the stats I bring in for the team. A teammate? Nothing a six-pack of beer can't solve. A friend? Well, haven't had many of those.

But with Levi . . . I'm a tangled web of fucking emotions. I want to push her down, like a preteen boy with a crush he doesn't know how to handle—other than to make her life miserable in hope of scoring some points. I want to apologize for being a sorry sack of shit who lashes out when he feels off kilter. I want to pull her to a stop and drag her into my arms and tell her that yesterday's conversation was the most genuine one I've had in years.

If ever.

And that scares the shit out of me.

"I'll take care of the interview," she says, her tone all kinds of huffy. "God knows you can't be trusted with words right now."

I yank open the double-wide doors and angle my body so she can skate past me. The scent of strawberries catches in my nose, and fuck me, but she smells delicious. Fresh and fruity. Like woman and sunshine and hopes and dreams all wrapped up with a perfectly tied bow.

"Levi, I—"

"*No.*" She whirls around, nearly sending me tripping over my own feet in a last ditch effort to keep from running her over. "No. I'm sorry, but I'm not okay with you being a jerk to me. Not ever, but *especially* not after last night."

The words *I'm sorry* sit on my tongue, but each time I begin to edge them out, she tromps right over them.

"I don't know all the details of your life and I'm not

going to pretend that I do, but I can say with *full* clarity that however fucked up you think you are in the head, none of that gives you any right to pull that bad attitude with me."

She's breathing so heavily her breasts are on the rise. Up and down, they move, holstering my attention even as I try to regain control of the situation.

"Levi—*Aspen*—"

"Abso-fucking-lutely not." Her hands fly at my chest, shoving me back. Or trying to. Like a rabbit attempting to move an eighteen-wheeler, I can't be budged. "You know which people get to call me Aspen? Family. Friends. You, *Coach*, are neither."

Venom.

She's spitting venom and I'm hard as a fucking rock, and if that doesn't prove that I'm not quite right in the head, then I honestly don't know what does.

I step in close, fully prepared to throw her over my shoulder so we can settle this in private, when she brings her foot down on mine. *Hard*. Definitely not an accident. The cute blonde from the pub has claws, I see.

Something about that makes me grin.

Which sets her off *completely*.

"You're my assistant," she snaps, chin thrust forward. "Does that make you feel good? To know that with a snap of my fingers I could have you fired?"

One foot in her direction. I lower my voice, aware of the echo in the empty hallway. "Sorry to disappoint, but you'd have to do a heck of a lot more than snap your fingers."

Her mouth pulls tight. "You don't think I could?"

Another step. "I think you've got a lot working in your favor being back in your hometown but getting rid of me isn't gonna be a win for you. You'll lose."

A sexy growl works its way up her throat. "I wish I could

clobber you with your ego. Let you feel the brunt of the burn."

"Think you're doing a fine enough job on your own." I quirk a brow, daring her to argue my point, then follow up with another step forward. "I haven't had a tongue lashing like this one in years."

I see the moment awareness hits her that I've backed her into a corner.

Lockers behind her, a wall to her left.

More lockers to the right, thanks to the *L* shape of the hallway.

Her heels collide with the bottom row of lockers, and there's a familiar, rattling metal sound that brings me straight back to my grade-school days.

"You've got nowhere to run, Coach," I drawl, planting my hands against the cool metal locker on either side of her head. I lean forward, pressing the weight of my frame into hers. "You gonna put me in my place?"

Lowering my head, I graze her earlobe with my teeth. She told me she wasn't anyone's toy. That's good. I'm not looking for a plaything. I'm not even sure *what* I'm looking for, but what I do know is this: I'm dying to taste that sweet, whip-smart mouth of hers. I want the fire that fuels her to belong to me, even if only for a single kiss.

I nudge the column of her throat with my nose. Rasp, "You gonna remind me that I'm your *subordinate* and I better heel before you punish me?"

A shudder wracks her body. "You called me a pain in the ass," she mutters breathlessly.

"Correction: I said that you crawled up my ass and died."

Slender fingers find the hem of my shirt, twining themselves up in the fabric. "I want to hate you."

I kiss her neck. Because this is what I should have done

the night that I met her. What I should have done the night
of the parent/staff meeting at the Golden Fleece. What I
should have done yesterday, when I sat in her courtyard and
wondered what she might do if I slipped my hands over her
naked thighs and pressed a kiss to her berry lips.

My mouth coasts down over her pulse. It quickens
under my touch. Pulses to a rhythm I know all too well, one
that races to the beat of: *What are we doing here? This is
crossing so many boundaries. We. Can't. Do. This.*

I obliterate every internal protest and husk out, "I want
to understand why I can't hate you."

And then I capture her cheek with my palm, holding her
in place, and slant my mouth over hers.

17

ASPEN

*T*he kiss is as rugged, as savage, as the man himself.

Blunt fingers curl toward the back of my skull while his thumbs crest my cheekbones, palms kissing the hollows of my cheeks. Dominic is big all over. I knew it when I met him but standing here now with my back pressed against a row of high school lockers and his muscular thigh wedged between my legs . . . it's overwhelming.

He's overwhelming.

And still I submit—to the sensations of his tongue driving into my mouth, reckless and aggressively intimate, and to the heat building within me.

When was the last time I felt like this? So needy, so damn desperate?

Years.

It's been years, if ever.

Long before I found Rick sleeping with another woman.

Long before he stopped climbing into bed beside me at night.

Long before the comfort he offered felt shallow and—

A gasp breaks free from my throat.

Dominic swallows it with a husky laugh, his mouth parting and his teeth nipping down on my bottom lip. He pulls away long enough to growl, "Wherever you went in that pretty head of yours, remember that you're with me right now. Only me," and then the kiss is back on and I feel like I'm floating.

Scratch that.

I *am* floating.

Hands spreading under my butt like a human-based safety net, Dominic hauls me up and into his arms. My back slams against the lockers again, and oh, God, but the jangle of metal clanging against metal brings me right back to high school.

Only, when I roamed these halls twenty-plus years ago, it wasn't in the arms of a mountain-sized Adonis.

Football practice, V-card status, homework—that was my M.O., back when I was seventeen and dreaming of playing in the big leagues. Can't say I'm dying to turn back the clock, especially when I feel a very stiff part of Dominic drag against the very soft part of me.

Oh, God, that feels so good.

I snatch the sunglasses off the top of his head, hooking them over the collar of my shirt. Snag his beloved baseball hat, too, and settle that bad boy on my head. Backward. Like I'm some sort of badass instead of a thirty-seven-year old single mom with stretch marks on my belly that do *not* go away no matter how much lotion I slather on them.

"Kiss me again," I beg, before clutching his shirt and using my grip to drag him forward. Our lips meet. Teeth clash. Tongues collide. And it feels glorious and messy, and is that him making that delicious growling noise in his throat?

It is.

I feel blessed to hear it.

With one hand still locked under my ass, he brings the other up to cup the back of my head. Pressure cranes my neck back, and it takes a moment for realization to kick in that he's tugging on the brim of the hat to put me where he wants me.

Vulnerable.

Neck exposed.

Prickly stubble grazes my cheek before his lips find the delicate line of my throat. A kiss. Hot breath dampens my skin, shooting shivers down my spine. Another kiss. This one lower, directly over my fluttering pulse. Again, another. Over the sweet, sensitive place where my neck and shoulder meet. A tongue flits out, tracing my flesh just before he nips the same spot, and I'm a goner.

Game over.

I jack my hips forward, seeking more of that hard pressure at the apex of my thighs, only to feel a plastic dial dig into my spine.

Lockers, right. High school, right.

Do I care?

Not in this moment. Not when Dominic DaSilva, of all people, is driving me off the cliff of insanity-induced lust.

Rolling my hips once more, I relish the curse that bursts from his mouth: "Fuck, not here. Classroom."

The lockers shimmy into silence as he spins us around, my legs locked around his lean waist. I kiss the underside of his chin, hearing the telltale click of a door opening. I lick the corner seam of his mouth when his ass hits a desk and he anchors me on top of him, so I'm straddling his lap. I tangle my fingers through his hair, marveling at its thickness, then release a moan when he grips my hips and roughly drags me flush against the length of his hard-on.

Dominic DaSilva is *truly* Hulk-sized all over.

God bless.

Inhaling sharply, my forehead drops to the hard plane of his shoulder.

There's the scent of grass and detergent and sweat, and something that's so uniquely Dominic that I wish I could bottle it up and keep it with me forever. For when this moment is over and locked away in a box of Feel Good Memories Never To Be Repeated Again.

"We're going to break the desk," I utter, raggedly.

"Does it look like I give a shit?" His hand frames my face, a wordless demand for me to lift my head and look him in the eye, and oh boy, but *no*, it does not actually look like he cares. Not about anything besides how our bodies feel moving against one another.

And it feels good, *so* inexplicably good.

Is this the way true desire is supposed to feel? Reckless and addicting, like at any given moment I'll shatter into a million little pieces? It didn't feel this way with Rick, not even once. I was young; he was much older. I listened when he said, "bend over," and I obeyed, awed that a man like him would ever pay a small-town girl like me any bit of attention, when he ordered, "get down on your knees."

I didn't own my sexuality with my ex-husband. I didn't force him to take my likes and needs into consideration, and I certainly never took control in the bedroom. First because I was too nervous and scared to make any sort of wrong move that he might find offensive, and then, later, because it was simply easier to do as he said, so it could all be done and over with that much sooner.

It was never like this. *I* was never like this.

Assertively, my hips grind down against Dominic to a sensual rhythm that feels both foreign and natural all at once. I feel my core clench when I tear my gaze away from Dominic's feverish expression to look south.

Obscene.

Everything about this illicit moment is one for the books.

My hands paw at his shirt, lifting the fabric so I can scour his rock-hard abs with my short, unpainted nails. His fingers have tugged down the waistband of my sweatpants—along with my underwear—and each time my hips rise up, riding the length of his erection that's still tucked away behind his shorts, my sweats lower another inch. Exposing the narrow landing strip of hair. Narrowly exposing even more. Another inch, and he'll see it all.

"You're the devil," I hear myself whimper, all too aware of where we are but unable to stop. "I went to school here."

Gently, he bites down on my earlobe. "And now you work here."

"You're ruining me."

His cock twitches against my core, like he enjoys our banter just as much as I do. "Nah," he grinds out, his mouth hovering deliciously over mine, "the way I look at it, you're the boss. And I'm just following your lead."

His statement is so absurd, so utterly out-of-left-field, that I laugh even as I moan because if he keeps doing *that* I'm gonna come. Right here, right now. And it will be gloriously—

"I'm blue da ba dee da ba die . . ."

Dominic's hand flexes against my butt. "What the hell is that?"

No.

No, no, *no.*

I clutch his face between my hands, planting my mouth on his for another heated, halfway-to-orgasm kiss.

Except that I move too fast.

Too abruptly.

There's a moment of pure panic when I know we're about to fall ass-to-the-ground, but I'm too wound up to think of anything but Dominic, lips, huge erection, sex, now. In that order. Then the dratted panic ensues as gravity proves almighty.

My arms pinwheel and the desk tips backward, and we land in a tangle of legs and elbows and sunglasses gone rogue.

"*Ooomf.*"

Dominic's arms wrap around me, catching the brunt of my fall like a true gentleman in disguise. We're poised at an awkward angle, his calves trussed up on the side of the metal desk like he's on the verge of being strung up on a rotating spit above a fire. I breathe in his London High polo, my legs sprawled out behind me. For the record, his chest is marvelous. Hard, no cushiony spring in sight. The stony muscle under my cheek is the stuff of legend.

"*I'm blue da ba dee da ba die!*"

The massive chest beneath me deflates as he grunts, "Your ass is singing *Blue* by Eiffel 65."

I fumble, arm behind my back, to grab my cell phone from my shorts pocket. Already knowing who it is, I say to Dominic, "I'm surprised you know the song."

"Who *doesn't* remember this song? It might as well have been the *Baby Shark* of the 90s."

Quirking a smile at his bad joke, I stare at the lit-up screen for only a second before pressing the little green telephone and letting my head droop like a wilted flower back onto Dominic's chest. *Hello there, Bad Decisions, so nice to be reacquainted.* "We're on our way."

"Do I even want to fucking know where the two of you went off to?" Adam shouts, loud enough to be heard halfway to Pittsburgh. "Is DaSilva dead? Is that what happened?"

Nothing about Dominic is remotely dead. No, sirree. His breathing is still ragged and his head is thrown back like he's desperate to finish what we started and one peek down at his shorts is all I need to know that he is *very* much alive. And hard. So very, very hard.

"Is this not the time to fill you in that I disposed of his body?" Regretfully, I hoist myself up onto my knees. "He's in the back garden that Principal Moyer loved so much two decades ago."

"*Levi.*"

"We're going," I assure my boss, watching avidly as Dominic rearranges his more-than-obvious erection before standing the desk back up on its four spindly legs. I'm surprised it lasted as long as it did. They sure do make them stronger now than they did back in my day. "I promise."

"*Now*, before I demote you and promote DaSilva just to see you both suffer."

The line goes dead.

I swallow, then tuck my phone back into my pocket. Swallow again because while the nerves took a hike during our heavy-duty make-out session, they're already back in full force.

*Hol*y crap.

We just did that.

I just did that.

"How would you get rid of my body?" Dominic asks after a small pause, his voice gruff.

My gaze snaps up to meet his. Relief grips my shoulders

when I see the humor flaring to life beneath his usual stoic expression. "Lye." I slip his hat off my head and, indicating for him to help a girl out a little and bend down some, I settle it on top of his. "Give it a few months and no one will ever know you were there."

He whistles low. "Savage."

I fake a hair-toss, keenly aware of my wobbling top knot. "I don't leave room for error."

"What would you make of the last fifteen minutes?" Dark eyes home in on my face, laser-focused as though he's trying to get a script for my brain. "Bad call in judgment?"

I lick my lips. Scoop up his sunglasses from the tile floor and hold them out for him to take. "In every which way," I answer with full honesty.

My personal bubble goes *pop!* as he steps in close. Lowers his head to kiss the line of my jaw. "You gonna let me finish what we started?"

Like my body has a mind of its own, I feel my head tip to the side, giving him more room to play. "Give me a good reason to say yes and I'll consider it."

Masculine fingers loop around the hem of my shirt, knotting the fabric and drawing me in sharply against his chest. "I can think of at least three off the cuff."

"So sure of yourself, are you?"

"Always." A small pause as we leave the scene of the crime. "You gonna tell me why your ringtone is *Blue*?"

I flash him a small grin. "Oh, that's just for Adam. Isn't he a cranky old bastard? Not that he's *old*, obviously, but you know what I mean. He's just a little—dare I say it—*blue* at heart."

"Surprisin' me once again, Coach. I like it." Dark, masculine laughter echoes off the lockered walls. "Have you picked out a ringtone for me?"

"Wouldn't you like to know."

"Give me a clue."

"Call me and find out for yourself."

Moments later, *Bad Company* from Five Finger Death Punch erupts from my butt pocket, and I laugh. I laugh so hard that I barely hear Dominic grumble "Low blow" from behind me, and I laugh so hard that my sides hurt and my cheeks pinch and I feel *good*.

Crazy what an insanely good kiss from a hot guy can do for your mood.

And Dominic's kiss? It was . . . magic. Dark and erotic and raw but magic all the same.

I've never had one like it—and though I'm loathe to admit it, something tells me I'll never have one like it again.

18

CELEBRITY TEA PRESENTS:

PUT A RING ON IT CONTESTANT DOMINIC DASILVA POPS UP
IN MAINE! WHY WE BELIEVE HE'S NURSING A BROKEN
HEART

ell, well, well, Dear Reader, how much can really change in a week's time, you ask? In the world of reality TV, the answer is everything. We last left off with ex-NFL player Dominic DaSilva getting fired from his job. (Ensue pitiful crying soundtrack). Based on a new article I discovered online last night . . . it seems Savannah Rose's heartbroken contestant is now living in Maine.

Yes, I said it. Maine.

The land of Red Lobster, quaint seaside towns, and rabid Red Sox fans.

Deegan Homer, a reporter for the New England Sports Advocate, had the luxury of interviewing DaSilva. In his words, the infamous former NFL tight end was, "Uncomfortable with the questions I asked, which were nothing out of the ordinary." At another point in the article, Homer describes DaSilva as, "tight-lipped and woefully distracted. He continued to allow Levi, the head coach of the London High Wildcats, to smooth over his rough answers and awkward transitions."

Now, Dear Reader, you might be thinking . . . Maybe DaSilva just had a bad day. We all have them—me less often than most, I must admit. (#HumbleBrag)

But I'm keen to argue against the whole "bad day" theory.

A source close to Savannah Rose recently revealed that, after word spread of DaSilva being dumped on proposal day, he then tracked down Savannah to win her back. Word is, of course, that she rejected his offer.

If I were in his position—thank God, I'm not—Maine would also look incredibly enticing.

Which brings us to my point exactly: despite some bad and reckless behavior on the show, DaSilva has always maintained a charming, devil-may-care air. He smiles and flirts and, Dear Reader, every time he lifts his shirt I once again find my reason for breathing.

Tight-lipped. Woefully distracted. Uncomfortable with the spotlight.

This isn't the Dominic DaSilva we've grown to love and adore over the last six weeks that Put A Ring On It *has aired on TV.*

So, I say to you, why else would DaSilva flee the state, if not to give his heart time to heal from Savannah's stinging rejection?

As always, Dear Reader, I'll be back next week with all the tea. Have an opinion about this whole dilemma? Drop it in the comments. Do you live in Maine and want to stalk the little town of London for the good of the cause? Drop me a line via email. Celebrity stalking is a joint effort, my friends, and when the celebrity involved is caught in a scandal . . . Well, you know what they say.

I'll sleep when I'm dead.

"*I*t's fucking bullshit."

"You know what's bullshit?" my good friend Nick Stamos retorts from my iPad, which I've got propped up on a tier of cardboard boxes for our video chat session. "That carpet. Jesus, my soul just withered and died on sight."

The glare I send his way—or the iPad's way, rather—goes unnoticed as he looks at something off camera. "Not the carpet." Although the carpet is hideous in every way possible, too. "That *Celebrity Tea Presents* asshole. He's bullshit."

Nick winces. "Mina and I saw the article this morning. It was . . ."

Usually, the mention of Nick's fiancée, Mina, would have me asking where she is and why she hasn't popped in to say hi yet. But I'm so tightly wound up that pleasantries have sailed right out the window. "Shit," I growl, my shoulders flexing as I rip out another section of awful shag carpeting, "that's what it is. A pathetic excuse for journalism."

"I was going to say it was a little harsh."

"That too."

"You gotta let it go, man. You know how many times they wrote about me and Mina before I popped the question and asked her to marry me? Look at it this way—it's your turn to shoulder the limelight now."

With a satisfying *shripppppp* the carpet comes free. "I'm done with the limelight. Why the hell do you think I moved to bumfuck-middle-of-nowhere Maine?"

"Because you like the ocean."

Truth.

"And because you enjoyed Maine when we went up to Bethel for that weekend away, even though you had to stand guard and watch your door all night," Nick adds with a chuckle.

Also the truth.

Mina's not-quite friend Sophia is a female menace with tentacles for limbs, sucking in all single men who make the mistake of entering her orbit. Nice girl, I guess, but not my type.

Even so, I enjoyed that weekend trip.

For the first time in years, I'd breathed a sigh of relief. There wasn't any paparazzi waiting to pop out of a bush or a laundromat or a dumpster and charge at me with their cameras. They didn't tail me from the grocery store to where I parked my car in the lot. They sure as hell didn't sneak around and grab pictures of me naked.

Maine is paradise.

The mountains. The winding rivers. The solitude.

And thanks to one reporter who's looking to do a little social climbing by ensuring his article goes viral, that paradise is now laid to waste.

It's only a matter of time before the paps find their way to quaint London.

My lungs clamp tight as I adjust my grasp on the carpet from another angle and give it a hardy pull. "How long do you think the school is going to allow me around underage kids when the media flocks here like rabid vultures?" It's a rhetorical question. Even if it wasn't, I don't give Nick long enough to come up with a satisfying answer. "Not long, Stamos. I'm gonna get my ass handed to me the first time a pap crosses school lines and pisses off a parent."

"Would it matter? You haven't said anything about London that gives me the impression that you're in it for the long haul." When I cut a glance his way, Nick holds up his hands. In one, he's gripping a hammer. Probably doing work on one of his many restoration projects, I'm sure. "I'm not going to pretend to know what it's like to be bad boy Dominic DaSilva—"

I roll my eyes at his overt sarcasm.

"But you've got the money, man. If the town isn't working out for you anymore, you can just . . . leave."

Two weeks ago I may have agreed with him.

Before Levi face-planted on my dick in front of an entire pub.

Before I had her ass grinding down on me in a deserted classroom like we were preteens instead of rapidly-hurtling-toward-middle-aged adults.

Before she looked me in the eye and dared me to acknowledge that unless I'm flipping the world a middle finger, I'm not satisfied with my life.

"Leaving isn't gonna work for me," I mutter, dropping to my haunches to grab my water bottle from the floor. The heat hasn't cooled off in the last few days, and I'm already envisioning stripping down to a pair of swim trunks later and making use of the private access down to the water.

A private access that links with Levi's halfway down to the beach.

Bottle perched on my knee, I ask, "You ever regret going on the show?"

For a beat, Nick's silent. Then, "Are you asking me if I regret losing my anonymity?" A small, minute pause that seems to stretch for far too long. "Or are you askin' if I regret Savannah Rose?"

We both know Nick wasn't feeling Savannah. Oh, he tried his best to make it work—but when he confided in me that they mutually decided to skip the overnight date, there was no denying that the passion wasn't there for them.

Hadn't been that way for me and Savannah.

I'd liked kissing her. More specifically, I'd liked the way she made me feel: like I, as a person, was more interesting than the money in my bank account and the football accolades attached to my name. With her, I felt . . . special. Here was this beauty out of New Orleans—a woman whose family is wealthy and influential—looking at me—a poor kid out of Cali who spent five years in and out of juvie by the time I was sixteen—like I had something worthy to offer her.

Except I wasn't worthy at all.

Because the producers had paid me to come on the show as a contestant and I never once turned down the six-figure check. Because my own boss had suggested I go on *Put A Ring On It* to help increase views for Sports 24/7 and I never once told him to fuck off, that saying yes meant I could fuck up someone else's life.

Bad Boy Dom.

The moniker is laughable.

The media—the *world*—has no clue how bad I am. Down to my core. Down even further to the rot in my veins that bleeds not red but black sludge, infecting everyone and everything.

So, yeah, I went on that overnight date with Savannah. I kissed her and reveled in the revelatory sensation of being with a woman who cared about *me*, and I forgot all about the dollar signs and the ratings and the freebie commercial runs the *Put A Ring On It* producers guaranteed Sports 24/7 every Wednesday night when new episodes would air.

Savannah stopped me just as I went to remove her pants.

Her hand on my shoulder, her fingers curled in a fist like she wasn't even sure she wanted to be touching me. And then it all went to shit—she'd overheard the producers talking about *me* and how surprised they were that I lasted as long as I did, and how great a liar I must be to keep all my dirty secrets under wraps.

She wanted me to leave, and I did, knowing full well that I had damned myself the moment I signed the NDA form and agreed to the terms of my casting.

Two days later, Savannah Rose dumped me when I asked her to take a chance—a real chance—on me. A month after that, I found myself standing on her front stoop with an apology already formed on my tongue.

I didn't ask her to change her mind about our relationship. Hell, I didn't even spend more than ten minutes inside her home before I was back in my rental car and driving to the closest ramshackle bar I could find.

Good guys with golden hearts like Nick deserve women like Savannah Rose.

Not guys like me.

"Savannah," I finally murmur, lifting my gaze so I can see Nick's face on the screen. "You regret her?"

Even though we're hundreds of miles apart, him in Boston, me here in London, I feel the weight of my best friend's stare. Like always, he looks like he's trying to work out a puzzle. Trying to figure me out.

"I can't regret her," he tells me, hammer resting against one shoulder. "If it weren't for her then I'd have no idea that Mina is everything I ever wanted or that she's the woman I want to marry and wake up to forever."

I nearly chuck my water bottle at the iPad. "Jesus fuck," I mutter, rolling my eyes as envy cuts through my system, "you know how disgusting the two of you are? Women get pregnant just by looking at you together."

Nick whistles. "That's a skill I'd like to add to my resume. Mina's gonna be pleased."

"As opposed to what? Being annoyed by your very presence? Tell her I can commiserate fully with that."

"She loves me."

"So you both keep telling me."

"Asshole." He throws his head back with a laugh. "I swear, between the two of you I'm surprised I'm not bleeding from all the verbal jabs."

"What can I say?" My shoulders hike up in a casual shrug. "We have a common target—you."

"In other words, you both love to fuck with me."

"At the risk of you turning back into Sour Puss McGhee, someone's got to. We keep you on your toes, her more so than me."

"Oh, oh right. Like you're one to talk, Mr. Woefully Distracted."

I grimace.

Unfortunately for Mr. Deegan Homer, I spent our entire interview distracted by one perky head football coach. The curve of her ass as she leaned forward in the chair, tucking one ankle behind the other, all demure-like. The straight line of her back as she talked about the team with pride and excitement. The bow of her upper lip that stretched a little unevenly when she smiled.

"DaSilva."

I snap to attention. "Yeah."

"What do you regret?" Nick asks, the words spoken low and carefully like he's aware of how easily they'll spook me.

I think of Levi dry-humping me like her life depended on it.

And then I think of the boys on my team—boys like Topher, who mentioned how much he wouldn't mind another round of mini-golf with hope in his blue eyes—who're downright thrilled to have me here to coach them. Not the charming Dominic. Or the unfeeling Dominic. Or the bad-to-the-bone Dominic.

But rather the Dominic who cares, the one who started Junior Buccaneers and spends more time than not working with charities across the country that are directly involved with kids in foster care.

That's the version of me that they see and idolize.

Tossing the capped bottle to the side, I turn to look back at my master bedroom. It's in complete upheaval—not that it bothers me. I've slept on the couch ever since I moved in. Same way I've slept on the couch at every place I've ever lived in for as long as I can remember.

"I regret believing that my life was so predictable that I had to do something insane, like go on a dating show, to prove to myself that I was still alive."

Nick's delayed response proves he doesn't get it.

Levi would, though.

Levi would understand all that I hadn't said in a heartbeat.

*M*oonlight slips through the drawn curtains when I feel a vibration coming from within the bedsheets.

With my face buried in my pillow, I flatten a hand and thump around for my phone. My alarm clock is only inches away on my nightstand, but without my glasses, the digital numbers are nothing but a blur of neon red.

I flip onto my back, eyes screwed tightly shut.

Feel around for another second and yes, right . . . *there.*

Not even bothering to look at the incoming caller, I answer and then tap the general vicinity on the screen where the speakerphone option is. Dropping the phone on my chest, I sleepily croak out, "'ellow?"

"Hey."

That voice.

My eyes spring open. "Dominic?"

"Yeah, it's . . . me."

I can almost imagine him repositioning his baseball hat on his head. Except that it's—

"What time is it?" I flop onto my side, taking my phone

with me as I snatch up the alarm clock and shove it front and center in my face. "Three. It's three in the morning and you're calling"—alarm bells go off in my head as panic settles in—"are you okay? Did something happen?" My legs scissor the sheets as I drop the clock back in its spot and shoot up in the bed. "Tell me what you need."

"I wanted to know if you might go for a swim with me."

I stop short of rolling out of my king-sized bed as his words sink in to my sleep-addled brain. He didn't say . . . No, he wouldn't *actually* be calling me this late at night—early in the morning?—to go for a . . .

"A swim," I say, drawing out each individual letter. "You just asked me to go swimming."

"I did, yeah."

I hear the rustle of sheets, and a visual of Dominic leisurely resting in bed hops into my brain. Black sheets—his favorite color—would be tangled around his hips, revealing the dark happy trail that could entice even the most innocent into doing naughty, sinful activities. His inky hair would be mussed, like he's combed his fingers through it all night. His chest . . . oh, he'd be shirtless, hard pectoral muscles all on display.

A feast for the gods.

Or, more specifically, a feast for me—one mere mortal woman who wouldn't mind partaking in a Dominic DaSilva buffet.

"Levi? You there?"

Slipping from the bed, I quietly pad over to my large window, which overlooks Frenchman Bay. I part the heavy curtains, allowing more moonlight to filter in. It turns the black shadows dancing in my room into warmer hues—soft blues, deep purples. Without my glasses on, I can't see much of anything besides blocks of color.

Holding the phone close to my mouth, I drop my voice to a whisper, then think better of it and untap the speakerphone button. Tuck the phone between my shoulder and my ear. "It's too late."

"You mean we've got practice in the morning."

8 a.m. sharp.

I need two cups of coffee, no cream, no sugar, on seven hours of sleep, to function like a normal human being. Never mind how much it would take to get me going after a nighttime jaunt in the chilly waters.

Not wanting to come right out and say no, I scramble for another reasonable excuse. "It's pitch-black out."

"That's part of the fun, Coach."

"Being eaten by a shark that I can't see coming is not my idea of a good time."

"How do you know? You ever tried it?"

I clap a hand over my mouth to stop the stem of laughter before I wake up Topher, whose bedroom is just down the hall. From behind my fingers, I burst out, "You're insane."

"I'm tryin' to have us meet in the middle."

"Is that so?"

"Yeah." His voice drops to a low, seductive rumble that I feel like a caress all the way down to my toes. "I told you that to feel alive I like to hit rock bottom first—"

"You do realize that rock bottom has a very different connotation when you're talking about open waters, right? I mean, there's rock bottom and then there's *ocean* bottom."

"—and you told *me* that you feel best when you're safe."

At the utter conviction in his tone, I lift my free hand and press it to my chest. Over my heart, which is beating as fast it did when he kissed me, up against a row of high school lockers, and stole my breath away.

Letting my lids fall shut, I simultaneously allow my forehead to kiss the cool glass window. "It's three in the morning. My son is sleeping down the hall. I'm all he's got, and while I appreciate you sort of promising to keep me safe from hangry sharks, I can't just sneak out of my house in the dead of night like I'm fifteen all over again."

The line descends into silence, long enough for me to question my decision to tell him no.

"Dom, I'm sorry. I—"

"I want your trust."

The unexpectedness of his words has me accidentally thwacking my forehead on the glass. *Ow*. I finger the knot, hoping it won't bruise tomorrow. It'll be just my luck if it does. "You have it, Dominic."

"Thirty minutes," he counters swiftly. "It's all I'm asking for. Five to get down to the water, five to get back up. Twenty out in the bay. I'll wear a watch—waterproof, obviously. I promise you, no dillydallying."

The fact that he—a six-foot-six football player who must weigh close to three-hundred pounds—used the word "dillydallying" makes me crack a grin. "Why are you pushing so hard for this?" I ask softly.

"Because there have been nights my entire life when I've felt so goddamn adrift, it threatens to pull me under." I hear his deep, indrawn breath, followed by a slow and steady exhale that brings goose bumps of awareness to my skin. "But tonight I don't want to feel alone and I don't want to feel like I'm in an ocean swimming all by myself without an anchor to keep me moored."

It hurts to breathe.

I know my lungs are in my chest and I know, logically, that they're healthy and pumping oxygen as they should be.

And yet, blood roars in my head and my heart pounds to a rhythm I don't quite know and for the first time in fifteen years, I feel my inner recklessness rearing its head and demanding its due.

I step back from the window and move toward my bedroom door. Cracking it open, I slip through on quiet feet, all the while Dominic waits on the other end of the line—in a house only twenty feet away from mine. I feel my way down the hall with a hand trailing the wall. Down past the bathroom Topher exclusively uses. Down past the guestroom Topher passed up when we first moved in because he claimed it was too big for just him.

We can keep that one open for when Mariah and my friends come to visit.

My boy—always looking out for others.

His door is shut, and I turn the knob with my heart in my throat.

For fifteen years, I've played it safe. I've stayed behind the metaphorical curtain and kept my own needs silent— sometimes out of fear, because I knew Rick was vindictive, and sometimes out of an effort to put my head down and keep hustling. Just because I was a young mother didn't mean I couldn't be the best one for Topher. When Rick started flaking out on us, I worked even harder to be everything my son needed.

Topher's snoring greets me, even though I still can't see a damn thing without my glasses. He's passed out cold, like always. Even as a newborn, he slept like a rock. He won't be up until his alarm has gone off twice and I'm ripping the sheets away from his curled-up body.

"Levi?" Dominic says softly in my ear as I back out of my son's room. "Forget I asked, okay? I'm not trying to make you do anything you don't want to do. I'm not that kinda guy. Maybe the three of us—me, you, and Topher—can go out

on the water this weekend. I'll grill some burgers or something. Make a day out of it or—"

I close Topher's bedroom door behind me and press my
back to the wood. I pray I'm not making a huge mistake
when I give in with a hushed, "Thirty minutes. Not a minute
longer."

Dominic's lingering pause tells me I've surprised him.
Then, "Thirty minutes, Coach. That's a promise."

21

DOMINIC

I wait for her by the hedge that separates our two courtyards.

Any moment now, I'm convinced my phone will ring and she'll tell me she's changed her mind. I wouldn't blame her. My request came out of left field for the both of us. One minute I was sprawled out on my couch, scrolling through the latest sports news—Tampa Bay news, in particular—while suffering a raging case of insomnia, and then I was searching my contacts and tapping on her name.

I held my breath as I heard the ringtone and prepared myself to hear the beep of her voicemail.

Crushed misplaced hope beneath the imaginary heel of my shoe when I allowed myself to stop and think about what I was really asking of her.

Dominic DaSilva, party of one.

Aspen Levi, team of two.

The fact that she said *yes* . . . Jesus fuck, it's hard to wrap my brain around it.

Probably why I'm standing here, preparing myself for

the inevitable when she comes to her senses and tells me to take a hike.

My ears prick up when I catch the sound of shoes crunching over gravel.

And my chest . . . my goddamn chest expands with the sort of relieved sigh I haven't experienced in years, since that long-ago day when I went to the Buccaneers as the third overall draft pick.

"You there, Coach?" The words emerge raspy and hope-ful. I should clear my throat, maybe say something else to reestablish the back-and-forth banter that's been the foun-dation of our relationship from the start, but so late at night . . . when all of London is asleep save for us . . . it seems disingenuous to pretend I don't need this moment.

Knowing that, even though I'm alone in the world—no family, few friends—Levi chose to meet me tonight is humbling.

Instead of answering, she simply walks toward me. Immediately, I sweep my gaze over her, from head to foot. Thankful for the moon being directly overhead, I take in her loose blond curls that dance around her shoulders and the black, square-framed glasses perched on her nose. Glasses that I didn't even know she needs.

She's bundled up in a wrap with a sash cinched at the waist. Bare, toned legs from the thigh down. A pair of flip-flops on her feet.

Beneath one arm, she holds two perfectly folded towels.

"Sorry," she says with a nervous laugh, "I'm such a mom." She pats the outer towel with her free hand. "Thought we might want to dry off when we're done."

God, she's beautiful.

With those nerdy glasses and the nervous way she tugs at the hem of her wrap and the moonlight turning her blond hair into strands of platinum and silver, she's absolutely stunning.

"I'm not gonna kiss you tonight," I blurt out, a far cry from the suave, charming version of myself that America has watched on TV every Wednesday night for weeks now.

With a finger to her glasses, she pushes the frame up the bridge of her nose. "Why not?"

I drop my gaze to my hands, which I stuff in the pockets of my swim trunks. *Just say the fucking words, man. Don't be a pussy.* I clear my throat. "Because I've always jumped into the sack with women I find attractive. I don't remember their names. I can't tell you a damn thing about them. I don't want tonight . . . I don't want us going out in the water to be about getting off."

If Levi's amused by my verbal fumbling, she doesn't show it.

She touches her fingers to my wrist, a light, tantalizing brush of skin on skin that hardens my dick even as it quickens my pulse. "I know exactly what you mean."

Something told me she would.

The glow from the moon highlights the path as we wind our way down to the beach, with me up front to lead the way. Her hand finds my naked back, the warmth of her skin chasing away the chill of the night. Stone pebbles kick up under my tennis shoes, and I lift a thin branch about halfway down, so she can duck under without smacking her head. In silence, we fall back into place.

Only this time I reach backward and grasp her hand in mine.

I hear her stifled gasp.

"This okay?" I husk out.

"I always figured you were the sort to take crazy liberties.

Glad to see you're not proving me wrong," she teases, squeezing my hand.

She doesn't let go.

A grin fights its way to my face.

The downward slope of the path evens out as pebble turns to sand. I wait for the moment when Levi realizes there's a kayak waiting, the same one I hauled to the beach earlier today in anticipation of an early morning workout before football practice tomorrow.

This isn't what I had in mind hours ago, when I balanced the kayak over my head and walked it down the path, but this is so much better.

"Is that a . . ." She trails off, setting the towels down on a cluster of rocks. Releasing my hand, she steps forward. "You have a kayak?"

I nod. "Bought it when I got the house." I kick off my shoes, aiming them for the rocks with our towels. "I figure you can go in the kayak, oar in hand to defend yourself from any sharks, and I'll go in the water."

"So I'll be safe."

She says it so matter-of-factly that my gaze leaps to her face. Though the clouds have slipped over the moon, casting her in shadow, I get the feeling she's serving me with a hard, searching glance. "Maybe another night you'll jump in the water with me."

"Maybe I will."

My cock stiffens in my swim trunks as I hear her fumbling around with her silk wrap, and I blame the clouds for stealing away the opportunity for me to get a real good look at Levi in nothing but her bathing suit.

I picture her in a one-piece. Something practical and simple.

Something *she* believes is fitting of someone who's a mom to wear.

Shock smacks me upside the head when she drifts closer and I catch a quick glimpse of skin. Thin straps are knotted at the back of her neck, and the bikini—*Jesus*, she's beautiful—she's wearing is nothing but two strips of cloth that cover the necessities.

I go from half-mast to full-blown erection in a matter of seconds.

She plucks at the waistband of her bottoms. "I had to dig deep in my closet for this," she says, her voice as soft and rhythmic as the waves lapping at the sand, "so it's a little on the small side."

Small is the perfect size.

Her figure is nothing but temptation. Heavy breasts and wide hips. Trim arms and legs that go on for fucking days— the high cut of her bikini bottoms only serves to make her legs look longer, leaner, and I'd give my right nut to feel them wrapped around my waist as I lower her to the sand and cover her body with mine.

"Dominic? You're . . . you're staring."

There's a note of hesitance in her voice that I instantly despise. To say nothing of the way she nervously fiddles with her bikini top strap, occasionally sneaking glances up at my face, like she's worried I disapprove.

The only thing I disapprove of is my promise that I won't be kissing her tonight.

I'm an idiot. A Grade-A idiot because how the hell am I supposed to keep my hands to myself when she looks like—

"Fucking perfection," I rasp, sweeping my gaze up to her face. "You're fucking perfection, Coach."

In every single way.

"You think so?"

Hell yes. Every part of me thinks so. My needy cock, my starved gaze, my hopeful heart. "Get in the kayak before I make a change of plans."

Like a temptress sent to drive me wild, her fingers graze my stomach. "And what plans might those be?"

I lower my voice, my own fingers seeking out the bikini bow at her hip. "Me putting you on all fours while I fuck you from behind."

She laughs softly. "For the record, I appreciate you offering to do me doggy-style. Less chance of sand getting into private places that way."

I tug on the string, loosening the bow in warning. One more pull and the knot will come free and I'll be entering paradise. It's tempting. My fingers glide under the knot, and there's no mistaking the way her hand flies to my wrist . . . and pulls me closer.

Oh, fuck.

In the shadowed night, my gaze collides with hers as my fingers dip south. I grip the knot between my index finger and thumb, and I'm sure she can feel the way my pulse is hammering at the base of my wrist. I promised her no kissing. I vowed to make this night about more than my need to strip her naked and sink into her sweet heat.

It takes every ounce of my self-control to not skim my palm down and cup her between her legs. Instead, I jerk her closer with my hand around her bikini strap top and, when I feel her hot breath on my chest, I do the goddamn gentlemanly thing: I re-tie the knot at her hip. Tight. That shit isn't coming undone anytime soon.

My hand slips down to squeeze the outside of her naked thigh. "Get in the kayak, Coach. We're going on an adventure and we're down to fifteen minutes."

Giggling, Levi sashays backward. "You're bossy,

Dominic," she tells me, one hand to the side of her black frames as she peers over at me. "I like it—a lot. Okay. Enough lollygagging. Let's do this."

I tuck my cell phone into one of my tennis shoes, then follow behind her. "Lollygagging?"

"Don't judge me. You used dillydallying the other day," she says, defending herself as she drops one foot, then the other, into the kayak. "Are you going to push me in?"

"That was the plan."

My hands find the curved edge of the kayak as I bend at the waist. And, because I'm not all that much of a true gentleman, I take advantage of the fact that Levi is facing away from me to readjust my hard-on. *Enjoy it now,* I want to tell it, *you're about to die a quick death.* At this time of night, the water is gonna be lukewarm at best. I'll be lucky if my nuts don't shrivel up on me.

"You know," Levi muses, "you're really good at this assistant thing."

"You thinkin' about giving me a raise?"

"Wish I could." She throws a glance over her shoulder at me. "But you'll have to settle for what I can give you."

It's a euphemism if I've ever heard one.

More like a promise.

A promise I wouldn't mind her keeping. I'm dying to know how she'll feel in my arms without clothes in the way. How her berry lips will taste after I've gone down on her and brought her in for a kiss. If she's as passionate in bed as she is on the field.

If our stint in the classroom is any indication, I have a feeling that passion isn't a problem for her. At least, it's not a problem for her when she's with me. I don't think I'll ever rid myself of the memory of her sweet ass rolling and moving while she straddled me on that desk.

Shoving aside all thoughts of the two of us together, I wait for her to get comfortable. When she's ready and waiting with her hands wrapped around the oars, I slowly push, allowing the kayak to glide into the water. My toes are the first to make contact and I experience a split second of regret. It's colder than I expected.

Suck it up, big guy.

The dark water sucks the kayak forward with the retreat of the current. Waves crash against my knees. The clouds part and the moonlight illuminates the surface of the water, revealing the swell of Levi's hips and the nip at her waist. Blonde curls tangle their way down her back, disheveled from sleep and the gentle wind coming in from the east.

I wish I could take a picture of her in this exact moment.

Her toned arms work to power the oars, relieving me to walk along behind her as the water rises to my waist and then up to my rib cage.

A chill settles in my chest as I kick off the sand, the burst of sudden momentum propelling the kayak deeper into the bay.

Levi's chest folds forward, then straightens again. "We should stop here," she says, sounding nervous. Her head swivels to the right and then the left as though she's trying to gather her bearings.

"A little farther." Where the ocean floor isn't directly within reach and I'm forced to sink or swim. "Don't let go of the oars."

Because this swim is meant to satisfy us both—me diving off into the unknown while she finds harbor in the familiar.

Another few yards and then I tell her to stop rowing. I kick my feet behind me, swimming until I'm alongside the kayak's profile instead of its rear. With one hand holding onto the edge so we don't separate, I tread water. Then I dunk my head backward, welcoming the water as it splashes over my face and wets my hair.

"What's your earliest memory of football?" Levi asks when I come back up for air.

Slicking my hair back and out of my face, I think on that, searching through the memories. Feel the blow to my gut when it surfaces because I don't . . . I don't want to share that piece of myself with Levi. I'm not proud of the way I lived my early years. I had a chip on my shoulder the size of the White Mountains and I made sure everyone around me knew it.

I ran with the wrong crowd.

Stole from good people who didn't deserve my bad behavior.

My earliest experience with football was just after I got out of my first round in juvie. I was an eleven-year-old punk with a tracking monitor locked around my ankle. I felt its weight with every step. Knew what would happen if I stepped outside of the marked perimeter of foster home number three.

Neighborhood kids played football in the street, just out of reach, while I watched from the kitchen window. They laughed and they shot the shit, and I don't really know how long I stood there, like a ghost seeking a connection with the living, except that eventually the elderly Mrs. Ramirez used her broom to swat at my feet, warning me that if I made one wrong move I'd find myself homeless.

Again.

"I've had football at the forefront of my life since I was a kid," Levi says, saving me from my own silence, the way she always tends to do. I appreciate her intuitiveness more than she'll ever know. "I used to think Dad was disappointed in the fact that I wasn't the baby boy the doctors promised him and my mom."

Feeling grateful for the reprieve she's given me, I swim a little to the left so I can better see her face. "Is your mom still alive? You never mention her."

Levi smiles wide. "Alive and kicking. She's always busy. The life of a social butterfly, I guess. She belongs to about a gazillion different clubs around here and if it weren't for Topher, I'm pretty sure I'd never see her."

"She sounds like a character."

"She's Mom." Her shoulders lift in a nonchalant shrug. "I can't complain. At least she loves me more than she loves Willow."

At the mention of her younger sister, I tip my head to the side in curiosity. "Your mom actually tells you that?"

"Tells me what?"

"That she loves you more than she loves your sister?"

Feminine laughter mingles with the rippling waves sweeping against the hull of the kayak. "Oh my God, no. I'm totally kidding. Even if she does have a favorite—and I think Willow and I both annoy her equally—she doesn't pick sides. She never has."

I'm suddenly beyond thankful that we're taking this swim in the middle of the night instead of the middle of the day. This way she can't see that my cheeks are burning red with embarrassment. Family interrelationships are pretty much out of my realm of expertise.

"Right." I splash the water with a flat palm. "Sorry. Stupid question."

The kayak tilts toward me as she leans her weight in my direction. "You know when you have a million things you want to say," she says gently, "but none of them sound right, even in your head?"

All the goddamn time.

"Talking isn't my strong suit." I reach up to grasp one of the oars. The kayak shimmies, twisting toward the left in a semicircle. "As you've probably figured out by now."

"You faked it well all those years on Sports 24/7."

My brows shoot up in surprise. "Don't tell me you watched every episode."

Levi pretends to fight for possession of the oar I'm holding, sending the kayak rocking back and forth. Laughter seeps out of me, chasing away the cold bite of the water when she drops her head back with a heavy sigh.

"One episode," she admits, as if it pains her. "Only one."

"Yeah?" I inch my hand up the oar, until my fingers graze hers and she's gasping at my icy touch. It might be early June, but the bay is still cold as shit. Ignoring the wrinkled sensation of my fingertips against the silk of her skin, I push for more information. "Which episode?"

"You're going to tip me over." Her thumb hooks around mine, a subtle warning for me to cut it out. "And it was about a year ago, maybe a little before that. You hosted a top-ten countdown of college players who showed potential to make it to the NFL but didn't for whatever reason."

I vaguely remember the one she's talking about. During my four-year stint with Sports 24/7, I rarely had the opportunity to throw my own ideas into the mix. Screenwriters held the upper hand and, as I learned early on, I was nothing but a well-paid face for the show. The episode Levi's referring to is a segment someone in the production room thought would be a major hit with our audience.

It wasn't.

"I waited for you to say my name."

At her ragged confession, my legs momentarily stop moving and my weight dips down, the salty water rushing up my nose. I power kick and spring back up like a released buoy. But the near drowning doesn't stop me from asking— no, demanding: "What did you say?"

"I sat there on my couch, you know. Topher was at practice and Rick, for once, was actually picking him up." Her shoulders shake and I'm not sure if she's feeling chilly or if the memories are too much to handle. "Anyway," she says, bending her knees to her chest and wrapping one free arm around her legs, "I knew it was unlikely I'd be mentioned. My insecurities rose up and I remember . . . I remember thinking to myself, *God, Aspen, the only reason you were note-worthy to begin with was because you're a woman playing a man's sport.*"

A woman playing a man's sport.

My gut twists unpleasantly and suddenly staying afloat feels that much more impossible. "Levi, I didn't know." How the *hell* didn't I know? Watching her on the field with the Wildcats, it's clear to anyone that she knows the sport well. Too well, some might say, for someone who only coaches the game. "I don't—"

"You didn't know for the same reason your show didn't mention me, Dominic. It's the same reason that Deegan Homer guy came and interviewed us and he spent forty minutes questioning *you* about your career. I was an accessory. On your show, I wasn't even that. I'm not going to say you all passed me over because I'm a woman, but I won't lie and say the thought didn't enter my head a time or two while I counted down the top ten right along with you."

Shame and fury squeeze my lungs. "No," I growl, using my weight to dip the kayak and force her to look at me. Not out at the bay or down at her knees—at *me*. "Don't ever use that word again." When she only stares back at me, clearly confused, I spit, "Accessory. Toy." She'd used the latter at the

Golden Fleece when she warned me against messing with her emotions. "You're not either of those things, Levi." Squeezing my eyes shut, I loosen my tight grip on the kayak. "I feel like a self-absorbed prick for not realizing you played ball in college."

"Dominic, you are somewhat of a—"

"An asshole," I finish for her, recognizing the teasing lilt to her voice and taking no offense. I deserve that jab and any others she throws at me because I shouldn't have assumed her knowledge of football was anything but personal experience showing itself on the field. Once again, she's surprised me. That in and of itself shouldn't be surprising. There hasn't been a single day since I met Levi that she hasn't proved me wrong in some way or another.

Call it my own intuition but I'm getting the feeling that the reason she was so upset about being left out of the top-ten countdown isn't only a matter of being pushed out of the sport because of her gender. With rust coating my every word, I order, "Tell me what happened."

She hangs her head, shame inscribed in her every feature. "I was stupid back then, Dominic. Naïve. Entranced by the idea that this mega-powerful general manager of a well-respected football team wanted *me.*"

I want her out of the kayak and in the water with me.

I want to be able to read the emotion in her gaze when she bares her soul.

I want her to know that even when you feel like you're drowning, all it takes is one second of reminding yourself of mind over matter—that one's head will always be smarter than the fickleness of one's heart—to know that you won't plummet to your death.

Aware that I sound way too gruff but unable to help it, I give it to her straight: "Levi—*Aspen*—he took advantage of you. That's what guys like Clarke do. You weren't naïve and you weren't stupid." Rick Clarke was a slick, older guy who'd preyed on Levi's innocence. It doesn't take a rocket scientist to put two and two together. I bet he romanced her real nice with dinners and parties and gifts—nothing too extravagant because Levi isn't the sort to be impressed with flashy things. He hooked her before she even knew she was being baited, and if I weren't swimming right now I'd be up in that kayak pulling her into my arms. Wanting to make sure she heard me, I repeat, "You weren't stupid, Levi."

She shakes her head. "When our marriage went south, I used to wonder what it was about me that first attracted him. And it wasn't for years that I realized that he liked only the *idea* of me. When I played for Boston College, I broke stats left and right. Local newspapers loved to talk about me —the first female kicker the NCAA had ever seen. They debated how the NFL would react to a player like me, someone who was just as good as any of my male counter-parts." She grips the oars, rowing them once like she's so agitated that she can't sit still. "I was an anomaly and Rick liked that. He liked to take what didn't belong to him— whatever caught his fancy—and bend it to his will, offering promises he would never keep and the sort of support that would make any twenty-one-year-old girl's head spin."

As much as it pains me to admit it, I'm not surprised that I didn't realize Levi played for BC.

She's two years older than me, and at eighteen, I was solely focused on leaving my shitty reputation behind and focusing on the end goal: getting drafted by the NFL. If a school didn't play mine on the regular, or at all, I paid it no attention. If you weren't in my face day in and day out, living and breathing the same air as me, I didn't pause to give a damn or learn anything more.

Classes. Practice. Games.

There was no room in my life for anything else to exist, even on the periphery.

"I dropped out of college when he knocked me up." At her confession, my heart sinks even as I train my gaze on her face. "All those years of putting in the work—gone. All those practices where I had to deal with the guys on the team giving me the cold shoulder, and making me feel like I was an outsider, and telling me that I didn't belong—none of it ended up mattering at all."

"*Jesus.*" Gripping the oar, I tug it out of her grasp so she can't try to outswim me. "How the hell did your parents allow you to marry a prick like Clarke?"

"They didn't." Another loose-limbed shrug, but the casualness of it is belied by the bone-weary fatigue in her voice. "I eloped with Rick like a total fool. Dropped out of BC during my senior year because Rick lived in Pittsburgh. He'd only been visiting London when we met, and I was so gung-ho about raising our baby together as a family. My mom begged me to reconsider, but I thought I was in love. People do all sorts of reckless things for the ones they love, right?"

I hear her utter self-loathing, and for the first time in my life, I hate that it's in this moment that my soul recognizes it's not so alone. Me and Levi, we aren't so very different.

Sure, she grew up here in beautiful little London surrounded by her family and I grew up in shithole neighborhood after shithole neighborhood in and around San Francisco, but at the bottom of it all . . . we've both survived insurmountable obstacles and come out on the other side to tell the tale.

We're one and the same—and I *hate* that.

I fucking hate to think of Levi hurting, especially at the hands of a scumbag like Clarke.

"My earliest memory of football is watching the kids in my neighborhood play on the street," I say, a notch above a husky murmur, to make sure she hears every word. "I'd just ended up in juvie for the first time. I robbed"—fuck, this is hard. I close my eyes against any possible disgust that I'll see in her face, even as I keep the biggest secret to myself—"a corner store, but that was the first tick on a whole lot of boxes that had me on the wrong side of the law."

She breathes out my name.

I do my best to pretend there's no pity in those three syllables.

"I was bad," I go on, kicking my feet a little faster, relishing the burn in my thighs and my calves. "Kicked out of school. Wearing an ankle monitor like I was some sort of prepubescent savage. I was already big for my age—looked closer to thirteen or fourteen. But I was in bad shape, heading straight for a career in misdemeanor crimes at best, federal charges at worst, and then I looked out the kitchen window and saw them all throwing the ball."

Hope burns in her voice when she asks, "Did you go out there and play?"

I laugh, the sound harsh and angry. "With that ankle monitor beeping every time I got close to the front door? Not a chance in hell. But I dreamed about it later that night. Every night after that, too. Football was my gateway out of the shithole that was my life."

I stole money for pads and gear.

I rode a shitty-ass bike that I found in a junkyard to and from practice, its janky wheels bumping along like I was riding a roller coaster and not the black mountain bike that had seen better days.

When I hit middle school and found that the gym was open until six at night, I toiled away every extra hour that I could, lifting weights and building up my core strength.

But a kid is only as successful as his environment allows him to be, and I spent more time in juvie than I spent out of it by the time I turned sixteen. When Louisiana State actually looked at me as a potential recruit during my senior year and took a chance on a poor, troubled kid from Cali, I cried.

Big fat tears that my ratted blanket soaked up while I slept on the couch of my last and final foster home.

I look up at the sky. The stars are duller now, the encroaching sun already starting to peek out over the horizon. We've stayed out here long past our allotted twenty minutes, and I . . . I—

"I'm grateful for you."

My head whips toward Levi. "What?"

She runs her tongue along her bottom lip, sending heat straight down to my groin. "It's something I started doing when I first married Rick—finding little things to be grateful for when everything else felt like it was crumbling down."

I swallow, hard.

"And you're grateful for me?" My voice is thick, guttural. I don't bother to clear it when I try to add a little levity to the conversation with a teasing, "Because you like how I kiss?"

"Because you remind me that life's not worth living if we aren't willing to take a risk."

Before I can even predict what she'll do next, she surprises me—yet again—by tossing her glasses into the kayak and jumping into the bay beside me. The pressure of her fall sends water splashing into my face, and I quickly re-grasp the side of the kayak before it floats away.

Levi bobs up next to me, slicking her hands back over her drenched blond hair.

A nervous smile pulls at her lips as she reaches out a hand and pats the air between us. "I'm blind as a bat without my glasses," is all she says, missing my face by about ten inches.

I hook an arm around her waist, keeping her afloat. The feel of her almost naked body slipping against mine? *Jesus fuck.* It's all I can do to keep hold of my restraint when I growl, "Get back in the kayak before you drown."

"You asked me to trust you."

My heart speeds up at a fast clip. "Aspen . . ." Her name is a warning and a request all at once. What the fuck is she thinking, launching herself into the water like that? "You're scared of sharks."

"You told me being scared is half the fun."

I don't know whether to wring her neck for throwing my words back in my face or drop my lips to hers for a hot kiss. Screw my vow to keep tonight platonic. In the end, I only manage a strangled laugh that catches in my throat. "You said it was pitch-black out."

Still caged to my side by my one arm, she points at my face. "I can't see a thing. Could be bright as day and I'd still be lost. Now, are you going to see me safely home like a gentleman or what?"

I'm pretty sure no one has ever labeled me a gentleman before.

A criminal? In my early days, yeah.

A smooth-talking playboy? Often enough.

A real good football player? Every day for the last decade and counting.

Never a gentleman, though. Not until now.

Not until Levi.

"You want to ride on my back?" I ask, because I'll be damned if I let a single thing happen to her.

"And take a free pass to the beach?" She sprays water at me with a flick of her fingers in the rippling tide. "I'm not afraid of a little hard work, *Coach*. I'll race you."

I'm never one to turn down a challenge.

Or, it seems, a friendly race through the dark waters of Frenchman Bay, with me pushing the kayak and Levi having no qualms about pretending she can't see me when she kicks me in the side or tries to shove me out of the way.

She's as devious as her son.

And I like it. More than I should.

We make it back to shore in one piece.

Except that I can't help but fear that a sliver of my useless heart has been stolen by the woman who flops onto her back as soon as we make it to the beach. Forgetting all about the sand that's now coating her skin, she asks me, "Can we come back out tomorrow night?"

I throw my head back and laugh freely. "You're a piece of work, Coach."

Her fingers brush my ankle as I tower over her. "Correction—as a wise man once told me, I'm something of a work in progress."

22

ASPEN

"*O*h, my God, look at *that* guy."

When Willow's finger darts in front of my face, I bat her arm away and discreetly lean back on my bar stool to scope out whoever *that* guy is. My sister's not one for subtlety, that's for sure, which I guess isn't a bad thing since we've skipped the Golden Fleece and opted for a night out in Bar Harbor, which is only a twenty-minute drive up the road from London.

The good thing about Bar Harbor?

Everyone's a stranger.

Since walking into The Red Ruby thirty minutes ago, I haven't recognized a single face. There's certainly something to be said for not having to play the Coach card tonight or the Levi card or *any* card, really, besides tossing back a drink or two and enjoying the evening for what it is. Freedom.

I'm grateful for having a night out with my sister where I can just relax.

Willow smacks my arm, hissing, "He's leaving!"

I sip my vodka and cranberry. No Guinness for me tonight. I learned that mistake *very* well the last time.

"That's what patrons do, Wills. They grab a cocktail, stay awhile, then leave when they're ready to go home."

"I'm going to get his number."

I choke back a laugh. "You're obsessive."

"And *you're* sexually frustrated," Willow counters with full-on sass. Momentarily forgetting about her target, she sips her cocktail and stares at me unerringly. "I still can't believe you went swimming with Dominic and didn't even get the D. I'm telling you, it's a travesty. Even *I* feel disappointed—I can only imagine how neglected your vagina must feel."

"Keep your voice down," I frantically whisper, shooting a glance to my left. A relieved sigh works its way up and out of my system when it's clear that no one has taken a seat beside me. *All the points go to Bar Harbor, of which I know zero people.* "I regret telling you anything."

"Liar. You so don't."

"I really, really do. Also, who uses the phrase *get the D* in their thirties?"

Willow tosses her hair over one shoulder, her lips pursed smugly. "Those of us who know what it feels like to get some dirty sex, dear sister. If you just"—here she makes an obscene hand gesture that honestly terrifies me—"let your reservations go, you'd probably have a good time together."

Since that single kiss at London High a few days ago, Dominic has kept our physicality on lockdown.

And I get it—I really, really do.

We work together. Technically, I'm his boss. It's unlikely that he's here in town for the long haul, and there's also the matter of Topher . . .

I'll never do to my son what his father has accomplished in the year that we've been divorced. Rick totes around new women like they're fashion accessories. He calls Topher while he's on his way home from a date—in other words, when he's *with* his date. He only wants to video chat when he has "company" over because, as he puts it, "Don't you want to meet my new girlfriend, bud? Don't tell Mom about this, yeah?" It's manipulative and it's disgusting, and while I know Rick doesn't want *me*, I think he's pissed that Topher chose to move to Maine with me instead of staying in Pittsburgh.

Punishing us both is the name of the game for my ex-husband, but what he doesn't seem to realize is the lasting damage he's doing to his son. Instead of thinking his dad is so "cool" to be hanging out with women who are just this side of legal, Topher asks if Rick is depressed or sad that we left. It doesn't help when Rick regularly forgets to check in, leaving Topher to sit by the phone for hours and wait for his call. All attempts on my end to whip my ex-husband into shape have gone unanswered.

Rick does what he wants to do and nothing else, literally and figuratively.

So while my ex-husband flaunts his menagerie of women around, including in front of his son, I haven't slept with a single soul.

Not one.

And yet . . .

"Is it wrong that I can't imagine myself having a fling?" I utter the damning words slowly, softly, so there's no chance Willow will ask me to repeat them. "I've never . . ." I shove my hands through my straight hair, dropping my chin to stare into my pink cocktail like it holds all the answers to the dating universe. *If only.* "Rick was my first, Wills. The guy before him was . . . well, unmemorable. You know that. I know that."

Surprisingly, Willow doesn't launch into a dramatic rant fit for an off-Broadway show. Hell, she doesn't even smile when she settles a hand over my forearm, her hot-pink nails a direct contrast to my pale skin.

"You're scared of commitment," she assesses succinctly.

I bark out a startled laugh. "I was married to Rick for fourteen years, Willow. I don't think commitment is my problem."

She arches her brow, taunting me. "Then let's call it like it is: you're scared of sex."

My eyes go wide as I jerk a glance over my shoulder. "Keep your voice down! You can't just . . . you can't just—"

"You have sexphobia."

Seeking alcoholic guidance, I drain the rest of my cocktail. The ice cubes rattle in the glass when I plunk it down on the bar top. Feeling heat dust my shoulders and warm my cheeks, I finally mutter, "That's not a real psychological term."

It's a pathetic retort and we both know it.

Willow lifts a finger to call for another round of drinks. Then she turns back to me, her blue eyes—so much like mine—curious and zeroed in on my face. "Don't forget that you spilled your guts out to me after you left Rick."

"Another reason to avoid Guinness for the rest of my life. It never, ever does me any favors."

She nudges me in the shoulder. "You can't base sex off what you had with Rick the Prick. I mean, look at me. I'm divorced. I'm still hitting the scene. I'm *living*."

"You're having enough orgasms for all of us."

"Don't hate." Accepting the drinks from the bartender, who slides them across the bar, Willow takes a hearty sip of her Manhattan through a black straw. Because that's the type of person my sister is: an EXWIFEY driving, straw-sipping, orgasm-obsessed woman. Quirky as she is, I can't help but admire her style.

"You know what your problem is?" she asks, twirling her straw around in her glass.

"I have a feeling you're gonna tell me no matter what."

Pointing the Manhattan in my direction, she says, "You left your sense of adventure behind the minute you said *I do.* You're thirty-seven, Aspen, not ninety-seven. Let's face it, I know a lot more ninety-seven-year-olds who are living harder than you are."

"I went swimming after midnight with the hot football player next door. I'm living, Wills."

"B*efore* that. I love you, so I'm just going to come out and say it . . . You're a little boring, sis."

My jaw promptly falls open. "*Boring*?"

"Boring," she confirms after another sip. "Wicked boring."

"I coach football!"

"Which you've done for ten years now. Maybe it was exciting and thrilling ten years ago, but at this point . . ." She fakes a yawn that has my eye twitching, I'm so flabbergasted. In a very unlike-Willow move, she swipes the back of her hand over her mouth, chirping, "Sorry, I think I caught some drool there."

I don't even know what to say. Is it true? Am I *boring?*

Sure, Dominic swam me out to Frenchman Bay while I rode in the kayak, but I jumped *in,* didn't I? And, even before that, didn't I hump him in a classroom? That's a risky move, I think. We could have been caught and I could have been fired and—

"You're thinking so hard your ears are steaming."

I snag Willow's glass and, pushing her dainty straw aside, take a large gulp of a *very* strong Manhattan. Spluttering, I cough into my bicep and shove her drink back in her direction. "What do you have in that? An extra shot?"

"Two," she says smugly, "because I'm living, Asp. And you should be living it up too. You're single, you have a great job, you're back *home,* and I've missed you."

I eye her speculatively. "Have you really?"

"Well, I've missed you picking up the tab whenever we go out."

At the humor in her gaze, I'm tempted to tug on her hair the way we used to do as kids. Life was so much simpler then. When I took a risk, it affected only me. Now I have Topher to think about. My baby boy means the world to me. In all those years of dealing with Rick, my baby boy *saved* me. He kept me going, he kept me strong, he kept me from leaping headfirst into a downward spiral of depression.

Sucking my bottom lip behind my teeth, I release the stiff set to my shoulders. "I know I'm not some wild rule-breaker or anything, but I don't . . . I *won't* regret Topher, even if getting pregnant changed everything for me."

I murmur the words low, more for myself than for my sister, but she's got the ears of a bat and hears me anyway. Settling a hand over mine, she clicks our glasses together in a quasi-toast. "No one said anything about regretting Topher. You're single-handedly responsible for how well-mannered and caring he is. *You* did that, not asshole Rick. I mean, I guess that also means it's your fault for turning him into a brat." When I shoot her a look that clearly reads as *really?* she scurries to add, "Kidding! Kidding. He's a lovable brat, that's what I meant to say. *Obviously.* Where is he tonight anyway?"

"A friend's house."

Bobby's house, actually. Meredith was all too pleased to have Topher come over and spend the night. It warms my heart to know that my boy is making friends. Visiting London over the years has been something of a rare occurrence. More often than not, my family came to Pittsburgh or we met up in New York City or Boston for some sightseeing. Secretly, I always thought Rick's aversion to coming back to Maine was because he regretted knocking me up and felt pressured to get hitched and put a ring on my finger. Mistresses may be easily tucked away and hidden from the public eye, but a baby? Not so easy at all.

And while Topher has none of Rick's bad qualities, he did inherit his father's charming personality. There's not a soul my baby boy has met that he hasn't befriended. Any other kid may have struggled with moving to a small town like London, but Topher . . . Well, he's always found a way to fit in, even when the odds are clearly stacked against him. I like to think that's a trait he inherited directly from me. More likely than not, it's something that is uniquely *him*.

When Willow excuses herself to—and I quote—"stalk that guy down before he really leaves," I check my phone, expecting to see a text from Topher. Okay, *hoping* to see a text from Topher.

Nada.

Figures. He's been talking about this sleepover all week, ever since Bobby issued the invitation on Tuesday.

Though I promised that I wouldn't bug him all night, I shoot off a quick text to him anyway:

Me: Kick Bobby's butt in Fortnite, kiddo. After all those charges on my card, I expect you to be an expert.

I wait only thirty seconds before my phone vibrates with an incoming message, and it's one that makes me both cringe and laugh out loud.

Topher: It's teaching me about credit, Ma. Just think what I'll be able to do in ten years. #PayUp

"Brat," I mutter good-naturedly under my breath.

Me: Don't stay up all night. Remember, you're helping me in the garden tomorrow.

Topher: I'd never forget

Me: ... I can smell your lie from here.

Topher: Not a lie, Mom. Just a fabrication of the truth.

Me: Big words can't distract me, dear son. Don't oversleep. I'll be by to pick you up at nine.

Topher: 9:30? And can we bring Harry home? His mom can't pick him up in the morning.

Me: Sure, and 9:15 is my final offer.

Topher: I think you hate me.

Me: I can't hate you. You're my favorite kid.

Topher: Mom, I'm your ONLY kid.

Me: Exactly.

Just as I move to pocket my phone, it vibrates again and I peer down at the screen, fully prepared for another incoming text from Topher.

Dominic.

My heart squeezes in anticipation.

Swiping to unlock my cell, I quickly read his message.

Dominic: I've entered hell. Send help.

Me: I'm surprised you need assistance. I thought you'd be welcomed there with open arms . . .

Dominic: Har har. You're hilarious.

Me: I've been told that on a few different occasions.

Me: Call my curiosity piqued, though. What's hell like nowadays? I don't make a habit of visiting regularly. All that soot and brimstone . . . not exactly my thing.

I glance up at the mirror behind the bar, only to find a huge grin on my face. It's been less than a week since Dominic kissed me. Ravaged me, more like. And it was . . . delicious, in the best possible way.

I want to feel his lips on mine again.

Willow thinks I'm sexphobic or however she put it, or that I'm afraid of commitment, but the truth is that I'm neither. I don't fear sex. I don't fear relationships. It's just that, in my experience, neither has particularly worked out in my favor. Rick never cared about my pleasure—and he certainly never prioritized it when we did sleep together. And commitments fracture. They shatter and they splinter, and if I had a penny for every time Rick promised me that "he'd do better," I'd be so loaded I could buy myself a private island.

At the vibration of my phone, I glance down and promptly choke out a laugh.

Oh, my God.

He looks *miserable*.

Seated at the bar of the Golden Fleece with his customary baseball cap in place—and with it flipped backward—Dominic scowls at the camera. Sharp jaw line. Slightly crooked nose, no doubt from a football injury at some point. I follow the line of his bulky shoulder to where he's pointing up above his head to the TV behind the bar.

The photo has frozen an image of Dominic on the screen, wearing nothing but a pair of briefs, alongside another twelve or thirteen guys who are all dressed in nothing but different forms of underwear. Briefs, boxers, tighty-whities. One guy is even decked out in a G-string, which terrifies me more than it arouses me. Plus, how the hell did he arrange his junk in that thing? Did he push it *back*?

You really don't need to be thinking like that.

My phone buzzes again.

Dominic: Shawn's turned my stint on *Put A Ring On It* into a betting bracket.

Another photo comes through, this one depicting a chalkboard posted up on the bar with a bunch of names scrawled in white.

Dominic's name is circled twice and boasts the least number of votes.

I bite down on my thumb, smiling so hard that my cheeks hurt.

Me: Looks like you're about to finally find out what it's like to come in last place after all these years. Are you a sore loser?

Dominic: Why don't you come by and find out?

My pulse quickens, my fingers frozen over the touch-screen keyboard. I could easily hop in my car and be at the Golden Fleece in less than twenty minutes. It's not like I think Willow will mind—one glance to where she ran off to shows her in heavy conversation with *that* guy.

Simply put, Willow is living and I'm . . . going to take a risk.

Like when I hopped off the kayak and into the water, just to shock Dominic.

I like surprising him. I particularly like keeping him on his toes.

And I'm tired of treating sex like it's something to be distrusted.

It's been four years. Four years of resisting Rick whenever he *did* try to slip into my bed at night and cuddle up beside me. As if he hadn't spent the previous night banging god-knows-who. As if he hadn't made me feel inadequate and less than in my own skin.

Once upon a time, I loved how I looked. Toned muscles that were put to work every day on the field. Short hair that I styled in a cute pixie cut to keep the strands out of my face when I played. Scars earned from scrimmages over the years—on my shins, on my hips, the one on my upper lip from a particularly bad play back in high school.

You're as skinny as a fucking boy.

You look like a dyke with that short hair.

You really want to test me, Levi? Who are they gonna believe in court when you say I pushed you down? Me . . . or you.

Rick stole fourteen years of my life. Fifteen if you count the last year, when I stayed in Pittsburgh and tried to be the better parent and allowed Topher easy access to the both of us.

Fifteen.

I can't—I *won't*—give my ex-husband another second.

With straight shoulders, I type out a short response to Dominic and hit SEND before I can chicken out and talk myself out of it.

Me: I'm in Bar Harbor with Willow. Give me thirty minutes.

Me: And Dominic?

His answer is immediate.

Dominic: Yeah, Coach?

Me: You better kiss me tonight.

23

DOMINIC

*T*he Golden Fleece is something else tonight.

Seated at the bar with my back to the pub, I nurse a Bud Light and check my watch for the second time in twenty minutes. Not that I'm counting or anything.

Part of me regrets offering Levi the invitation to join me. After all, it's not every day you invite one woman to hang out while you're attempting to romance another one on reality TV. Tonight's *Put A Ring On It* episode was filmed over six months ago—and this particular snippet recorded even before that—but it's still uncomfortable.

Painfully awkward.

Yeah, that's a better way to put having to relive me and twelve other dudes sporting nothing but our underwear and drenched skin while Savannah Rose, who's been blind-folded, plays connect the dots between what set of abs belongs to which contestant.

Put A Ring On It is nothing if not B-Grade entertainment.

Like I'm privy to an inevitable train wreck, I watch Savannah feel up my buddy Nick. Her nails barely scrape across his stomach—like she's too nervous to even consider going for a full fondle—before she turns around and announces, "This is Mario!" Slam the buzzer. Throw up the red flag. Both Nick and Mario, a body builder out of Miami, step out of line and retreat to the "loser's" bench.

Savannah presses a hand to the blindfold. "I got it wrong again, didn't I?"

The pub erupts with laughter.

I take a pull of my beer and mentally prepare myself for the moment when Savannah reaches me in the lineup. Based on the fantasy-league board sitting beside the bar, there's going to be an uproar when I "win" the wet abs contest in approximately . . . oh, four minutes and some change, depending on how the producers edited the footage.

Fact is, until tonight I had no idea how much money the Golden Fleece was raking in with this new fantasy league Shawn started. The pot alone is worth more than three-thousand dollars with the buy-in at fifty bucks. Which means sixty Londoners have already joined the bracket—with more tagging along every week.

It'd be hilarious if it wasn't also absolutely ridiculous.

Maybe I should ask Levi to meet me somewhere else.

A heavy hand on my shoulder dissolves my plans for escape. "DaSilva."

Spinning on my bar stool, I eye the unfamiliar guy in front of me. *Might be a football parent.* I force a big smile, hoping it'll get the job done. "Hey." I put out my hand for him to shake. "Is your kid on the Wildcats?"

He grips my hand tight enough to cut off blood circulation, pumping it up and down two times over. "Me? Have a kid? Not a chance, man." His laugh is as boisterous and terrifying as his handshake. "Nah, I came over here because me and the guys"—he jerks his thumb over one shoulder

—"are taking this *Put A Ring On It* thing to the next level. Fantasy-league intel." Like he's a bookie in need of information, he whips out his phone and types, types, types. Glances up at me, then swings his gaze over to the TV. "I'm trying to wrangle enough of my buddies to join that I can walk away from this thing with a new paint job for my sailboat. Anyway, since you're sitting here . . . gonna guess you didn't win."

We have a new Sherlock in town, ladies and gents.

Biting back a stinging retort, I drop one arm to the bar, my beer dangling from my index finger and thumb. "Sorry to disappoint . . ."

"Oliver," he supplies eagerly.

"Oliver." I force his name out from between gritted teeth. "But I signed an NDA when I got on the show. Much as I'd love to give you a leg up, I'm not looking to be sued." I tilt my head to the side, eyeing him critically. "You feel me?"

Oliver shakes his head, his longish hair flopping every which way. "C'mon, man, all I need is a hint. That's it." He holds up his phone, wiggling it side to side. "My bets are on that Greek guy."

Nick would have a field day with this conversation. I make a mental note to bring it up to him next weekend, when he's in town to help with some of my house's much-needed renovation.

Slowly, I drawl, "Stamos is a solid choice."

"Yeah? You think?" Oliver's expression brightens. "Everyone else at the table is convinced it's gonna go to that investment broker out of Kansas." Almost sheepishly, he amends, "I mean, *some* of them think you pulled the big win. Hey, could I get your autograph for the wife? She's a big fan."

That investment broker out of Kansas didn't make it past eight ring ceremonies.

Not that it's my business to divulge that information—I'm not lying about the NDA. The producers may have been selfish idiots in many other respects, but they knew their job inside and out.

Then again, they still managed to let the biggest reality-show scandal hit the media long before airing even began.

It's always a hot topic when your star bachelorette walks away, single, on a show designed to end with a proposal and a ring.

Grabbing a napkin from the plastic dispenser and a pen from the forgotten receipt, over to my right, I sign my name as I always do: *Dom DaSilva. Never settle for the mundane.*

Oliver thanks me profusely then scurries off to his table.

Ten bucks says he's as single as a doorknob and seconds away from bartering off my signature to the highest bidder.

Sure enough, I see wallets coming free of pockets moments later.

"Fucking typical."

"Hello to you too?" comes a breathless feminine voice off to my right, followed by the thud of weight hitting the bar stool a second later. I catch the delicate aroma of her perfume before I see her face: subtle lavender, and a deeper note of some herb I'll never know how to pronounce. I'm a football player—not a member of Mensa.

To my surprise, Levi leans in, her nostrils puffing with three successive inhalations. "No brimstone that I can detect." She lifts her chin, inhaling deeply like she's starved for me. "I'm almost disappointed."

Based on how quickly a smirk finds its way onto my face, Levi might as well be the antidote to my pissy mood. "*Disappointed?*" I tap my beer bottle to my chest. "Don't worry,

Coach, I'm more than willing to bring you to the Underworld for a spin."

She pats my forearm, her fingers lingering noticeably before she splays her fingers over the bar. "My very own Charon," she purrs with subtle sarcasm, "how very generous of you."

"I can be generous when I want to be." I shift on the stool, angling myself to get a good look at her. Whereas her blue eyes are almost always tinged with sadness, today they're on fire. Needy. Absolutely present. My cock thickens behind my zipper, the relentless bastard. "Didn't I swim you and that kayak out into the bay?"

The curve of her bottom lip deepens. "I rowed myself, thank you very much."

Humor eases the always-present pressure in my chest. Setting my beer bottle down so I can free both hands, I drop my forearm to the bar and invade Levi's personal bubble. *Pop.* My eyes fall to her lips. Fuck, I want her. We've played the cat-and-mouse game for days now. Correction: we've been at it for *weeks.*

Flirting. Teasing.

A weaker man would have buckled and given in on that very first night.

"What's the most unexpected thing you've ever done?" she asks, catching me off guard.

"Ever?" I echo, my eyes locked on hers. So damn blue they're almost black in the candlelit pub. "Or recently?"

"In the last year."

I tilt my head toward the TV behind me. "Besides going on a dating show, you mean?"

As though it pains her to think of me with someone else, her brows furrow. "Yeah, besides that."

Giving her question only a moment's thought, I lift a hand

to her face. Cup her jaw, my thumb tracing the hairline scar that bisects her upper lip. "It's ridiculous how much I crave touching you," I utter in a low voice, unable to look away. Not even Savannah Rose had a grip on me like this. I liked Savannah. I cared about what she thought of me. I wanted to be the sort of man she looked at and thought, *Yeah, he fits in my world.*

With Levi, worlds aren't even a factor.

I crave the feel of her skin on mine.

I want to know what's going on in her head at all times, even when she'll push and prod at my walls until I'm being just as vulnerable.

I like knowing that soft as she is, as warm as she can be, she's a total hard-ass too.

Shaking my head—and shoving those thoughts away—I drag my thumb across her plump bottom lip, mussing up the shiny gloss she's wearing. She blinks up at me, and damn it if I don't love the look of her smudged lip gloss paired with her big blue eyes. *A perfect match.* Yeah, I wouldn't mind being the one to dirty her up real good.

Focus.

"I went skydiving a few months ago," I finally answer. And, knowing that Levi is the sort of person who always pushes for more, I elaborate without her asking for it: "When you're free-fallin' like that, no one gives a shit about who you are or what you've accomplished in life or where you're from. End of the day, it's you, a parachute, and the rush of wind in your ears."

Levi reaches for my beer and pulls back only long enough for a sip. "Give me something else," she prods, bottle neck dangling from between two slender fingers. "Doesn't have to be something recent."

Casting a quick glance over to the people filtering into

the pub—it's still relatively early for a weekend night—I cup the back of my neck, idly rubbing the muscles there. "I'm gonna go with the trip I took after my physical therapist gave me the go-ahead with my leg." I knock the heel of my right boot against the bar stool's leg. "You ever heard of Hua Shan in China?"

Levi takes another drag of my beer. "Can't say that I have. Is it a monastery or something?"

"Better. So much better." Remembering the edge of anticipation that had my lungs pumping for days in advance, I scoot forward so she won't miss a word. "Hua Shan is a mountain ridge. An adrenaline junkie's dream. Loads of articles have coined it the world's most dangerous hike." I lift a hand, illustrating the invisible line of a sharp peak. "Narrow paths are carved into the mountain side, and there are these . . . real narrow planks that are bolted to the cliffside."

"It sounds . . . dangerous."

I flash her a small grin. "I prefer to think of it as thrilling."

"You would, Mr. Living On The Edge."

"You tellin' me that you wouldn't risk it all for the best sunset in the world?"

She doesn't even bother to hide her eye roll. "C'mon. For a *sunset?* That doesn't seem very . . . you."

"Why? Because I'm a jock?"

"That's not what I said. *I'm* a jock, too. Or I was, I guess. You just don't seem the sort to stop and enjoy something as poetic as a sunset or a sunrise or anything, really, that doesn't involve—Dominic, are you listening?"

"Multitasking," I answer as I open the internet tab on my phone. With quick fingers, I plug in a website that I've kept a secret for years now. It's been no one's business but mine and I've always preferred it that way.

To the world, I'm Dominic DaSilva: world-renowned athlete, TV host, bad boy extraordinaire.

I'm not denying any of that.

But a small part of me will always be that kid who felt invisible and neglected. Who watched the world pass him by and vowed, even if only to himself, that one day the world would be his for the taking, if he only dared to reach for it.

Silently, I pass my phone over to Levi, who takes it carefully after setting aside the beer. I pick up the Bud Light automatically, seeking *something* to busy myself with as I wait for her to connect the dots—to see more of me than I've ever allowed another person.

I hear her sharp, indrawn breath at the same time I watch her thumbs swipe up.

"You took these?" she asks, awe coating every word.

Ignoring the unfamiliar bundle of nerves in my stomach, I dip my chin. "Yeah. I did."

Her head bows as she continues to scroll. "Dominic . . ."

My heart pounds a mile a minute. "They're not professionally done, obviously. I bought a camera but it's not like I know what the fuck I'm doing with it—"

"Where is this?" She shoves the phone in my direction, pointing at the screen. "I don't recognize it."

"Tyulenovo." At her blank stare, I stifle a grin. "It's in northern Bulgaria, along the Balkan Sea. See?" My hand engulfs hers, my thumb sandwiched between her fingers as I swipe up to view the next picture. Craggy cliffs, turquoise, turbulent waters, and a thirty-foot-plus drop that terrified me as much as it spurred me on. I can almost recall the rush of adrenaline that gripped my lungs like a vice when I made the jump. "People come from all over the world to cliff jump from this exact spot."

"Insane people, you mean."

"I think the term you're lookin' for is 'adrenaline junkie.'"

Shooting me an indecipherable glance, Levi angles the phone so we can both see the screen. With her thumb hooked under mine, she encourages me to scroll up with a little nudge. "There," she says, "where was that?"

Narrow gravel roads winding along protruding mountains. Hot rain pelting my back as I gripped the bike's handlebars. Stinging calves by the time I finished the path. "Death Road in Bolivia. My heart was in my throat the entire ride. It was . . . awesome."

"Awesome," she mocks sarcastically under her breath, "meanwhile, I would have peed myself."

I knock my knee against hers. "I wouldn't judge you if you did."

"No?"

"Of course not."

She narrows her eyes, disbelief warring with humor in their sapphire depths. "Really."

"Yup." I draw out the word, popping the *p* just to see that flicker of humor truly spark to life. "We're in this together. Two coaches taking on the world—"

"Or at least this corner of Maine."

"—and I wouldn't let you suffer that embarrassment alone." Cocking my head, I lower my voice playfully. "Nah, Coach, I would have pissed myself right along with you. That's teamwork right there."

Levi promptly drops her head, chin to her chest, and just when I'm convinced that she's going to tell me to screw off for being weird, she laughs. She laughs so hard that her shoulders shake with the force of her mirth and she begins to turn heads. Crazy as it sounds, I revel in the girlish sound.

I can hear Savannah Rose calling my former castmates forward at the ring ceremony. Hear my name said, too: "Will you accept this ring, Dom?" Savannah asks and then there's my husky response, "Yeah, of course I do."

The pub's patrons, Oliver included, erupt into a series of excited catcalling. No doubt some of them have won this week's fantasy league stats by having me stick around for another seven days.

But it's Levi who captures my sole attention. Levi who's making my dead heart leap and my damn cock stiffen, even though I'm in a very public place with a number of people who probably wouldn't mind earning themselves a little extra cash by going to *Celebrity Tea Presents* or another shitty gossip rag with information about what I'm up to these days.

I slip off the bar stool, then barricade Levi's body with mine so she's off-limits to Oliver and his buddies. I don't give a shit what they say about me—it's nothing I haven't heard before or won't hear again—but I'm not dragging Levi into this mess with me. Not here, where everyone can speculate about what might be going on with London High's head and assistant coaches.

"Where's Topher?" I ask, a plan already forming in my head.

"At Bobby's for the night with Timmy and Kevin. Harry, too." Levi peers up at me, my phone still clasped in her hand. "Why?"

"Because you're coming with me."

"Oh, am I now?"

"Yeah."

I snag my phone from her and pocket it in my jeans. I want to do so much more than that, too. Spread her legs wide and step in between them, her calves looped around my thighs as I angle her for my cock. Feel her nails scrape my shoulders as I lower my head and find her pert nipple with my mouth. Cup the weight of her breast and know, without a single trace of worry, that Levi is with me for *me* and not because of who I am. Who I *was*.

Boldly, I watch as Levi's hands tremble while she adjusts her top, as if she's gathering her wits about her and coming to a decision I'm not privy to. Her straight blond hair falls forward, a physical shield that closes me off from her expression.

And then . . . and then air comes slow and reedy through my nose when it hits me.

The straps of her shirt hang loose around her biceps, exposing the upper swells of her breasts and the fine lace of her bra.

She's signaling exactly what she wants from me tonight . . . and I'm gonna give it to her—but on my terms.

Just as I need to find peace in the calm, she's craving a taste of the insanity. I heard the tremor of excitement in her voice when she looked through my photos. Saw the longing for *more* that she desperately tried to hide behind questioning why I do such outrageous things.

I cliff dive, and I climb mountains on planks as wide as my forearm, and I risk biking straight off a mountain because it makes me feel as though my fate is entirely in my hands. It's mine to take and mine to destroy and there's something empowering about risking it all and knowing that it's your own free will and mental strength that sees you safely to the other side.

"You trust me, Coach?" I ask softly.

She blinks up at me, wetting her bottom lip in a way that has my jeans feeling too damn tight. "The last time you asked me that, I found myself in a kayak at three in the morning."

I make a point of checking the time on my gold Rolex. "It's only ten, which means we've got some time before you run the risk of turning into a pumpkin." Shoulders raised to keep everyone else out of our conversation, my gaze never wavers from hers. "Do you trust me."

Not a question.

She licks her lips again, but nothing about it is sexual. She's nervous, I can tell. Being nervous is good—you can't win if you don't take a leap of faith. Slowly, she inclines her head in the smallest, most imperceptible nod I've ever seen. "You going to feed me to the sharks?"

"Can't make any promises."

"Will you make me one promise?"

"Name it."

Her throat visibly constricts. "Call me Aspen . . . just for tonight."

Fuck.

It's my turn to find it difficult to swallow. Harder, still, to keep my distance when I'm uncomfortably aware of multiple pairs of eyes tracking our every move. Londoners are curious, and I'm . . . I'm freefalling.

"Yeah," I manage to choke out, my voice thick with emotion, "I can do that."

24

ASPEN

*A*side from a quick pit stop by our houses—me to drop off my car and Dominic to grab some "necessities," as he called them, from his place—we get on the road.

Only, I'm blindfolded.

Blindfolded, like a scene out of *Fifty Shades of Grey*. "I feel like Ana," I whisper, because it's hard not to whisper when the world feels out of reach and you're completely dependent on another person to make sure you don't, I don't know, *die.*

Dominic's voice is nothing but heat and amusement. "Ana, who?"

"*Fifty Shades of Grey?*" At the ensuing silence, I try again. "E.L. James? Famous romance author?" Still nothing. Figures—*men.* "She writes erotica. BDSM-type stuff."

"Whips and cages and chains, oh my."

The words emerge so droll that I can't help but shake my head. Already I'm itching to rip off the blindfold and breathe through the low pulse of anxiety clinging to my skin. "Have you ever tried it?"

"Bondage?"

"Don't sound so shocked. Clearly you have an affinity for blindfolds."

Husky laughter echoes in the cab of the truck. "Let's not get it twisted here, Coach—you're wearing an old T-shirt wrapped around your head. And nah, I'm not interested in any of that."

"You're not going to tell me why?" If nothing else, the blindfold has given me the gift of no filter. It's absolutely liberating, even if my nerves haven't quit me yet. I press my knees together, my hands clasped in my lap as I listen to the gentle whir of the wind speed past the car. "I feel like most guys wouldn't mind tying a woman up."

"I don't need ropes, Aspen."

Pleasure, as sharp and insistent as the moment he kissed me, gathers between my legs—and all because he used my name. My *first* name. It sounds like heaven dipped in orgasms coming out of his mouth. Sweeter, even, like an endearment. Baby. Sugarplum. *Aspen.*

I almost beg him to say it again.

I don't, but only because he continues talking in that rough, deep timbre that could convince even a nun to ditch her habit, it's so sensually wicked.

"If I want to pin you down, I'll do it with my hands locked around your wrists. If I want to see your ass turn pink, I'll skip the paddle and use my palm." A heavy, masculine hand curves possessively over the back of my skull and I feel him tighten the knot of the blindfold. "And if I'm dyin' to see your eyes squeeze shut because you don't know if you can take anymore, I'll cut out all the toys and put you on your knees instead, slipping my cock between those berry lips of yours."

Oh.

My.

God.

Without my sight, my hearing is so much more acute. There's nothing but the sound of tires rolling over a smooth road and my uneven breathing for company. I squirm in the passenger's seat, my thighs rubbing together. Two of my fingers arch toward my throat to skate over my skin.

"What're you doing?"

"Checking my pulse." *There*, at the base of my neck. Between my legs, my clit throbs to the same fluttering beat. He's turning me inside out. Stringing me along like a cat in heat. *Deep breaths.* "You can't just say things like that—"

"Does it scare you?"

I sink down on my seat. "*You* scare me."

"Why?"

"Because we've known each other for all of two weeks and already I've let you lead me out into the ocean, blindfold me, and then put those *images* in my head. What will I let you do to me next? Where do I draw the line? I feel like . . . I feel like . . ."

"You're alive."

My unadorned fingers flex in my lap. "Yes."

He drums a catchy beat on the steering wheel. "You know how I feel every time I do something insane?" I can almost envision him throwing up bunny quotes around the word "insane." The way he says it, the way I've heard him toss the word around about himself in the past, tells me it belongs to a much bigger story. Something he's not ready to reveal yet. "I feel like you do right now, Aspen."

Feeling bold, and curious to know if I can hear joy displace his always-present cynicism, I tease, "You feel like your panties are wet?"

And I *do*.

I hear the back of his head collide with the seat and the deep rumble of his laughter, and call *me* insane, but I swear I can hear a wicked smile curve his lips. Breathtaking. That's how he sounds—breathtakingly handsome.

I imagine his teeth grazing his bottom lip when he murmurs, "How do you always manage to surprise me?"

"Maybe because I'm demolishing every stereotype you had of me." Holding up a hand that I can't see beyond the black fabric, I tick off each finger as I speak. "Young woman married to a much older man. Accidental pregnancy. Female football coach. Divorced and not bitter—okay, sometimes a little bitter." I pause, four fingers curled into my palm with my thumb still standing tall. "Any others I should add?"

"Yeah."

My heart clenches. Idiot. *Idiot.* Why wouldn't he take the opportunity to list his misconceptions of me? God knows that I've been judging him for years. I've used his bad behavior as a lesson to my players multiple times over. More shamefully, I believed everything Rick ever said about Dominic, never digging deeper than whatever rumors hit the gossip circuits.

"I won't break," I edge out, blinking quickly behind the blindfold. Whatever he thought of me when we first met, I can take it. Sticks and stones and all that. "Go ahead."

The trucks slows to a crawl. My seat belt tightens across my chest as Dominic cuts the ignition. I wait, breath drawn, for the jangle of keys—only to feel the pressure of his big frame leaning over me, one hand gripping my thigh.

Oh, boy.

Ears straining for a hint of what's to come, I catch the click of the passenger's side door opening and then there's no mistaking the way my hair is carefully tucked behind my ear and his lips brush my ear to order, "Get out."

I tilt my head, surprised. "But you didn't—you didn't tell me what other judgments you made about me."

"Because I don't have one."

Despite my lack of sight, my eyes shift back and forth. "I'm confused."

"This is for you."

His hand glides up, up, up my thigh, the pressure of his thumb deepening the higher he moves. It's sensual and heavenly and *oh, God.* My hand flies out to grip the door handle. My heels dig into the floor as my hips lift. Just enough to see if his hand will shift from the crease of my hip and cup the apex of my thighs. It doesn't. *He* doesn't. I nearly whimper. Clearly, he wants me out of this car but I can't, for the life of me, find the strength to get out. Not when it means he'll stop touching me.

In that commanding, deep voice of his, he continues, "Took a risk and married a man you loved. Got knocked up and gave birth to a pretty awesome kid. Defeated the odds and took a job that historically belongs in a man's world. Bravely divorced a shit-bag of a human being." I feel the slope of his nose against my profile, then the softest, most tantalizing, brush of his mouth over mine. "Wants to take risks but fears that the time for all that is over because you've hit the ripe old age of thirty-seven . . . Did I miss one?"

My mouth gapes open. My lungs cease pumping.

"Dominic, I—"

He cuts me off with a kiss. Unlike the first, this one is rough. Demanding. That hand resting at the crease of my hip bone squeezes tightly and his thumb sweeps over the center seam of my jeans. I gasp into his mouth, and it's all the permission he needs to take the kiss from a ten to a twenty.

Dangerous.

In this moment with his T-shirt caging my sight and his hands on my body, I feel dangerous. Weightless. An adrenaline junkie who's finally found her perfect fix.

I cup his stubbled cheeks, finding them effortlessly, though I still exist in the dark. Moaning into his mouth, I beg shamelessly for more. *Take me*, I whisper to no one, my fingers scraping down the length of his throat. *Want me*, I think wildly, as I clutch his T-shirt and flick my tongue against his. *Make me yours*, my soul sings, when his hand leaves my thigh to coast north, under the fabric of my shirt and farther up more, until his fingers skate over the underwire of my bra and I'm all but shimmying in place to get it off.

I arch my back, giving him plenty of space to fiddle with the clasp.

He traces the line of my bra over my rib cage. Dances his fingers down the pearls of my spine. Presses me forward, until finally, yes, yes, *yes.*

The bra comes free, my breasts lowering without their satin-bound cage to keep them perky. Momentary panic supersedes all desire. I don't know what kind of women Dominic sleeps with, but I can't imagine they're like me. Nearing forty. Breasts that lost their pep sometime in the last few years. A belly that's not nearly as tight and flat as it once was when I led the country in made-field goals.

It was one thing to sleep with Rick. Strained as our relationship was, especially in the last few years, he witnessed the changes to my body as I experienced them myself. Dominic . . . Dominic wasn't privy to any of that. Will he be turned off by the cellulite? Will he call this off the moment he notices the puckered scar from my long-ago C-section? I don't think I could bear to see disgust flit over his rugged features.

I grasp his hand, the one that's not all up under my shirt. "I don't think I can do this."

My shirt goes tight around my chest as he pulls my bra off completely. Strapless. *Dammit.* Just another reason to hate them.

This is too much.

All of it is too much.

"Get out of the car, Aspen."

My head jerks toward the sound of his voice. "What?"

"You heard me."

"You took my bra!" I exclaim indignantly.

"And I'm gonna take a hell of a lot more from you tonight." My seat belt abruptly loosens, then rappels up, like he's undone the clasp. Sure enough, I feel the webbed polyester jam under my armpit. "Those judgments I listed off? Those are the one's you're holding against *yourself*. Yeah, you can frown all you want. You can even tell me to fuck off, if it makes you feel any better. But that won't prove me wrong. So what's it gonna be? You going to give your inner self the big, ol' middle finger, Dominic DaSilva-style? Or are you going to ask me to take off that blindfold and drive you home where you'll crawl into your safe bed and read a sexy book and dream of all the things you *wish* you could be doing, if you dared to take a risk?"

Blood roars in my head.

Sweat dampens my palms.

The seat belt clings as it meets its maker, and I reach out a hand, fumbling for the door handle.

I'm grateful for feeling safe after all these years with Rick.

I'm grateful for returning home to London, even knowing not everyone in town would be happy to see me back.

I'm grateful to Dominic-friggin'-DaSilva for essentially telling me to put on my big girl panties and live my best, most adventurous, life.

The door swings open and my shoes greet what feels like dirt. It's slightly spongy. Not nearly as compact as cement.

Dominic's voice coming from the driver's seat halts me in my tracks. "You know how I figured you'd get out of the truck?"

I look over my shoulder, seeing nothing but various shades of black. "Why?"

"Because there's nothing you enjoy more than flipping me the bird, Aspen, and this will be the most satisfying middle finger you've ever given." A door slams shut, and then I catch the sound of heavy footfalls coming around the front of the truck. "Now hold my hand and let me lead the way. It's time to take you on a midnight hike you'll never forget."

25

DOMINIC

*C*adillac Mountain is nothing but shadows at this time of night.

Broken twigs beneath our shoes.

Grasping branches raking through our hair.

But the air up here . . . Fuck, it's good. Crisp. Light. Forgiving in a way that only Mother Nature can be.

I followed my GPS on the way up to Mount Desert Island's tallest peak, putting the sucker on mute so Levi wouldn't overhear the British lady giving me directions to Summit Road. I haven't had the chance to hike Cadillac Mountain yet, but I've skimmed enough articles online to know what to expect as we enter the trails.

Like an old friend, adrenaline guides me down the narrow dirt path. Slung over my back is a bag stuffed with an oversized blanket, two bottles of water, and two hastily made turkey sandwiches. I hold a flashlight in one hand and Levi in the other.

I don't know what it says about me that the anticipation of stripping Levi naked is just as thrilling as heading to the Super Bowl—if not more.

"Are we almost there?" Her voice breaks through the still of the night.

"Almost."

During the day, this trail is apparently well-used. The soil is jampacked after being stomped on for hours on end, and the overlook site we're heading to is usually teeming with tourists searching out a peek of the bay and the surrounding islands.

"Do you think we'll get caught?" Levi asks.

"If you haven't been cuffed at least once, are you really living?"

"*So* not funny."

"Would you be opposed to me cuffing you?"

"I thought you said your sexual prowess doesn't require accessories?"

At her flippant tone, I chuckle. It's the most I've laughed in years, if ever. *I don't want it to end.* "It doesn't need anything besides me, myself, and I."

The flashlight casts a wide scope, revealing the overlook I read about: flat stones lining the perimeter of the cliff that were supposedly formed during the last Ice Age; a sharp drop that leads straight to injury, at best, death, at worst. Trees protect the otherwise grassy, enclosed space, offering natural privacy.

"I swear to God, Dominic, your ego is just—"

Her weight collides with my back, sending the both of us stumbling forward. Looping an arm around her waist, I haul her upright and flush against me. The T-shirt covers her from forehead to nose. Taking advantage of the fact that she can't see me coming, I maneuver the flashlight so it's not shining into our faces and then capture her lips with mine.

She sighs, immediately softening into my frame. I feel her fingers skim the waistband of my jeans, under the hem of my shirt. Goose bumps that I'd like to blame on the slight breeze flare up on my skin, making a liar out of me. Levi does this to me, not the wind. And she does it every damn time.

I crowd her space, leveraging her backward with my arm hooked around the base of her spine. *More.* More of those breathy mewls of hers. More of her fingers flirting with the button of my jeans. More, more, more. I'm an adrenaline junkie looking for his next fix, and I get my perfect hit every time she's in my arms.

It takes every ounce of self-control not to sink deeper into the kiss. With a rumble of protest in my chest, I pull back and taunt, "Don't be shy now. My ego is what?"

"Big."

"Yeah?"

"Oh, yeah."

"Perfect." I tug on her shirt. "Time to take this bad boy off."

There's just enough moonlight for me to see her blanch. "I'll be topless!"

"That's a guarantee."

"Anyone could see me."

"It's almost midnight," I say, struggling not to laugh at her expense. Aspen Levi has got a *long* way to go before she's pulling the sort of stunts I do, but I'm more than willing to rise to the challenge and take it slow with her. Slow is good. Slow is . . . *not as predictable as I used to think.* "Who's gonna see you? A bear?"

"Oh my God, don't even play with me like that."

"Sharks," I muse, my thumb finding her ear and playfully tugging on her lobe, "bears. Is there anything you're not worried about eating you?"

"You?"

I can't smother the mirth this time. I let it out, knowing that there's not a soul out in these woods at this time of night. Skimming my hand down to her jawline, I press my forehead to hers. Her uneven breath flutters across my lips. "That's where you're wrong, Asp. I am going to eat you. I'm gonna slick my tongue right over your lips then suck on your clit so damn hard, bears will be the last thing on your mind."

I don't know which one of us is more shocked.

The fact that I called her *Asp* or how very obvious my intent is for tonight's activities.

Either way, it seems I don't have to worry.

Levi whips her blouse right over the top of her head, careful to keep the T-shirt blindfold in place. She saucily twirls her shirt around one finger, then attempts to pat down my chest. When she finds me, she hooks the fabric around the back of my neck and reels me in.

"Have you looked yet?" she teases nervously, and it doesn't take a rocket scientist to know what she's talking about.

I haven't looked—but not for a lack of trying.

Who's the idiot who didn't think this all the way through? *That'd be me*. Because Levi's naked chest is currently nothing but shadows and an indecipherable silhouette.

This was the plan. I picked Cadillac Mountain because I knew it would push Levi out of her comfort zone, but only so far. Shadows are safe. They're low risk and keep everyone on equal playing field.

Except that I can't see a thing.

Her slender hand grabs mine and—Jesus *fuck*—lays it across her full breast. I choke at the same time I try to breathe through my nose. "Aspen—"

The flashlight falls from my hand to the grass.

I planned to guide her into this moment. Romance her —no matter the fact that romance has never been my thing. I'd sweet-talk her out of her clothes, one by one, until the blanket cushioned her from the ground and my body shielded her from the sky, wandering bears, and anything else that might go bump in the night.

Only, I'm strung so damn tight from that bold move of hers that . . .

I rip my backpack off, slinging it down one arm and unzipping it a heartbeat later. The water can wait; the food can too. But the blanket . . . my fingers grasp the soft material and I waste no time in flicking it open and laying it flat over the ground.

"What was that?" Her hands comb through the air, searching for answers that she can't see. "It sounded like a sheet or a tarp maybe?"

It feels difficult to breathe. Throat tight, I manage a guttural, "A blanket. It was a blanket," before nudging my backpack closed with my foot.

"Did you . . . did you pack a *care* package for us?" comes Levi's soft question, and even though she's the one blindfolded and shirtless, I suddenly feel just as exposed. Just as naked.

Because this is not what I do.

Taking care of another person, seeing to their comfort first, is *not what I do.*

My limbs are frozen, my heart thudding erratically, when she kicks off her shoes and feels around for a hint of soft fabric. The discarded flashlight illuminates her calves, her searching toes, and then, as she sinks to the ground, her knees cushioned by the blanket. She sweeps her knuckles forward as if to confirm her suspicions.

I'm bad boy, cynical Dominic DaSilva, and I planned us a romantic interlude under the stars.

I'm completely out of my element here.

I clear my throat. "Levi—"

"No." The flat of her palms fumble around on the blanket as she pats around. "You promised me."

My lids fall shut. "*Aspen*."

"I take a risk; you take a risk." Her hand finds my bent knee. "That's how this works. I won't be vulnerable without you, Dominic. I've done that. I lived that life for *years*, and I won't do it again. Not for you, not for anyone."

"Rick." I might as well spit out his name, the way it trips off my tongue like something to be spurned and cast out.

She doesn't say yes, not quite. But her hands continue their upward glide, until she's settled snuggly in the *V* of my spread thighs and her fingers are climbing higher and the heels of her palms are dragging over my quads. She pops the button of my jeans. "So, what's it going to be?" she says, throwing my own words back in my face. "You going to do this with me—be all the way in—or are you going to drive me home and tuck me into my safe bed that won't have you anywhere near it?"

My head drops back, eyes seeking out the thousands of stars twinkling in the clear night sky. I think back to all the times I've searched out the universe as I am now. Back with that goddamn ankle monitor tracking me like a savage, when there was nothing left to do but look out my window and make a wish on a fake shooting star. At every hotel we stayed at during my Tampa Bay years, when I'd find myself stepping outside and wondering the point of life when all the stats and Super Bowl rings and victories did nothing to alleviate how wrecked I felt inside. My last night on *Put A Ring On It*, when I overheard the producers and crew laughing about how they were positive Savannah Rose would accept Nick's proposal over mine.

Since birth, loneliness has tagged me as its victim.

Not anymore.

I can't—I won't—give up this chance to be with Levi, just because I'm fucked up in the head.

Tonight, she belongs to me.

Like the savage I used to be, I tear off her blindfold and toss it aside. Reach behind me, fingers grasping the back of my shirt, and yank it over my head. Pull her flush against me, hard chest to hard nipples, and holy shit, she feels like bliss and salvation all wrapped up in a package designed to make me lose my mind.

"*Yes.*"

I hear her whimper just before I crush our lips together. My tongue wars with hers, meeting in an aggressive kiss that draws a groan from deep within my chest. I don't go easy on her, but . . . Levi, I know she can handle me. *All* of me. I spear my fingers through her hair, tugging sharply on the strands until her head is canted back and I'm free to kiss all that soft skin bared only for me.

"Say my name, Aspen," I growl, my lips finding the curve of her jaw. I flick my tongue out, then move south to uncharted territory. "Say that you want me, that you want *this.*"

I cup her breast, my thumb cresting over her puckered nipple. And aw, fuck, *that moan.* It's the sexiest sound I've ever heard, and I almost come right then and there in my jeans, like a prepubescent jerking off for the first time. It doesn't help that her hands clutch the back of my neck to keep me close or that anytime I trace the rough pads of my fingers over her, that moan of hers comes again.

It's all I can do not to unzip my jeans and give myself a little relief.

One glance up at her shadowed features and my priorities storm back in line: I'm gonna make Levi come so hard, she'll be feeling me between her legs for days.

"Say it," I demand again, pinching her nipple. I drop my mouth there to soothe the sting away, before I do it all again.

"*Dominic.*"

Her voice cracks on the second syllable of my name and I hiss when her nails bite into my scalp. Hooking one arm around her back, I lower her so that she sits at an angle that forces her to trust me, to give me her full weight to hold— and then I feast. I lave at one stiff nipple, swirling my tongue. Her back muscles twitch under my palm and, with my other hand, I track the curve of her waist. *Beautiful.* That's how she feels in my arms, how she tastes in my mouth.

Levi arches her spine. "I've never . . . oh, my God, please don't stop."

And because I like keeping her on her toes, I change up my rhythm and scrape my teeth against the sensitive nub. I swallow a grin when she gasps, her fingers scrabbling for purchase on my shoulders.

"You've never what? Tell me, Asp. What have you never felt before?"

"This good," she whimpers, devastation and euphoria lacing those two words like a tightly wound knot. "I've never . . . not once . . . oh, God. I can't think straight."

Somehow, in the matter of weeks, Levi and I have learned to communicate through a language no one else knows. It sounds cheesy, and hell, if I had even summoned the thought six months ago, I would have checked myself into the closest psych clinic. Except that it isn't cheesy at all

—I hear all that she isn't saying, and my temper goes through the roof.

It's bad enough that Rick Clarke took other women to his bed, but it's downright cruel that he never made his wife feel beautiful and wanted.

But his loss is my gain, and I don't hesitate when I pull back long enough to unbutton her jeans. With a finger to the center of her chest, I push her all the way down. Her butt collides with the blanket, and then I get to work stripping off her pants.

"You, too," she says into the night. "If I take a risk, you take a risk. Remember?"

I drop the jeans off to the side, then find her slim ankles with my hands. Guide my palms up over smooth skin and strong calves. "Oh, I remember, but you're going to have to wait for that. Have a little patience."

"Patience is overrated."

"You won't feel that way in a minute." Settling myself between her legs, I spread them wide with an assertive hand. "Plus, I don't wear underwear."

"*Oh.*"

"Mhmm." Slipping my palms under her thighs, I lift them onto my shoulders. I'm staring down the barrel of heaven right now. Me, myself, and the sweetest heat known to mankind. I'm starved for a taste of her, right there where she's the softest. My thumbs sweep over her inner thighs. "You find that patience yet?"

"No underwear at all?" is all she asks, so lightly that the words might as well flit away with the breeze.

"None," I confirm, pressing a soft kiss to the quivering flesh on the inside of her knee. "Nada." Another kiss, farther up her leg. "Zilch." And, before she can issue any more protests about my lack of underwear, I hitch a finger around her panties and move the fabric to the side. Lower my head and exhale, easy and controlled, right over her bare pussy.

"Oh, *God*."

Yeah, I have her exactly where she belongs.

At my mercy.

Begging for my touch.

Desperate for *me*.

Ignoring the fact that her thighs are damn near squeezing my head into oblivion, I use my free hand to spread her lips. Her legs loosen, as if she's caught on that she's nearly throttling me, and I chuckle. "Found some of that patience?"

"Go . . . go easy on me," she says in a whisper, "this . . . Rick never . . . Crap, you know what I mean."

Everything in me goes ramrod still.

"Never?" It barely constitutes as a question, my teeth are gritted so hard.

"Never."

Breathe in, breathe out.

"Good," I growl, "because this first belongs to me. *Only* me."

Her hips rise off the ground when I touch my tongue to her clit. Her cry pierces the night, and if I had a single romantic bone in my body, I'd also say that it pierces my heart. Slashes it in half, stitches it back together, good as new, and pops it back into my chest for me to use again.

I groan at the taste of her. A whole lotta sweet. A little tart. *Just like her*. I take it easy, tempting her with the promise of more but keeping the pressure light. The elastic band of her underwear cuts into my knuckles, but I don't stop for even a second to remove it. Not when I've got Levi begging me to "keep doing that." Like there was any other option the second her shirt came off and my cock turned so stiff my vision blurred. No. Other. Option. My tongue slides along her crease, slipping into her core.

Another cry that echoes off the mountain.

Her legs tremble on either side of me, and I'm faced with the truth: maybe I'm the first one to go down on her, but she's the first one to make sex feel like something more than just getting off.

I want to take my time.

I want to make her come all over my face, and then shove her right back up the same damn mountain so I can watch her splinter apart all over again. Never has fucking felt more selfish. Feeling her heels dig into my back? Hearing her keening moans? Knowing that I'm the first and only guy to ever feast on her like she's my own personal buffet? Yeah, all kinds of selfish on my part.

I've never been accused of being a gentleman.

Needing more, I thrust a finger deep inside her.

"*Oh!*"

I enter her with another finger, just to see her belly seesaw with heavy breaths and her hands fist the blanket. Like I said, selfish.

"Dominic." Her hands fly off the ground to clamp down on my forearms. She pulls fruitlessly. "I need you. *Please.*"

I lap at her clit, applying enough pressure to send her hips on the rise again.

Her panting echoes in my ears. "No, that's not what I mean. You. I need *you.*"

"What part of me?" I taunt, before swirling my tongue over the sensitive nub again. "Say the words for me, Coach."

She pauses only a moment before caving with an aggravated cry. "Your cock, you jerk. *Now.*"

With one last lick at her clit, I slide her legs from my shoulders. "Take off your underwear," I order, already fumbling in my jeans' pocket for the condom in my wallet. I tuck the square foil between my teeth, keeping it safe as I kick off my pants and shoes before dropping to my knees. I can't see a damn thing but I feel the cool breeze against my erection, and then I feel even more when Levi's dainty fingers unexpectedly wrap around my length.

"*Aspen.*"

Fire races down my spine when her lips delicately kiss the tip of my cock. It's sweet and tender and then she might as well cut me at the knees. She sucks me in. *All the way down.* A gurgling noise erupts from her mouth as I hit the back of her throat, and *oh, fuck.* Control spirals out of reach. It's gone the instant she peels back long enough to praise, "I love the way you taste," and then goes back to lapping at the leaking, swollen head.

I'm going to die.

All these years of risking my life in dozens of different ways, and I'm gonna end up with an obituary in the newspaper that reads: *Died of a heart attack at the age of thirty-five. Cause: amazing blow job. Where: on a mountain top. Regrets: only that he didn't last long to finish the job.*

Frantically, I rake my fingers through her hair. "No more," I groan, "you keep that up and I'm going to come . . . *Jesus*, Aspen."

I cup the back of her head, unable to keep from thrusting forward. I don't want to hurt her. I don't want to scare her. But nothing—*nothing*—has ever felt so good as her mouth sucking me off. Her hand and lips meet in the middle of my cock, coming together again and again to turn my vision sideways and wreak havoc on my body.

When she finally does pull away, it's with the sassiest retort I've ever heard: "Say it, Dominic," she purrs, her fingers dancing their way up my flat, ridged stomach, "say how much you want this."

"I want *you*," I confess raggedly.

I rip the condom open with my teeth, roll the latex down over my already hypersensitive erection, then climb on top of her. In all my life, I've always stuck to positions that put women facing away from me. Doggy-style. Reverse cowgirl. Doesn't matter how it got done, so long as I didn't need to make that connection.

Callous.

Asshole.

Unfeeling.

I can't be any of that tonight, not with her. Levi. *Aspen*.

Wrapping her legs around my waist, I prop myself up with a hand to the left of her head. Guide my cock to her pussy, already hissing between my teeth because I know this woman is going to ruin me forever as soon as I thrust inside.

"I'm big," I warn her, not cockily just stating the facts.

She hooks her hands over my shoulders. "I know."

"I'm not gonna be able to take it slow."

"I know that too."

"I'll try. I don't want to hurt you—"

"Stop talking and make me feel good, will you?"

This woman . . . she was made for me.

I enter her with a single stroke. Her nails dig into my shoulders, but I hardly feel it. I don't feel anything but the sensation of her tight pussy milking my dick. Needing to feel her walls clamp down on me again, I draw back and flex my hips forward.

"*Again*," she whimpers, her legs reflexively tightening around me. "Again."

So I do.

I hook one arm under one of her legs, hiking it up so I can thrust even deeper. With the flashlight uselessly pointing toward the copse of tress, I revel in the shadows cast by the moon overhead. The chance to be open without risk of being judged. I kiss Levi's chest. Her collarbone. I whisper in her ear, promising that I'm gonna deliver her straight to fucking heaven with an orgasm so good she'll never forget it.

She'll never forget *me.*

She clasps my face between my hands, kissing me squarely on the mouth as though she knows my features so well that she doesn't even need the light to find me. I suck on her tongue, and I piston my hips forward, and I silently damn myself for taking this step with her. There's no coming back from this moment. Each thrust feeds my addiction. Each gasp that leaves her mouth is another reason for me to make it my sole mission in life to see Levi come. Daily.

My mouth finds hers in a demanding kiss and for the first time in my life, I let myself *feel.* Feel the need that tightens my balls and puts my orgasm at the ready. Feel the way Levi isn't content with letting me put in all the work— her hips rise to meet mine, over and over again. Feel the emotion that surges forth when she whispers in my ear that she's never felt so good as she does underneath me.

Ruined.

It's the perfect word for how I feel when she comes around my cock, my name on her lips. I drive my hips forward, hitting her at the perfect angle, and there's no stopping the inevitable when her sex clenches my dick like a vise. With a guttural groan, I hurtle into the oblivion right along with her.

Her arms circle my back, sweeping her palms down my spine in a gentle gesture.

Safe.

The word settles in beside *ruin*, then kicks the latter to the curb. Try as I do to stifle it back into the dark depths of my soul, it flips me the bird with mocking gusto.

Levi threads her fingers through my hair.

And she breathes out a quiet laugh into my neck.

"You took a risk and got your reward," I murmur into her skin, that goddamn word refusing to take a hike and leave me alone. *Safe.* So stupid and silly, and yet I can't deny the shudder that wracks my limbs when she kisses my forehead. "How do you feel?"

"Like I'm on Cloud Nine."

"Good," I grunt. "That's real good."

But Levi is Levi, and I'm not surprised when she forces me to look up at her, even though I can't make out her features. "And how do you feel?" she asks.

I answer honestly, in the only way I know how: "I feel like I've won the Super Bowl all over again."

A soft kiss meets my forehead. "I know exactly what you mean."

Yeah. I knew she would.

26

ASPEN

"*M*om, can I drive to practice today?"

I meet my son's excited gaze as we pack up all our stuff for a day full of scrimmaging. Unfortunately for him, my stomach has formed a hard lump of *hell to the no.* I've yet to recover from the last time he got behind the wheel, and I'm not sure I ever will. Bikes are a good method of transportation. Eco-friendly, no revving engine . . . Really, they're perfect for fifteen-year-old boys determined to turn their mothers' hair completely gray.

"Mom? Can I?"

"You do remember what happened the last time you drove us, don't you?"

Topher tugs on his earlobe. "It's just a minor scratch. Plus, I promised Coach DaSilva I'd help out with his house to pay him back."

"You did?" I grab the car keys off the entryway table before Topher can get any fast ideas. "When?"

"The day he took me mini-golfing. You should come with us next time." Topher snags my duffel bag, as well as his own, and hikes them up onto his shoulders. The benefit of giving birth to sons who grow like weeds. "I totally caught onto his act when we played last weekend."

"What act?"

I'm starting to sound like a parrot—not that it stops me from asking questions. Since our night up on Cadillac Mountain late last week, Dominic and I have done our best to keep what's going on between us quiet. Although I'm not entirely sure what *is* going on. While our late-night phone calls and round-the-clock texting scream *It's a relationship!* there hasn't been ample opportunity to sort it all out. I spent the entire weekend with Topher, and there's been no more sneaking out all night on my part. Once was risky, twice was downright stupid but . . . three times? As tempted as I am to throw caution to the wind, I don't want Topher thinking that tiptoeing around is acceptable behavior.

Leading by example has never been more difficult.

Especially when my nosey, *sexy* next-door neighbor has made it a habit to knock on my bedroom window every evening for a midnight kiss out in my courtyard. A heady, toe-curling kiss that ends with my back pressed against my house and Dominic's thigh wedged between my legs. Twice now he's gotten me off that way, his hand clamped over my mouth to keep me quiet and a dry-humping session that leads straight to orgasmic oblivion.

Dominic DaSilva has made being bad feel so incredibly *good*.

With Topher ambling down the brick-cobbled walkway to my Honda, I shut the front door behind me and immediately scope out Dominic's driveway. His truck is gone, which means he's probably on his way to the school already. With a firm hand, I kick the anticipation of seeing him to the curb and unlock my car.

"Toph?"

We both climb in, him relegated to the passenger's side while I take the wheel. Cracking open a Gatorade bottle that he brought along, Topher guzzles half of it with all the aptitude of a teenager who doesn't care about a thing called calories. Swiping the back of his hand across his mouth, he leans back in the seat. "I mean, I could tell he was trying to go easy on me. He'd fake a hit and let the ball take five tries to make the hole, that sort of thing. At least, he did in the beginning."

"And by the end?" I ask, already sensing where this is going. After all, Dominic did call my baby boy a swindler. I've never been so proud.

"It was an all-out battle, Mom, and it was *awesome*! I still won because I don't think mini-golf is his thing, but he came up with all these crazy rules for us. Like, instead of trying to get a hole-in-one, we had to hit a specific bush on the course or skip the ball over a small stream. It was insane."

Insane. A word that seems to exclusively belong to Dominic alone.

After last weekend up on Cadillac Mountain, I think I've grown an affinity for the insane.

I think I've grown an affinity for him.

Or a crush. A *harmless* crush. Who wouldn't, though? The man's an enigma to those he doesn't know, and now that he's shown me pieces of himself, is it any wonder that I want to learn more? I mean, I never would have guessed by looking at him or even seeing him on TV that he has a secret love for photography.

Dominic is a puzzle comprised of mismatched pieces and I think he prefers it that way.

I slide a glance over to Topher, who's practically bouncing in his seat with excess energy. His leg jiggles up and down, his Gatorade going for a joy ride since it's balanced on his knee. "You seem to like him. Coach DaSilva, I mean."

"Oh, yeah. Did I tell you that he's letting me call him Dom when we aren't at practice?"

No, I definitely did *not* know that. "Is that so?"

"Yep! It was the spoils for whoever won at mini-golf. If I won, I could call him Dom."

"And if he won?"

"Which would never have happened because you taught me better," Topher says, cracking himself up. "But, yeah, if he won then he said that he got to take me and you out for dinner."

Like a date?

Butterflies flutter to life in my stomach. It's no good to think *what if*'s—Dominic hadn't won at mini-golf and after our heart-to-heart that day, he hadn't mentioned dinner. But still the thought of us sitting down at one of the little restaurants that line the shore brings a huge smile to my face.

Feeling giddy for the first time in years, I turn onto Main Street. "Maybe we could have Coach DaSilva over for dinner sometime this week? How does that sound?"

I don't remember the last time I've seen Topher brimming with such excitement. He blows up at the front of his hair, then gives up, exclaiming, "Ma, that would be so much fun. Maybe we can all play football on the street? You can show Dom how badass you are with the ball."

I pretend to hack up a lung at his B-bomb.

"Sorry," he mutters, swatting at his hair again, "I meant to say how *great* you are with the ball."

"Thank you." Lifting one hand off the wheel, I poke him in the side. "One day you can curse and do whatever you want, but today is not that day."

"Is it *ever*?"

I grin. If I had both hands free, I'd rub them together evilly. "Nope."

"Mom?"

At the trepidation in his voice, I glance over at him. "What's up, baby?"

"Is it wrong . . . is it bad of me that I had more fun hanging out with Coach DaSilva than I do with Dad?"

It's a good thing I'm not sharing any of that power drink because if I was, it'd be all over my dashboard. As it is, I come up spluttering all on my own. *Pull yourself together!* "Toph, bud, of course it's not wrong." Parenting needs to come with a rulebook. A how-to rulebook that tackles everything from changing diapers to the first time your kid asks about masturbating—that conversation nearly put me in an early grave—to times like now, when your kid feels guilty because his daddy is a prick and yet he still sticks up for him. Shaking my head to clear my thoughts, I add, "But you have to remember that every person has their own personality. Coach DaSilva might like to get out there and play mini-golf with you, but you can't forget how many hours you spent with your Dad playing video games. That's the thing you two do together, remember?"

Out of the corner of my eye, I watch my son slink down in the seat, dejection written all over his face. "I remember."

"And remember how he built that treehouse for you?"

"Mom, he hired someone to do that."

Dammit. He's so right. I quickly backtrack. "Of course he did. Because he wanted it to be the best treehouse you've ever seen. The best and the biggest. Your dad is many things, kid, but a builder is not one of them."

"He's also not a good husband."

Cue sudden heart attack. Including one almost side swerve into an innocent fire hydrant.

Think, think, *think!*

"Your dad's relationship with me has nothing to do with the one he has with you, okay? We might not be in love with each other anymore but make no mistake, baby, he loves *you*."

"I think he loves his mistresses more."

Forget the fire hydrant, suddenly Main Street has become a living, breathing whack-a-mole setting. Pedestrians are all over the place—tourists, from the looks of them—which means I've entered a game of *don't-hit-the-jaywalker* while my brain promptly hits the fritz. "Where in the world did you learn that word? Because I know I've never used it."

Topher side-eyes me like the teenager he is. "It's called the internet."

A visual of Not-Dominic having sex pops up into my head. Which totally proves my point when I argue, "I don't know what you're looking up on the internet, bud, but you're about to be slapped with a parental lock you'll never figure out how to take off."

"You're going to ban me from Buzzfeed?"

Goddamn Buzzfeed. What the hell is that site writing about nowadays, anyway? "Yes, yes I will. Especially if it has you slinging the word mistress around."

"But that's what they are!" His voice cracks and splinters my heart in the process. "Dad cheated on you and that's what they're called. I'm fifteen, Mom, not five."

It takes every effort on my part not to slam my head against the steering wheel repeatedly, all in the hope that I'll somehow turn back time and start this crappy Monday morning over again. "What your dad did is wrong, baby. I won't pretend otherwise. If you make a commitment to a person, it comes with expectations—loyalty and faithfulness being two of them. But none of that changes how he feels about you."

"Then why didn't he put up a fight when I said I wanted to move to London with you?"

Like a gaping fish, my mouth flaps open and closed.

Since the divorce and Topher's and my more recent move to Maine, I've always assumed that Rick made the decision he knew was best for Topher. Had our son stayed in Pittsburgh, he would have been left in the hands of babysitters more days than not. My in-laws passed within months of each other when I turned thirty-one, and Rick is an only child. Coming with me to London was in Topher's best interest—Rick knew that, I knew that, and although we fought about many different topics, who Topher would live with was never one of them.

Plus, it's not as though Rick contested in court when the matter of custody came up. He requested all major holidays —except for those when he travels with the Steelers—and I agreed.

Pulling into the school's parking lot, I find a free spot near the walkway down to the football field. After I park, I turn to Topher and plant my hand on the headrest of the passenger's seat. "Dad did what he thought was best for you. He travels all the time and if you'd stayed with him . . ." I reach up to push back those locks of hair that always fall in front of his eyes. "He misses you, Toph. I'm sure he's missing you right now, and if you don't think that, then you don't know your dad at all."

Topher eyes me like I've sprouted monkey ears and a bushy donkey's tail. Skepticism radiates from every one of his teenage pores and he doesn't even bother to hide his eye roll. "Sure, Mom. Okay."

He cranks open the car door, one foot already drifting out to freedom.

I grab his forearm before he can escape. Give him an encouraging smile that I hope alleviates the tension building within him. "How about you send him a picture of the field when you get down there, huh? Or even a video he can watch while he eats lunch at work."

My baby boy gives a half-hearted shrug. "I guess I could."

"You should. Maybe we can even make a team video today—something all the kids can show off to their parents. How does that sound?"

A little of Topher's earlier enthusiasm comes frolicking back. "We should do a choreographed dance. Something that will trend online."

I bop him playfully on the head. "What did I say about the internet?"

"No Buzzfeed. But this wouldn't be Buzzfeed!"

Topher Levi Clarke is nothing if not persuasive. Waving him off, I tell him I'll be right behind him.

I wait until he's out of sight and cutting around the corner to where the football field is, and then promptly call Rick. I don't make a habit of calling him often, unless it has something to do with Topher—and after this morning's conversation, Topher is my only priority.

This is not a social call.

My ex-husband's ringback sings in my ear, a four-string symphony soundtrack that I know he likes to use to make himself seem posh and elite. Truth is, Rick Clarke is a Detroit native who grew up with close to nothing and connived his way to the top of the sports management food chain. The man has more money than he could spend in a lifetime, women flinging themselves at him every hour of the day, even though he's in his mid-fifties now, and owns four houses across the country. To say nothing of his beloved private jet that he purchased when he received his seven-figure bonus with the Steelers. And yet he still can't find a single damn minute to call his son to say three simple words: *I love you.*

The violin takes on a solo run and I drum my fingers impatiently on my thigh.

It lurches back in with the rest of its orchestra family, only for unexpected knocking on my window to send my phone flying from my hands.

"Crap!"

I fumble for it midair, like I'm back in football, and catch it with a smooth one-handed grab.

"This is Rick Clarke, GM of the Pittsburgh Steelers. Leave a message after the beep and I'll get back to you when I can."

Knowing its futile—Rick rarely returns my phone calls —I flick my gaze to the window, only to see a stranger standing there, waving at me like a lunatic. I hold up a finger, pointing to my phone for the man to give me a second.

"Rick, it's me again. Aspen. I know you're probably busy, but please give Topher a call at some point today. I mentioned this the last time I called but he . . . he really misses you, and I think he'd feel better if he heard your voice. Two minutes, that's all he needs. All right, I'm gonna go. Please don't forget to call. Thanks."

With a placating smile to the gentleman, who's yet to stop waving at me, I toss my phone into my duffel, yank it out from the backseat and then maneuver myself out of the car.

I give the man a swift onceover: neatly parted brown hair, white T-shirt, jeans, sneakers. Totally normal-looking.

Maybe he's a football dad? Leveraging my work duffel higher up on my shoulder, I spare him another scrutinizing glance, taking note of the drawstring bag he's holding down by his side. "I'm so sorry, do we know each other?"

"Yes! Well, you don't know *me* exactly."

Because that's not creepy at all. I shoot a quick look over to where the fields are located, debating how fast I can run if it comes down to it. "Are you one of the parents?"

"Parents?" His eyes go comically wide. "Oh, the *parents*. Of the kids. Oh, no. I've sworn off children forever. Little devils, honestly. Don't you think?"

There have been multiple times in the last fifteen years that I've looked at my son and thought he might actually be the spawn of Satan—but coming from a stranger? That's not going to fly with me.

I hold up my hands in silent warning. "Listen, it's great to, uh, meet you, but I'm going to have to ask you to leave. Unless you're a parent to one of my players or a journalist looking to write an article about the team, you can't stay—"

"Oh, but I *am* a journalist!" Before I have the chance to turn away, or even process what's happening, a flash goes off in my face. "See? Totally a journalist." Another bright flash that causes little black dots to dance in my vision. "I read all about you in that *NESA* article—the one Deegan Homer wrote? After that, I just knew I had to come and talk to the Wildcats myself. Anyway, I'd love to do a quick interview with Dominic DaSilva. Is he around?"

The man tries to sidestep me.

Not on my watch.

In my sneakers, I'm as tall as he is, something I use to my advantage when I head him off and stand in his way. "You can't go down there."

That jovial grin on his face slowly goes flat. "It's public property. Sure I can."

Warning bells sound off in my head like BB guns gone wild.

"It's a *school*, Mr. Whoever-You-Are, so no you can't go down there. Do you have written permission from our athletic director for an interview? I bet you don't, which means if you even *think* about cutting around me, I'll have cops out here so fast you won't even know what hit you."

Simply to prove that I'm willing to back my talk with a whole lot of action, I riffle through my bag for my phone. 9-1-1. I hover a finger over the green telephone, fully prepared to send this crazy dude straight to the Mount Desert Island county jail. "Don't test me. I'll do it."

He mutters something unflattering under his breath. Takes a single step back. "You know, when I read that article about you in *NESA*, I figured you were a lesbian. A girl coach? Yeah, you gotta be into pussy."

What? Does he think I haven't heard that before? I spent almost all of high school with every guy thinking I was into chicks. I dealt with Rick, who, when drunk, liked to tell me that he knew the reason why I was such a "dead fish" in bed: because I was secretly lesbian. Apparently, that was as far as his creativity went for explaining my increasing lack of attraction to him. Rick's self-worth is as inflated as his bank account.

Men can be such narcissists.

Tempted as I am to raise my hands like claws, just to see if the man will go screaming in the other direction, I lower my finger, hovering just above the call button. "Not to cut this heart-to-heart short, but I've got about a gazillion other things I'd rather be doing. Talking to you is not one of them."

Another flash goes off in my face. It's so disorienting I jerk my chin back, blinking repeatedly. Who the hell does this guy think he is? The friggin' camera police?

"*Seriously*?" I snap angrily. "I tried to play nice, but game time is officially over. You need to leave. Right now."

He whirls around, drawstring bag smacking against his thigh as he breaks into a quick-paced jog. One minute I'm debating the merits of chasing after him to tackle him to the ground, and the next I'm watching nothing but taillights as he revs his engine like a total tool and speeds onto the main road like the devil itself is chasing down his car.

I push away the mental image of a bunch of children dancing around a bonfire dressed in Halloween devil costumes, then immediately turn for the fields.

During my marriage to Rick, I watched players for the Steelers be hounded by the media. On the rare occasion that I attended an event with my ex-husband, it was hard to miss the so-called journalists who stood outside on the road, snapping pictures of whatever they could.

But I've never experienced the paparazzi phenomena for myself. I purposely stayed away from the craziness of celebrity athlete culture and stuck to what I did best: coaching middle school football and then later the high schoolers of a small town just outside of Pittsburgh. The only people who cared about those kids were their parents, the nearby rival teams, and the local newspaper that usually dedicated a single column to Hancock High's wins and losses.

London High is similar to Hancock in that way.

There's only one variable between the Tigers and the Wildcats. A man who dresses in all black, wears a tattered baseball cap that has seen better days, and has a body that could make an angel weep.

"Hey," he calls out now, jogging over to me from where he was leading the team warm-up. "Everything all right? Topher got here almost twenty minutes ago."

I meet Dominic's concerned gaze. "Houston, we have a problem and that problem is . . . you."

27

DOMINIC

"*I*'ll resign."

Brien shoots me an exasperated look. "You're not resigning." He glances over to Levi, who is camped out in the chair next to mine. "How was practice today?"

"Practice was great. The kids are doing great. I'm doing great." She turns in her chair to face me, a *don't-mess-with-me* look hardening her expression. "*You're* not quitting."

Jesus fuck, not her too.

Reaching up for my hat, I toss it on Brien's desk, then scrub my hands over my face. "You guys really think that douchebag from earlier is going to be the last pap to show up here? If you do, then you're delusional."

Levi snatches one of my hands and tugs it away from my jaw. She watches me earnestly, a hopeful gleam in her blue eyes. "All we need to do is reconfigure the way we do things. Just because one jerk showed up in town doesn't mean we're about to face down the White Walkers."

Though it feels absurd given the severity of the situation, I can't help but laugh at her pop-culture reference. "Are you really comparing the paparazzi to an undead army from *Game of Thrones*?"

Her playful smile nearly knocks the wind out of me. "You have a problem with that?"

"Not even a little."

Brien bangs a fist down on his desk, then looks from me to Levi and then back to me again. He wags a finger, pointing to each of us. "What's going on here?"

Levi's hand untangles from mine. "Nothing! Definitely nothing."

I don't remember reading the contract I signed well enough to know if sleeping with a coworker is on the Don't Do This list. I'll have to look for my copy, which is somewhere in my house buried beneath all sorts of equipment in prep of Nick coming up this weekend to help with some of the major renovations.

"You two are getting along surprisingly well," Brien drawls, finally taking his seat. "Which is yet another reason why you can't quit, DaSilva. One pap isn't gonna make a difference down the line."

"It's never only one, though." Hands on my thighs, I inhale sharply. "They're like vultures circling. They show up at your house, at your gym, *in* your gym. Thanks to that *Celebrity Tea Presents* asshole, they all know I'm here in London."

"*Celebrity Tea Presents*?" asks Levi, her brows raised in question. "I don't think I've ever heard of them."

"It's a him," I say. "An anonymous him but a him nonetheless."

Brien swivels his chair toward the desktop monitor. His fingers fly across the keyboard—he taught typing here at London High before moving over to the sports department —before he exclaims, "Here we go. *Celebrity Tea Presents*.

First thing that pops up on Google."

"No surprise there," I mutter. "He's the leech on all of Hollywood."

"Uh, guys?"

At Brien's uneasy tone, I jerk my gaze up. "What is it?"

He doesn't say a word, only turns the monitor so both Levi and I can get a good look at the screen. One glimpse of the headline and my stomach sinks like a rock free-falling down to the bottom of the ocean.

"*Celebrity Tea Presents:* **BREAKING NEWS** *Is* Put A Ring On It's *Dominic DaSilva Mending His Broken Heart By Sleeping with A Married Woman?*"

Silence permeates the office for only a half-second before Levi's voice fills it. Only, it's not Levi sitting next to me who's talking but a clip of her on the computer screen: "*Not to cut this heart-to-heart short, but I've got about a gazillion other things I'd rather be doing. Talking to you is not one of them.*"

The footage cuts to her livid expression—blazing blue eyes, pursed mouth, furrowed brows—before swerving down and zooming in on the concrete, as though the person with the camera is taking off.

Beside me, Levi scoots to the front of her seat, bracing her hands on the desk. "How did he get that I'm *married*? I haven't even worn my wedding band in three years."

Three years. Is that how long it's been since she decided to divorce Clarke? As much as I want to pause the conversation and ask, I cut straight to the chase: "I doubt the pap even knows who you are. It's clickbait, simple as that. The dude that showed up here probably sent whatever he had over to *Celebrity Tea Presents* the minute he left the school. Then Mr. Anonymous Asshole himself whipped together an article he knows will stop people mid-scroll."

Her fingers curl into a fist. "Adam, read the rest."

My college buddy winces. "I don't think I should."

"Yes, you should." Levi stares him down, unblinking. "Or I'll come over there and read it for myself."

Scratching his ear, Brien sighs. "You're as stubborn as your dad was, you know that?"

"I'll take that as a compliment. Now read."

Hand to the monitor, Brien angles it toward him. "Okay. Buckle up, kiddos, here we go." With a click of his mouse, he leans forward and clears his throat. "*Dear Reader, let me start off by saying YOU ROCK! I put out the call, hoping that one of you might be able to find out more deets on our favorite football player, Dominic DaSilva, and not only did one L.A. native come through but he did so in style!*" Brien glances over at me. "At least you're his favorite football player?"

Unceremoniously, I scratch my forehead with my middle finger. "You're more than welcome to take my place whenever you want."

"I'll pass, thanks." He scrunches his nose, ducking his head out of the way like he's trying to avoid the curse of my middle finger. "Okay, where were we?"

"Finding out why the hell they think I'm married," Levi cuts in, tension radiating from every inch of her. "Hopefully sometime before I turn thirty-eight."

Brien quirks a half-smile. "How close are you?"

"Stop procrastinating, will you?"

He leans his head one way, cracking his neck, then does so in the other direction. "Sorry, I'm one of those people who *hates* awkwardness. It's worse than nails on a chalkboard." As if sensing our mutual impatience, he breaks down. "Fuck it, okay! Okay. You asked for it. He then writes, *According to our source, who flew all the way to London, Maine, in the name of spilling the tea, DaSilva is romantically involved with the woman seen in the video posted above. Who is she? Our source didn't get her name, but a little reverse image search, tagged with some online digging from yours truly, reveals her name to be Aspen Clarke, wife of Richard Clarke. If you're like me and thinking, who the F is Richard Clarke? Never fear, Google is here to save the day. Clarke is the long-time general manager of the Pittsburgh Steelers, and, are you ready for some extra hot TEA? At one point, DaSilva was even in talks with the Steelers for a trade. Our source claims he witnessed both DaSilva and Aspen at a local hotspot over the weekend. Picture of the very obvious canoodling session is below. Now, before I wrap up our daily dose of hot football gods, may I just add . . . the tea may be spilled but a scandal is a-brewing, ladies and gents. Stay tuned for more updates. Also . . . Savannah Rose who?"*

Brien hasn't even stopped reading before I breathe out, "For fuck's sake."

Is nothing sacred anymore? Is there no place in the world that a guy can escape to without having to worry about being stalked by a hoard of fame-seeking assholes? More importantly, who the hell is willing to bend their morals so badly that they'll gladly ruin an innocent woman's life for the sake of clicks on a virtual page?

Levi doesn't deserve this shit.

I open my mouth, fully prepared to tell her exactly that, when Brien stomps right over me: "I'll ask you both one more time. Are you two sleeping together?"

Shit. Fuck. *Dammit.*

At any other time in my life, I wouldn't think twice about coming clean. But coming clean puts Levi's job on the line. While I don't need the money, she does. I won't be the reason she gets fired today.

"No."

"Yes, we are."

My gaze darts to her stubborn, beautiful face. "*Aspen.* What the hell are you doing?"

She doesn't spare me a glance. "It was one time," she announces blithely, like she's discussing the color of her shirt or what she ate for dinner or anything, really, besides the fact that we fucked on top of a mountain and it was the best experience of my life. "But yes, we had sex."

The tension in my neck increases tenfold. "Brien, what she's trying to tell you—and is failing at, by the way—is—"

"And I'd like to have sex with him again."

"Jesus fucking Christ," I grunt, my knuckles digging into my eye sockets. When I drop my hands three seconds later, the office hasn't changed. Brien still looks shell-shocked, Levi is calm as can be, and I . . . I want to pour myself a beer and pretend this isn't happening. "He's going to fire you, you know that, right?"

Levi pats my forearm consolingly. "He won't."

"He will."

"*He's* sitting right here," Brien butts in, his expression, for once, unreadable.

Folding one leg over the other at the knee, Levi leans in close to me. "Want to know how I got this job?" she says, not even bothering to keep her voice low.

"Football."

"That, and also because I teach History."

I blink, slowly. "Probably one too many concussions to the head over the years, but I'm not following."

Levi's chin tilts toward Brien. "Tell him who also teaches History here at London High."

One great, big sigh that I swear I can feel from this side of the desk. "My wife does. *Did.*" At my blank stare, he clarifies, "We decided at the end of the school year that she should stay home with the kids going forward. We were paying through the roof for babysitters and daycare and, honest to God, but she's been wanting to grow this knitting club she started—"

"With my mom," Levi pipes up, a finger raised. "They're obsessed."

Brien's shoulders droop. "So obsessed."

"I think they use it as an excuse to get everyone together and drink wine all night."

"Either that or they're calling in male strippers."

I hold up a hand. "Wait. Hold on. Forget about the male strippers for a second." I look at my old LSU roommate-slash-teammate. "I didn't realize you worked with Sara. You told me that you two met at the gym."

Levi elbows me in the side. "The *school* gym. Which means if they can hook up and then get married with no penalties from the school, we can do the same." When my eyes widen, she hastily adds, "Hook up. *Hook up.* Who said anything about marriage?"

Brien taps the desktop monitor. "Technically, this guy did."

"Well, I'm not—married, that is. Maybe I should send this *Celebrity Tea Presents* fellow my divorce papers? Along with the bill for how much my damn lawyer cost me?"

Although my brain is still locked on the M-word, I shake my head. "Won't do any bit of good. Once he sinks his teeth in, it's game over."

She nibbles on her bottom lip, and damn if my cock doesn't stir with interest. "I don't think I like this guy."

I laugh, head tipped back. "Join the club, Coach. Join the fucking club."

"So, what do we do then?"

A month ago, I ran. I ran all the way from California to Maine, hoping I'd find some semblance of normality in a tiny town situated on a strip of beachfront property. I don't think what I've found comes close to being normal, but running again means leaving Levi, and for the first time in my life, I don't want to see myself out the door.

It's not love.

I don't know what love is. But Levi feels like safety and the biggest adrenaline high I've ever encountered, all rolled into one.

So I'm not going anywhere.

I settle my hat back on my head, squaring off the brim, and then fold my arms over my chest. "We're gonna get to fundraising so we can take the team on that camping trip you want to happen so badly. And we're gonna do it in a big way—with a calendar spread."

"Oh, Good God," Brien groans, closing his eyes. "I heard about that. DaSilva, I might turn a blind eye to you and Levi doing whatever the hell you're doing together, but I'm sure as shit not signing off on a calendar that has you wearing nothing but an appropriately placed sock."

"I'm not talking about me or that stupid sock."

"The team," Levi murmurs from beside me, "you're talking about the team and then with you as the—"

I nod.

Yeah, with me as the photographer.

Refusing to acknowledge the way my heart pounds a little too fast, I ask roughly, "You in?"

The curve of her smile is the sweetest encouragement I've ever felt. "Will there be sharks and bears?"

"I'll see what I can come up with."

"Then yes," she murmurs, "I'm in."

28

ASPEN

*T*he boys on the team are beyond ecstatic about the chance to sell calendars with their faces on them.

Their mothers, on the other hand? Not so much.

Sitting at my kitchen table, I flip to the next parent signature form and spy another scribbled comment at the bottom corner of the page: *Any chance Coach DaSilva will go shirtless, at least? ~ Belinda Wilde.*

Wilde. Wild. How fitting.

Cross-checking with my spreadsheet, I tick off Matthew Wilde from my list, marking him as good to go. Then I return to the forms, moving onto the next. This time the note is scribbled beside the date: *Let me know if you need any help with anything. In college, I always helped my sorority with putting together our fundraisers. P.S., wine date soon? – Meredith.*

I worried about returning home to London. I was gone for so long that returning felt a bit like London was an alien planet and I had no idea if my oxygen would work here.

Over the last month, it's gradually begun to feel like home again.

Would it feel that way if it weren't for Dominic?

The thought is completely unbidden, but I turn it over in my head anyway. In the grand scheme of things, I haven't known my next-door neighbor for long at all. A matter of weeks, person to person. Years, I guess, if you take into account all those times Rick brought him up in conversation, long before Dominic retired from the NFL.

That Dominic and my Dominic feel like two completely different people.

My Dominic.

I certainly don't own him, and I'm not even sure we're dating. Isn't that something I should talk to Topher about first? Sure, he *likes* Dominic—as a coach and a friend. If Dominic and I make things official, he would be . . . a stepdad. Maybe. One day. If things get that far, which I'm not sure they ever will.

That would entail Dominic sticking around long-term. While I know he's feeling the London vibes right now, who's to say that he'll want to stay forever?

Ignoring the way my heart palpitates at the prospect of him leaving, I turn to the next form. No pointed comment this time, thank you, universe, but wait . . . I drag the paper closer, my glasses slipping down the bridge of my nose, and look from student signature to parent signature.

Harry Blackwater.

Heather Blackwater.

I lean back in my chair, turning my head to call out, "Topher! Baby, can you come in here a second?"

"*Mooommm!* What did we say about you calling me baby?" he shouts back, seconds before I hear his feet moving across the hardwood floor in the hallway. A second pair of footsteps join in—Timmy came over to hang out today—before they're both standing in the entryway to the kitchen.

The younger boy shifts his hands behind his back, like he's standing in military formation. "I told Chris that I think it's cool that you still call him baby. My mom calls me *hey, you.*"

My brows shoot up. "Chris?"

"Yeah." Completely oblivious to my confusion, Timmy points to Topher. "He's been trying it out. Seeing if he likes it as a nickname."

Topher grimaces. "Ma, it's just that . . ." His hands come up, wringing together. "Okay, so when I went mini-golfing with Dom-*Coach* DaSilva, I asked him what he thought about my name."

"Why in the world would you do that?"

"Because he's a *guy*, Mom. And even if you haven't noticed it, some of the seniors make fun of it. Topher, I mean."

"What he's saying is that they make fun of him for answering to the nickname Topher," Timmy explains, his head bobbing up and down. "I get it. I want to go by Tim, but I can't get anyone to jump on board. It *sucks.*"

My gaze volleys back to my son, who's watching me like I should *totally* be getting where he's coming from. His eyes implore me to understand when he continues, "So I asked Coach DaSilva, like, what do you think about my name? And he said, *It's not bad.* But I could hear it in his voice that he was acting, just like when he pretended to be bad at mini-golf, so I asked him again, and this time he goes, *Listen, kid, I'm not one to talk because I don't even know who I'm named after or if my mom just picked Dominic out of a hat, but Topher . . . Topher's a bit of a pansy name. Chris is strong, though. Manly.*"

A pansy name.

If Dominic were standing in front of me right now, I'd punch him in the gut. *Stepdad*? The man can't even pull himself together to tell a kid that he's perfect as he is!

"Topher," I start slowly, choosing my words carefully, "you can't go by the name Chris."

"Sure I can." He grins widely at me, all teenage confidence. "It's called choosing your own identity. I want to be a Chris."

I choke back a laugh. "You can't. I mean, you can later on if you want but it's going to take time and money." When he only stares at me, confusion shining in his blue eyes, I say, "Topher is your given name on your birth certificate, buddy. Not Christopher. Not Chris. Just Topher."

"Just Topher," he echoes as though in a fog.

"Man, that sucks," Timmy says, punching my son in the arm. "I can still call you Chris, if you want? No one has to know."

"But I'll know." Topher drops his arms to his side in complete defeat. "Mom always says it's not good to lie. It's beneath us."

That's my baby boy.

"Speaking of not lying . . ." Gesturing for him to come forward, I point to Harry Blackwater's parent form. These signatures . . . they are way too similar to simply be a coincidence. The block letters are more in tune with a sixteen-year-old boy's handwriting than an adult woman's penmanship. "Mrs. Blackwater. Has Harry mentioned anything about her?"

Topher and Timmy exchange a look, and my Mom radar goes haywire.

I point to the chairs opposite me. "Sit."

Grumbling, Topher plops down into the closest chair. "You weren't supposed to find out."

"I told you we should have had someone else fake her signature," Timmy mutters out of the corner of his mouth. "My mom would have done it."

From where I'm sitting, this does not look good.

"Would have done *what*, Tim? Sign Harry's release form?"

When his lips clamp shut, I home in on my own kid. "Topher. What's wrong with Heather Blackwater?"

"There's nothing *wrong* with her, exactly," Topher says, squirming in his chair, "it's just that—"

"Don't break the Bro Code!" Timmy hisses, lightly punching Topher in the arm again. "You promised Harry."

"We don't lie in this house." I lift a brow, daring Topher to argue otherwise. "So you're going to tell me why I'm looking at two signatures that have clearly been signed by the same person, and you're going to tell me right now."

Topher, recognizing my hard tone, visibly caves. Shoulders slumped, he whispers, "Mrs. Blackwater said she had to take care of something in Portland. That's what she told Harry, anyway. She's been gone two weeks."

"And Harry's dad?" I ask, even though I already know I'm not going to like the answer.

"He died a few years ago. Harry said he was real sick."

I look at both boys, flicking my gaze between the two of them. "And where has Harry been staying for the last two weeks?"

"With me and Mom," Timmy answers quietly, "and with Bobby, and also with Kevin. We ask our parents if he can spend the night and they say yes."

They say yes.

Meanwhile, they have no idea what exactly they're saying yes to.

I push my seat back. "C'mon, we're going for a ride."

Timmy blanches. "You're not bringing me home, are you? I'm sorry we lied. But my mom . . . my mom—"

Not wanting to freak him out, I cross over to his side and pull him in for a quick hug. I may be a coach to these boys, but some of them need so much more than a person to tell them to do another round of push-ups. "I'm not sending you home, kid. Your mom is working late in Bar Harbor, I know. You can still sleep over."

His frame relaxes immediately. "Thank you, Coach. No more lying. I mean it."

"I'm holding you to that."

I usher both teenage boys into my car with Topher settling in the passenger's seat. Shoving his phone forward, so I can plug it into my dashboard, Timmy asks for me to play some random band that I've never heard of before.

Against the backdrop of what used to be called techno music and is now, according to the boys in my car, referred to as EDM, I put my plan into motion: "Now which one of you is going to tell me whose house Harry is staying at tonight?"

"Kevin's," they answer in unison.

"Great! Now buckle up, boys, and someone tell me where to go."

I don't know what I'm doing here.

I don't know what my plan is, save for bringing Harry back to my place. That's as far as I've gone in my head.

But all I can visualize are my friend Mariah's three adopted children, all of whom were left to fend for themselves before they ended up in Pittsburgh's foster-care system. I remember their hopeful faces the first time I met them, before the adoptions were finalized, when they tried as hard as they could to be invisible in Mariah's house. Like if she didn't hear them, if she didn't see them, then maybe she wouldn't send them away.

I can't imagine leaving a random child that I don't know to survive on their own, never mind one of my own players. It goes against everything I believe in. I coach because I want to teach these kids responsibility. I coach because I want them to have the life skills—football and otherwise—to reach for their dreams while simultaneously learning when to push hard on the gas pedal and when to ease up and enjoy the view. I coach because I love kids—their enthusiasm and their hopes and dreams—and because after Topher's birth, Rick refused to have another baby.

Topher's enough for me, he always said.

I think the truth is much more convoluted, though I know I stayed with him early on in our marriage because I hoped he would change his mind. And because I refused to believe that he had so blatantly lied to me when we first met.

What man marries a woman and vows to fill every day with happiness and love, only to take pleasure in tearing it all down?

Rick Clarke.

Who knowingly makes his wife miserable and then won't even agree to sign the divorce papers, year after year?

Rick "the Prick" Clarke, that's who.

It was only by chance that I found out one of my players at Hancock High needed to swap school districts because of a change in foster homes. Unwilling to let my player go without fighting for him to stay within Hancock town lines, I sought out Mariah's contact with child services. The male social worker never touched me, nothing more than to shake my hand, but Rick came home to the two of us sitting at the kitchen table together and went off on a bender.

He brought two women home that night—the first time he ever broke his hotel-only cheating policy—and Topher found his dad in bed with them the very next morning.

I filed for divorce two weeks later.

Miracle of all miracles, Rick finally stopped putting up a fight.

"Mom?" Topher asks from beside me. "What are you going to do when we get to Kevin's?"

I keep my gaze locked on the darkening road ahead of the car. "I'm going to bring Harry home."

Our home.

At least until I figure out what's going on with Heather Blackwater.

29

DOMINIC

$\mathcal{T}$he lights are on at Levi's place when I pull into my driveway.

I look over at the two pizza boxes sitting on my passenger's seat. Funny what a few weeks can do for a person's mood when life isn't taking a massive shit on you. Or maybe it's got nothing to do with the universe playing nice and everything to do with playing nice with the sexy woman next door.

With only three days left to go until the calendar shoot, I've been all over London introducing myself to local business owners. Though my photography has always been reserved for mostly landscapes and architecture of the locations I've visited over the last four years, I'm strangely pumped up about trying something new.

And what I really want to see are the Wildcats playing ball all over the city.

In my head, it's a fucking masterpiece. Players getting ready to hike the ball inside London's infamous Cookies and Joe Diner that dates back to the 1950's. In another shot, I want Harry, the football whisperer, in mid-throw at

the base of the Ferris wheel down by the pier while
Topher, seated on the Ferris wheel, pretends to catch the
football. Maybe have Bobby and some of the D-men lined
up on the beach, the sand kicking up as they move in
formation.

The calendar may have started as a joke centered
around me and my dick, but I'm running with the overall
idea and thinking of ways that include both my team and
London life.

I know not every kid will make the JV or varsity cut, but
football—for me—gave me my first family. It's a bond
created not by blood but by common interests, and if I can
do something to help these kids find that family . . . then,
yeah, I'm gonna pull out all the stops.

Stops that included calling my old Sports 24/7 boss,
Steven Fairfax, to see if he might be willing to run a special
about the calendar and, on a much larger scale, high school
football across the country.

And even though I hate the man's guts for firing me, for
something the network forced me to undertake, I'm thrilled
he said yes.

Yes.

Three little letters that'll guarantee we sell enough
calendars that every kid on the team will be able to make
the camping trip without needing to ask their parents for a
dime.

I grab the celebratory pizza boxes, then jump out of my
truck.

There's a pep to my step as I head for Levi's brick walkway. I have the entire weekend mapped out, including
someone to do their hair. Not that any of the boys need a
haircut, but, hey, maybe some of them will want one after I
introduce them to Nick's fiancée, Mina, who is a hairstylist

down in Boston. Once I unloaded my plans on Nick, Mina happily agreed to come along and help out too.

Stepping onto Levi's taco-themed welcome mat, I ring the doorbell and hang back, pizza boxes tucked under one arm.

"Coming!"

The door swings open a moment later, and, with a wide grin on my face, I lean my shoulder against the frame. "We've got to stop meeting like this, Coach," I drawl.

Levi doesn't laugh like I expect her to, though she does smile weakly when she takes in the pizza boxes. "Food?"

I quickly scope out the entryway above her head. No Topher. Not wasting a moment, I cradle her face with my free hand and lower my mouth to hers. Heat flares up within me, and it's all I can do not to throw the pizza into the nearby hedges and kiss her the way I want to.

All-consuming, with her straddling my face while I feast on that hot pussy of hers.

My cock stiffens in my shorts.

Cursing under my breath, I pull back and touch my forehead to hers. "I have good news."

Her blue eyes search mine. "I have . . . I have—" Her fingers grip my T-shirt, coiling the fabric sharply between her knuckles. "I have a Harry."

My brows pull together. "The football whisperer? Harry's in your house?"

"Is that really what you call him?"

"The kid's gonna go far, Asp. If there's one thing I know how to spot after all these years, it's natural skill. Harry has it in spades."

That makes her pause. "And Topher? Does he have it too?"

I kiss her forehead gently. "Sometimes natural skill can

get you in trouble—you lack the hustle. Topher's like me. Dogged determination. Aggressive ambition. There's no right or wrong way up the ladder. It all comes down to sheer will and hard work." Fingers brushing her hip, I murmur, "You know how that goes, Ms. Lou Groza. Not every day someone I know has won the award for the best kicker in the NCAA."

A pretty blush stains her cheeks. "You looked me up?"

"Had to know what sort of talent I was up against. I'm a little disappointed LSU and BC never played against each other in the bowl game. Just imagine the meet cute we could have had if we'd run into each other years ago."

It's a solid attempt to make her laugh and it works. Her smile brightens even as she rolls her eyes. "The fact that you said *meet cute* is right up there with *dillydally*."

"Speak for yourself, Ms. Lollygag."

"I think I like Ms. Lou Groza better."

I step forward, pushing her back into the house. "I knew you would. You're as competitive as I am. I'm still bruised from the night we went swimming. Do you know how pointy your elbows are?"

"You big baby."

I glance over at her, not even bothering to hide my shit-eating grin. "Endearments, huh? Imagine what you'll be calling me after I make you come again."

"*Dominic!*"

"Nah, we've already reached a first-name basis, Aspen." I sidestep around her, pizza boxes raised high, so I don't knock her knickknacks off the entryway table. "Now how about we take this to the kitchen table. Call in Topher and Harry. We'll figure out whatever is going on."

"Tim is here too."

"Timmy, you mean?"

She gives a loose-limbed shrug. "He wants to be called Tim now." She pauses, hand on my arm. "By the way, did you happen to tell Topher that he's got a . . . how did he put it? *A pansy name*?"

The grin I give her is all boyish innocence. "Pansy name? Nah, Coach, that wasn't me." Her eyes narrow suspiciously and I bop her on the nose, just to mess with her. "I believe the way I phrased it to him was, *what kind of hippie-dippie name is that*?"

She rubs her hand over her mouth, raking her gaze up and down my frame like she doesn't know what to do with me. "I should hate you for telling my son to go by the name Chris."

"Now *that* I didn't say. The only Chris's I've ever met are douchebags."

"Is that so?"

"No," I murmur, trying hard not to laugh, "but you hated me less for a solid ten seconds when I said that, didn't you?"

"I . . . I—"

I lift my brows, waiting. "You . . . ?"

"You're a piece of work."

"A work in progress," I counter with a wink. "Ninety-percent completed, ten-percent chaos."

She shakes her head, her blond hair falling forward to frame her face. "Ten-percent chaos. There must be something dreadfully wrong with me that that's the part of you I like best."

"I'm willing to roll the dice and say that you don't regret that fact at all."

I REGRET EVERYTHING.

At the very least, I regret not having a beer to pop open once Harry sits down at the table and spills the beans.

"Harry," Levi interjects, her pizza all but forgotten on her plate, "I don't understand. Why would your mom leave in the first place?"

The football whisperer shovels pizza into his mouth like he hasn't eaten in days. Which is entirely possible, given the fact that he's been couch-surfing at all of his teammates' houses. "I don't think she left-left. She . . . she does this sometimes. But she always comes back."

He glances at Timmy, as though looking for backup. Clearly wanting to help his buddy out, Timmy bobs his head in confirmation. "I think she's sad. Ever since your dad . . . you know."

Finding out Harry's dad passed away from a heart attack the same year I retired from the NFL felt like a punch to the gut. For as long as I've been wandering the world, looking for something that makes me feel alive, this kid has been trying to find a safe place to call home. Red-haired, green-eyed, and pale-skinned, he's the polar opposite of me in every single way.

And yet, when he looks at me, I see myself staring back. The eleven-year-old version of myself. The hunger. The fear. The desperation that led me to do stupid things because I wanted to fit in—to find a family—and also because I was so damn tired of being shuffled from house to house, San Francisco suburb to San Francisco suburb.

Until one day, a group of older boys asked me to rob a convenience store with them. They wanted the money from the register. I didn't know what I wanted. Money didn't sound like a bad idea. Money meant food, security, brotherhood—at least, it did if I ran with those kids.

They handed me a gun and I took it.

Like an eleven-year-old idiot, who thinks he knows everything there is to know about the world.

I stormed into that convenience store, trembling all the way down to my tattered shoes, and pointed the gun at the clerk. Like I was some big, bad baller who mugged people instead of the parentless, oftentimes homeless kid whose stomach growled late at night and who had only ever known the comfort of a couch and never a bed.

Unfortunately, waving guns around like I did is a sure-fire, guaranteed way to find yourself in juvenile detention. It's also a first-step indoctrination to things like wearing ankle monitors because society deems you a criminal, skipping school when the "boys" need you to help them out with risky, stupid shit, and learning, the hard way, that making something of yourself after years of only making trouble will be a herculean task you'll fail more times than not.

Feeling like there's an anvil on my chest that I can't shake off, I grind out, "You don't want to be me, kid."

Everyone at the table, including Levi, looks at me.

Grasping the glass of milk from beside my plate, I pretend it's a Bud Light and drain it in one go. "My dad died, too." Drug overdose, from what I understand. I found it in the San Francisco online newspaper archives when I was at LSU. "I was two at the time. I never knew him."

"Coach," Harry says, pizza slice hovering halfway to his mouth, "I'm sorry, but I don't know what that has to do with me."

"Let him tell you this."

It's Levi who utters the words, and I search out her gaze diagonal from me. *Thank you*, I want to tell her. And sure enough, it's like I can read her without speaking. *I have you*, those blue eyes of hers tell me. *I have you and I trust you.*

I swallow, hard. Drop my eyes to my untouched pizza before I push the plate away. "What little I know of my mother isn't fit for mixed company. But she left when I was five and never came back."

"My mom will come back," Harry cuts in vehemently. "She always comes back. Sometimes she needs some time away to think—to, I don't know, do whatever she does, but she never leaves for that long."

I don't beat around the bush. "Has she ever been gone for two weeks before?"

Slowly, Harry shakes his head. He whispers, "No," like it's the last thing he wants to admit.

"And I bet this time, when she was gone longer than expected, you stayed in your house alone, didn't you?"

Harry's eyes don't waver from my face. "Yeah."

"How long?"

"Six days. That's . . . that's the longest she's ever been gone before."

It takes me a moment to realize that Levi has gathered up Topher and Timmy and left the kitchen. Their plates are gone, along with one of the pizza boxes, and I want to thank her for giving Harry privacy. A cataclysmic moment like this isn't easy to admit even to yourself, never mind in front of a group of people.

When I hear Topher's familiar voice shushing someone, I know they haven't gone far. The three of them are probably listening in, and that's okay too. Harry's gonna need people in his corner and he can't go wrong in trusting Levi or Topher. Timmy, too. At practice, I've watched the younger boy take a page out of Topher's book and talk to the teammates who tend to stick to themselves.

Taking off my ball cap, I toss it on the table and run a hand through my hair. "Harry, I don't know how much you know about all of this, but you can't keep crashing on your friends' couches."

"I know." His ears turn a burnished red that matches the color of his hair. "And I know that you and Coach Levi are gonna need to tell the police about what's going on."

I remember the first time the cops walked into our tired apartment with its creaky steps and moldy walls. I'd stayed there for a little under a month before a neighbor reported my mom as missing. She wasn't missing—just chose a different lifestyle, one that didn't include her five-year-old son. The police had all agreed that it was a miracle I'd survived that long. But that was me to a T: scrappy and resilient to the bitter end.

"We'll go down there together," I tell Harry, keeping my tone level, the same way I always talked to the kids who matched with Junior Buccaneers. Like frightened animals, kids can be skittish. I know I used to be. "Me and you. How's that sound?"

"Did they take you away?" His shoulders curl in tightly, a sixteen-year-old reduced to the emotions of someone so much younger. I know how he feels. Acutely. "When the police came, did they put you in . . . foster care?"

There's little point in lying to him. "Yeah, Harry, they did. But I was only five. No dad, a mom who had left for good. No other family to take me in. Our situations aren't nearly the same. Your aunt, she comes to some of the practices, doesn't she?"

Looking startled, as if surprised to know I've been paying attention, Harry bites down on his thumb. "Yeah. My great-aunt. She's . . . weird."

Weird isn't synonymous with awful. Clearly, the woman cares enough about her great-nephew to show up to our scrimmages and cheer him on. "Does she know that your mom leaves?" When Harry shakes his head, I sigh. "Kid, just because she's weird doesn't mean she's not family. What's so weird about her?"

"Her house smells like cat pee."

Unfortunate, but not the end of the world. "What else?"

Harry flicks his gaze away from my face, as though he's thinking hard on that. "She really, *really* likes takeout."

I bark out a laugh. "Harry, most of the world prefers takeout. You know how well this pizza joint knows me?" I point to the boxes. "I order out from them at least three times a week."

"She also has dolls! Weird, creepy dolls. Coach, I swear their beady little eyes follow me whenever I sleep at her house."

I can't stem the laughter reverberating in my chest. It rolls out of me, boisterous and hearty. "Do they talk?" I manage on a short breath.

"I think some of them do . . . maybe. One time, when I was a kid, I ripped out their batteries and they still didn't stop talking. Aunt Gloria is *weird*."

"Well, we can't have you staying there then." I bump a fist against the table, rattling my silverware. "Who knows, kid? One day you might be at practice when those dolls kidnap you to another planet."

Finally, that pinched, fearful look dissipates from his face. "You're making fun of me."

"All I'm saying is, there are worse things out there in the world than cat pee, takeout, and creepy dolls." Dropping my voice to a serious note, I lean forward, propped up on my forearms. "I don't want you to ever have to face those worse things, kid. I don't want you to ever go through what I went through."

"When you went into foster care . . . did you like the families they put you with?"

I think of Mrs. Ramirez and the countless other people I stayed with until I graduated high school. Only one home resonated with me—the last one I ever lived in before I turned eighteen. Mr. and Mrs. Halloway. Elderly couple in their seventies. Good-natured souls. They'd had their hands full with me, but they knew how to harness my anger and bad attitude. Football was my saving grace, and, in a way, it was theirs too. Both the team and the game kept me out of trouble.

"Some," I say evenly. "But every person I lived with made me who I am today. And if I wasn't me, then I wouldn't be here right now, sitting at this table with you."

*T*he boys, including Harry Blackwater, are tucked in bed when I sneak out my back door sometime around one in the morning.

I don't know what Dominic told the police about Heather Blackwater or Harry's crazy aunt who I never noticed attending our practices. But Dominic noticed—the man who the world views as unfeeling, saw what I failed to. Even more, he spoke to Harry on a wavelength I never could, getting to the heart of the matter within mere minutes. When Dominic dropped Harry off at my house, it was with a faraway glaze to his dark eyes and a softly spoken, "I'll pick him up in the morning and bring him to his aunt's. We already filled her in about what's going on at the station."

He left as quickly as he appeared.

So here I am.

Barefoot, dressed in the same clothes from earlier, skirting around the shoulder-high hedges that separate our two courtyards. Turnaround is fair play—if Dominic thinks he can stop by whenever he wants, then I can certainly return the favor.

Using the flashlight on my phone to guide the way, I hurry across his neatly trimmed lawn. Unlike my house, there aren't any French doors to peer into, so I'm forced to knock on the single back door and wait like a total lurker.

"C'mon, Dominic," I mutter, bouncing from one foot to the other in my impatience. I knock again, adding a little *ratta-ta-ta* for fun.

Hello, my name is Aspen Levi and I come to your house in the middle of the night bearing show tunes.

Imagine all the restraining orders I'd get with a calling card like that.

With my hand balled into a fist, I thump on the door again to the rhythm of Eiffel 65's *Blue*. I'm midway through the chorus when the door squeaks open and a set of bulky arms haul me inside.

The door shuts behind me.

My back is shoved against it.

Surprised, I lose grip of my phone as it falls to the floor. In the same moment, aggressive masculine lips find mine in the dark.

Oh, yes.

This isn't what I came over for but it's certainly what my body needs.

I thread my fingers through Dominic's dark hair, rising up on my toes so I can meet his kiss fully. His palm finds the base of my spine, and he groans, the sound so seductive that I answer with a needy whimper.

He drags me closer, until his hard-on is like a brand on my stomach and my breasts are squished flat against his chest. Fingers slip into the back of my shorts, ignoring my panties—they're fun ones today, with the words "Not Today,

Satan" printed on them—so he can fill his palms with the curve of my ass.

A single squeeze and my legs tremble where I stand.

I grip his shoulders for leverage. Moan into his mouth when his hand slips farther south to cup me right *there*, where I'm hot and needy, and oh, God, he needs to warn a girl before he goes straight for the grand prize.

"Fuck, Aspen," he growls against my mouth, "you're so damn wet."

Gasping when his finger strokes my clit without preamble, I clutch his biceps and hold on for dear life. "You have that effect on me."

"Oh, yeah?" His wicked fingers don't apply any more pressure, keeping the grazing touches light and airy and simply *not enough*. "What else do I do to you?" he taunts, his lips finding the column of my throat. Teeth nip my skin, then suck the sting away.

My core clenches. My toes curl. My head . . . "You turn my brain to mush."

"Sounds messy." As if wanting to determine if what I say is true, he pushes two thick fingers inside me, curling them just so.

I cry out, my head tipped back. And, sure enough, it's as though he's reduced me to nothing but his thrusting fingers and the rapid rate of my pulse and the feel of his massive body caging me against his back door.

It feels *wonderful*.

Wild.

Reckless.

"Keep talkin', Coach," he works out on a heavy breath, the word *coach* sounding more like an endearment than a reminder of who we are and how we found each other. "You stop, I stop."

"That's cruel," I pant, rolling my hips to keep rhythm with his ministrations, "and so unfair."

"That's life." Slowly, he drags the pads of his fingers through my wetness. "It's cruel. It's unfair. And that's what makes it beautiful."

To my surprise, he drops to his haunches and promptly makes quick work of my shorts and underwear. They're down around my ankles, and then completely gone, before I can even utter his name. And then he's tracing the line of my leg with his fingers, up, up, up, until he palms my thigh and pushes my leg off the floor.

The sole of my foot lands on his broad shoulder.

I'm not sure if I've ever been more exposed.

I whisper his name, a question in every syllable, but he cuts straight to the chase, as he always does: "You stop talking, I stop too. Those are the rules. Good luck."

Good luck?

"Sometimes, you're still the same jerk who told me that he wasn't trying to pick anyone up at the bar—*ohhh,* okay." His tongue slicks from my entrance to my clit, never missing a beat. I can talk. However long he needs, I can . . . My lids fall shut against the dim lighting filtering in from another part of the house. "I lied. I so lied. You were wonderful that night. A true gentleman."

His hands clasp my hips, nailing my ass to the door so I can't escape his tongue.

The man is out of his mind if he thinks I'm going anywhere.

Cupping the back of his head, I fumble for words. "Have I mentioned how I figured out about your no-underwear policy before you fessed up? Because I-I totally noticed—" I break off, unable to sheathe a moan when he circles his tongue over my clit. We may be indoors but I'm seeing stars.

Thousands of them. "Y-You would do drills with the team and I . . . I couldn't stop myself from noticing how *free* you were. Down there. If you know what I mean."

He chuckles, then pauses to husk out, "dirty girl." His hot breath wafts over my sex and damn it if that doesn't feel magical too.

Dirty girl.

I don't feel dirty.

I feel reborn.

Positively fantastic with each swirl of his tongue, and—

No. No!

Keep talking. That's right. All I need to do is turn into Chatty Cathy and we'll go right back to it.

"I have another confession and this one is embarrassing, but so long as you keep doing *that*, I'll spill all my dirty secrets."

I'm instantly treated to the heady sensation of his fingers getting reacquainted with my core. Dominic scissors his fingers, and I nearly break down. *It feels amazing.* That I'm holding my weight up at all is a miracle. My hips grind down on his fingers, then roll upwards against his tongue. My breathing comes shallow.

As much as I want to beg him to please get on with it, I agreed to the game.

And I always set out to win.

"I looked you up," I breathe out, biting down on my bottom lip. "That day you took Topher mini-golfing, I looked you up." Sensing his gaze on me, I don't stop rambling in fear of him pulling away. "Turns out, you're so famous that people . . . people role-play as you."

He sinks a third finger inside me, stretching me almost impossibly wide, and those sparkling stars come back with a vengeance. "Where?"

Welp, here we go.

"Porn."

One second he's there and wrapping ribbons of pleasure around me, and then he's gone.

Gone!

"Oh, c'mon," I cry out, "you said keep talking and I did. In fact, I even told you something incredibly embarrassing about myself—*oh!*"

I'm upside down. Literally, upside down with Dominic's shorts-clad bubble butt in my face as he storms through the house. My breasts provide padding against his muscular back, although they also attempt to strangle me. For what it's worth, bras do *not* work wonders when you're dangling over a man's shoulders.

"Too much?" I ask, using my hands to keep my boobs away from my face. "Should I mention that you're in much better shape? Also, you have a bigger penis. You know, in case that was a question that popped into your head when you decided to throw me over your shoulder like a rag doll."

He pauses in what looks to be the living room. A lamp is on in the corner, and from my angle, I can see a couch and a coffee table. The couch has pillows—bed pillows, not the living room accessory kind—and a comforter. Does he *sleep* out here?

One boob slips from my grip and knocks me in the chin.

Double-Ds were a dream of mine before Topher. A goal, if you will. Then I gave birth, gained thirty pounds, and can't even be carried like a damsel in distress without being suffocated by one of my own tits.

There is something dreadfully ironic about this scenario.

"For the record," I say, putting Boob A—the left one, it's

always the left—back into place, "he didn't dirty-talk like you. By which I mean, you do a *much* better job."

"Aspen?"

My heart positively flutters at hearing him using my first name. "Yes, Dominic?"

"You drive me batshit crazy."

And then I fall, somehow angled just right so my back lands on a cushioned foam mattress that has no sheets or pillows. I bounce once, twice, and then twist my head in time to watch Dominic undress. Thanks to the overhead light, I have a front-row seat to the way he pulls off his T-shirt, fingers grasping the fabric at the back of his neck. One by one, his abs are revealed. I count them all because I'm a stickler for certain things.

Eight.

Eight.

And, oh boy, but he's got a single tattoo. The number twelve printed across his lower rib cage in Roman numerals. Twelve . . . the number on his jersey from when he played for Tampa Bay.

I wonder what he might do if I get on my hands and knees and lick every one of those glorious ridges. I give it only a moment's consideration before I'm shuffling onto all fours and crawling over to where he stands beside the bed.

The unused bed.

Under my hands and shins, the mattress truly feels brand new.

Not that I give it much thought once I cup his butt, squeezing each cheek, then kiss the lowermost abdominal muscle. His skin twitches and I grin. Oh, how *lovely* it feels to give him a taste of his own medicine.

I trace my tongue over the sharply ridged line of his stomach.

"Shit." His fingers sink into my loose hair, following the curve to the back of my skull. "Aspen."

Up, up, up, I go with my tongue. *How do you like it now, Dominic?* Out loud, I casually suggest, "Keep talking or I'll stop. Weren't those the rules?"

His guttural laugh might as well be a furnace inside my chest, it warms me from the inside out. "Batshit crazy," he reaffirms, but he doesn't move his hands and I take that as the go ahead. "And I fucking love every moment of you surprising me, Asp. Every. Single. Moment."

I cup his erection through his shorts, smiling to myself when his breath hitches and his grasp on me tightens.

Dominic DaSilva at my mercy is the best gift of all.

I follow the waistband of his shorts with my mouth, pressing little kisses here and there. When I reach the drawstring tie, I don't bother to undo it. Instead, I kneel down onto my heels and lower my face, kissing my way over the heavy ridge of his cock concealed by the fabric.

A sharp, masculine gasp greets my ears.

And then, "The only time I've slept in a bed since I was a kid is when we traveled for games and when I was on *Put A Ring On It*. No other option. A couch feels temporary. Like I always have one foot out the door—fuck, fuck, *fuck,* that feels so good." I lick my way up the length of his erection, pulling his shorts down at the same time, so when I kiss the tip, it's all Dominic. Every last bit of him. "I, shit—I can't think."

"Try," I tell him, just before I take him all the way into my mouth.

1-Aspen; 0-Dominic.

I like this game.

"I don't do permanent. I don't do predictability. But you . . . I've thought of nothing but fucking you in a real bed, with you riding my cock before I flip you over onto your knees and take you from behind." His hand shifts to the top of my head, and I don't issue a single protest when he applies pressure. "You're turnin' me inside out, Coach, and I'm trying . . . Jesus fuck, I'm trying to turn it right back around but I can't. You're the first thing I think about when I wake up, and I experience a hundred different moments throughout the day when I—oh, God. More, baby, give me more of that."

More of that is me taking him all the way to the back of my throat. It hurts to breathe. But the *baby* he whispered raggedly spurs me on, and I bob my head. Twist my hand around the base of his cock and squeeze tightly before slicking my palm up to meet my mouth.

My eyes water but I'm not sure if it's due to how deep I'm swallowing him or how precious his words are, especially when I know how rare they are for him to ever admit out loud.

Hands link under my armpits, and I have the wherewithal to go with it as I'm gently rolled onto my side. I hear the tear of a condom wrapper and then it's Dominic's big body weighting down the mattress behind me. With my back to his front, he hooks my left leg up and back over his hip, spreading me wide. I feel the blunt head of his cock at my entrance, as well as his flexing fingers on my hip.

In my ear, he husks out, "Last chance for you to tell me to stop."

I arch my back, twisting my head so I can see his face. "Why would I ever do that?"

His throat works with a rough swallow. "Because I don't think I can let you go."

It's as much a declaration of love as he's ever given—I read the truth, and the fear, in his familiar black eyes. But beyond that, I see hope simmering there. It catches my breath. Shatters my heart. I nod, shakily, and press two fingers to that dimpled chin. "I trust you," I whisper to him.

In my heart, I say three very different words.

I love you.

It's too much too soon. I made that mistake with Rick, falling for the façade without getting to know the person behind all the fancy, polished walls. Except that it feels *right* with Dominic. It feels right when he thrusts deep inside me, angling his hips so every drive forward pulls a cry from my lips. It feels right when his fingers smooth down over my not-so-toned belly to rub my clit in tiny, electrifying strokes that feel like heaven on earth.

And it feels so incredibly right when I grip the mattress that has no sheets because he bought it for me—for us— and my hand skids when my palm turns sweaty.

Dominic loops his other arm under my head, providing a literal man-made pillow.

"So good, baby," he groans in my ear, sliding in and out of me on a sensual, toe-curling glide, "every time I touch you, you feel so good."

He can win this round.

I can't find any words. They've vacated my brain, even if they haven't left my heart, and I'm nothing but a string of moans and sighs, each one pitched a little higher than the last.

"Come all over me," Dominic grunts by my ear, his finger rubbing my clit faster, the plunge of his hips driving ever deeper inside me. "Let yourself go, baby. I know you want to give in."

He pulls out, so much so that the tip of his cock nearly leaves me, and then thrusts in so hard, so swiftly, that I see stars.

Literal stars.

Or maybe not so literal, but it doesn't matter because the orgasm is sweeping over me, and I grab at Dominic's wrist to still those sensual circles because everything is so hypersensitive that I feel like I'm about to come out of my skin.

Devilish.

That's how Dominic's chuckle sounds as he firmly grips my hips, rolls me over onto my stomach, and enters me on a single thrust. The bedroom is empty, save for the bed, and one very well-positioned mirror that catches our reflection.

My hair is a mess and my cheeks are red and my lips are parted, but it's Dominic who steals the show. His arms are tight ropes of muscle, his torso nothing but solid planes of rock-hard strength. With broad hands, he holds my hips as he pumps into me, never relinquishing the rhythm that catches my breath even now, when I'm already satiated and simply enjoying the ride.

Breathtakingly handsome.

He bites down on his bottom lip, his hips plunging forward. Once, twice, and then I feel each imprint of his fingers on my flesh as he drops his head forward, his gaze locked on the place where he's entering me again and again.

"You ruin me," he groans on a short breath, and whatever he might have said next is lost to his orgasm. He comes with his head thrown back, the veins in his neck tensely visible. Devastating. That's how this moment feels, like we're cracking down our last barriers and accepting whatever comes next.

Briefly, he turns me onto my back before collapsing down on top of me, his arms engulfing either side of my shoulders. "I'm fucked in the head," he rumbles, his cheek against my own, like he's trying to force me to see the *real* him, the one that will send me scurrying far, far away. "I sleep on the couch and I bought this bed because I wanted to have sex with you in it."

I tiptoe my fingers up his spine. "And the mirror?"

"I found it at one of those consignment shops down on Main Street yesterday." A small pause. "I wanted to take you from behind and still see your face."

A giggle warms my chest. "You're a gentleman through and through."

"I bought sheets, too. I planned to put them on the bed before I had you over."

Is it too cheesy to hug him? It doesn't matter. I flatten my palms on his back and squeeze him tight. "Are you trying to romance me, Coach DaSilva?"

His chuckle is low and sexy, the kind of laughter I want to hear every morning when I wake up. "Honestly," he says, brushing my hair back from my face, "I have no idea what the hell I'm doing. But I'm hoping if I throw a shit ton of darts, one of them will hit bull's-eye."

"Dominic?"

"Yeah?"

I think back to what I overheard him say to Harry, about not regretting the path his life has taken because it's led him here to London. It led him here to *me*. "I'm glad Savannah Rose didn't get to keep you." Swallowing past the vulnerable knot of fear, I add quietly, "And selfish as it is, I'm happy your job fired you."

"It's not selfish."

"It is."

"It's not." His hand sweeps possessively down my side. "Because only one of us gets to be selfish, and I've already taken the position." His fingers turn evil, tickling me. "Face it, Asp, you can't have everything." He pulls me underneath him, so he's straddling my waist but keeping his weight from being too much. "Head coach," he teases, his fingers merciless in their quest, "badass mom who rescues kids who need saving. Let the little people around here have the chance to make a name for themselves, would you?"

Laughter gurgles up within me. I twist, trying to get away from those tickling fingers, but I can't squirm quite far enough. "Fine! Fine, I'll give something up. Name your price!"

The tickling ceases, and when I meet his searing gaze, I already know what he's going to ask for: "You, me, and this bed for one more round. And then I'll send you home. Tomorrow we'll go back to real life and talk about Harry and the calendar, and the fact that you don't see why we need to have the kids running miles with me every morning to build up their endurance . . . but for right now, you're mine. Deal?"

I smile up at him, my heart so full that I fear it might burst. "Deal."

31

DOMINIC

*I*f there's one thing I learned on *Put A Ring On It*, it's that Nick Stamos takes his job very seriously.

When he and Mina pull up to my house on Friday afternoon, it's in a white van with *Stamos Restoration and Co.* printed across the side in blue lettering. Of all the guys I met on the show, Nick is the only one I talk to regularly.

The bastard is a pretty boy through and through, though I doubt he sees himself that way. He works with his hands for a living, a blue-collar worker all the way through, and if he had even a little of the same temperament as the rest of the show's contestants, he'd have ditched his home-improvement act and signed with some of the modeling agencies that I know would pick him up in a heartbeat.

But that's not Nick's speed. Not even a little bit.

Slipping my hands into the front pockets of my worn jeans, I bump Topher in the shoulder. "You ready to put your mouth where your shitty driving is, kid?"

From the other side of Topher, Timmy pipes up, "I thought the saying goes, are you ready to put your money where your mouth is?"

"It would go like that," Levi's son grumbles good-naturedly, "if I had any cash."

To my left, Harry throws up a hand. "Wait. I thought we were getting paid for today's gig?"

I hook an arm around the football whisperer's neck and scratch his head with my knuckles, noogie-style. "You and Tim get money. Not-Chris on the other hand . . ."

Topher groans, squeezing his eyes shut. "Coach, I'm sorry I lied about the Chris thing. I just thought it sounded cooler! I seriously thought my real name was Christopher. I panicked and—"

"Pointed the finger at me." I nod, releasing Harry so I can repeat the process all over again with the lanky kid who looks nothing like his mother save for his blue eyes. "I don't blame you, kid. Your mother is a scary person." I drop my voice to a mock-whisper. "I can handle it when she punches me."

His mouth drops open. "She *punched* you?"

Levi has done a lot to me. She's kissed me with so much passion behind her touch I feel eviscerated, she's put me in my place when I turn broody, she's . . . Well, it's probably not a good idea to think about her going down on me when I'm talking with her son.

I squeeze Topher's shoulder. "She has not, in fact, punched me though I'm positive she considered it when you rammed into my truck."

"Scraped," he interjects earnestly, "I *scraped* your truck. Big difference."

"What the hell happened to your truck, DaSilva?" Nick asks, sauntering toward us with Mina's hand clasped in his. "It looks like it fought a war with a bear and lost."

Chuckling low, I amble forward to greet my friends. "It fought a war with a Topher and lost." I grip Nick's hand, slapping him on the back in a quick hug. Then turn to his pink-haired fiancée, Mina. Her dark eyes flash up at me, and though I never met her before a few months ago, our friendship was instant. She leaps up at me, and I catch her around the waist in a twirling hug. When I set her down, I turn to the three teenage boys who are waiting to be introduced. "That one," I murmur, pointing to Topher's lanky frame, "is a Topher."

He smiles weakly, shrugging his narrow shoulders. "I mean, at least I won? Maybe I need a medal or something."

"How about a hammer?" I suggest.

"You know, that works too."

Grinning at him, I quickly introduce my friends to my players. Each one of them is gracious and open. Tim shakes Nick's hand and then shyly hugs Mina. Topher, the most outgoing out of the three, hugs them both like he's known them his entire life. And Harry, who's been staying with his Aunt Gloria while the cops search for his mom down in Portland, loses the frown as soon as he sees all of the power tools Nick hauls out of the van.

"These are so cool!" he exclaims, swinging a sledgehammer around like he's on the verge of joining the Celtic Olympics and hurling tree trunks across a field. "It looks like Thor's hammer."

Mina laughs. "I can see it." When Nick peers over at her, she cocks her head playfully. "What, you know I love me some Chris Hemsworth."

"So long as you love me more," he tells her, ignoring the equipment in his arms in favor of bending over to plant a kiss on her mouth.

When Nick catches me eyeing them, he points the load in his arms in my direction. "What? You aren't going to tell us that we're sickening?"

Maybe I would have a month ago—before I met a blond-haired football coach who called me an asshole. "Does it make you feel all warm and fuzzy inside when I do?"

"I felt all warm and fuzzy inside when I saw Natasha in a bikini the other day," Topher cuts in, leaning down to wrap his hands around the wheelbarrow's wooden arms. Straightening to his full height, he looks over at me. "I think she has a boyfriend though."

My tongue suddenly feels thick in my mouth. "I-I—"

"If she *didn't* have a boyfriend, I'd want to ask her out," he continues, completely oblivious to the fact that I'm at a total loss for words.

If he was just another player on the team, I'd slap him on the back and call it a day. But this is Levi's son, her baby boy, and I don't know whether to bubble-wrap him so he can't even *see* this Natasha girl ever again or dump him on his mom's taco welcome mat and tell her I'm out of my element.

As though sensing my internal struggle, Mina brushes past me to bump Topher over so she can grasp one of the wheelbarrow's arms, leaving him to hold the other. "What do you think about Natasha's friends? Any single cuties?"

"Well, there is this one girl . . ."

Together they move up my driveway with Tim and Harry tagging along behind them.

A hand comes down on my shoulder, startling me.

"I've never seen you speechless before." Nick. *Right.*

With my eye still on Topher, I bend and grab the tarp we'll be laying down over my floor while we go to town demolishing the walls. "His mom would kill him if she heard him talking about a girl's bikini top."

"Who's his mom?"

"Levi." I don't know why I fail to introduce her as Aspen

other than the fact that her first name has slowly begun to feel like my way of connecting with her on a level no one else does. "She's my coworker. Boss." I shake my head. "She's the head coach for London High. She lives next door."

Nick's head swivels as he looks between Levi's cute Cape Cod-style home to the 1950's ranch to the left of my house. "Cape Cod? She's got good taste."

Trust the home-restoration guy to make judgments based on how much he likes a house. Granted, he wouldn't be wrong about Levi. She tastes fantastic too.

"You should see the inside of the place. She's got this nautical theme going on, and it fits her personality to perfection."

"Yeah?"

I nod. "She's out with her sister right now, but when she gets back I'll see if she can give you a tour. We could ask Topher, but . . . he's on punishment duty. You know, the whole bear-claw thing."

"I'm surprised you haven't gotten it fixed yet."

"Just been busy." Not that I haven't had the time to bring it to the shop. I have, I just . . . haven't gone. For whatever reason. "Figure when I bring in the truck, I'll do Levi's Honda next."

"You're sleeping with her, aren't you."

Not a question.

Slinging the heavy tarps over one shoulder, I motion for him to hand me the remaining bucket of tools we'll need for demolition day. "A gentleman doesn't kiss and tell."

Nick snorts under his breath. "Since when are you repping the gentleman title?"

I slide a glance his way. "You can't be the only good guy around here, man."

"Are you a good guy?"

"Fuck no. But . . ." I kick my chin toward Levi's house. "She makes me feel like I could be. Does that answer your question?"

"Not even close." The van's doors slam shut, and then he's at my side, my own Greek fairy-godfather looking to sprinkle some romantic fairy magic on me. "You love her yet?"

My lungs threaten to pop and deflate right there in my chest. Choking on nothing but the salty breeze from the bay, I glower at my best friend. "Jesus, don't ask me that."

"Because you're scared the answer is yes?"

With Topher and the other boys laughing inside my house with Mina, I want to tell Nick the truth: that I've never loved another person, not even Savannah Rose, and I have zero experience with the emotion. All I know is that I'm willing to do anything to keep Levi from kicking me to the curb.

If love is fearing that she'll send me packing, then yeah . . . I'm fucking terrified.

But not scared enough to walk away from her and Topher and this small coastal town that feels like home in a way nothing else ever has.

32

ASPEN

A knock on my open front door has me yanking my head up from where I'm packing my bag for today's Wildcats photoshoot and heading to answer it.

Mina.

It has to be. Topher spent all last night talking about how awesome Dominic's Boston friends are, including the pink-haired Mina who advised him to, and I quote, "Ask the shy girl out in his friend group."

Sweeping my gaze over her, I take in her vibrant hair and olive skin, along with the funky tie-dye T-shirt she's wearing and the frayed cut-off shorts. She looks hip and sassy and everything I used to be before I married Rick.

Offering her a grin, I wipe my hands on my boring khaki shorts. "Hey! You must be Mina."

Her features warm with a genuine smile. "And *you* must be Levi, Dom's girlfriend." I must visibly make an *oh-shit* face, because she waves me off with a laugh. "He didn't call you that, but Nick and I know him way too well. He's smitten."

"I . . ."

Before I can even prepare myself for it, she wraps her arms around me in a tight hug like we've known each other for years. "I've honestly never seen him smile so much. And, based on the amount of times your name came up in conversation yesterday, I figure you're the reason why."

I don't even know what to say, other than to pull a total teenage-girl move and beg her to tell me everything. Shameless? Absolutely.

As though sensing my inner turmoil—do I embarrass myself completely by demanding the details or pretend I'm cool, slick, and unfazed—she releases me, only to whip out her phone. "Nick and I kept count. Thirty-seven times." She shoves the phone in my face, and sure enough, there are multiple rows of tally marks drawn out in virtual pink ink. "Don't mind us, but we're totally taking bets today."

"On what?"

Her smile is sly. "How long Dominic lasts before he cracks and kisses you." Pocketing her phone again, she takes in the entryway of my house. "Nick put his money on six hours, but I figured I'd come over and do a little re-con. You know, ask how long he goes without laying one on you when you're together."

Mina's frank attitude is almost mesmerizing. I thought *I* was ballsy, but, holy crap, she takes the prize for sure. Sensing a kindred spirit, I finish zipping my backpack before slinging it over one shoulder. "When we're alone? Five minutes. If we're around the team and he's trying to be professional? We're looking at an hour, tops. He tends to get creative."

He's kissed me behind the bleachers during practice.

He's followed me into the girl's bathroom in the school, corralling me into a stall so he can sneak a kiss without worrying about prying eyes.

When we took Harry and Topher out for dinner the day after I picked him up from Kevin's house, Dominic asked me to help him pick a song on the jukebox, just so he could stand behind me, his hands greedily fisting my hips, and grind his erection into my ass.

The man is absolutely shameless . . . and I live for the excitement of watching him wrack his brain to figure out ways to get me alone.

It's the most fun I've had in *years*.

Conscious of the time, I ask Mina if she wants a ride to the first stop of the day and she takes me up on it, no questions asked. Along the way, she fills me in on how Dominic asked her to take care of the boys' hair for the photoshoot.

He's thought of everything.

The mapped-out stops throughout town. Cookies and Joe Diner. The Ferris wheel down by the pier. The same overlook he brought me to up on Cadillac Mountain. The sandy beach just around the corner from the tail end of Main Street.

The boys' parents have been assigned designated spots to meet Dominic for the photos, and for the kids whose parents can't make it today, I've taken on the role of chauffeur. I may be the head coach, but Dominic . . . he's as good as I am at what we do, if not better. I never would have thought to include the town as the backdrop for the calendar. I never would have asked local businesses to sponsor the project and agree to sell the calendar at their shops.

That hustle is all Dominic.

When Mina and I pull up at Cookies and Joe Diner's tin façade, I park the car and turn to my pink-haired passenger. "This is going to sound like a totally random question, but when you said Nick . . . would that be Nick, like the one from *Put A Ring On It*?"

Mina's dark eyes zero in on my face. "You watch the show?"

"Sometimes." I shrug, feeling my cheeks burn. I'm sure if I touched my fingers to my skin they would come away singed. "It's a train wreck that I couldn't help but turn on when it first started last month."

"I'm guessing you stopped watching right around the time you met Dom?"

Guilty. So, so guilty. "It's not nearly as much fun now, though everyone in town eats it up. They even have a fantasy league going down every Wednesday night at the Golden Fleece. At this point, I wouldn't be surprised if half the town is in on it."

Her lips form a round *O*. "Seriously? Oh, my God, that is *awesome*. And totally genius!"

I'm sure Shawn thinks so. From what I understand, he's the one that pulled the whole thing together. The Golden Fleece is probably raking in thousands of dollars every week, all because Londoners can't resist watching one of their own up on TV. After weeks of putting his blood, sweat, and tears into the high school football team, Dominic has gone from out-of-town celebrity to a London transplant, like many others who have moved here over the years.

Plus, when I played for Boston College, all my parents' friends put together a betting-pool website, just so they'd have a personal stake in me winning games. Londoners are loyal to their core—and if they like you, they bet on you. Dominic has been welcomed into the fold, London-style.

Scraping together what confidence I have, I ask, "Have you ever . . . met her? Savannah Rose, I mean."

"Savannah?" Mina pulls her pink hair over one shoulder. "No. I mean, I guess I could if I wanted to. Nick's on good terms with her. I'm sure we'll speak at the reunion show in August—I *totally* plan to go. Between us, I sort of live for the gossip rags."

Will Dominic bring me to the reunion show? Are we even that far along in our relationship? We certainly aren't engaged—or even dating—the way Nick and Mina are. Shoving down the stupid, useless insecurities, I slip the keys from the ignition. "Thank you. It's stupid to even ask; I just figured . . . you dated Nick after the show wrapped up filming, and I thought, maybe, you might have some—"

"Advice?" At my small nod, Mina laughs softly. "Girl, we might not know each other but Dom? Maybe he hasn't told you yet—probably because he doesn't even know how to admit it to himself—but he adores you." She points to her phone as she pops the door open. "Thirty-seven times. Thirty-seven! Also, if you want to try and plant a kiss on him sometime around noon today that would be *perfect*."

I laugh. "I'll see what I can do."

∞

In the end, Nick wins the Kiss Bet.

Thanks to time spent shuffling kids around from location to location, I don't have the chance to catch up with Dominic until hours later. It's the Ferris wheel photo op, the last stop of the day, and as I climb out of my car with Harry getting out of the passenger's side, my gaze immediately searches for a Hulk-sized man wearing a backward ball cap.

"Oh, there he is!" Harry loops a backpack over his shoulder, then jogs toward the group of people standing at the base of the Ferris wheel.

Dominic turns, a camera held in his hands, and I'll be lying if I say my heart doesn't thump a little too fast at the sight of him. He's dressed in his customary "Dominic

Uniform." Dark everywhere, jeans, T-shirt, that hat he wears to death. Though, when I stroll closer, it's hard to miss the tired lines creasing his rugged face.

He's running himself ragged.

The way he is now—intense and super-focused—might as well be a replica of the Dominic that trained with the Bucs and came out with two Super Bowl rings and what feels like a gazillion MVP awards. Except that we're coaching high school ball, not the pro's, and this calendar is supposed to be fun for *everyone* involved, not only the kids.

Glancing to my right, where the Ferris wheel's longtime operator, Mr. McKerron, is sitting with his head bowed, like he's reading something or sneaking in a nap on the job, I scurry over and put my hands on the booth. "Mr. McKerron!"

The sun glistens off his shiny bald head as he looks up at me. Gradually, a slow smile grows behind his bushy, gray beard. Arthur McKerron can't be a day under seventy-five. "Well, look-ee who we have here! Aspen Levi. I haven't seen you since you were yay-high"—he holds up a flat hand, leveling it off at his waist—"and crying your little heart out because you were terrified to go up on The Monster."

Terrified is putting it mildly.

I'd clung to my mother's leg and refused to let go, like a monkey hanging from a tree limb.

Hand shielding my eyes from the setting sun, I peer up at the Ferris wheel. "You guys really haven't changed the name in twenty years?"

"Now why would we do that? It's a tourist attraction. You can see it clear across the bay."

Growing up, The Monster and I developed a mutual hate-hate relationship. You know the worst time to discover a fear of heights? When you're strapped to a mechanical wheel, nicknamed "The Monster," with nowhere to hide.

I shiver at the memories.

Switching my focus back to Arthur, I paste an *I've-got-this* smile on my face. "So, I was thinking—"

"A dangerous activity," he says with a mischievous twinkle in his eye. No wonder he hasn't sought out a different job. The Monster is a perfect fit for him. I swear he takes an almost sadistic pleasure in watching little children shout for their parents at the top of that damn wheel. "Go on, Miss Levi."

"Before we wrap up the photo shoot, would it be possible for us to run a round for whoever wants to go for a ride?" I think of the determined set to Dominic's mouth. "I think it could do everyone some good to cut loose for twenty minutes."

Arthur flips his magazine closed. "And how fast would you like The Monster to go?"

My stomach threatens to upheave my breakfast. There is no way I'm stepping foot on that thing. Already the cinnamon bun I grabbed an hour ago for a snack is shimmying in my belly, ready to show up for the cause if needed. "Slow. *Really* slow."

"Kids prefer the thrill."

"I'm not sure—"

"C'mon, Miss Levi. Do you want to be the reason they smile for the rest of the day or not? Also, how are you going to let them up on The Monster without being a good coach and leading the fun brigade yourself?"

I've been strong-armed by a seventy-five-year-old hustler and he knows it.

With a pep to his step, Arthur McKerron ushers me along to the group and tells everyone to pair off into twos. I find myself heading for Topher, but then he catches my eye, twiddles his fingers at me, and whirls around to go find one of his buddies.

I've been ditched by my own son.

Feeling like the last kid picked in freshman-year gym class, I stand in the shadow of The Monster and watch everyone find their other half. Mina loops her arm with Nick, staring up at him with an adoring expression on her face. They're ridiculously cute together. Harry chooses Tim, while Topher bumps fists with Bobby. Matthew Wilde looks miserable when his mother, Belinda, tucks her hand into her fourteen-year-old's grip and keeps him rooted by her side. Even Timmy's mom, who surprised me by helping out all day, since she requested off from both jobs, hurries to claim Meredith before another parent steals her away.

I'm an island floating in the middle of the ocean.

Then again, this is ideal. What's the fun in tackling The Monster when you have to do it alone? Not fun at all. Clearly, I'll need to pass on the ride and hang out with Arthur instead. *Perfect.*

"Waiting for me, Coach?"

Oh, boy.

My heart pounds a mile a minute at hearing that dark, smoky voice. Dominic doesn't hold my hand, not in front of the team and all the parents, but I feel his heat at my back as his hand folds over my shoulder.

"I've missed you," he husks out, bowing his head so he speaks directly into my ear. "You know, I haven't been on one of these things in at least twenty-five years. And the last time I did, it certainly wasn't with a girl as pretty as you."

Flattery means nothing in the face of The Monster.

I open my mouth, fully prepared to let Dominic down gently and, oh, I don't know, suggest we sneak away to the unicorn carousel instead, when Arthur ruins everything. "You!" he shouts, pointing two fingers at me and Dominic. "You two go up together."

I dig my heels into the cement as Mr. Super Bowl Champion himself swoops forward like he's ready to tackle another team for the ring. Dominic is all in and I am so, *so* out. When he realizes I'm not at his side, he turns on his heel and plants his hands on his hips.

"You gonna let me go up there alone?" he asks, serving me with a daring onceover.

Coward, that one looks reads. *Find the bite of the thrill.*

It's one thing to have sex on top of a mountain when I'm more than thirty feet away from the edge of a cliff. Another thing entirely to put my fate in a monstrosity nicknamed The Monster.

Arthur skirts past me, ducking his head to whisper, "Don't make me tell all your players what happened when you were seven."

My jaw drops. "That's blackmail!"

"No, Miss Levi, it's called telling you to have a little bit of fun. Now get up there. I can't put anyone else on board until I strap the both of you in."

Like I'm being led like a lamb to the slaughter, the soles of my sneakers drag across the concrete. I would face down a million clowns before one round on this thing. Dramatic, maybe, but what isn't dramatic at all is the way my temples pound and my head feels all sorts of woozy. I don't want to do this. I *really* don't want to do this, but then I hear Topher call out, "Be brave, Mom!" and any option of fleeing goes right out the window.

I can be brave—right?

Show the team and my son and crazy, sadistic Arthur McKerron that I can *do* this.

Except, as I sit beside Dominic and fold my hands in my lap, my split-second bolt of bravery has apparently taken off for greener pastures. *I'm going to be sick.* Sweat dampens my palms as Arthur clicks the seat belt across our laps, then folds down the metal bar that is meant, I guess, to provide the illusion of safety. He waves good-naturedly, wishes us luck, and practically skips away to rope some other sucker into taking a ride on The Monster.

Tall as Dominic is, he has no choice but to sprawl out his legs before us. Actually, there might be such a thing as *too* tall for this ride. He drapes an arm over my shoulder, his body positioned for maximum room, while his right thigh presses into my left. Never mind the fact that his massive, six-foot-six frame is cramped beside me, he still manages to look insanely comfortable and delicious while I'm on the verge of a meltdown. Suddenly, this moment feels not unlike our first one at the Golden Fleece. Face-into-crotch falling, notwithstanding, of course.

"The pictures are comin' out well," he says. Nothing about his expression signifies that he's as freaked out as I am about the sudden jerk of the Ferris wheel as we inch up, up, up so the next seat can be filled.

"Mhmm."

My hands clutch the metal bar in a death grip.

Clang. Clang. Clang.

"You're the reason this is even happening, you know. I'm not talking about the dick-in-a-sock thing either. I mean, honest to God, Asp, I've never had the courage or even the interest to show my pictures to anyone before I met you."

"Uh-huh."

Clang. Clang. CLANG.

The Monster jolts to a stop. I don't know how high up we are. My eyes are closed and, oh, God, why do our seats have to *swing* like that? Back and forth and back and forth, and there's no doubt about it: I'm going to vomit that cinnamon bun *everywhere*. That's just if I'm lucky, too. More likely than not, I'm going to die up here. Heart attack. Definitely a heart attack.

"Maybe we should have everyone over tonight for a pizza party. Not like I haven't given Pizzeria Athena enough business already. But, you know, I really want the team to feel like we're all a family, like how we took care of Harry. Did you see his aunt joined us earlier at Cookies and Joe Diner? Anyway, swimming at a private beach never hurt anyone. Could be good for morale—Aspen, you okay?"

Clang.

Clang.

Clang.

We're chugging our way up again. Higher, higher.

"I need to get off of here."

"Here?" Dominic echoes.

"The Monster." *Clang! Clang! Clang!* "I need to get off The Monster."

"You mean the Ferris wheel?"

I nod. At least, I think I'm nodding. With my eyes closed and The Monster rotating around, gathering its victims from the loading zone, it feels like I'm floating.

"Aspen, baby, don't tell me . . . Are you afraid of heights?"

My hands fist the metal bar. "Are you laughing at me?"

And then . . . and then I feel it. The arm that's wrapped around me is shaking. His big body is shaking. The friggin' seat is *shaking*.

I'm going to kill him.

"Dominic," I mutter, my mouth completely dry as anxiety spikes, "stop. Stop laughing. We're going to fall. The bolts are going to come loose and—*oh, my God.*"

The seat swings. Back and forth.

Clang. Clang. Clang.

More swinging, and suddenly I know it's him. *He's* doing this. Teasing me. Playing with my emotions.

"I hate you," I whisper out from between gritted teeth. "I hate you so much."

I feel his lips on my exposed shoulder, and then hear his velvety voice by my ear. "You don't, Asp. You don't hate me at all. But you're gonna hate yourself if you have to suffer the wrath of The Monster and can't even enjoy the view."

"I've lived in London most of my life. I've seen the view."

"Not like this." His hand rounds the back of my head, smoothing down the flyaway strands. "How are you gonna tell me you're such a badass if you can't handle opening your eyes on a Ferris wheel? How are we going to go skydiving together?"

My heart pitter-patters at the thought of us making plans for a life outside of the Wildcats. Then, it picks up speed at the mere thought of skydiving. Never going to happen. Weakly, I utter, "Topher will go with you."

"Topher's a great sidekick but you, Coach—you can't be my partner-in-crime if you don't go for the gold when it's right in front of you." His hot breath coasts over my cheek as he kisses my temple. "Take the risk, earn the reward."

"What's the reward?" I ask, but already my eyes are peeling open. I'm close to hyperventilating and there's nothing I want more than to be back on solid ground. And then I see there's a hand in front of my face, blocking the promised view.

"Breathe for me, baby," comes his soft command.

I suck in air sharply, filling my lungs.

"Now breathe it out."

Out it goes, my chest deflating with the exhalation.

"You good?"

I hear the clanging of The Monster's metal gears. Hear the boys—Topher, too—below us hollering about something off in the distance. A yacht, I think. Seeking the strength from Dominic's arm wrapped around me, I nod.

He pulls his hand away, dropping it to my thigh. "Check out your reward."

We're at the tippity-top of the Ferris wheel, some hundred feet off the ground. Maybe less. Maybe more. I can't bring myself to swing my gaze down and take in all the tourists mingling around on the pier and looking like ant-people.

But the horizon, that I can see.

And it is . . . *breathtaking.*

Sailboats coast along the deep blue waters, their crisp, white sails flapping in the wind. Farther out, the yacht Topher was shouting about heads east toward Bar Harbor. It's long and sleek and glistens under the setting sun. I swallow, hard, then glance west. The islands across from London appear like green jewels, enticing me to stare a little harder and make out the houses nestled between the trees.

I count them all: one, two, four . . . seven.

"Not so bad, is it?" Dominic drawls, the dratted jerk sounding all too satisfied with himself.

"It could be worse."

"Yeah? How?"

I meet his dark gaze. "I didn't pee my pants this time."

Slowly, his mouth curves up in a delicious grin. "I'm sorry"—he puts one hand to his ear, leaning in—"I could have sworn you said *this* time."

And so under a sky painted pink and purple and yellow, with my heart in my throat and my panties wet but for an entirely different reason than fear, I regale Dominic DaSilva,

Super Bowl ring champion, sports news anchor, about the one time I rode The Monster and peed on myself. When I get to the part that includes the riders below me hollering about it starting to rain, I try to uphold whatever pride I have left: "I was only seven. It was a shock to us all."

He loses it.

Head thrown back, eyes squeezed shut, sexy laughter tumbling out of him.

Life has never been so good.

33

CELEBRITY TEA PRESENTS:

WILDCAT LOGIC: WHEN DESPERATE EX-NFL PLAYERS
BECOME AMATEUR PHOTOGRAPHERS

ear Reader, I'm sure this is not an article you ever anticipated reading. Between us, it's not one I anticipated writing either, but here we are. (No, really, here we are).

As you may have guessed from the headline, retired NFL player Dominic DaSilva has traded in his football jersey for a cell phone camera app. Now, before you start thinking, "WOW! Harsh," let me just say . . . don't you find it a little odd that Sports 24/7 created an entire TV segment about high school football of all things, of which fifteen minutes of the half-hour episode were dedicated to Maine's London High School? After all, it's not every day that a sports network goes out of their way to highlight a small town in the middle of nowhere that also happens to be the place where their former employee now works.

I'm spilling the T-E-A, sister.

Here. We. Go.

For the sake of getting right to it, I won't mince words: I think DaSilva is so keen to be in the limelight, he'll do anything to get his name and face in front of people. Let us look at the facts, shall we?

1. *After retiring from the NFL, DaSilva promptly was hired by ESPN's top competitor, Sports 24/7, in which he hosted his own show for roughly four years. I don't watch sports—unless the athletes are swimmers and wearing speedos, of course—so I can't say whether or not DaSilva was any good. For the purpose of playing nice, let's say he did an ahhhmazing job and deserves a daytime Emmy. Moving on.*

2. *Hot or not, the man went from living in Los Angeles, where he had his pick of women, to going on ANOTHER TV show, all in the hope of keeping his name lit up in neon letters, as well as locked and loaded in everyone's mouths. Since* Put A Ring On It *began airing a little more than a month ago, Dominic DaSilva's name has remained in the top five trending hashtags on Twitter. No easy feat, that. I tip my hat off to you, Mr. DaSilva; you sure know how to make the right moves, boo.*

3. *As has been mentioned in earlier installments of* Celebrity Tea Presents, *it's been reported—though never confirmed—that America's favorite tight end went on* Put A Ring On It *for all the wrong reasons. In the land of romantic dating shows, "the wrong reasons" might as well be the equivalent of Satan breathing on the back of your neck. It's also synonymous with "money-grabbing jerkoff." You heard it here first.*

4. *Heartbroken, single and recently unemployed, DaSilva moved across the country to a small, Podunk town in Maine, only to come crawling back to his old employer for some extra attention in the form of a segment practically dedicated to London High School, where he now coaches football. I firmly believe that*

this move, more than any other, showcases DaSilva's true intent. Is he any good at photography? Honestly, who cares. (I don't). Does this calendar, however, display an underhandedness to stay relevant within Hollywood? These are the facts as I look at them, Dear Reader.

5. *Just in case we've forgotten: Aspen Clarke. The girl is married. Enough said.*

Truly, I don't need any more examples to prove what we already know: Savannah Rose made the right choice in sending this social climber home. She can do better. So much better.

Will I still be tuning in to tonight's episode of Put A Ring On It, *however? You bet I will. Reporting on the insanity of Hollywood is a job, honey, and Daddy needs to pay his electric bill.*

Consider the tea piping hot and poured, Dear Reader.

I'll see you tomorrow for more juicy celebrity gossip.

34

ASPEN

"*There* we go, boys!" Clapping my hands, I run along the edge of the field as Bobby breaks through the linemen. "Yes, Bobby! Perfect! Go, go, go!"

Across the field, Dominic shouts at his players to pull themselves together.

We're at odds.

Total enemies.

Well, at least until the whistle blows for our next water break.

We've been scrimmaging all morning, and after nearly four weeks of working the kids day in and day out, Monday through Friday, the magic is starting to happen.

It. Is. *Glorious*.

The sounds of pads colliding might as well be music to my ears as Bobby fakes a left, then skirts to the right. Matthew and Kevin, two incoming freshmen, who will probably find themselves on JV at the end of the summer, sprint toward Bobby and the football. Like I drilled into them over and over again in the last month, both boys explode from the hips and lift Bobby straight off the ground.

"Hell fucking yeah!" Dominic calls from the other side of the play, pumping a fist in the air. "Now *that's* what I'm talking about, boys! There we go!" He claps his hands, completely missing the fact that he just dropped an F-bomb, then cups his hands around his mouth and hollers my name.

"Yo, Aspen!"

Aspen, not Levi.

He's been doing that more often than not lately.

Although he's too far away for me to make out his expression, there's no denying the utter glee in his voice when he bellows, "How do you like them apples?!"

Only a man like Dominic DaSilva would dare quote Matt Damon on sacred football ground.

I snatch the whistle from where it hangs on my lanyard and tuck it between my lips. *Tweet! Tweet!*

Everyone halts in their tracks, save for Dominic, who stalks across the field with that swagger of his that should be deemed illegal in all fifty states. "Gather up, boys!" Once I have everyone's attention, I drop the whistle and fold my arms over my chest. "Since Coach DaSilva here thinks his smack talk is going to make us quake in our cleats"—all my offensive line, including Topher, boo like the awesome kids they are—"I think it's only right that we put him in the game."

Chirping crickets are louder than the response I'm given.

Then Topher shoots up a hand, his mouth guard hanging from the corner of his mouth. "Wait, like he'll *play* with us?"

I point to the metal bleachers where we regularly set up shop. "Flag football. I don't need any of you being pummeled by the Hulk over there."

One glance at Dominic shows him smirking and

rubbing his hands together like an evil scientist. Or a retired NFL player who spent years in a league where acquired injuries became equivalent to notches on a bed post.

Harry hooks his fingers over the cage of his helmet. "I'm *so* in."

"Me too!" calls out Bobby, who's still holding the football under his armpit.

Timmy slinks an arm over Matthew's padded shoulders. "I mean, if he comes my way, I'm just gonna take cover." He points up at Matt's face. "That's where you come in, my friend. You can take him."

Matt, who stands almost at six feet tall, though he only recently turned fourteen, curls his gloved hands into a set of vicious claws and growls, "Gooooooo Wildcats!"

Unfortunately for him, puberty is a real pain in the ass and his voice cracks on the last syllable. I smother a laugh amidst manly guffaws. Dominic ambles toward the incoming freshman, pops him on the back with a friendly thump, and says, "Don't worry, kid. Happened to me until I was twenty, at least."

One hard glance at Dominic's face and I know he's fibbing, but some of Matt's redness clears and the grin Dominic gives our JV-hopeful is nothing but kind understanding.

Be still, my heart.

Then he turns on me, that smile leveling out as it turns challenging.

I back up a step. "I don't like that look, Coach."

"You should," he drawls, approaching me like a panther hunting its prey. Once at my side, he turns to face the team. "Who thinks Coach Levi should join the game?"

Some of the kids exchange hesitant looks.

Except for Topher, who sends me a subtle wink. "Oh, I don't know if you guys want to take it that far."

Bobby, falling for my son's ploy, tosses the football up in the air before catching it again. "What? You don't think we can take her?"

"I don't think you can." Topher points to the faint scar in his right eyebrow. "You know how I got this?" Everyone stares at him, waiting. "I got it because my mom taught me everything I know about ball. Every day after school we ran drills together in front of our house. One time, she threw the ball—perfect spiral, guys, *perfect*—and I was so dead set on getting it, I ran right into a tree."

Timmy gapes. "Did you get the ball?"

"Of course I got the ball," my son scoffs. "*Then* I hit the tree."

"So, she's in then." Dominic nabs the football from Bobby's grasp. "We're flagging it up, boys and woman. Get yourselves ready and then meet back here."

I manage two steps toward the bleachers before fingers hook in the waistband of my shorts and tug me backward. Sandalwood. *Dominic.* Putting on my best *go-get-'em* expression, I face him with a smirk that feels more playful than arrogant.

"Wanting to say a few last words?" I taunt, poking him in his hard as steel chest.

He grasps my finger, lifting my hand to his mouth. Heat floods my core, and, oh man, he should *not* be looking at me like that when we're surrounded by teenagers. His dark eyes skirt right, then left, before he drops a single kiss to the inside of my wrist. "Yeah," he murmurs with a silky edge, "don't think I'm gonna go easy on you, Coach."

I stand up taller, spine straight, and take that final step between us. Chest to chest, I tilt my head back and stare him down. "Don't think I'm going to go easy on *you*. I feed off the fear of my enemies."

His chuckle is nothing but hot sex and tangled sheets. "That threat ever work for you?"

"Not even a little."

"I didn't think so." He gives me a gentle push toward the bleachers, the tips of his fingers coming dangerously close to the curve of my butt. When I flash him a warning glance, he pulls back boyishly and stares at his hands like they've personally betrayed him. "No ass grabbing at practice," he berates, rolling his eyes. "Jesus, it's like they don't know any better."

Absolutely ridiculous—but my smile lingers long after I've suited up with my orange flag belt looped around my hips. Since not everyone can join in at once, Dominic and I agree to play twice, first with Group A and then with Group B, who, led by Timmy, forces everyone to into some sort of choreographed cheerleading on the sidelines that has everyone rolling with laughter.

For the sake of getting me in the game longer than the normal kicker, I join the defense as one of the linebackers on the scrimmage line.

I hitch my sweats at the knees, getting down low to the ground.

One glance up puts me at eye level with Topher.

He waggles his eyebrows. "Heya, Mom."

I give him by best mean-mugging glare. "Don't forget who taught you everything you know."

"I won't"—*tweet!*—"oops! Got a ball to catch. See you!"

And then he's off, dashing to the right as he hightails it down the field. I pause only momentarily to admire his excellent form, then push forward, my knees extending as I sprint past Bobby, who's playing wide receiver to Dominic's quarterback.

Because, of course, the Hulk would play QB among his teenage disciples.

"Fall back, Harry!" he shouts now, bouncing up on his toes in that way only professional players do. He's as heavy as a bull and still manages to prance around the field like he's as limber and delicate as a ballerina.

I wait for Dominic to make the pass, my gaze following the arc of the ball as it spirals toward Harry's hands—and then dart forward, yanking one of the orange flags from the teenager's belt.

"Crap!"

Patting Harry's shoulder in commiseration, I look to Dominic and wait for him to catch my eye. When he does, I lift my hand, middle and index fingers straight, and bring them to my eyes in the classic, *I see you* gesture.

With his ball cap facing backward, there's no hiding the way his brows draw inward. He claps his hands, shouting, "Again!"

For a second time, I face off against Topher, whose eyes are narrowed as he drops into position.

I blow him a kiss. "No greeting this time, bud?"

Tweet!

It's been years since I've played football with anyone but Topher in our front yard, but it all comes back to me instinctively. Sure, I'm a little heavier than I was in college—and that's saying nothing about how much harder it is to run with larger, post-baby boobs. But the groove . . . I still have it.

In spades.

Spotting Dominic's intent as he eyes Bobby midway down the field, I change gears and haul ass toward the end zone.

Ten yards.

Five yards.

I look up, expecting to see the ball coming straight down over my head into Bobby's waiting arms when I hear, "Boo-yeah!" come from my left. *Oh, no.* Thighs protesting my abrupt pivot, I watch in awe as Dominic sprints down the field to make the touchdown. Like he's back at Raymond James Stadium playing for the Bucs, he kisses the football and runs in a semicircle, playing to a crowd of teenage boys who worship the ground he walks on.

Then he turns my way, football cradled to his chest, and mimics my earlier threat with his free hand: *I see you.*

"Game on," he mouths for me only.

I love you.

I mouth the three little words to his back, once he's jogging up the field and bumping fists with his teenage teammates.

Not wanting to be outdone, I call for a timeout where I explain the plan. "Like we practiced, guys. Break through the fold and get to the QB. We're gonna take him down."

Matthew lifts a finger. "Can I hit him?"

"It's flag football, Matt. No, you can't tackle him." I clap my hands together. "Okay, let's do this."

Like a unit prepared for battle, we all fall in line.

It's me and Topher, round three.

"I love you," I tell him, just to see him squirm when his teammates overhear me.

He makes a face, groaning, "*Mom.*"

Tweet!

"See-ya, son!"

And then I'm off once again. Lo and behold, the boys stick to the plan. Kevin and another boy, Jason, aren't able to hold the tight formation and I dive right through them.

Pivot on my heels to change trajectory and head straight for Dominic, my arms pumping, my lungs heaving like they haven't in years. Adrenaline fuels me as Dominic arcs his throwing arm back, his gaze locked on someone down the field—I rip off the flag at his hip with such gusto his shorts nearly come down in the process.

Unfortunately, I have so much momentum, stopping isn't an option.

I plow into him, driving us both to the turf with a resounding *thud*.

"Oh, c'mon, Coach!" Matthew shouts at me as I see stars. "You said we couldn't hit him!"

Dominic grunts beneath me, and then I feel his hand around my pelvic bone. "Don't move," he warns, "or everyone is gonna get a real good glimpse of little DaSilva."

I freeze, muscles locking. *Do. Not. Laugh.* It seems a futile cause, especially when I choke out, "I wouldn't call him *little*, per se."

"You're trouble, Coach. You know that?" He hikes his shorts up, lifting me off the ground as he pulls the waistband around his hips. "Big. Fat. Trouble—"

"Dad?"

Topher.

Planting a hand on Dominic's chest, I shove myself up.

"Dad!" I hear Topher shout.

I land on my butt, but there's no mistaking the way my son rushes across the field to the oh-so-familiar figure strolling toward us like he doesn't have a care in the world.

No.

Rick "the Prick" Clarke has descended on London all over again.

35

ASPEN

*B*lood roars in my head.

Why is he here?

Why is he here?

For years, I played the good-cop card. Every time Rick failed to show up to one of Topher's football games, I promised him that Dad had a big surprise coming in the mail for him. I bought Topher video games. Football gear. A basketball hoop for the driveway. Each present that arrived at our house was signed by Rick, courtesy of his personal assistant, Patty.

In our house, we have only one rule: never lie.

And I broke it time and time again, all to ensure Topher never saw beneath the slick veneer Rick wears oh too well.

One day, I figured Topher would learn the truth. One day, which I always hoped would never actually come, and if it did, I prayed for it to be sometime in my baby boy's twenties or thirties—later, when he was older, so he would be more emotionally equipped to handle the devastation.

I never expected it to happen now, on a high school football field surrounded by his peers.

My heart shatters when Topher throws his lanky arms around Rick's shoulders and Rick doesn't return the gesture. Like a statue, he stands there, accepting the affection as though it's his right, before gingerly removing Topher's arms and stepping to the side.

Altogether, the hug lasts less than five seconds.

For a teenage boy who's always craved his father's attention, five seconds is all it takes for devastation to settle in.

Topher's expression crumbles at Rick's casual ambivalence.

Fuck you, Rick. Fuck. You.

"Aspen."

A hand grasps my bicep, but I shake it off. "Dominic, not right now. Please—"

"*Aspen.*"

I whip around, frustration boiling to the surface as though I'm a pot that's been set to heat for far too long. "*What?*"

Black eyes flit from me to the team. "Take Topher and go home. I'll deal with the kids." He gives me a little shake, staring down at me. "Tell me something you're grateful for —right now."

Right now? He wants me to count one of my lucky blessings right *now?*

I slick my tongue over my bottom lip, struggling to come up with something when my ex-husband is upsetting my son and my emotions are fired up and ready to make Rick rue the day he was ever born.

Dominic's grip tightens around my shoulders. "I'm grateful for *you*," he tells me, his voice low, urgent, "because it wasn't until you that I knew love wasn't a figment of imagination. I see it—every time you look at Topher and your players."

Every time you look at me, his dark gaze implores.

I swallow, hard. "Dom—"

And then the voice of my nightmares interrupts us, and sneers, "You always were about that easy pussy, weren't you, DaSilva?"

36

DOMINIC

*R*ichard Clarke has the stereotypical appearance of a used car salesman.

Slick, brown hair that reminds me of Topher's, but instead of hanging in front of his face, Clarke's is smoothed back over what I want to imagine is a bald spot.

He's dressed in a navy-blue suit, no matter the fact that he's standing on a football field. The fabric is clearly tailored, with silver thread and silver cufflinks and a matching silver handkerchief tucked away for safekeeping in his breast pocket.

Leather loafers that no doubt cost as much as my ramshackle investment property.

He looks exactly the same now as he did when he flew to Tampa and invited me to a business lunch, the particulars of which have never escaped me. Even then, during a time when I took sponsorships from companies whose morals didn't align with my own, all for the sake of a healthy paycheck, I looked Rick Clarke in the eye and knew I would never take this man up on his offer.

The fact that he just insinuated Levi is an easy lay hasn't

escaped me and my hands ball tightly at my sides. I want to ram my fist into his perfect nose. Watch the blood spurt out from his nostrils and see his eyes go wide when he realizes that I'm about to make his life a living hell.

I step forward menacingly, fully prepared to deck him.

Only, instead of being intimidated by my size, he only smirks. Then plucks at his jacket sleeves, brushing away nonexistent lint. "I wouldn't do that," he says pleasantly, "or are you trying to teach your team that violence is an acceptable method of communication?"

The pointed reminder, that we have forty-plus teenage eyes trained on us, is the only reason I don't lay him out cold where he stands.

Speaking slowly, so he doesn't miss a word, I demand, "You're crashing practice, Clarke. Couldn't find it in yourself to wait out the last thirty minutes in your car?"

Though I outsize him by at least six inches, Clarke doesn't shirk back in fear. Nor does he once spare a glance toward Levi.

Fucking prick.

Levi bumps me out of the way, fury embedded in her stiff movements as she confronts her douchebag ex-husband. "I'm going to let your comment slide, Rick—but only because I don't give a damn what you think of me." Her nostrils flare. "But that doesn't excuse you shrugging your son off just now. How could you *do* that? He misses you."

"He's fine, Levi."

Her jaw visibly tightens. "He's called you every day for the last month and a half."

"And we've spoken," Clarke says calmly, like they're discussing the weather and not their fifteen-year-old boy who looks like his dog has just been stomped on by an elephant. "Once a week, every Friday at 3 p.m."

I've never seen Levi more livid. The pulse in her temple jumpstarts, fluttering fast. "You're lying," she seethes, breathing heavily. "Topher wouldn't lie about something like you never calling him."

"Topher is a teenager, and teenagers lie. Now"—Clarke's black eyes cut to my face—"I'm in the mood for a beer. DaSilva, care to join me?"

Over my dead fucking body.

The words are on the tip of my tongue, ready to fly, when I spot the boys watching the three of us. Timmy has his shoulder pressed up against Topher's in silent camaraderie. On the other side of Levi's son are Harry and Bobby. All are sporting serious, flat mouths and hard eyes. All witnessed Clarke brush off his only son.

Just as they all watched Levi unravel the moment her ex-husband showed up.

They might not know who this man is, but they know enough to recognize when things are on a one-lane track to shit creek.

Jesus *fuck*.

The last thing I want to do is spend any amount of time with Rick Clarke, especially after that nasty comment of his, but this . . . this is what you do for the people you care for, right? You put their best interests before your own. You take the hurt and the frustration and bear it so they don't have to.

Purposely, I turn to Levi and subtly brush my fingers over her knuckles. "Aspen, wrap up practice, will you?"

Her eyes promise murder if I go with her ex-husband.

Better me than her. I don't trust the asshole farther than I can throw him—which says a lot because I played both tight end and quarterback at LSU. Brien hated that I was his backup. I always did love to needle him and pretend I'd steal his position.

"*Aspen.*"

She jerks away, her body poised to strike. "Sure, yeah. I can do that, *Coach.*" Storming away, she hollers to the guys to strip off their flag belts and prepare for conditioning.

Pissed or not, hopefully she'll realize I'm subjecting myself to Rick's company so she won't have to. Because she needs to bring Topher home and comfort him after his dad's stinging rejection.

Clarke, cold as stone, raises a single brow as he watches his ex-wife with an inscrutable expression. I want to sling back an arm and knock him out cold. Instead, I shove his shoulder with mine, locker-room style, and head for the parking lot. I don't say a word.

He wanted a beer? Fine.

But that doesn't mean we have to do a damn bit of talking—and it sure as hell doesn't mean I can't take him behind a bar and bust his face in.

37

ASPEN

"*I* hate him!"

I barely get my front door closed before Topher erupts, throwing his duffel bag on the floor with unleashed anger.

I hate him too. More than you'll ever know.

I keep the words locked up inside myself, the way I've done for years now. I've never wanted to be the mother who talks poorly about her ex-husband. No, I want Topher to make his own decisions and come to his own way of thinking, but with Rick cold-shouldering him on the field . . . I feel the embarrassment radiating off my son in waves.

"Baby," I murmur softly, pointing to the couch, "come sit down. Please."

Topher's shoulders hunch forward. "You don't understand. You *don't get it!*"

My heart splinters as I watch him pace the living room like a caged animal. All his life, Topher has been the gentlest soul. He doesn't yell and he rarely throws tantrums, even when I ground him for pulling stupid stunts, but this . . . this bottled-up rage. This isn't *him*.

"I need you to make me understand, Toph." I sit first, hoping it'll convince him to follow my lead. I pat the cushion beside me. "Make me see."

Although he doesn't sit, he swarms into the living room with his hands clamped behind his dark head, arms bent like chicken wings. Then, on a short, pentup breath, he exhales, "Dad asked me to stay with him."

My world goes dark.

Just like that, the living room tips sideways and I grip the couch cushion, like it might somehow keep me upright, and I blink back the sudden onslaught of tears. *Don't cry in front of him, girl. Keep yourself together!*

Easier said than done.

I know that mothers are separated from their children every day.

I know that—and I know that Rick, deep down, must miss his only son, but I . . . I—

A sob breaks from my soul, and I cover my mouth with my hand to keep it down. Suppress it. Force it so deep within my heart that Topher sees me as only calm and collected, willing to accept whatever decision he's made.

Please don't leave me.

I shush the inner begging and raise my gaze to meet my son's. Swallowing down all my inner flailing, I manage a warbled, "I'm sure he misses you, baby. We both love you so much."

"He doesn't."

"He *does*."

Topher tugs at his hair, pulling sharply. And then he explodes, kicking at the coffee table with the sole of his shoe. "*Why do you defend him?*"

I'm wholly unprepared for the question.

My chin snaps back in shock. "Topher, I'm not *defending* him."

Another kick, though this one misses the table's leg. "You *are*. You always do! Anytime I ask you about him, you say the same thing. Your dad loves you, baby," Topher mimics in a high-pitched voice, "he's just busy." He laughs, the sound hard and piercing. "Yeah, he's busy, Mom. He's busy cheating on you and you—and you just *accepted it*. For years."

I feel the blood drain from my face.

Tingles come to life in my legs, in my arms. Like a prisoner of my own making, I sit with my tongue tied—because nothing I say will sound good. I either expose Rick for the asshole he is, or I try to salvage any relationship he'll ever have with his son . . . despite the fact that he doesn't seem to care.

A virtual Grandfather's clock pops up in my head, taunting me with its passing hands and ticking time.

I don't know what to do.

Rubbing my lips together, buying myself time, I squeeze my thighs with my hands. "Topher, it's not so easy to explain. All you need to know is that I love you and Daddy loves you and—"

"No lying."

I wouldn't be surprised if blood stops circulating to my feet, my grip on my knees is so tight.

"You told me," Topher says, dropping his butt to the coffee table and sitting down right in front of me, "that we have one rule in our home. *No lying.*"

He has me backed into a corner and he knows it.

Breathing slowly through my nose, I scrub at my tears with the heel of my palm. As much as I want to keep this secret from Topher, I won't let Rick ruin the relationship I have with my son. Topher is my world, and I . . . God, I would have died so many times over during my marriage if I hadn't had him to brighten my day. Some people look to God or angels or other all-powerful beings for guidance—all I ever needed was Topher to show me the path to take. Like I told Dominic, my son is my secret weapon. And my secret weapon kept me alive even in the darkest times of my life.

"Your dad . . ." God, I don't want to say this. My throat feels too tight, my chest even tighter. "I don't know how many times I filed for divorce, Toph. I could lie and give you an exact number, but the truth is, I lost count."

He visibly swallows. "Then why would you stay?"

Briefly, I lower my lids.

I'm grateful for moving to London with Topher.

I'm grateful he's made such great friends.

I'm grateful that he met Dominic, who can show him what it's like to be a good, honest man with a kind heart.

"Mom?"

I open my eyes and give him the truth: "Because I wouldn't have had you."

"I-I don't understand."

Flexing my hands, I stare at my unpainted nails and try not to hear *his* voice: *Can't you fucking dress like a woman for once? It's like I'm sleeping with a goddamn man.*

Rick enjoyed chasing a legend in the making.

He also found pervasive pleasure in destroying every-thing that made me special.

"Bud, sometimes . . ." I struggle for words, wishing they would come on demand. As one might expect, they don't, and I'm left to fumble my way through the murky darkness. "Sometimes when people have a lot of money, they do things that are wrong." Crap. That's not right. Cursing under my breath, I try again. "What I'm trying to say is, Daddy is worth a lot, Toph. A *lot*. Enough that he made it so I could leave, but if I did, he kept full custody of you. I couldn't . . . I couldn't do that, baby. I couldn't leave you behind."

It's why I started coaching. Because I needed my own money—I had no college degree at that point; I had no life skills aside from football. I begged Rick to let me work, faking a need to be out of the house and doing something on my own.

I always suspected he knew how desperate I was to succeed, all so I could pay for a high-class lawyer and leave him. High-class because with Rick's seven-figure paycheck, I didn't stand a chance against him with anything less. He called judges friends, lawyers his best buddies, people across the country his close confidantes.

And he made the matter of Topher's custody the one thing that would keep me locked to his side for years. He didn't want me, but he didn't want anyone else to have me either.

A bird whose feathers were clipped prematurely, then shoved into a gilded cage with no hope for escape.

I haven't breathed—*really* breathed—in fifteen years, not since I returned to London.

Blue eyes, the same shade as my own, well up with tears. "So you stayed with him because of me?"

"Yes."

I would have stayed longer, too, but Topher's shock at finding two women in Rick's bed a year ago proved to be the one thing that unlocked the keys to my prison. No judge could rule that Rick was fit to parent a child when he was rarely home, couldn't even remember his son's phone number, and brought home strange women every night.

Reaching out, my hands find Topher's. "I would do anything for you. *Anything*, Topher. Do you hear me?"

His fingers interlace with mine, holding tight. "I don't want to go back to Pittsburgh, Mom. I want to stay *here*, with you and Coach DaSilva and Aunt Willow and my friends. Dad told me before we moved that you would end up sending . . . sending me back." His nose twitches, like he's trying to hold back the tears. "Please don't."

Rick said that, did he?

Temper spiking, I drop to my knees and hug Topher around the waist. "Never. You're never going back unless you want to."

38

DOMINIC

*T*he Golden Fleece has taken the *Put A Ring On It* fantasy league to new levels.

The minute I walk into the pub, I spot my face in a blown-up, cardboard cutout along the far side of the wall, near the jukebox. Beside fake me is a matching cutout of Nick Stamos and the other eight contestants who have yet to be sent home by Savannah Rose.

"Like it?" Shawn asks, a damp rag slung over one shoulder as he wipes down a glass with a dry towel. "A gift from an anonymous donor."

I let out a low whistle. "Fancy gift."

"That's what I said when Fed-Ex dropped it off on Monday." The bartender eyes me, slicking up, raking down. "I can't imagine who the hell would spend money on something so absolutely ridiculous."

"You post them on the Golden Fleece's social media accounts yet?" I ask, all smooth obliviousness.

"Of course we did. What, do you think I'm not willing to make some extra cash by bringing all of Mount Desert into this fantasy league? We're tripling our usual Wednesday revenue."

I grip his shoulder, offering him a sly grin. "Then my work here is done."

"I knew it was you!"

I mime zipping my mouth shut. "Anonymous donor who loves fantasy-league sports." Tapping my head, I point at Shawn. "You hear me?"

The elderly bartender salutes me. "I hear you. And while no one is around, let me just say thank you."

Grimacing, I grunt, "You might want to hold off on the grateful schtick."

"You're not so bad, once you get under all that black— Jesus Christ, what the hell is Rick Clarke doing here?"

Like the devil himself has been summoned, Clarke appears beside me. "He's meeting me."

Shawn shoots me a look that could stop a man in his tracks.

Lucky for him, this isn't a social call.

I'm gonna let Clarke have his beer and then I'm gonna send him packing so fast he won't even know what hit him. No one fucks with Levi or Topher, especially not him.

"Two beers," I tell Shawn. "We won't be long."

"You don't even know why I asked you to meet me," Clarke interjects, trailing behind when I head for the closest booth. I let Levi's ex take the seat that leaves his back open to the door.

Sitting diagonally, so my legs can extend out to the left of the table, I drape my arms over the back of the booth. "We're not here for socializing," I growl, my voice resolutely hard. "I said pretty much all I have to say to you in an email that's probably rotting away in your inbox."

"Ah, the email." Clarke undoes the top two buttons of his suit jacket. "It's funny, of course."

Knowing I'm being baited into conversation, I bite out, "What's funny?"

"That email." Shaking his head, the older man strips off his jacket and lays it across the table. "Did you know that Levi read it? Her response to your . . . crassness was illuminating."

My molars might disintegrate to dust, I'm grinding them so bad. "Illuminating."

"Yes, illuminating." Clarke leans back, issuing a no-named thank you when Shawn drops off our beers. "She said you were bullish."

Ignoring the condensation on the glass, I bring the Bud Light up to my mouth. "An improvement over what she called me when we first met in person . . . right here in this bar."

A tick pulses to life in his jaw.

Bingo.

When he first rolled up on the field, I didn't want to believe it, but it's all too clear that Rick Clarke is here for one reason only: to keep me away from his ex-wife. I'm not entirely sure how he knows about us, though I have to assume that someone showed him the articles from *Celebrity Tea Presents*, particularly the one where they called her Aspen Clarke and claimed she's still married to the asshole sitting across from me.

From between gritted teeth, Clarke edges out, "And what, exactly, did she call you?"

I smile at him, all wide and toothy—because I know it'll piss him off. "An asshole."

His dark eyes, so unlike Topher's, widen marginally. "And that doesn't anger you?"

I like to think of it as our own special blend of foreplay.

Since there's no chance in hell I'm ever gonna admit that to her ex-husband, I merely shrug my shoulders and opt for another sip of beer. I dangle the bottle loosely from my index finger and thumb. "Why fight it when it's true—you feel me? Now"—I point the base of the bottle toward him —"what the hell are you really doing here in London, Clarke? And don't give me that bullshit about wanting to see your son. I saw how you reacted to Topher out there, and you should be feeling lucky as fuck right now that I'm not looking to sit behind bars again anytime soon."

The *I've-been-locked-up* card is not one I pull often.

But it has its time and place, and this is one of them. At six-foot-six, I could do major damage to Clarke without breaking a sweat.

He knows it.

I know it.

He clears his throat awkwardly.

I sit my ass back in the booth, beer bottle in my hand, and don't say a word.

Sometimes, silence is the best intimidation tactic.

I learned that in juvie too.

Clarke clasps his Bud Light between his hands. "I'd like to offer you a job."

A job. That's . . . unexpected. And incredibly unwanted.

When I lift my brows, encouraging him to move on or get out, his fingers reflexively squeeze the bottle's glass neck. "As a recruiter for the Steelers. Clearly, you have a passion for coaching." He glances around at the pub, taking in the sparse décor and the candles seated at every table. "But staying here in Maine is a waste of your talents."

I make a dramatic show of sitting up straighter. "You really think so?"

"Do I?" Clarke echoes, a hint of emotion finally coating his tone. "You've won two Super Bowl rings. You're the Heisman trophy winner from college. The MVP winner from half of your seasons, at least, while you played for the Bucs. Do I *think* so?"

Once upon a time, someone listing off my accolades would have inspired a sense of excitement and fulfillment within me. After all, when you have no sense of self-worth, it always feels real nice to be the recipient of good, old-fashioned praise.

Eighteen-year-old me would have been a puddle of goo right now.

Thirty-five-year-old me only takes another sip of my beer, purposely dragging out my response to make the man sweat. "I'm not looking to play matchmaker."

Clarke sits forward in the booth. "I'm not saying anything about matchmaking with the players, DaSilva. I'm talking about you leaving this Podunk, small-ass town and doing something with your life."

I like this Podunk, small-ass town.

And crazy as it may seem, I feel like working with the Wildcats blends all of my interests. Football, working with kids and making a difference in their lives, *Levi.*

"Coordinator, then." Some of the lackluster enthusiasm in Clarke's face dilutes. That tick in his jaw comes roaring back, and this time his nostrils flare too. "All right, special teams. How does that sound? I can't promise you a top coaching position, but something smaller to start out? That I can do easily."

I put my beer down. Plant my hands flat on the table and jut my chin forward. "Cut the goddamn bullshit, Clarke. You're not offering this job out of the goodness of your heart. So why don't you tell me the real reason you came all the way to this small-ass, *Podunk* town?"

I'm no idiot. I know why he's here, but I want to hear him say it.

I want him to show, once again, that he's a controlling bastard who thinks he can play God with a snap of his fingers and a promise to give a man what *he* thinks we all want. I didn't want his offer of pussy and money and fame seven years ago, and I certainly don't want anything he's offering now.

Dark eyes level on my face, unwavering. "Levi—"

"Is not yours."

With the front door to the Golden Fleece propped open and all the blinds drawn back, there's no hiding the rage that twists Clarke's features. "I don't know what you think is going to transpire between you and Levi, but I can promise this: you'll get sick of her soon enough." His knuckles whiten around the bottle's glass neck. "The woman you see now? That is *my* doing. Her long blond hair? Me. She looked like a dyke when I met her. Her big tits and the meat on her bones? *Me.* Fucking her for the first five years of our marriage was like screwing a man." His mouth twists angrily. "Anytime she stepped out of line, I put her in her place. So, when you're fucking her and thinking she's the woman of your dreams, just remember I had her first. Everything you like about her, I created. I took her out of this goddamn town and made her who she is. *I* did that."

Put her in her place.

The last time I punched someone, the producers on *Put A Ring On It* asked me to get physical with another one of the contestants. The altercation was mapped out in advance. Me defending my so-called honor against a sniveling prick out of Kansas. I refused. The investment broker didn't.

When you see a fist swinging in your direction, though, it's only human nature to strike back. And, I did—hard—with one upper right hook to the chin.

Down he blows.

Staring at Rick Clarke now, my knuckles are already tingling with the want for retribution. But this isn't a bare knuckle fight on low-grade reality TV. It's real life. And until this moment, I never realized the scope of misery that Levi suffered being married to this jackass.

The mental abuse she no doubt suffered.

The manipulative tactics and the destruction of her psyche.

Without even asking her, I know why she stayed. I know why she put up with it all, even as her ex-husband changed everything about her.

Topher.

My own mother walked out on me when I was five-years-old and never looked back.

Levi survived fourteen fucking years with this fool because her son needed her.

I've never met another person like her. No one else in the world is as good as she is, as pure and driven and loving and kind. And I'm one lucky asshole that she looks at me and sees someone worthy of standing by her side.

My ass comes off the seat. Tension like I haven't felt in years, since that long-ago day in my childhood that put me on a path straight to hell, turns my blood cold. "Say it again."

Suffocating in his own ego, Clarke doesn't even have the wits about him to realize I'm walking a very tight rope that ends with my fist battering his face. He follows suit, straightening from the booth and getting in my face. "I fucked her, DaSilva. I fucked with her mind and I fucked with her body, and once Topher agrees to move back to Pittsburgh with me, I'll fuck with her heart too, you—"

Crack!

Arm cocked back and rearing to go, I look from my balled fist to Clarke's stunned expression to Levi standing just behind her ex-husband, her glass bottle shattered and spewing beer like a fountain of alcoholic debauchery all over his head.

I love her.

It's certainly not the most appropriate time to realize it, considering she just bashed her ex-husband over the head with a bottle of Bud Light, but I've never done anything in my life by the books. Why start with the way I fall in love? Her blond hair is in disarray around her face and her skin glistens with beer. She takes my goddamn breath away.

Like the goddess of justice, she tosses the broken bottle to the ground. "That's for thinking for one friggin' second that you could *ever* manipulate our son into playing your stupid games."

Clutching his head, Clarke stumbles out of the booth. "You crazy fucking bitch."

"You're right," Levi hisses, her normally delicate features severe in her fury. "I *am* a crazy fucking bitch—I put up with you for far longer than I ever should have, no matter what you held over my head. You plucked me out of this town like I was your treat of the month and then you spent the next fourteen years *ruining me*."

If she's expecting Clarke to show any remorse, she doesn't get it.

He only laughs harshly, like a lunatic, and tears a hand away from his skull to point a bloodied finger at her face. "Did you walk in too late to hear this part? I *made* you, Levi." He wavers to the right, looking green in the face. "I dressed you up and stripped you down and you should be thanking me for all I've done for you."

"You're wrong."

I glance over at the bar, expecting to see Shawn prepared to throw down the hatchet but he's not behind the bar. Figures the longtime bartender would take his break the minute shit's about to hit the fan.

Sauntering toward Levi on visibly weak legs, he taunts, "I made you, sweetheart. You were nothing before me."

Fuck this.

Before he can advance any farther, I grab the neck of Clarke's damp button-down shirt and pull—hard. With his balance already shot from the hit to his head, Levi's ex-husband careens backward, arms pinwheeling almost comically. I step to the side when he topples to the floor.

How the mighty fall.

"I was *someone*, Rick," Levi bursts, her face contorting with frustration. "I had dreams long before you showed up, and you know what? Let me say thank you." She sweeps forward, her eyes flinty, the toes of her shoes practically stomping on her ex. "*Thank you* for being such an asshole. You opened the unlikeliest doors for me: I discovered that I love coaching. I learned what I want out of a relationship and what I don't. And you gave me my most important mission in life: to make sure that your son turns out to be nothing like you. So, thank you—because you took a twenty-one-year-old woman and made her strong and invincible, and I. Love. Me."

"Poor, little Aspen Levi," Clarke mocks as he crawls onto his feet to stand, "trying to be brave. Do you remember what happened when you first told me no—"

I don't have the time to stop it. One second I'm twisting

at the waist with the intention of grabbing Clarke to shut him the hell up, and then Levi is doing it for me.

Thud!

Oh. *Shit.*

Clarke falls to his ass as Levi sucker punches her ex-husband in the gut. She's fuming, blue eyes large and murderous in her face. *Time for this to end.* I'm reaching into the fray, intent on yanking Levi away before she does any lasting damage and we have a lawsuit on our hands, when I hear it:

"Oh shit, is that Rick 'the Prick' Clarke?"

I twist to stare at the newcomers, only to find Oliver standing not ten feet away with two buddies. He stares at me, holding onto a flailing Levi, and I stare at him. He turns to his friend, and says, "Hold my beer, Stuart."

Stuart, the friend, narrows his eyes. "Are you hurt, Levi?"

Her biceps tense under my grip. "And you care *why*? You told me your wife was dead just to mess with me."

Do they know each other? And what the hell—he pretended his wife was dead? I don't have the chance to ask the question before the third dude exclaims, "Wait, she's *bleeding!*"

"Fuck that dude," Oliver growls at the same time Stuart snaps, "Hold our beers, Sam, no one fucks with a Levi but us," before promptly thrusting his and Oliver's beer bottles to the third guy.

And then . . . and then straight mayhem ensues.

Londoners storm the Golden Fleece, and if this was the eighteenth century and not the twenty-first, today's festivities would result in someone being drawn and quartered out on the town square.

No one fucks with a Levi.

I manage to snag her T-shirt before she can launch

herself forward all over again. With little finesse, I drag her back and into my chest.

"Dominic, let me go!"

"Not a chance, baby. I saved you a front-row seat."

Chairs fly.

Clarke, red-faced and shaky on his feet, throws half-hearted swings at the Londoners out to defend one of their own.

There's something almost poetic in the deliverance of sweet justice.

Hey, I might be a man in love but I'm still the same old Dominic DaSilva.

Sirens screech outside and then two officers jam through the front door. Over the heads of everyone brawling, including Shawn, I watch as the dark-haired officer re-holsters his gun and sighs. "Jesus Christ," he calls out, "who the hell started this?"

All fingers point to Rick, who, in turn, jabs a finger in Levi's direction.

"Goddammit," the other officer grunts, "my wife's gonna kill me if I show up late and miss Savannah Rose's one-on-one dates this week."

39

ASPEN

$\mathcal{T}$he Mount Desert Island County Jail smells like roses and killed dreams.

The roses make sense: I spotted a vase when Officer Temler brought me in, my wrists cuffed.

The killed dreams make sense too. My holding cell is only ten feet away from the front desk, which means I hear every blistering second of Rick calling his lawyer to make bond. On his way out, he stops in front of my cell. His precious suit is drenched in beer, and there's a cut on his temple from a Bud Light shard. I should regret hitting him over the head with a bottle. I should regret it—but I can't. Because this man, who I once loved with everything that I was, turned me into a shadow of myself. He tore me down and used my own son to keep me in place, and a single bottle—which barely glanced his head, mind you—doesn't come anywhere close to the number of betrayals he dropped at my feet in the last fifteen years.

"Have you come to gloat that you're walking free?" I ask, never letting my gaze waver from his familiar face. I let this man touch me. I let this man *inside* me. And yet he stands there like a stranger, the bars of my cell the physical divide that's metaphorically separated us for years. When he remains quiet, I huff out a frustrated laugh. "I'm done, Rick. Done with you and your selfishness."

"My lawyer asked if I wanted to pay your bond," he finally mutters, looking uncomfortable as he tugs on his suit cuffs, "I said I would."

I meet his gaze. "No."

"You'd seriously rather sit in that cell? Are you kidding me, Levi?"

I pat the cot I've been camped out on since being led in here. "Let me phrase this differently for you: I don't want to see you again. Not in London, not anywhere. If you have an issue, take it up with my lawyer. As for Topher, I suggest learning how to repair your relationship with your son. I'm not doing it for you anymore. You want him to think you're honorable? You want him to *love* you?" I drop my elbows to my thighs. "Then show him you care. Or else one day you'll wake up and realize that you're alone and you'll have no one to blame for that but yourself."

His expression stiffens. But Rick doesn't do vulnerability, and if my warning has any impact on him, he doesn't say it. Instead, he only issues me his usual cold-hearted farewell: "See you when I see you, Levi."

He strides off down the hallway, and I can't help but snort "good riddance" under my breath.

I hope he's sorry. I hope he gets on his private jet back to Pittsburgh and stays there forever. I've spent years sheltering Topher from the truth but, considering I'm drenched with booze and sitting in a jail cell, I think it's safe to say I've reached the end of my rope.

If Topher decides to speak with his dad after this, I won't stop him.

But I'm done. Finished. *Finite.*

Oh, my God, I'm in jail.

Unlike Rick, I wasn't given the opportunity to make my one call, which seems a little unconstitutional if you ask me. I mean, I've seen enough *NCIS* episodes on TV to know that everyone deserves one call.

Right?

As the adrenaline coursing through my system eases, I can't help but wonder how long I'll be stuck behind bars. Eternity is a hell of a long time to pay penance for smashing a bottle of cheap beer over your ex-husband's head.

I wrack my brain, trying to remember how long people serve for battery charges. *NCIS* is proving useless. All I know are formations for football drills, special teams tips, and random facts about US History that could bore an officer to death. *Thank you, online college degree.*

It's not enough. I left Topher with my mom and the knitting club, so at least I know my baby boy will be cared for. But what about Harry—the police are still searching for his mom—and Timmy and Bobby? Hope dwindles like a melted candlewick. I still haven't taken Meredith up on her offer to grab some wine.

The sound of footsteps jerks my head up, and I scramble off the narrow cot to wait by the caged door to plead my case. *It better not be Rick again for round three.*

"Hello!" Resigned to the fact that I've officially hit rock bottom at the ripe old age of thirty-seven, I rattle the bars. "Hey! Hey, Officer—please, I'm sorry. You have to understand how sorry I am." The footsteps grow louder, nearer. "I need to make a phone call. Doesn't everyone get one call? I need to—"

Like the son of Lucifer himself, Dominic saunters into the small hall outside my cell. Dressed in all black, he swirls a key around one finger, looking relaxed and amused and—Oh, my God, he is *not* whistling right now.

But he is, and he's whistling a tune I know all too well.

Five Finger Death Punch's *Bad Company*—the song I made his personal ringtone after the day Topher crashed my car into his truck.

The whistling stops, and then Dominic catches the keys mid-swing.

"You know," he murmurs, voice low, "I never thought I'd find myself in lockup again after my last stint. But here we are—mind if I take a seat?" He points to a bench that looks like it's seen better days.

Not that it stops him from sitting down anyway. The bench's legs whine, protesting the onslaught of Dominic's bulky weight, but he only pats the empty space beside him and tests its strength by shimmying his lower half, the same way he did up on The Monster to mess with me.

Slowly, succinctly, I force the words out of my mouth: "Are you here to save me?"

"Save you?" he echoes, straightening the bill of his black hat as he relaxes against the wall, his long legs sprawled out before him. He folds his hands over his flat stomach. "Nah, Coach, you save yourself every day. You don't need me to play knight in shining armor. You're a badass all on your own."

Confused, I stare at him blankly. "Then why are you here?"

He swings those keys again, a taunting circle that catches my eye. "I'm gonna tell you a little story. That work for you?" The jangle of the keys stops when they hit his palm and he gestures to the bars. "Not that you can really go anywhere. It seems you're at my disposal, baby."

My eyes narrow on him as my fingers curl around the metal bars. "*Dominic . . .*"

"You know that I ended up behind bars because I robbed a corner store. What I didn't tell you is that I did so at gunpoint. Yeah, I heard that gasp, Coach. It's okay—we both already know I'm not up for a running at being America's next sweetheart."

He scrubs a hand along his jawline, and I track that move with my stomach twisting unpleasantly. I knew he'd been in trouble with the law in his youth—he'd told me himself and Google always comes through with a few strokes on the keyboard—but nowhere had I read . . . *that* about the gun.

Mouth dry, I edge out, "You never said how old you were."

Dominic tilts his head slightly, those expressive dark eyes rooted to my face. "Eleven. Old enough to know better, young enough to think I wouldn't get caught." His hand falls to his thigh, the keys clattering like chimes blowing in the breeze. In here, behind these bars, it feels so very hard to breathe. "You take a kid who has nothing—has no one—and he'll do just about anything to fit in. Don't pretend you don't see it with the kids you've coached over the last decade. Hope is a fragile thread, baby. You know that, too, don't you? After living with a man like Clarke, hope is what kept you going."

I lick my lips, wishing I had water to quench my suddenly parched throat. "Topher," I rasp, "Topher is what kept me going."

A small smile flits to his face, like my response is one that soothes him. "I had football." He says it simply, without averting his gaze. "I had football and random people's couches and a bike I stole from a junkyard to get me to and from practice. Until I ended up with Mr. and Mrs. Halloway after my last stint in juvie, I stole whatever gear I needed to play the game. Because football was my way out. Football was gonna save me, and that fragile thread of hope, Asp, it thickened. Strengthened."

"But?" I whisper.

His gaze heats, the palm of his hand curling tightly around the keys. "But inside I was still that helpless little kid, abandoned by his mother in an apartment for twenty-seven days. Lonely. Starving. Unwanted." His Adam's apple bobs down the length of his throat. "I once read somewhere that a kid's most formative years are from birth to twelve years old. Maybe that's bullshit. Maybe it's not. I don't really know. All I know is that I've lived my life with hope in one hand and self-destruction in the other. I've traveled the world, I've played with the best athletes this country will ever see, and you know . . . you know the only thought I had when I came down wrong on my leg?"

I don't need to ask him to elaborate about what he's talking about.

Because I know the game of football inside and out.

Because the first time we met, I was watching that 2015 game at the Golden Fleece, and whispered, "Not even assholes deserve that."

Aware that I'm clinging to the metal bars like I'm on the verge of attempting to crawl through the narrow slats, I take a deep, stabilizing breath. Then, "Make me see."

It's what I told him when he sat down in my courtyard and bared a corner of his soul. *Let me in*, my hearts sings now. *Trust me.*

Jaw tight, Dominic confesses, "Let me die."

I whimper, hands closing over my mouth because I can see the truth in his searing gaze. I hear it in the dark rumble of his voice, and I squeeze my eyes shut. Pressure builds behind my eyelids, but still Dominic doesn't stop.

He gives me no reprieve.

"That fragile thread of hope was gone. I was tired. Fucking exhausted with being in my head and wondering why I could have everything at my fingertips—money, houses, cars, women—and none of it mattered. I rode a bike down Devil's Road, half hoping I'd crash and burn. I climbed a mountain in China, wondering with every other step if the plank of wood beneath my feet would crumble and give out. But roaches"—he lets out a dark, caustic laugh—"they stick around. They survive, even when nothing else does. And then I met you."

Peeling my eyes open, conscious of the tears slipping down my cheeks, I meet his gaze. His rugged features, once so impassive that his ambivalence drove me insane, are cracked wide open. He hides nothing from me: not the way his mouth trembles as he tries to smile or how his eyes glisten, his own tears ready to spill.

To the world, Dominic DaSilva is a bad-boy charmer, a smooth-voiced asshole, a football-playing legend.

To me, he is this man.

Open. Vulnerable. Trusting.

"And then I met you," he rasps thickly, "a woman with sapphire eyes and the sweetest laugh that kept my ass on that bar stool when I knew better than to stay. Even when Topher banged up your car, you didn't yell at him. I watched you bring snacks every day for the boys, even though every granola bar and carrot bag came out of your own pocket—but you couldn't bear to see any of them go hungry. You showed everyone such *love*, and I . . . I wanted that, baby. I wanted to feel loved by you and you better believe that scared the shit out of me."

"Dominic, I do. I lov—"

He cuts me off with an abrupt shake of his head, holding one hand up. "Let me finish. Please."

I nod, no matter the fact that these bars are in my way and I'm desperate to go to him.

Clearing his throat, he goes on. "When I saw Clarke striding across that field, I wanted to nail him to a wall. Knock him down. Put him through misery because he'd done that to you for fourteen fucking years." His mouth curves in an amused smirk. "Except that you knocked him down yourself—because that's the sort of woman *you* are. Everything about you is vivid. Your smile, the pitch of your laugh, to the way you constantly surprise me." A soft, husky chuckle that goes straight to my core. "I enjoy every single minute of being shocked by you. You put me in my place, and I . . . Well, I never expected the words *I love you* to pop into my head just as you bashed a bottle on your ex-husband's head like a total badass, but there you have it. Figures I wouldn't fall for a normal woman who only wants flowers and a date."

He stands, rising to his full height. My chin tips back, so I can keep my gaze zeroed in on his face. "I got you, instead," he tells me, ambling closer, until his hands are on either side of mine on the bars and he's leaning down so that my whole world is nothing but his black eyes. "A badass football player. The best damn coach this town has ever seen. A mother who will go through hell and back for her son. And a woman . . ." His throat constricts. "A woman who saw a broken man, and instead of walking away, you pushed me back into the light—a place I never even knew existed. I love you, Aspen Levi. I love you so fucking much and, honestly, I'm only a little sorry that I waited until you were in prison to tell you, but no time like the present, right?"

I hear nothing but the sound of blood roaring in my head.

And his confession on repeat: *I love you, Aspen Levi. I love you, Aspen Levi.*

"Fifteen years ago, I thought I fell for a man who spun fairytales and promises he'd never keep." When Dominic opens his mouth, I touch my finger to his lips, silently asking for him to give me this. "Topher kept me sane. Topher kept me moving. I wanted out. I wanted to *live*—but shackles don't always come in the form of physical handcuffs. Sometimes they're more subtle, like a ring on your finger."

I catch Dominic's hand, holding his fingers through the bars and flip his hand over, palm down, so I can find his ring finger. It's bare, just like mine, and I kiss it. Once. Twice. "Coming back to London terrified me. I'd left this place behind, thinking I was about to embark on this crazy adventure. And I came back fifteen years later, with darkness in my heart. Except that you're wrong about me." I glance up, and our eyes lock. "Topher kept me breathing, but you . . . you brought me back to life. I love you, Dominic. I love you so, so much."

"Jesus fuck, Aspen."

My smile is all kinds of wobbly at hearing the familiar curse. "Let me out of here so I can kiss you."

And then that devilish grin I've come to know all too well tugs at his lips. He pulls back, just far enough to wiggle the keys. "Let you out?" he teases roughly. "And here I was gonna suggest that I make use of your conjugal-rights visitation."

I can't stop my jaw from dropping open. "Conjugal *rights*?"

His dark eyes flash with humor. "You ever done it in a prison, baby?"

I laugh, even as I fight back the tears because how . . . how did I deserve a man who'll find the hilarity in every situation—even when I'm locked up in jail? Pushing my fingers as far as they can go through the cage, I point at his hand. "If you love me like you say you do, you'll use those keys and take me home."

"I *do* love you." He catches the tips of my fingers and dips his head to kiss them one by one. "Thing is, I won't make it home. So I'm thinking—even though I'm new at this relationship thing—that we should practice our compromising skills. I suggest the truck as middle ground. What do you say?"

"I say you're crazy."

"Is that a yes, Coach?"

"It's a yes, you jerk. Now get me out of here!"

40

DOMINIC
TWO WEEKS LATER

The Athlete's Reckoning
I'm No Hero by Dominic DaSilva

*Y*eah, you read that right.
  I'm. No. Hero.
  Here's what I am:
A two-time Super Bowl champion.

MVP winner—seven seasons.

Heisman Trophy winner.

An alleged football god. (I don't regularly call myself this, but we'll go with the approximately 10,241 searches that popped up with my name when I typed "football god" into Google).

A former host of a sports show.

Those are the facts—minus the football-god one—but they don't make me infallible. I'm human, just like you. I make mistakes, just like you. I break hearts and do stupid shit and have regrets—Just. Like. You.

If you've been in the limelight for any amount of time, you start to learn certain things. When a magazine or a gossip rag drags your name through the mud, you're told to take it at face value. They don't know the real you. When rumors catch fire and you're standing in line at the grocery store, only to see your face staring back from a tabloid magazine, you're told to feel grateful that you're getting any attention at all.

Attention means money and money is always good.

I used to think so.

Hell, there wasn't much I wouldn't do for a paycheck.

Go on a dating TV show for a six-figure bonus from my job? Done.

Accept even more cash slipped under the table from said dating show, just so they could get a "celebrity" on the books and ramp up audience numbers? Check that shit off, I'm there.

I repeat: I'm no hero.

I've crossed so many lines that, ultimately, I got my ass kicked to the curb by a woman with a sweet heart who only wanted to find love. I deserved that rejection. Maybe I even deserve to have my name dragged through the mud all over again by sites like Celebrity Tea Presents *and others.*

Maybe I deserve that.

But innocent people don't.

My girlfriend doesn't.

Her teenage son doesn't.

Savannah Rose—the sweetheart mentioned above—did not sign up to have her name thrown into the trash, right alongside mine, just because she went about an unorthodox way to find her other half.

When I contacted The Athlete's Reckoning *about my plans for this article, they advised me that I'm committing career suicide.*

I told them I don't care.

Maybe I'm in the minority for signing up to a dating show, but I am not *alone in having my privacy and the privacy of those around me ripped to shreds. I'm done keeping quiet. I'm done pretending I don't give a shit.*

And I'm certainly done with finding out that my best friend, my other half, was accosted in a parking lot by a pap looking to make a quick buck off what my name can buy him. Do this again and there'll be hell to pay.

So, call this article career suicide. Call it whatever you want.

I'm a retired NFL player who coaches high school football.

I'm a guy in love with a girl, who wants to make sure nothing happens to her or her son.

But I'm no hero—and I don't play a gentleman's game when my loved ones are threatened.

These are the facts.

T<small>UCKING THE PHONE BETWEEN MY EAR AND SHOULDER</small>, I <small>STARE</small> at the article on my laptop as I wait for the click of the call to signal it being picked up. I expected to be a hell of a lot more nervous than I am. It's not every day that I call an ex— is she really an ex? Tough call—to say thank you after she gave me permission to blast her name in a public forum like *The Athlete's Reckoning.*

"Hello?"

Eight months. That's how long it's been since I left *Put A Ring On It* and heard Savannah Rose's voice for the last time. She doesn't sound a damn bit different.

"Savannah, hey." I tap my fingers on the top of my laptop. "It's me, Dom."

"Oh! Dom." She sounds short of breath in my ear, like I've caught her mid-workout. "I didn't expect you to call."

There's an audible bang on the other end of the line, then what sounds like a door slamming closed. *What the hell is going on over there?* I shake my head to clear it, even though she can't see me. "I know. Sorry, this is"—awkward, slightly uncomfortable, all of the above?—"probably bad timing. You might be busy."

"No! No, of course not. Not busy at all."

"Are you sure? You sound like . . ."

"I'm on the treadmill," she quips, perkier than I've ever heard her before. "Yep, totally on the treadmill. What's going on? Did the article go live?"

I cast a quick glance back to my laptop. "It's live and rolling. I just wanted to say thank you again, for giving me the go-ahead with this. I don't want to make things harder for you, but I—"

"You're looking out for Aspen." Her voice gentles. "And Topher. How are they—okay?"

Savannah Rose may not have been the woman for me, but she's a damn good person. I screwed her over. Lied to her for most of the show about why I was there, and here she is . . . doing me a solid. There aren't many people like her out there in the world, and the familiar razor edge of guilt slices through me.

She put her life on hold to go on *Put A Ring On It* and she walked away from it with nothing but scandal and heartbreak.

"They're good, yeah. Thank you for asking. And I'm sorry, again, for being that asshole no one wants on the show. I know you said before that it's okay—I just really want you to know how sorry I am. It was a shit thing for me to do. I regret it, taking the money . . . and going on the show in the first place."

"It's all water under the bridge, I promise! Listen, Dom, I have to—"

Did she just giggle?

"Savannah, you good over there?"

"Yes, totally good!" Then a hushed, "Owen, stop!"

Owen? My brows draw together. "Wait, wasn't there an Owen on the show?" I ask, cutting over the sounds of what has got to be whispering. "The one you kicked off on the first night?"

"Dom, I'm so sorry. This isn't a good time. The treadmill, it's"—an unmistakable whimper cuts through the line—"it's really giving me a hard time today. Gotta go! It was great talking to you!"

The line goes dead.

Staring at the blinking numbers at the top of my screen —forty-five seconds, that's how long we talked—I mutter, "What the ever-loving fuck just happened?"

Owen . . . Owen, I don't remember his last name but there was no forgetting Savannah's epic throw down on the show—the one and only time she ever lost her cool, including when I came clean.

Clicking out of my article on *The Athlete's Reckoning*, I type "Put A Ring On It Owen Savannah" into the search-engine bar.

Thank you, Google.

The first thing to pop up is a YouTube video. Immediately, I tap on it, my phone tossed on the coffee table, and watch a clip from the first episode of the season. For the sake of my own sanity, I've stayed away from all the aired episodes. But this . . . I swear I'm not making shit up.

How many Owens can Savannah Rose possibly know?

"Dominic?"

I glance over my shoulder to watch Levi sail in through my back door. Holding out my arm for her, she doesn't miss a beat. She parks her sweet ass on my lap, her arm looped around the back of my neck, and kisses my forehead.

Is it manly if I admit that my heart fucking melts whenever she does that?

Not that I care.

"What are we watching?" she asks.

I shake my head, still feeling like I've been hit by a Mack truck. "Hell if I know. I think . . . I think Savannah Rose might be seeing this guy."

Levi leans forward, tugging me with her, as she practically puts her nose to the screen. "*Owen?* You think she—I mean, before you ask . . . I *did* watch this episode. I was bored and lonely and we hadn't met yet, so clearly I was not watching and salivating over you."

I kiss her mouth, cupping her jaw as I do. My tongue dances with hers, and I lick her bottom lip because I know it makes her ticklish. She shivers in my arms. *Jackpot.* I pull back. "We both know you watched because you think I'm hot."

"Correction, I do now but I didn't then."

"Liar."

"I don't lie," she says sweetly, "except for whenever you try to cook dinner. Then I lie—with gusto."

In mock-affront, I gasp loudly. "You tell me my food tastes great!"

"You can't cook, Dominic. It's not one of your many talents."

"Topher likes it when I grill."

"I think Topher likes it when there's open fire." She slips down to the floor, situating herself between my knees. "Speaking of Topher, the two of us were talking and . . . we both think you need a place to stay while you rehab this house."

I drop my chin, keeping my gaze trained on hers as she

slants her palms over my upper thighs. "Baby," I husk out, "are you asking me to move in?"

Blue eyes drop to my crotch. "It's acceptable if you take the guestroom."

I hook a finger under her chin. Keep my voice low and steady when I murmur, "You're relegating me to the guestroom?"

Her smile twitches even as her fingers move to the waistband of my jeans. "Not a chance," she teases me, "but I'd be lying if I said I didn't enjoy the look on your face when you thought I was telling you the truth."

I tackle her onto the floor, leveraging my body over hers. Whichever Owen Savannah Rose is talking to is not my problem.

My problem is the sexy, beautiful blonde squirming beneath me and begging me to take pity.

I lower my face, dropping a kiss to her lips. "I don't do pity, Coach," I murmur in her ear, "but with risk comes great reward . . . and for you, I'm thinking orgasms."

41

CELEBRITY TEA PRESENTS:

THE DAY WE BANNED DOMINIC DASILVA

ear Reader, it has come to my attention that I've been threatened by one Dominic DaSilva. THREAT-ENED. I started this blog ten years ago. Never in that amount of time has someone dared to come after me.

I report what I see as the truth.

I entertain you, Dear Reader, because it brings me joy.

I'm funny.

Well-informed.

Meticulous in my reporting.

And I'm pissed.

Dear Reader, it's not often that I'm left speechless. In fact, since a fan forwarded me that article THAT SHALL NOT BE DISCUSSED HERE, I have sat down to write this post at least a dozen times.

I am emotionally drained.

Entirely distraught.

I've never, not once in ten years of operating Celebrity Tea Presents, *felt so out of sorts. (So out of sorts that I binge-watched* The Notebook *fifteen times in the last seventy-two hours, simply so I could feel better about the number of tissues I've used).*

It must be said: I have never banned a celebrity from being discussed on my site. All tea is good tea. But this . . . DaSilva took it too far. The hate comments piling up from goddamn football fans is absolutely horrid, and I apologize to you, Dear Reader, for needing to disable all comments for the time being.

I hope you understand my pain.

Before I crawl back over to the TV to watch The Notebook *for a sixteenth time, I have only a few choice words to say:*

Fuck you, Dominic DaSilva.

We'll be back to our regularly scheduled programming next week.

EPILOGUE
ASPEN

One Month Later

"*And then*, the terrifying beast rose up from the lake and looked at the woods and thought . . . I smell them. The rotting stench of football, and I shall eat one of you!" Matthew Wilde throws up a pair of "claws" and growls like he's the savage beast from his story.

Feeling the heat from the bonfire on my face, I hide a laugh as the boys all start to grumble their disappointment.

"Dude, *that's* all you've got?" Kevin shouts from the other side of the fire.

"I think I just peed myself," Timmy says, jumping up from the log he's been perched on for the last forty minutes. He cups his crotch crassly. "Just kidding! No pee. For real, Wilde, that was pitiful."

Matthew, being the good soul that he is, points one of his Party City claws at Tim. "*My* scary story was pitiful? Bro, you burped out the chorus to the *Twilight* theme song."

I raise my s'mores cooking stick in the air. "I thought it was scary."

Heat that has nothing to do with the fire and everything to do with Dominic warms me from the inside out as he uses the evening light to his advantage and slips a hand between my tightly clamped thighs. "You think everything's scary," he rumbles out, his chin coming very close to perching on my shoulder. "Ferris wheels, sharks, bears— speaking of bears . . ." He shifts away to call out, "Gloria, will you wrangle the teens into the bunks with Meredith? I need to ask Coach Levi to look over something for me."

Aunt Gloria, who has become somewhat of a beloved secretarial assistant since Harry moved in with her, bobs her head. "You got it, boss."

Dominic nudges me in the side. "See?" he taunts, and though the night sky hides his upper face, I know he's laughing at me. "She calls me boss. Aunt Gloria knows what's up."

"Aunt Gloria," I say, rolling my eyes, "also likes the cash you slip her every week to help care for Harry."

"I have no idea what you're talking about."

"Sure you don't."

Except that he totally does.

The police found Heather Blackwater in a halfway home down in Portland two weeks ago, and though Dominic tries to brush it all off as a concern that isn't ours, it's impossible to miss the way he's firmly planted himself in Harry's life. He pays Gloria for all of Harry's football gear and never misses the opportunity to bring Harry to practice when his great-aunt can't do so herself. He stopped all work on his house to bring in Nick Stamos and his crew and direct them to Gloria's place for some remodeling.

Dominic isn't taking any risks with Harry, and at least three times a week, the redheaded teenager is over at our house and hanging out with Topher.

My heart squeezes at the thought of my son, and I scour the kids all gathered around the fire to find him. He's sitting with his legs crossed at the ankles, his chin resting on his bent knees. The matter with Rick dampened his bright smile—particularly when Rick gave up all parental custody to me—but we're working to bring back his pep.

Dominic, especially.

Following practice, they spend their days swimming in the bay and playing basketball out on the street. They binge Netflix shows that I have no interest in watching—moto gearheads are not my thing—and I've walked into the living room multiple times to see my son passed out on one side of the couch and Dominic sleeping on the other.

As if sensing my stare, Topher lifts his head and catches my eye.

I love you, I mouth to him, hoping the fire is bright enough that he'll notice what I've said.

He smiles, a soft, boyish grin that warms my heart. *Love you, Mom.*

It's what I need. *All* I need.

My team around me, Topher, Dominic.

If this is what true happiness feels like, then I never want to leave this camp.

"Come with me," Dominic urges quietly, his hands already tugging me up onto my feet. "I gotta show you something."

"Are you sure we should leave?"

"Gloria and Meredith can handle the kids," he says, leading me toward the cabins we've rented for the weekend. "And if they can't, Brien will step in."

I laugh at that. "Adam hasn't even left his car since he got here earlier."

"He doesn't do bugs."

"What a pansy."

A hard palm swats my butt, and I jump. Twirling around, I put up my hands. "Whoa now, mister—"

"You asked for a bear."

"Not even once. Remember, I fear them."

"You don't fear me."

I cock my head, staring up at him as I walk backward. "Should I?"

"Yes."

And then he's looped an arm around my thighs and I'm over his shoulder—*again*—as he breaks into a light jog.

"Dominic." I pound a fist on his hard butt cheek. There's barely any give. *So unfair.* "Dominic, you have to put me down."

"Negative, Coach." He doesn't even sound winded as he cuts across the dark field to where the staff cabin is located. "I have to show you something."

I stare down at the grass as it passes me by, his sneakers churning up dirt. "You're going to offer to show me your penis, aren't you?"

His husky laughter is music to my ears. "Ye of little faith, baby."

Only once we reach the cabin does he drop me from his shoulder, righting me again on my feet. The world goes topsy-turvy from being upside down to right side up, but then Dominic is backing me up into the dark cabin. He flicks the switch by the front door, flooding the interior with light.

When I booked these cabins, it was with the money the team made from the calendar. It sold thousands of copies. Quite literally, thousands. Even more surprising was when high school football teams across the country began shooting their own calendars.

It's a blessing and a curse.

Every time we spot another calendar gain viral traction online, Dominic buys fifty copies. His house—the one he doesn't even live in anymore—has become a storage unit for football calendars of teams he doesn't even know.

Leaning into him, I kiss his arm. "I love you, you know."

The grin he gives me is nothing but desire and adoration. "I love *you*."

Then he drops his mouth to mine, and I'm gone, as I always am, when he kisses me. I arch into him, my palms splayed over his rib cage. The kiss feels like hope and promise and love, and I give into it completely, hopping up into Dominic's arms and knowing he'll catch me no matter what.

Sure enough, he does, with his hands hooked under my ass and a masculine chuckle easing between us. "Here I thought I'd have to romance you a little or at least swear that no one is gonna come in here."

I tilt my head to the side, giving him ample room to kiss his way down my neck. "I saw you whispering with Meredith and Aunt Gloria. You were scheming."

"I have no idea what you're talking about."

The cabin is nothing but rows of bunk beds. Not that that stops Dominic from carrying me over to the closest one. He props my back against a wooden ladder that leads to the top bunk, and promptly orders, "Hold on, Coach."

Hold on?

Hold on to *what*?

My shorts are gone in the next breath, ripped down my legs until they hang loosely around my ankles. Oh, yes please. I love it when Dominic gets handsy. "Did you see it?" I ask, already breathless, as he traces his tongue along the inside crease of my hip bone.

Black eyes dart up to my face. "See what?"

"Underwear."

With one hand to my pelvis, like he honestly thinks I'm going to disappear on him, he peers down at the discarded panties on the floor. Flicks his fingers over the fabric so he can see the black font that reads: *Property of Football God.*

His shoulders shake with mirth. "You better fucking believe it, baby."

And then he surprises me completely, standing tall and inching his waistband down.

I wiggle my brows. "Are we already getting to the good stuff?"

He wags a finger at me. "Hey, now, everything we do together is the good stuff." The waistband of his shorts lowers, treating me to my very first visual of Dominic in briefs. He only reveals a few scant inches of the underwear but, much to my delight, I can see enough to admire how the black fabric cups his impressive erection like a faithful lover. And that dark happy trail dipping into paradise? God, he's delicious. And mine, *all* mine.

Wait.

I blink.

Why is he wearing briefs?

The shorts drop to the floor with a shove of his fingers and—

Oh. My. God.

I laugh so hard that the only thing holding me up is the ladder. "You didn't," I whisper, pressing my palms to my aching cheeks.

Dominic points to the words written across the briefs.

Belongs to Football Legend. Below the white print is an arrow leading down to his dick.

Without a hint of shame, he shrugs his broad shoulders. "I saw your order come in and couldn't let you one-up me."

This—this right here is true love.

Laughing at all times of the day, knowing that your other half is going to pull some crazy stunt because there's nothing he enjoys more than rising up to a challenge—especially when I'm the one issuing it.

"C'mere,' I tell him, holding out my arms.

He doesn't need any more convincing.

He slants his mouth over mine as he corrals me onto the bottom bunk. My butt hits the firm mattress first, and then Dominic's hand is at my shoulder and pushing, pushing, pushing until I'm sprawled out on the twin-sized bed. He follows me down, leveraging his big body over mine. *Yes.* I hook my legs around the backs of his thighs when our kiss turns frantic. Tongues sliding, lips wet. Dominic tastes like s'mores, and I lick at his lips when he tugs back to catch his breath.

His chest reverberates with a groan. Yeah, he likes it when I push him and take control of his pleasure. Wanting to hear sexy noise rumble out of him again, I strain my bare hips so I can get as close to him as possible.

Dammit, the briefs are in the way.

"I'm never wearing them again," he grumbles against my neck. "Good in theory, bad in practice."

With tight, efficient movements, he strips the material off and throws it onto the floor. Freed from its confines, his thick cock bobs against his lower pelvis. The swollen head is already leaking pre-cum. My mouth waters, and I don't care what that says about me. I'm openly desperate for this man, and I don't care who knows how much I love him.

Dominic's fingers find my thighs. Sharply, he spreads them even wider. So wide that my right knee is actually pulled into my chest while my left hangs over the side of the bed. There's nothing at all I can do about my body's response when Dominic rakes me with such a thorough once-over that my sex clenches in anticipation.

He studies me like he wants to devour me whole.

And I want to be devoured.

The thought alone is sensual enough that I throw my arms open and silently invite him in. Into my bed, into my body, into my heart.

His calloused palms squeeze my inner thighs and then he gives me his full weight. Air escapes my lungs upon impact, but that doesn't stop me from dragging his head close so I can sip on his full lips.

Perfect.

The length of his hard cock slicks through my wet folds, a slow, sensual back and forth that pulls a moan from deep in my soul. He never once enters me. It's torture and yet divine, exquisite pleasure and still hell on earth.

Merciless. That's the only word to describe how he takes pleasure in seeing me squirm beneath him. And squirm I do, needing more, needing him inside me.

"I love you," I whimper.

He glides against me again, but this time he takes his cock in hand and rubs the head against my swollen clit.

"Oh, my—"

Dominic cuts me off with a feverish kiss. He sucks on my bottom lip. Drags his hard-on through my wetness. Huffs out a low, sexy laugh when I thrash my head on the pillow and beg him to just give me what I want.

He doesn't.

Instead he ducks his head to lift my shirt up, up, up, until my chest is exposed and his mouth finds my nipple.

Paradise.

This must be what paradise feels like.

"I'm grateful," I moan, not above fisting the bedsheets as I try to remember how to use my brain. *You can do this.* "I'm so grateful you walked into the Golden Fleece and turned me down."

In response, he only sucks harder. Until my toes are curling and my head is digging back into the pillows. The tip of his cock slips into me, a slight pressure that promises so much pleasure, before he pulls back out.

Pulls. Out.

"You are the *worst*."

He releases a throaty chuckle that elicits shivers down my spine. "You don't mean that."

"I do"—I nod eagerly, molding my fingers over the crown of his head—"I so, so do."

Clearly wanting to drive me over the edge of insanity, he slowly thrusts inside me. The tip. *Only* the tip. I've never felt so empty without him.

I turn my face to the side, slamming my eyes shut. "I thought you loved me."

"I do, baby," he croons like the jerk he is, pushing in, giving me a little more of his length, before retreating all over again. "I love you, even when you lie and tell me my cooking is the best thing you've ever tasted. I love you, despite the fact that you leave your laundry all over the floor and pretend not to notice when I stick it in the washer. I'll love you forever, but especially when you challenge me to midnight swims in the bay and try to drown me every single time."

His cock drives deeper with every thrust. *Yes, yes, yes.* My legs flex against the bedsheets. Dropping my hands, I grip the pillow behind my head and pray for patience. Dominic is the antithesis of predictability. He thrives off surprise and shock, and he lives for the moments when he can tease me into diving into the ten-percent chaos with him.

I wrap my legs around his lower back, catching him off guard. We both hiss as he sinks to the hilt within me.

"Jesus fuck," he grunts, dark eyes glittering with lust. I wait for it, that moment when the panic sets in and he realizes—"Shit, Asp, no condom. I'm so sorry."

I don't let him retreat. Tightening my calves and my thighs, I hold him immobile as he props himself up on his forearms. Just to mess with him, I nip the shell of his ear. "I went on the pill."

A wicked smile swiftly tugs at his mouth. Then, "God, I love you."

And then there's no more talking, only thrusting hips and grasping fingers. Our mouths fuse, and I don't giggle when our teeth clack together or even when he forgets we're rocking it out on the bottom bunk when he tries to sit up. He smacks his head on the metal springs of the top bunk.

"You're mine," he rasps, tugging my knees up so they're flush with my chest and he can hit that sweet spot just *there*. "Mine," he repeats, his hips slamming forward and sparking heat inside my veins, "mine to love"—he kisses my mouth, sloppy and desperate—"mine to hold"—his hand cups my breast, his thumb flicking over the hard peak—"and mine to fuck."

I cry out the moment his fingers travel over my rib cage, down the slope of my stomach, to stroke my clit. He's filling me up and owning my body and it feels so good. My hips lift off the mattress as I meet him thrust for thrust. "Please, please—"

He gives it to me.

The orgasm rocks me to my core, turning me inside out.

I hold onto him tightly, clinging to his broad shoulders, as I crane my neck and come undone.

He shatters a moment later, my name gritted out from between his teeth, his hips pistoning forward with wild abandon as he spills himself inside me.

It's euphoric.

Downright life-changing.

I kiss Dominic's stubbled cheek, his dimpled chin, wherever I can reach.

It's not until we've come down from the high that he urges me back into my clothes with a swat to my ass.

"I thought you showed me all I need to see?" I point to his semi-hard erection.

Laughing, he only shakes his head like I'm too much for him. "Outside—now—before the kids come find us."

"*Now* you're worried about the kids finding us?"

Laughing, but still trusting him implicitly, I follow by his side, my hand engulfed in his, as he leads me around to the back of the cabin. The moon is out tonight, its illumination turning the lake silver and the woods a dusty gray. I made the right decision in bringing the team out here to wrap up summer camp.

They needed it.

I needed it.

Angling me so that my back is to the cabin and I'm facing the silver lake not ten yards away, Dominic says, "Look up."

I blink, startled. "Look up at what?"

"You'll see."

"Because that doesn't sound ominous at all."

"*Aspen.*"

I hold up my hands. "Okay, okay! I'm looking up." I tip my head back, my gaze soaking up the sky. Stars twinkle like

little gemstones. I cast my attention east, toward London—
though we're a good hundred miles away from my little
hometown on Frenchman Bay.

Wait.

My eyes narrow. Is that . . .?

"Dominic! Oh, my God, it's a shooting star!"

"You should make a wish."

Make a wish? What to wish for when I have everything I
already want? I've never been so happy as I have been this
last month. Life is good. Life is sweet. Life is . . .

I close my eyes, briefly, and let myself be whisked away
on the fairy tale of wish-making, exactly like Dad had me
and Willow do whenever we were feeling sad as kids.

I wish . . .

I wish . . .

My hands find my belly, and I hide a grin.

"Did you make your wish?" Dominic asks, his presence
hot at my back.

"I did." I stare up at the sky for one more moment, then
add, "I made two."

"Cheater."

"Swindler," I correct with a little laugh. "The first was
that I wished you would kiss me tonight."

I turn, expecting to see him standing in front of me—
and then glance down. My hands fly to my mouth when I
see him on his knees.

On *one* knee.

"Dominic—"

His hands shift forward, flirting with the moonlight to
reveal the velvet box he's holding. "I promise to kiss you every
night for the rest of your life," he vows, popping the box open to
reveal a ring. The details are lost to the shadows and all I make

out are a yellow stone and glittering diamonds. I don't even care that it's not fully visible, nestled in the black velvet as it is —it's *beautiful.* "I promise to always put you and Topher first."

"Topher! Does Topher—"

Dominic chuckles huskily. "Topher helped me pick out the ring."

"Oh. *Oh.*"

"I promise," he continues smoothly, plucking the ring out of the box and holding it up, "to remind you that you may be my boss on the field but you like it when I boss you around in the bedroom."

"Oh, my God, you're crazy."

"I also promise to accept the fact that Guinness somehow makes you drunker than a skunk, and that somehow, whenever you have some, you end up face-first in my lap."

I'm a hot mess. A crying, hot mess.

"I don't have the ability to plan for shooting stars but clearly the universe is looking out for me on this one. That was a great touch. Also, for what it's worth, I have another pair of briefs in my duffel bag that reads *Football Husband,* but I thought that might be a little too obvious. I'll save them for our wedding night."

My cheeks are warm, my limbs are shaking, and I have never, in my life, felt so treasured and loved as I do right now. "Yes!" I cry out. "Yes, I'll marry you!"

Dominic dips his head, a deliciously smug smile spreading across his face. "Baby, I haven't popped the question yet."

"Just *yes!* My answer is yes."

"I planned this whole thing out, you know. I want to see it all through."

"You can really just put the ring on my finger. I won't oppose."

He draws in a sharp breath, and then . . . Pops. The. Question.

Only, it's not the question I anticipated.

I stare down at him, brows creeping toward my hairline. "I'm sorry, I'm going to need you to repeat that for me."

Dominic blinks up at me, all wide-eyed innocence. "Aspen, will you"—my breath catches—"do me the great honor of changing my ringtone on your phone? *Bad Company* isn't a good fit anymore."

The problem with falling in love with a broken man is that when he becomes *un*broken, he suddenly thinks he's a comedian.

I stick out my left hand.

As I knew he would, he slides the most beautiful ring I've ever sort-of seen onto my fourth finger. He picked it out for me, with Topher's help, which makes it perfect. *Perfect for me.* In a shaky voice that is so not like him, Dominic finally asks, "Will you marry me, Coach?"

This time, I don't answer with words.

I drop to my knees before him and I plant a kiss on his lips, pouring all of my love for him into my touch. I frame his handsome face with my hands and breathe in everything this man is to me: my safe haven, my partner in crime, my reason to smile every morning that I wake up in his arms and he pushes me to embark on another insane adventure with him by my side.

My heart pounds so erratically that I almost miss his ragged whisper, "Thank you for making me see."

"See what?" I ask against his mouth, refusing to let him go.

"How I can love you more every day, and I will still never have enough of you."

The End

꩜

Thank you so much for reading Dom & Aspen's love story! I absolutely adore these two, and couldn't quite walk away from them once I reached The End, which means I totally wrote another epilogue for them set three years in the future. **Discover what Aspen wished for under the stars in this exclusive bonus content:** https://www.marialuis.org/kiss-me-tonight

What To Read Next?

Love Me Tonight (Put A Ring On It, #3) **is now available and features our favorite bachelorette!** Savannah Rose is about to be swept off her feet by the one man she shouldn't want . . .

Swipe right for an exclusive excerpt of this steamy and forbidden friends-to-lovers romance!

LOVE ME TOMORROW TEASER

Keep reading for a sneak peek of Love Me Tomorrow, the third and final book in the Put A Ring On It *series—featuring Owen Harvey & Savannah Rose.*

SAVANNAH

With feet that feel heavy like iron anvils, I trudge to my marked spot on the circular driveway. The grand mansion is to my back, the waiting limo to my front. I have absolutely zero expectations that the next five guys will rev my engine, so to speak, but Matilda's question continues to nag me: *If your dream man could step out of that limo, what would he look like?*

Temptation. The word slips through my mind and clings fiercely. My dream man would look like temptation.

"Savannah, you ready?"

After a quick thumbs up to Joe, I pin a serene smile in place like the debutante I once was.

Press my shoulders back.

Pray with every bit of my soul that even if the next guy to

climb out of that limo isn't my dream man, hopefully he'll be someone I find attractive—or, at the very least, someone who will do a damn good job of convincing me that although I don't *want* to be on a dating show, I made the right decision in honoring my contract by showing up.

The glossy limo door swings open and a pair of black-leather dress shoes hit the stone driveway. One foot, then the other, and maybe I'm crazy or already tipsy on too much champagne, but my stomach dips with anticipation.

Begrudging anticipation, but anticipation nonetheless.

Black slacks appear, and I curse the set director for placing me near the walkway leading up to the mansion. Case in point: my view is nothing but limbs. But yeah, this guy—whoever he is—he's got great legs. Thick thighs that strain the fabric of his pants. Tall-looking, too. Definitely taller than I am.

Wanting a better look, I shift up onto my tiptoes, the rasp of my sequined dress against the cobblestones echoing loudly in my ears.

Tattooed hands are revealed next. Thick, masculine fingers. A palm that could easily span the width of my back, tugging me close for a romantic dance, or a hot kiss, or a gravelly whisper in my ear.

I never cared for tattoos, not before *him*. Not before I watched him work diligently on every person who walked into his parlor. Not before I sat on that flat table, aware that I was rebelling in a way that I never had before, and felt the weight of his big hands coasting over my skin to mark me with black, irreversible ink.

I swallow hard and remind myself that Los Angeles is thousands of miles away from New Orleans.

Pull yourself together, Rose.

And maybe I would have been able to, if the man exiting

the limo hadn't stepped into the soft light just then and thrown my already teetering world straight into the abyss of chaos.

My dream man.

In the span of a heartbeat, I soak in his familiar face. The dark, tousled hair. The dark, close-shaven beard. The dark, bottomless eyes that always seem to anticipate my every move—even when I wish he couldn't read me at all. The tattoos that creep up to the collar of his black suit, and cling to the base of his thick throat.

I'm accustomed to seeing him in jeans and flannel shirts but decked out in a tailored, black suit like he is now . . . God, he looks raw.

Savage.

Powerful.

What is he doing *here?*

Instinctively, I step back—off the *X* taped to the stone beneath my feet and away from the man who isn't supposed to be anywhere but in his tattoo shop on Bourbon Street.

Certainly not here. With me.

Amelie.

My sister's face flashes in my mind's eye and I wrangle my rapidly beating heart into submission, pushing the traitorous thing down until the pounding in my ears is nothing but ambivalent white noise.

He doesn't heed the shock that's no doubt kicked my placid smile to the curb.

No.

Without taking those glittering black eyes off me, he ambles close, all loose limbs and simmering confidence, until we're breathing the same air, taking up the same space, existing in the same moment.

Temptation.

Goddamn temptation.

"Give me your hand."

It's all he says but spoken in that rough New Orleans drawl of his, it's both a request and a command all at once.

Flustered, my gaze shoots over to the crew, to all the cameras trained in our direction. The lights are damn near blinding but there's no mistaking the way Joe sits on the literal edge of his seat, looking enraptured by the scene unfolding before him.

One thing is clear: no one is going to help me out of this.

It didn't occur to me until just now how very public this experience will be. And I'm no idiot: Joe Devonsson will gleefully air this moment all over America in just a few short months, rubbing his hands together in anticipation of skyrocketing ratings. Then everyone will know, just by looking at my face, that I feel like I've been pummeled by an eighteen-wheeler.

I lower my voice, my hands balled into tight fists down by my sides to keep them from visibly trembling. "You shouldn't be here."

His sharp jaw clenches tight. "I'm exactly where I'm supposed to be."

I'm short on breath. I want to blame it on the too-tight dress. I want to blame it on the California weather, but it's late November and the air is cool, for once, without even a hint of humidity. I want to blame my lightheadedness on anything *but* the man standing a hand's width away, looking like the Prince of Darkness.

For a little over a year now, our relationship has been casual. Friends, no matter how often I found myself looking at him a little too long or secretly admiring the wide breadth of his shoulders or finding reasons to meet up with him that shouldn't have existed after he'd dated Amelie.

And now he's *here*.

Standing less than two feet away and stealing all my damn air.

My chin angles north with false bravado. "You can't stay."

Catching me completely off guard, he steps in close, demolishing the distance between us, and hooks an inked finger under my chin. My chest caves with need, lust, awareness. Although I'll never admit it out loud, my knees quiver, too. *Quiver!* Like I'm some sort of teenage girl faced with her first crush, instead of a thirty-four-year-old woman who knows her own mind and manages thirteen restaurants all over New Orleans.

I should move away. Shove him back. Demand that the producers kick him off the premises.

He doesn't give me the chance to do any of those things.

Moving methodically, like he's expecting me to scramble backward, he lowers his head and grazes his cheek against mine. I feel the bristles of his beard, the softness of his lips as they find the shell of my ear. His hand leaves my chin to clasp the back of my neck with a familiarity that reaches into my soul and twists, hard.

"No more running, Rose." The warmth of his breath elicits a shiver down my spine, my surname sounding like nothing less than a forbidden endearment dripping off his tongue. "Give me a chance. Give *us* a chance."

But there are no chances, not for us.

He lets me go and it's a miracle I remain standing on my own two feet, my legs feel so weak. A small smile plays on his full lips—a mouth I've never once kissed—before he turns away, heading up the walkway to the mansion.

My fingers curl, nails biting sharply into my palm.

He's my kryptonite. My weakness. And the one man who is decidedly off-limits to me—forever.

This . . . *flirtation* that we have going on? It has to end.

Tonight.

Ignoring the cameras and the knowledge that one day this moment will broadcast all over the country, I squeeze my eyes and make a decision: I need to let him go. I need to let him go and move on and let myself fall in love . . .

With someone who isn't Owen Harvey.

Click here and binge Love Me Tomorrow!
The Put A Ring On It series is available on ebook and paperback.

DEAR FABULOUS READER

Hi there! I so hope you enjoyed *Kiss Me Tonight*, and if you are new to my books, welcome to the family!

In the back of all my books, I love to include a Dear Fabulous Reader section that talks about what locations from the book can be visited in real life or what sparked my inspiration for a particular plot point. (I like to think of it as the Extras on DVD's, LOL).

As always, we'll hit it up bullet-point style—enjoy!

- It seems only fitting (and most important, I think) to begin with Dominic's upbringing. It must be said that not every child in foster care has the experience Dominic had—I know so many amazing foster parents, including family members of mine. But writing Dominic's character went deeper than that...for me, writing Dominic came as a direct result in listening to Mr. Luis come home from work (he is a police officer in New Orleans) and talk about the children he comes across on his job. Children who, yes, find themselves stumbling down the wrong path. The ten-year-old who has a rap sheet a mile long and an ankle monitor that goes with him everywhere. My heart broke (and breaks still) every time I heard Mr. Luis wish there was something he could do—or say—to get through to those kids. Something that would be the catalyst needed to give them something to strive for, something to believe in. For me, Dominic was born out of those late night conversations of discussing what we can personally do to make a difference. Dominic's childhood was not easy, it was not kind, but it is the childhood that so many face—and tough as the subject is to read, it is only that much harder to survive.

- Shelby Osborne. Becca Longo. Katie Hnida. April Goss. And now, Antoinette "Toni" Harris. These are all women who have gone on to play football at the collegiate level in the last decade—and Toni, the latest in the lineup of female greats—is determined to be the first to make it to the NFL. (Read about her here). In creating Aspen's character, I knew that I wanted to delve into the world of women who dream of playing in the NFL. What challenges do they face, stuck in a world dominated by (as Aspen said), "cocks and balls?" What sort of inner strength does it take to really come out on top and defy the odds stacked against you? I, for one, will be rooting for Harris!

- Remember when Topher claimed his Driver's Ed instructor spent all class talking about running through a forest of pot? Well, I'm here to announce that "Mike" is real and that story came from my own Driver Ed's class. It was too good to pass up, and to this day, I've never forgotten the two hours we spent learning about how he ran from the cops and ended up smoking weed with a couple he'd never met before. For the record: I still learned to drive just fine! LOL!

- What goes into a name? Well, in the case of Rick . . . a whole lot! In writing his character, I knew that I wanted to really delve into the world of Hollywood where much-older men prey on young women. I've always been fascinated with the women themselves—what happens when those women aren't so young anymore? If they do leave their spouse, what sort of lingering effect remains on their psyche? But picking a name for a character like Aspen's ex was hard. No one likes a villain. Which is how I came by Rick "the Prick." Years ago, my dad worked for a company (name most certainly redacted, LOL) and he had a boss named Dick. It should be noted that no one liked Dick. But one afternoon he, my dad, and the whole department sat in for a meeting. Dick, as Dick tended to do, got flustered about something and turned to the thirty-plus people in the room and announced, "I've never been a Rick, I've never been a Richard, I've just always been a Dick." Did he realize what he'd said? No, not at all—meanwhile everyone else tried to rein in their laughter. I couldn't resist paying a little homage to Dick in my own little way, fifteen years later :)

- London, Maine. While London is completely

fictional, I based our coastal town on "nearby" Bar Harbor. Beautiful. Quaint. An absolute escape from the rest of the world. I highly recommend visiting if you ever find yourself in that neck of the woods! Cadillac Mountain is a must!

- Speaking of London, the Golden Fleece is a merge of my two favorite bars in the world: Lafitte's Blacksmith Shop in New Orleans and the Golden Fleece (the one and only original!) in York, England. Like Lafitte's, my Golden Fleece is lit only by candlelight. And, like the OG Golden Fleece, London's version is very much fashioned/designed in the same Tudor style. You can't go wrong in visiting either—although I'd be remiss if I forgot to mention that cardboard cutouts of Dominic DaSilva will not be found at either establishment. I'm as sorry about this as you are, LOL.

- Ferris wheels—majestic amusement park rides, aren't they? Until, you know, you discover your other half is terrified of heights when you're already strapped in. Like Aspen, I'm not the *biggest* fan of heights. As it turns out, neither is Mr. Luis! Unfortunately, this is apparently something neither of us ever disclosed to one another in ten-plus years of our relationship— not until this past Christmas when we were each pretending to be *totally cool* with going on one. Yeah. We quickly realized our own mistake when it was too late to get off. I loved the idea so much, I decided to put it into a book!

- And, last—*The Athlete's Reckoning* is actually

based on the real-life online journal called *The Players' Tribune.* If you've never had a read, I highly suggest it! It's an inside look into the minds and thoughts of so many high-profile athletes. Some articles look back to a particular game while others truly reminisce about how an event went so very wrong. For me, I knew I wanted Dominic to find his voice—and this was the perfect way to do it.

As always, there are many more but here is just a sampling! If you're thinking . . . that seems rather fascinating and I want to know more, you are always so welcome to reach out! Pretty much, nothing makes me happier =)

Much love,

Maria

ACKNOWLEDGMENTS

I can't say thank you enough to everyone who helped make *Kiss Me Tonight* what it is today. Of all my books, this one was by far the most fun to write—and it's safe to say that I don't think I'll ever get over Dominic & Aspen!

Najla—you are the queen! Thank you for designing a cover that made not only me scream in excitement but readers too.

Kathy—Dom & Aspen wouldn't be here without your encouragement and support. Thank you for always pushing me to better my craft, to give more of myself to these characters, and never accepting less than they deserve.

Brenda—I would be so lost without your friendship! Thank you for always keeping me steady, sending me words of encouragement, and reading this book before anyone else.

Viper—you are amazing! Thank you, more than anything, for two years of friendship and two years of you reading my work in its raw (and terrifying) form.

Ratula—girl, I adore you! Dom & Aspen thank you. I

thank you. Pretty much, this book would be a shell of itself without your words of wisdom. You are the best.

Dawn and Tandy—you are the reason this book sparkles and shines!

Dani—I'm so glad to call you a partner-in-crime in the book world. Thank you for sticking with me and believing in my work!

To my besties/family/awesome-sauce friends Tina, Sam, Terra, Jami, Amie, Jess, Jen, Joslyn, and to my girls in 30 Days to 60k and Indie AF, this author journey would be so much less exciting without you. Also, I'd probably never get anything done without you pushing me along.

To my VIPers and to all my friends in BBA, just know that every one of you has changed my life for the better. This series is just as much for you as it is for me, and thank you so much for coming along on the ride.

And, lastly, to you Dear Reader, for picking up this book and giving me a chance. Thank you for allowing me the chance to live my dream—my very own permanent longing —as a storyteller.

Much love,
Maria

ALSO BY MARIA LUIS

ABOUT THE AUTHOR

Maria Luis is the author of sexy contemporary romances.

Historian by day and romance novelist by night, Maria lives in New Orleans, and loves bringing the city's cultural flair into her books. When Maria isn't frantically typing with coffee in hand, she can be found binging on reality TV, going on adventures with her other half and two pups, or plotting her next flirty romance.

∞

Stalk Maria in the Wild at the following!
Join Maria's Newsletter
Join Maria's Facebook Reader Group